BOOKS BY KIM SMEJKAL

Ink in the Blood
Curse of the Divine

KIM SMEJKAL

INK IN THE BLOOD

HOUGHTON MIFFLIN HARCOURT
BOSTON   NEW YORK

hmhbooks.com

The text was set in Dante MT Std.

Cover design by Jessica Handelman

Interior design by Kaitlin Yang

The Library of Congress has cataloged the hardcover edition as follows:

Names: Smejkal, Kim, author.

Title: Ink in the blood / by Kim Smejkal.

Description: Boston ; New York : Houghton Mifflin Harcourt , [2020] |
Summary: Celia and Anya, friends who use tattoo magic to send divine
messages, must rely on one another to survive when they discover the
fake deity they serve is very real—and very angry.

Identifiers: LCCN 2019001116 (print) | LCCN 2019002955 (ebook) |

Subjects: | CYAC: Magic—Fiction. | Tattooing—Fiction. |
Goddesses—Fiction. | Fantasy.

Classification: LCC PZ7.1.S5945 (ebook) | LCC PZ7.1.S5945 Ink 2020 (print) |
DDC [Fic]—dc23

LC record available at https://lccn.loc.gov/2019001116

ISBN: 978-1-328-55705-6 hardcover

ISBN: 978-0-358-34893-1 paperback

Manufactured in the United States of America

DOC 10 9 8 7 6 5 4 3 2 1

4500815629

FOR MY DĚDA,
LADISLAV MALEK,
WHO BELIEVED I WAS A WRITER
LONG BEFORE I DID

PROLOGUE

The tattoo appeared around Celia's ankle in the night. The magic woke her, the pain alarmed her, her mothers comforted her.

The thin black line summoned her to serve the Divine. It meant Celia was special.

So Celia asked for a chocolate. She figured the worst her mothers could say was no (like always), but if they were ever going to say yes, it would be when they were so proud of her they couldn't stop crying.

But first they asked her to tell them the Divine's story. Celia was already six years old and knew the story well enough. Standing in front of the hearth so the snaps and crackles of the fire would add to the performance, she cleared her throat and began.

A thousand years ago, a child found a magic box with some magic ink. With that special ink, the child tattooed people without touching them: when she drew a temporary line on her own skin, it became a permanent line on someone else's. Didn't matter how far away they were, either.

It was as if the child could talk directly to the angels. Her tattoos were mystical, and her messages were . . . *pure.* She wanted to help people make good choices.

Her mothers nodded and smiled. So far, so good.

But a few people got scared because the tattoos were so personal. Of course, they were *meant* to be personal. Those scared people got even more scared, and a few of them drowned that long-ago child. Held her underwater until she stopped breathing. They didn't want her tattoos.

Celia inhaled. She hated that part.

But the child didn't leave. Not really. She transformed into the Divine, still guiding us with her ink from afar.

Here, but not *here.* Celia fluttered her hands in the air vaguely. It was just like whoever had drawn her tattoo was here, but not *here.*

Then another child tried to claim the ink as hers. She tried to trick people. This was Diavala.

Celia loved saying that name, stretching it out, a word of whispered screams: *Deee-aaah-vaaah-laaaaah* . . .

But the clever faithfuls weren't fooled. They exposed the second child's treachery and killed her too. Diavala joined the Divine in that other realm, and they've battled for souls ever since: Diavala trying to lure people to hell, the Divine guiding them toward heaven with her magic tattoos. One day, when the Divine can best Diavala for good, she will return to us.

Celia bowed and politely asked for that chocolate.

Her mothers didn't give her *one*; they banged on neighbors' doors for hours, collecting as many sweets as they could. It became quite a party.

The next day, even after her mothers took her to the temple and left her there, Celia felt their love. She'd almost gotten sick from all of it.

If they were honored that their child had been called to serve the Divine, it had to be a good thing. It didn't even occur to Celia to think it would be anything other than wonderful.

That's how stupid she'd been.

ACT 1

CHAPTER 1

ANOTHER QUESTION MARK BLOOMED ON CELIA'S FOREARM, bigger and bolder than the others. The ink unfurled in an oily black stretched-out tentacle, wrist to elbow, the dot on the bottom a furious splatter. An hour ago Celia had still tried to hide Anya's messages by tugging her shirtsleeve down. An hour ago she'd still cared that she was in a busy shisha lounge, surrounded by people who might notice the strangeness of Divine tattoos appearing, then vanishing, on her skin.

But lovely absinthe made cares like that disappear.

Celia pressed her finger to the angry splotch on the bottom. *I'd tell you where I am, Anny, if only I knew!* Her gaze drifted over the haphazard collection of empty glasses on the table in front of her. "Huzzah, absinthe."

The rest of the room was alive with clusters of pretty people doing flirty things: enjoying their drinks and smoke, unwinding after a long day of doing whatever it was normal people did all day. Shimmering tenors, as individual as fingerprints and much more visible, shone around each body. Tenors were usually the boldest thing about a person's look, but there in the lounge their glint and vibrancy blended in the fog of shisha smoke that swirled from the colorful hookahs. Glasses clinked, laughter swelled, and everything fluttered: colorful sleeves, loose pants, long hair, light from a hundred candles, jingly jewelry hanging from ears and wrists and necks.

With her black everything—short hair, suspenders, tie, top hat, attitude—Celia stuck out like a monochrome stain amid all the color and life. Judging by the lounge owner's fluency in scowls, they'd finally noticed.

Not bothering to right her awkward sprawl, Celia smiled as they approached.

Or maybe it wasn't a smile, but a frown.

Whichever way was up. Whichever way was down.

"Time to move on," they said, their voice a deep baritone.

No, time to take a hostage. Pulling the hookah to the floor, Celia clamped the large bowl between her legs and hugged tight around its neck. They wouldn't muscle her out with so much expensive blown glass at risk. "A few more blasts, good soul," she said, jiggling the mouthpiece in her hand and then putting it to her lips.

The smoke trapped in the bowl tasted like all the people who'd touched the pipe that day, swirling together. *Dia*, how long had she been sitting there, doing nothing but staring?

The owner raised their caterpillar eyebrows as Celia struggled to hold in a violent cough. "You've had the green fairy; you've had some shisha. Now out you go, Lalita."

A flush crept up Celia's neck. *Fragile bird, my nimble little ass.*

A few people had turned their attention toward the standoff, and as Celia hugged her hookah tighter, the lounge owner's lips formed a grim line. "Here, hire a gondola and get home."

As they dropped her own kropi back on the table—each copper coin etched with the creepy four-faced image of the Divine—the edge of a black tattoo peeked out from under their sleeve. Both reminders of "home," the place no amount of absinthe could erase. Their big hands found her armpits. They lifted her up, an arm wrapped around her waist, and eased her out of the lounge.

On the wet street, mist replaced pink smoke, darkness replaced candlelight, gray streets replaced warmth and color. Someone shouted nonsense or poetry from a nearby balcony, their voice echoing in the night. As they rambled about a love gone wrong, (or perhaps their cat was missing?), Celia considered transforming the lament into a duet. *Woe to the inklings who cannot escape! Mumble, mumble, rhymes with escape . . .*

Another voice interrupted. "Cece!"

Anya. That same angry friend who'd messaged Celia all night. A twinge of guilt flared to life, and Celia stifled the urge to dart back into the lounge.

As she strode toward Celia and the owner of the lounge, Anya's black hair lapped at her shoulders in tidy waves, her midnight-blue top hat perched perfectly straight. A buttoned-up trench coat flared out behind her thighs, and her umbrella doubled as a walking stick, tapping a rhythm into the cobblestones. Anya looked perfectly composed. Then, and always.

Long and low, Anya muttered *"Dia . . ."* under her breath as she approached. The lounge owner startled at the curse, dropped Celia's arm, and took a step back, reacting as if Celia was the devil Anya had just named. Their look of shock was quickly replaced by one of anger and *youth these days . . . no respect.* They turned and stalked back into their bar, violently brushing the stain of blasphemers off their coats as they went. If Celia's loitering hadn't banned her from coming back, Anya's curse just had.

Stifling a smirk, Celia bowed. "My love, my love, you've found me. The smoke was pink tonight. The shisha was happy." She swore the smoke changed color depending on the shisha's mood, logic be damned.

Anya steered her away, but they made it only around the first corner before Celia grabbed the nearest wall and painted her boots with a swirl of green fairy absinthe. *Huh, looks exactly the same coming up as going down.* She knocked her feet against the brick wall and wondered if someone would lick it later, grateful for a free drink.

Anya rubbed Celia's back, her words tight despite the calming gesture. "You're a disgusting creature, Celia Sand."

That wasn't news. Groaning, she pushed away from the wall and prepared herself for the lecture.

The air around Anya flickered in an aura of red hues. Everyone projected a tenor — an oscillating personal spectrum of gender in myriad colors. Tenors showed something infinite about a person and gave it over to concrete, manageable language: He, They, She, or No Thanks to Any of That. There were as many tenors as people in the world, and Anya's tenor burned so familiar that Celia would have recognized it in a crowd of thousands. She knew Anya better than she knew herself, which meant that even before meeting Anya's gaze, Celia knew she'd find a withering stare.

"You're almost at the docks," Anya said, grinding her teeth so the sound crunched its way up Celia's spine.

Celia blinked in surprise—and a fair bit of pride—that she'd made it so far from the temple without remembering any of it. That explained the stronger than usual stench of fish.

"I know you got my messages," Anya said. "Why did you ignore them?"

"I didn't have my quill?" Celia ventured.

Inklings always had a quill. Usually many. One day Celia and Anya would wake up to find the raven feather fused to their fingers.

More horrible grinding, Anya's whole jaw working hard until her nostrils flared with a deliberate exhale. About the biggest tantrum Anya was capable of throwing.

But no lecture came. Instead, "You have to get back."

It took a moment for Celia to process Anya's words. "What? Another one?" Her mind sputtered. She'd assumed that after the afternoon she'd had, she wouldn't be missed for a while. She should have known better.

Anya nodded, and Celia's cloud of guilt blossomed into a wild thing, growing heavier as Anya turned tender: tucking Celia's hair behind her ears, straightening her top hat (a losing battle), and adjusting her blouse.

"Vomit everywhere," Anya whispered. She wiped her fingers on the bricks beside them, her frustration fading away to sighs. She wrapped an arm around Celia's smaller shoulders and squeezed. "You can't keep doing this to me, Cece. When it's over, when you're okay, I need to know." Only a short lecture, then. A familiar one.

Celia stared blankly, ignoring the occasional claps of arguments or drunken laughter assaulting her on the otherwise dead streets. The buildings were tightly pressed together and built upward, competing for space amid a crisscross of canals and bridges. More gondolas than rickshaws ferried the few people still about. So much water everywhere: it fell endlessly from the sky, was constantly underfoot, and . . .

Earlier that day, the temple had punished Celia with water. Cleansing, they called it: only a little, strategically poured, but enough to perfectly mimic drowning. The stories said that the Divine had drowned a millennium ago, which somehow justified repeating the horror on misbehaving inklings.

The punishment itself didn't last long. A few minutes after she'd stood up from the wooden floor, soaking and gasping, Celia could have found Anya and told her it was over. She should have. But it wasn't the first time she'd experienced that particular punishment, and it wouldn't be the last, so what if the point was that she was never okay?

Celia took Anya's hand and laced their fingers together, squinting into the creeping fog swirling over the canal and searching for a wayward gondolier for hire. If she could stretch her gaze around corners and westward, away from the Lassina Sea that hemmed them in, the stagnant Asuran canal must eventually find a real river. Far beyond the masses of buildings, docks, and mold, the land would gradually lift around her. Eventually they would leave the sogginess of Illinia behind and enter Kinallen, with its famous plateaus and spectacular hills. She tried to imagine it—crisp, dry air, bright sunshine, green cliffs, a country so breathtaking poets wrote songs about it—but it was like trying to savor a slice of ripe, rare apricot on your tongue while standing at the gallows.

The temple had more work for her: another Divine tattoo to complete, another person's life to affect. If she took too long to answer the summons, she just might end the night as she'd started it: on a wooden plank floor with water pouring down her nose and throat, breaking off breath.

Woe to the inklings who cannot escape . . .

The prow of a dilapidated gondola broke through the thick gray fog—all peeling red paint, rotten wood, and ragged gondolier at the helm to match. His tenor flickered in silver hues, its natural brilliance dulled by the heavy air. Celia raised her arm to him. "Does anything rhyme with escape?" she asked Anya.

Taking poetic license, Anya came up with quite a list as she stepped onto the boat: "Scrape, reshape, agape, agitate."

She helped Celia in, continuing, "Translate, mistake, urinate, charade . . ." as the gondola sailed off into the mist.

Any of Anya's words could have fit into the next line.

♦ ♦ ♦

The Profetan temple stood atop the only hill in the waterlogged delta. Every alleyway, building, and canal in Asura boasted a good view of the looming stone turrets and waving flags. The algae-coated bulk was the city's pride, the biggest red dot on every map of Illinia.

The giant statue of the Divine—the temple's marble crown—perched on the highest tower, up so high it pierced through clouds. Human shaped enough to be familiar, inhuman enough to be sinister, the omniscient Divine was depicted as a robed figure with one head but four faces, each facing a different horizon. The Divine's outstretched hands had one palm facing up to the angeli in the heavens and the other turned toward the diavoli of hell.

Each face and both palms boasted one large eye.

Those six eyes, gazing into all worldly horizons and the hidden realms of the afterlife, somehow comforted believers, as if omniscience equaled altruism. Celia had realized long ago that the Divine was either wildly malicious or didn't exist to see anything at all. If she was so pure, all-knowing, and compassionate, how could she let her own religion turn so crooked?

Where the Divine supposedly guided the temple's followers toward heaven, Diavala, the wicked trickster, lured victims toward hell. Carved into the same marble centerpiece as the Divine, Diavala peeked out in anguish from beneath the Divine's robes. Reaching one crooked hand out for help, her lips hung open as if she'd been squashed mid-sentence.

The pathetic look was part of Diavala's con, but Celia had

always related to her position. She tipped her hat to Diavala in greeting, since *her* existence was far more likely.

Then she tipped her hat to the guards, who let them in after checking their expertly forged permission papers. Authentic passes giving inklings permission to leave the temple grounds were as rare as an Illinian sunny day, but the guards didn't know that.

Arm in arm, Celia and Anya approached the main square. Their footsteps slowed, their chins dropped, their heartbeats dimmed, the temple and terrible statue casting its familiar heavy blanket over them. Even so late into the night, the perpetual hive of activity proved that those serving the Divine never paused for sleep. The lamplight throughout the square reflected off the damp cobblestones and lengthened the shadows of the rushing crowd.

How fast people moved showed the temple pecking order. The long-robed mistico—the holiest and most powerful of the Divine's workers—walked as if they waded through water, graceful and composed. They could travel with their eyes closed and not bump into anything; paths cleared for them. Everyone else who contributed to the maintenance of the temple, such as guards, cooks, and servants, strode around with purposeful steps, no-nonsense. At the bottom of the hierarchy, inklings such as Celia and Anya scurried like mice, weaving around those destined to walk in straighter lines. Inklings possessed the only real magic in the world, but that didn't count for much. They had only enough of it to prop everyone else up on their backs.

On the bright side, being so low meant not having to wear a uniform. The temple relied on clothing donations for inklings, and as a result of a healthy benefactor rivalry, inklings were probably the sharpest-dressed underlings in the world. If Celia ever had to forfeit her top hat for a robe, that would be the last straw.

Celia and Anya didn't walk any faster once the crowd swallowed them. A small cluster of apprentice inklings passed, each sporting dark circles under their eyes and balancing a stack of books and papers with tired arms. "But can the tattoo change *size* once we send it to the receiver's body?" one asked. The others were too tired to answer his desperate questions. They must have been the oldest eight-year-olds in Illinia.

"Celia!" A raven-haired apprentice trailing at the back of the group lit up, shrugging their shoulders and bobbing, trying to wave a greeting without the use of their arms. "Celia! Celia!"

Anya chuckled and lifted her hand in a wave. "They were frantic earlier," she said, and called out, "Hey, Wallis. Yes, we see you!"

Wallis was torn, clearly debating whether they should abandon their group. Their gaze swung with the beat of a metronome between their friends and the two older inklings.

Celia didn't know whether to laugh or cry. For whatever reason, small, bubbly Wallis *liked* her. "You'd better study hard, Flea!" Celia called, gesturing for them to keep moving. "Off you go."

Walking backwards to keep eye contact, Wallis nodded. After only a brief hesitation Celia crossed her fingers and held them up to her chest, exactly what Wallis had been waiting for. Their entire face stretched into a wide smile before turning around to catch up with their group.

Looked like Celia was telling bedtime stories to the fleas again. Whereas full-fledged inklings slept alone in small, stark rooms, apparently needing no company except their Divine, the apprentices still had communal dorms. They were a rapt audience for Celia to unleash her imagination on.

And somehow that particular flea had a keen ability to wheedle story time out of Celia more often than not.

Anya delivered Celia all the way to the doors that led to the workroom. "Tomorrow might not suck," she said with a sarcastic smile. So casual, as if she hadn't had to break a dozen rules in order to make sure that Celia answered the summons that night. Celia didn't believe in the Divine, the all-knowing, and she highly doubted Diavala, the pitiful step stool, but if she stretched her imagination, she could believe in angels and devils; for years, Anya had been too good to be true.

Celia inhaled deeply and straightened her top hat (again). Only a little vomit still clung to her boots—just enough to scandalize whoever noticed it, but not enough to get a full reprimand.

The line between what they could and couldn't get away with had taken ten years to sketch out, but both she and Anya had it perfectly memorized.

CHAPTER 2

SET DEEP IN THE BACK OF THE TEMPLE, DOWN TIGHT HALL-ways and as isolated as possible, the inkling workroom had high ceilings, rows of tables, and endless bookshelves. For functionality, the three exterior walls were entirely made of glass to allow as much natural light as possible given Illinia's cloudy climate, but it also made the space aesthetically beautiful. Something Celia suspected rankled the mistico daily.

That night, a small swarm of inklings worked under the dancing flames of the lamps, flickers reflecting off the windows like fireflies. Quiet breathing and the scratching of quills on skin created a melancholy music. They all diligently ignored Celia, Yusef at the neighboring table flushing rose red from the effort. She didn't blame them; someone who got into trouble as often as she did made friendship with her a perilous idea.

Another inkling, Dante, shot her a full-body eyeroll when he took in her disheveled appearance.

Stupid Dante. His smug face made Celia want to break all the rules at once. After making sure no one else was looking, she took out her favorite finger, just for him. He pretended not to notice.

High Mistico Benedict—who'd personally poured the water over Celia's face earlier, adding a cloth to create an extra good seal—moved around like a wraith: inspecting, humming, clenching his jaw, frowning. His bald head, light eyes, and pallor, contrasted against the midnight black of his robe, made his face glow like a searchlight. His sharp, handsome features looked as if they were carved from the same marble as his Divine, too perfect and cold, as though the sculptor had forgotten that people had flaws. There was only one High Mistico at a time, the position passing from one to the next in a closed-door ceremony that ended with the previous High Mistico literally dying at the feet of the new.

If you were a believer, every message from the Divine to her people passed through him like a conduit from the heavens to earth. His hand wrote out every order for inklings to convey through a tattoo, but he had nothing to do with the content. He was the highest authority on Profeta, the most revered and respected, the only one who could hear the Divine's will and speak for her.

If you weren't a believer, he was someone who read a lot of reports, listened to a lot of complaints, and issued a lot of commands. A manager, but the most powerful one in Illinia.

Celia and Anya were in the nonbeliever group, but they were the Illinian minority, and what they'd always found most troubling about Benedict is that they weren't sure which category—conduit or manager—he would have placed himself in.

Either way, it was a station for the most devout and fervent, and Benedict was the youngest High Mistico in Profeta's history. Everyone under him was afraid of him, which meant that everyone was afraid of him. Yusef turned even redder as Benedict hovered behind his chair.

Dante returned to tattooing his upper thigh, the side clasps of his tight trousers unbuttoned to expose his skin, his hand moving in sweeping arcs as he created his newest masterpiece. Most sketched on their own arms or legs. If an order demanded a back, neck, or (shudder) rear-end tattoo, people inked on their partners. One couple in the corner, Allea and Ferrin, worked on a lower-back tattoo, the inker dipping precariously low on his subject. As much as Celia loved Anya, she was grateful they'd never had to go that far south on each other, but Allea and Ferrin were by far the oldest inklings at the temple, well past middle age, and Celia supposed modesty only lasted so long.

High Mistico Benedict's iron gaze bore into Celia as she approached him. He was probably debating whether to lecture her now or later. Finally, with a stoic nod, he handed her the Divine order for Fiona Jenoah of Asura—someone she didn't know, but would now mark for life—before continuing his patrol.

Celia exhaled hard, willing her heart to resettle so she could work.

Below a list of Fiona's personal details, the note said: "Her vanity will kill her marriage. Her wandering eyes will force her children to wander down her same path."

A big part of inkling training was deciphering prose: Fiona of Asura wanted to leave her partner. The Divine wanted her to know that this would ruin her family.

Celia now needed to translate the warning into art, something this stranger would understand. She tapped her raven quill on the table and bit her lip.

How to ink the omen?

She pressed the quill to her forearm, ignored the slicing pain as the magic took hold under her skin, and drew.

A hand mirror slowly took shape on Celia's arm.

The tattoo would transfer to Fiona only when Celia commanded it. And it would appear line by line, exactly as Celia had drawn it, so she planned each stroke with precision. After receiving her own inked omen in the dead of night, Celia knew that execution was part of the show.

Celia imagined Fiona sitting up in her bed, sleep-mussed and confused about the pain at first, then realization mixing with fascination as she peered at the image forming on her skin. Celia always tried to make it as flawless a performance as possible. No long pauses to draw out the suspense. No unnecessary lines to confuse the image. Clean and pretty. It would stain Fiona's skin forever, so it was the least Celia could do.

An hour later, as a final touch, Celia inscribed—*Family is everything*—inside the face of the mirror. A sentiment Celia wholeheartedly agreed with, thinking of Anya, but still, if Fiona had some other view of the world, who had the right to tell her otherwise? In Illinia, Profeta did.

Dante hovered over her shoulder, his pants all buttoned up, his work done for the night. Celia didn't know how long he'd been standing there, and she didn't much care. "You leave too much room for misinterpretation," he whispered. He would have drawn a couple holding hands or embracing, something more literal, to keep Fiona from leaving.

Exactly, she thought, assessing the finished image. "Thanks for your unwanted opinion, Dante. It's something I can always count on."

A smile slowly crept over his face, cocky and abrasive and screaming *Your stupidity is breathtaking, Cece,* and they stared at each other for a beat before he turned away. If they were fated to be allies and enemies at the same time, that meant they were nothing: the good and the bad canceled each other out. Still, it was exhausting.

She sighed, her gaze lingering on her inked initials: *CS.* Small, subtle, and disguised enough within the artwork that she wouldn't die for them. Hopefully.

Tiny as they were, those letters meant something big.

An innocent conversation with one of the cooks had given Celia the idea a couple of weeks before. Teresia, chopping and slicing so fast Celia didn't understand how she still had all her fingers, had divulged a secret with a merry wink as the earthy smell of turnips surrounded them. "I put a drop of honey in everything I prepare. Though you'll never taste it, it reassures me to know it's there, a little kiss in your bellies. My apology for whatever unpalatable monstrosity Chef Foureta makes you choke down that day."

Teresia had laughed it off as the foolishness of old age, but Celia knew that any honey in the pantries would be reserved for mistico and important guests. Those were stolen kisses. Something little meaning something big.

And like a drop of honey in a pot of turnip stew, Celia's initials said, *I'm sorry your skin has to be my canvas. Forgive me for marking you up and affecting the course of your life.*

This new habit of signing her work made her nerves hum.

She waved her sore arm toward High Mistico Benedict. He nodded after inspecting it, then intoned the same benediction as always. "The Divine has spoken—"

With his monotonous voice droning on, Celia willed the image on her arm to transfer to Fiona. With nothing more than a thought—a nudge to channel the tattoo from inkling to recipient—they became two strangers connected by inky magic. Celia watched the hand mirror disappear as the ink moved to Fiona's skin.

When her arm was bare and unmarked once more, Celia severed the link, releasing her remaining hold on the magic. She ignored the brief flash of euphoria that always came afterward; it felt disturbingly as if the ink was *excited* to be allowed into a new body.

"—the people will listen," he finished.

Mistico Benedict's unnecessary blessing only ensured that a

mistico had the last word, but it was a ritual Celia quite appreciated, because it meant that they didn't have time to see beyond the landscape of her art to the tiny, sacrilegious details. Like alternate meanings. Or initials.

As she walked out of the workroom, the exhaustion after completing a job already taking hold, Celia gave her own benediction. *Fiona Jenoah of Asura, I hope you wander wherever the hell you want. Make some mistakes. That fresh ink is just a picture to appreciate however you'd like.*

"Inkling Sand?" High Mistico Benedict called after her.

Quills stilled as every inkling in the room looked up, faint traces of alarm lighting every face. Celia stopped and closed her eyes for the briefest moment before turning slowly. Her artistic rebellions were already balanced on a hair-thin wire, but signing her initials was risky to another degree. One of these days the wire would snap . . .

"It took you over an hour to answer the summons."

She nodded and kept her head bowed. Right. She'd almost forgotten the first transgression—being tardy seemed so insignificant compared with heresy. She gestured at her boots for authenticity, glad that relief could look so much like deference. "I was quite ill, Solemn Mistico. It has passed." With groveling body language, she gave him what he wanted. "It won't happen again."

High Mistico Benedict didn't acknowledge her apology. As the silence stretched on, Celia's initial wave of relief soured. As stony as she'd become over the years, droplets of sweat pooled on her skin, her shoulders shook, and her heart did that funny thing where it skipped around. Unbidden, she began fiddling with the slim leather cord around her wrist: a gift from a long-dead friend, a reminder of reality. The *Book of Profeta* clearly laid out punishments—calculated dagger cuts, water torture, executions—but you never knew where your crime fell on the spectrum according to High Mistico Benedict.

That morning, she'd delivered coffee to a mistico council meeting. At one end of the table, Ruler Vacilando blustered about the upcoming Ascension celebration and how it had to be perfection incarnate. She'd ruled Illinia for the last forty years, and the evidence lingered all over her body: full sleeves of tattoos, undulating images across her back, and just as many likely covering the front. One crept up her neck, enveloping the left side of her face like a bad rash.

At the other end of the table, the mistico council, led by Benedict, nodded agreement to everything that fell from Ruler Vacilando's mouth. A strange relationship, either symbiotic or parasitic or both, and confusing enough that Celia was never sure who was truly in charge of Illinia.

She should have paid more attention to her task instead of observing the scene playing out in front of her. She should have remembered that Ruler Vacilando liked her coffee black, not sugared.

For her coffee mistake she'd received water torture, so what would she get for taking her time answering a summons? As she manipulated her worn leather bracelet—turning, rubbing, turning again—it warmed under her fingertips.

But High Mistico Benedict only flicked his wrist, dismissing her. Starbursts of relief flooded her vision. She knew the line; she hadn't crossed it. But just before leaving the workroom, Celia glanced back to see that he was still watching her.

Her heart rioted all over again, and she knew she wouldn't sleep well that night.

Even before Benedict had risen in rank, he'd been Celia's personal demon. Ever since her first day at the temple he'd followed her around with those hard eyes. She'd stood in the large square, stone everywhere, and waited to be assessed with a bunch of other wide-eyed six- and seven-year-olds. The heavy clouds dripped sporadically, hinting at the deluge they would eventually unleash.

With a cool, strong wind blowing, she'd curled into herself for warmth as the big people in robes hovered and discussed. She counted the cobblestones at her feet. Watched trickles of water race between the cracks.

A tiny river of rain led to a pair of little black shoes tentatively creeping into the empty spot beside her. When Celia looked up to see who belonged to those shoes, she saw a child with huge dark blue eyes fringed with long lashes. "What's your name?" the child whispered, keeping her eyes trained on the mistico.

Startled—were they allowed to talk?—Celia could only respond with a gap-toothed smile.

When she got a smack on her arm as repayment, Celia squawked, "What was that for?"

"Do you even know what's going on here?" So this other child was a know-it-all.

"Yes. We're going to be inklings." It was the first time the word had fallen from Celia's tongue. She'd been chosen by the Divine herself, the proof of it in the fresh tattoo on her ankle.

"We'll never see our families again," the child said with heat, and then Celia understood that her new friend's shaking was not nervousness, but anger.

"That's not true." Celia hit her back. "My name's Celia. It means heaven. What's yours?"

"I haven't picked it yet."

Most children didn't choose their names until they were older, but Celia had been impatient. She didn't like her mothers calling her Kid, as there were a dozen Kids on their street already.

Her old street, anyway.

Old worries.

Celia studied her new friend's tenor—the glinting frame around the face, shoulders, and chest—and saw quite clearly that *she* was the proper pronoun for her right now. Celia's own tenor held enough bronze flickers to make her wonder if someday she might use *they* pronouns, or maybe she'd swing between using she and they pronouns as time passed. "I've always liked the name Anna—"

A robed mistico had turned to strike Celia, so she stuttered the name, turning Anna into An-yaaaaah.

But seconds later the child muttered, "Anya's perfect," as if the mistico's disapproval was exactly what she needed.

"We might get Lupita as a tutor," Anya said, nudging her pointy chin toward the calm, smiling, gray-haired one Celia had crossed her fingers for. How did Anya know so much about this place?

"I hope so."

"No." Anya shook her head hard. "My parents said she's the worst. Only sweet on the outside."

A faint uncertainty nudged at Celia. Anya's anger and her parents' warning hinted at a different story from the one Celia had received.

But Celia stared up at the mistico who'd hit her, fairly sure he was the worst. Young and pretty, iron-cold eyes, and an arrow-straight spine. "I'm due a pair with this batch," he said.

Socks, dice, gloves—those were things that came in pairs. Muffins and cookies came in a batch. Not children.

Mistico Lupita calmly stated, "You're not ready for apprentices yet, Benedict. Continue with your own training first, and we'll reassess the possibility of a promotion with the next round."

"That's *four years* from now."

"It's four years from now." Mistico Lupita's tone said end of story.

Scuffling boots, a long, loud wail, and laughter cut through their disagreement.

A young mistico with hair as pale as wheat turned a corner, blazing toward them with guards close behind. She shrieked and laughed, pulling her clutching hands away from her head with fistfuls of her own hair.

Celia flinched and shut her eyes.

With Mistico Lupita shouting orders to the guards over the screaming mistico, the entire courtyard had erupted in sound.

But it was the smell that scared Celia the most. The fair-haired mistico grabbed her, her breath foul enough to rot an apple, her tenor pressing close and feeling like a threat as it invaded Celia's space. With her slim fingers gripping Celia's shoulders painfully, her screams turned into a song. "It's all games, darling. It's all lies."

The guards grabbed the mistico and pulled her back. Mistico Lupita bowed her head reverently, her whispered prayers and benedictions in the background. In the foreground, the wild mistico delivered one more line: "You lose when your bones hum from the inside . . ."

Humming bones? Celia inhaled sharply and cupped her hand around her wrist—searching for any quaking that shouldn't be there—and shared a frightened look with Anya. That sounded painful. Wrong.

Calmly, a prayer still on his lips, Mistico Benedict took a bottle from a pocket in his robes, poured its contents on a rag, and pressed it to the wailing mistico's nose and mouth. The voice-shredding screams stopped abruptly as she lost consciousness. Before the echoes of her song had faded, before Celia could even register the metallic glint of the blade in Mistico Benedict's hand or where it had come from, a red river streamed from slices on the wild mistico's throat.

Somewhere close, a child screamed. That sound stopped abruptly too.

The guards dragged away the now forever quiet mistico, the temple doors slamming behind them.

Lupita finished her prayer and took the blood-soaked knife from Benedict, wiping it with her own cloth as she continued her lecture on his suitability for apprentices.

As if nothing at all had just happened.

As if someone who'd needed help hadn't just been *killed*.

Beside her, Anya shivered so violently her teeth knocked together. Her chin was tilted up, her fists balled at her sides, her eyes open but unfocused. It looked like she was fighting hard to keep a scream from escaping.

Which meant, maybe, that the killling had been real.

The little vein that bulged on Mistico Benedict's smooth forehead pulsed harder when he noticed Celia staring at him again. "What's significant about the Flogging?" he demanded.

Words stuck. The vein on his forehead was all Celia could see.

Mistico Lupita stepped forward. "The Solemn Mistico asked you a question, child." Her voice was kind. She smiled as she continued to wipe the blade. "You have to answer."

Celia recited what she knew, stammering her way through. "A child said she was the Divine returned to the mortal realm. She knew a lot of strange things and almost got away with it, people almost believed her, but she couldn't command the ink. She was flogged to death with a nine-tailed whip. It was actually Diavala, trying to trick us. We have to watch out for her."

Benedict slapped her upside the head, her black hair falling in her eyes from the blow.

When she tried to push it away, another smack.

"I asked for the *significance*."

Celia's lip quivered, mats of stray hair hiding her eyes. She didn't dare brush it away again. "I don't know what that means."

Beside her, Anya whispered, "Solemn Mistico."

"Solemn Mistico," Celia added.

"Well, you're clever." Mistico Benedict turned to Anya, his boots swiveling on the cobblestones to face the other direction. "Perhaps you should answer for her."

Celia sniffled and tried to hold in her crying. The screams and wails of the rotten mistico still burned her ears. *Humming bones, humming bones . . .* That silver blade, that red neck, that casual ending of life. The new smells—rotten apple, sweetness from the rag, the dull, metallic smell of blood—mixing with the rain.

Anya hesitated before she said, "Only the Divine commands the ink."

A tsk of approval. Mistico Benedict hit Celia again for good measure, yanking the first sob out. She'd already snotted and blubbered everywhere, all over her hair. That made her cry more.

But so quietly.

She tried to be smart like Anya. She watched Mistico Benedict's boots walk away and let her mewling whimper escape only when the mistico was far enough away. She still didn't move her hair.

Somewhere in the bowels of their new home, the fair-haired mistico's bones weren't humming anymore. They weren't doing anything at all, and never would again. Another child had started crying, begging for his parents. And another. Maybe they'd always been, and Celia hadn't heard, so caught up inside herself. The kind-looking, sweet poison of Mistico Lupita ignored everything except her task of sorting children. Celia's head hurt from the blows of the iron-eyed Mistico Benedict. She was covered in snot and couldn't stop crying.

Anya hooked her pinky around Celia's, as if they did it all the time.

And nothing had ever felt so dangerous.

CHAPTER 3

THE FAIR-HAIRED MISTICO HAD BEEN THE FIRST CELIA AND Anya had seen with the Touch, but there'd been many since. Apparently, the screams meant rapture more than suffering. The Touch was coveted insanity, the closest you could get to the Divine. Death was a final release into her arms.

Humming bones, madness, lies, and blades: the hidden benefits of life inside the temple.

Exhausted from work and still hung over from the night before, Celia tripped her way toward the dining hall the next evening, using Wallis's shoulder for support. She plopped herself on a bench and put her head down on the table with a moan.

Wallis, bless them, fetched both of their suppers. "Have you seen the new tapestry?" they asked, their smile big and toothy, and nudged their dimpled chin toward the back wall, where workers struggled to hang the behemoth rug. "I helped tassel it." They pointed to a spot on the bottom left corner where all the white tassels seemed marginally shorter than the rest of the fringe.

"Well, your work is exceptional. And this year's piece sure is . . ." Celia considered the panels. "Breathtakingly prosaic."

Wallis furrowed their brow as they ate their bland (honey-kissed) stew. "What does that mean?"

Celia meant that Ruler Vacilando commissioned a new piece for the Ascension celebration every year, but no matter the medium, the images didn't change.

Panel 4: Birth. A landscape of the hill where the child oracle had first used the ink to guide the people, with lines of pilgrims winding their way to see her. The same hill on which the temple now perched.

Panel 3: Ascension. After her murder, the child oracle left the mortal realm. Representing this moment is the familiar image of the four-faced, six-eyed robed figure, seeing into all human directions and into the realms of the afterlife. Above her head is a lightning bolt, symbolic of her transformation to Other.

Panel 2: The Flogging. Always nice and graphic. A blunt portrayal of the damage a nine-tailed whip can inflict on a body. A warning to be on guard for Diavala's trickery.

Panel 1: The Return. Similar in composition to the Ascension—a lightning bolt, a figure—except the figure is entirely human. Her features are always obscured, lending to the mystery, but people would know she truly walked earth again because her own ink would proclaim it.

Celia meant that those four images were already everywhere, from Illinia's coins to public buildings to crests, and she meant that Profeta stood on four rickety legs, one of which hadn't even happened yet, and why didn't everyone see how shaky the table was?

She said, "I wish they'd take the opportunity to be more creative, that's all. Although Diavala's flogging even has crimson blood and gore woven in to boost the effect. That's great attention to detail."

Wallis shrugged. "I guess." They started to eat, unbothered. Wallis's faith hadn't been stolen by monstrous doubt their very first time at the temple, and Celia refused to push them there. She had a feeling Wallis would get there on their own anyway.

"Have you seen Anya?" Celia asked. It wasn't unusual for them not to see each other all day, depending on their rotation of chores or work orders, but they almost always met for supper.

Through a mouthful of stew Wallis mumbled, "Oh, Anya said you need to check out the light crooked path."

Celia choked and almost fell backwards. "What?"

Wallis's eyes widened before their face rearranged itself into a confused frown. "She was looking for you at the baths and seemed rushed. I have no idea where she meant. Maybe that path from the dorms to the big fountain?"

Celia garbled out a goodbye, already on her way out of the hall. She checked her speed so as not to raise any suspicious eyebrows. *"The crooked path becomes light."* The phrase came from Lupita's favorite poem about freedom and independence . . . and escape. Lupita had told them that when she came up with a plan to help them leave the temple—and it was always *when*, never *if*, despite the odds—she'd use that as the signal.

Celia swallowed, trying to get the last lump of food down, her mind racing in a hundred different directions, each one chasing *escape, escape, escape.* She tried to temper her excitement with a healthy dose of levelheadedness: their old tutor wasn't to be relied on for much anymore, beyond inappropriate cackles and lewd jokes. *Could be nothing, nothing, nothing . . .*

She headed straight for the crypt.

The dead didn't hold opinions about rules, so the crypt had been Celia's and Anya's preferred entrance and exit for years when they didn't want to announce their movement at the front gates. A basement maze of stone pillars, recessed rooms, and rows upon rows of gleaming white skulls on shelves, most people avoided it.

Celia wasn't most people. She and the head skullkeeper had been in love once, as much as thirteen-year-olds can be in love, and they still held an extra-squishy soft spot for each other. The crypts were a safe space because Zuni was there, despite the gruesome decorations.

"There you are." Zuni's face flushed red when Celia found her in a dark corner of the processing room. "I didn't want to be halfway through prepping a skull when you showed up."

Celia smiled at her, her heart pinging at the thought that Zuni had been waiting for her. Zuni didn't return the gesture — losing her smile was the cost of moving, decapitating, and burning dead people all day, every day, for years — but the corners of her mouth softened whenever she met Celia's eyes. A reflex that time couldn't tame.

Celia grabbed the handles of the closest wheelbarrow, trying to ignore the sheet-covered body inside. Profeta kept only the skulls of the Touched and didn't bother keeping any part of a heretic — so there was a lot of excess for Zuni to burn outside.

They walked side by side up the ramp, the barrow's wheels squeaking like a family of rats. Celia had never asked how, exactly, Zuni did her work, and Zuni had never offered the information. The pyres seemed straightforward enough, but the skull cleaning could very well have been done by rats. Or beetles. Or acid.

It was a mystery Celia didn't particularly want the answer to and one Zuni guarded closely. Zuni refused to take an apprentice, saying that her knowledge was her only safeguard against ending up on a pyre herself. After Ruler Vacilando had appealed for "heartier stock" to work in the Divine's service, Zuni's family, butchers by trade, had walked away from her with the temple's gratitude, a yearly stipend from the state, one fewer mouth to feed, and a feeling of righteous self-sacrifice. That was how Zuni had described it three years ago, and time hadn't softened her opinion. The reason she and Celia had hit it off so well? Equally jaded.

"Did you ever consider that by leaving from the same exit as the dead, it's like you're doing test runs?" Zuni asked. She leaned over to fold a flopping arm back into the barrow, then feigned a shiver as she met Celia's eyes. "*So* morbid, Celia." Celia started laughing, almost dumping the contents of the barrow completely. But her breath hitched as Zuni leaned closer, the air between them overtaken by Zuni's tenor. The swarming colors haloing Zuni's face proved the limitation of words: even the continuum of *she* lacked all depth for her. The air around her could be deep reds similar to Anya's, or silvers similar to Dante's, or any combination of reds and silvers, pale or vivid. Deep reds always dominated, but most of Zuni's internal landscape swayed, constantly in flux along the long continuum of her. It had been an impossible game for Celia, trying to find a pattern to it.

She'd leaped at any excuse to stare at Zuni, really. Still did.

When Celia pushed through the heavy outer door with the front of the barrow, sunlight assaulted them. So rare in Illinia for the sun to peek out from behind clouds that it momentarily stunned both of them.

"You might even see a sunset," Celia said, squinting. "What a night to spend outside burning heretics."

Compact rows of pale grave markers gleamed, the farthest ones bright specks of white on the horizon—the long-ago dead, before the cemetery had run out of room. Anya, waiting for Celia under a distant tree at the edge of the temple grounds, waved.

Zuni pulled Celia in for a quick, one-armed hug. "Have a drink for me?"

Celia grabbed her arm and turned the half hug into a full hug, the scent of death that always lingered on Zuni a particular comfort when paired with her warm embrace. "I'll find you a feather."

The freckles on Zuni's nose folded over themselves as she scrunched her face and looked away, the closest she ever came to a smile, and something that looked as if it physically hurt her. "Thanks, Cece."

Birds didn't come near the temple, not even to the tree-filled cemetery. Celia figured their light, hollow bones must be particularly sensitive to the occasional humming skeleton, and they were smart enough to stay away.

Zuni hadn't seen a bird in three full years.

Rich Asurans could afford homes on stilts, but most lived on the unavoidable water in rows of docked houseboats. As Celia and Anya sat in the prow of a gondola, weaving through canal after canal toward Lupita's, Anya's stomach revolted predictably. In another life, Anya would have been Asura's harbormaster: methodical, precise, organized, and able to coordinate everything without ever touching water herself.

They paid the gondolier with their last two kropi as he muttered curses tangled with gratitude that most of Anya's illness had made it to the canal and he didn't have to clean much from the bottom of his boat.

The dip and sway of Lupita's floating home wouldn't help, but Anya soldiered on.

"Lupita!" Celia called after they let themselves in. "Do we have a treat for you!" She wandered into the cluttered kitchen, lighting some lamps to fend off the bleak atmosphere, and began clearing off surfaces. *Slowly, slowly, calm down, this might be nothing, don't hope too much.*

Lupita had moved to the houseboat after leaving the temple, and five years of depression hung heavy in the air. Her loss of faith had been sudden and sharp—a knife cut or a plunge underwater—and it had broken her in significant ways.

Celia wore a reminder of it around her wrist: that worn leather bracelet from her friend Salome. At eleven, Celia had stolen a bunch of inkling quills, intending to snap them all. It was a protest she knew would get her killed, but in the heat of the moment her thoughts were violent, filled with rage, unconcerned with consequence. She'd broken only one—Salome's—before she calmed down enough to realize that she might get all the inklings in trouble. Water torture for everyone, perhaps, for the mystery of the broken quills.

She had to tell the truth about what she'd done, so she was the only one who suffered for it.

She'd found Mistico Lupita and High Mistico Benedict. They'd listened to her wailing confession, and High Mistico Benedict had calmly nodded. Then he ordered Mistico Lupita to execute Salome.

"Celia just admitted her crime," Lupita had argued. Though never one to shrink away from rules and order, Lupita hadn't been able to slot his command into any Profetan logic. Her thoughts seemed to spin around terms like *unjust, spiteful, unrighteous,* unsure where to land.

"She did," Benedict had said. "But this is an opportunity to teach her what true remorse feels like."

And because at that point High Mistico Benedict outranked her, outranked everyone except the Divine herself, Lupita had done it. And as Salome died at her hand, Lupita's spinning thoughts had landed on one absolute word: *wrong*.

The Divine she loved would never choose someone like Benedict to be Profeta's leader, so there was something wrong with the Divine she loved or with the institution the followers of the Divine had created. Either way, Lupita's world crumbled. One moment she was a devoted emissary of the Divine, the next she was confused and doubting, shoulder to shoulder with Celia and Anya.

And just as trapped.

For Salome, they'd gotten Lupita, and though they loved Lupita now, it had been a shit trade. Salome had been a sparkle, and Lupita would be the first to admit she was a stain.

Anya plopped her satchel on the table and flopped into a chair. Before she'd snuck out of the temple, she'd acquired bread, a small hock of salted meat, and a few vegetables from Teresia in the kitchens. Celia got to work on the meal as Anya mustered up the energy to roam the rickety three-story house-boat to find Lupita.

Since leaving the temple, the former mistico had lived on a liquid diet of absinthe, rum, and the occasional dram of juniper gin, joking that she'd live forever due to pickling. When Celia and Anya began their apprenticeship with her, she'd already been ancient. Ten years later, and she hadn't aged a day, so maybe her pickling method had merit. Still, they tried to feed her solid food whenever they could.

"And do I have a treat for you, my lovelies!" Lupita's withered voice called from somewhere upstairs. "But if I could just have a set of eyes, that would be wonderful."

Anya groaned. "She can't find her pants again."

Celia chuckled as she concentrated on slicing potatoes without slicing her fingers, imagining Teresia doing the very same thing at that moment in the temple. Musical howls from a distant dog gave her something to concentrate on besides the hard beat of her heart.

"I heard that!" Lupita called. "But it's actually my brassiere I've misplaced. These things need to be well tucked in or they're liable to knock someone out with all their overexcited swinging."

Anya laughed as she stood. "Even better."

Finding the brassiere and tucking in Lupita's overexcited breasts proved a difficult task, and the stew was already boiling when Anya came down with Lupita on her arm.

"Smells lovely!" Lupita exclaimed.

"Ugh, onions." Anya clutched her stomach and paled to starch white.

Lupita felt her way to the window, her clawed hands gripping counters and tracing over clutter, and opened it to let out the scented air. Her mutilated eyes swiveled, perpetually bloodshot, one crisp green iris pulled down and out as if it bled. Her gaze never landed on anything, which deeply unnerved most people.

Since Celia and Anya had been there when she'd gouged out her eyes, they considered the healed version a vast improvement.

Being a mistico, just like being an inkling, was a lifetime deal. No one walked away from service. The day Lupita bought her freedom, she'd drained an entire bottle of gin in the span of minutes. Then, while drifting in that numb sweet spot just before blacking out, she'd plunged short, blunt knives into her eyes. She hadn't screamed, but her hiss had sounded very much like *Sssssssaaaaloooohh* . . .

She'd passed out before finishing the name, her remorse dying on her tongue. Celia had had to clean and bandage her wounds because Anya was throwing up too violently to help. It still gave Anya nightmares years later, but Celia only remembered thinking, *Hope this works.*

It had. Lupita had done no wrong, according to Profeta—no heresy, no subversion—so they couldn't bring forth their chloroform and daggers. Instead, they tossed her to the streets and treated her as if she'd never existed. Acceptably pious, but useless to them as a visual arts tutor.

On bad days, Celia still managed to be pissed off at her. Not because it had taken her so long to see the horrors of the temple, but for joining them only to leave them behind.

Jealousy was a strange beast.

"Hey, can I have this?" Celia had already cleared off the small table so they could sit around it, and she reached across and pressed the small feather she'd found under a caterpillar jar into Lupita's wrinkled hands.

"It's from a scarlet ibis." Lupita nodded sagely. "Or a phoenix, perhaps. Either way, red and magical and rare. But you may have it because I love you that much."

The feather was blue, from a common bluebird. Celia shared a smile with Anya.

"Well!" Lupita clapped her hands as an exclamation point. "I have *giant* news." Her gnarled hands did a little dance in the air. "Let me set the stage, dear ones."

They both recognized Lupita-speak for a heavy dose of irrelevant information. The story would get interesting only with the words, *All of that is to say . . .*

Feeling better yet? Celia scrawled the words on her arm with her quill, watched them appear on Anya's; then, instead of severing the link like she had with Fiona and allowing the words to become permanent, she commanded the ink to return to her, as if she'd changed her mind about releasing it. The evidence of her question disappeared, both their arms unmarked.

Anya answered, *A little. Don't suppose we can walk home?*

How can you live in a city full of water and get seasick?

Shut—

Lupita cleared her throat, yanking the budding smile right off Celia's face. "You think I can't hear you scratching into yourselves? I have the ears of a bat." Lupita's voice dipped into grave-deep territory. "You're careful with it, right? No one knows you've figured out this loophole?"

It was heresy to use the Divine's ink for anything other than Divine tattoos, but *loophole* made their covert communication sound innocent. Almost positive, like a reward for brave experimentation. If the Divine was omniscient, how could they get away time and time again with manipulating her ink like this? Keeping the secret meant staying alive, so Celia and Anya were very careful. Lupita knew about it now only because they'd told her.

"Of course no one knows." Anya tossed a smirk in Celia's direction. They'd become professionals at using the ink right under the mistico's noses.

"Good," Lupita said. "Because I refuse to mourn you." After an overdramatic pause, she resumed her rambling story.

At this rate, they'd never find out Lupita's news. Their stew got colder and colder as they sipped and poked at it, nerves firing harder the longer they waited. There was a distinct possibility that even if Lupita *had* found them a way out, they might not like it. Celia wasn't strong enough to pay for her freedom with her eyes.

She slashed a quick line down her arm with her quill and gave the ink a mental nudge so it understood her will. The same line rose on Lupita's blotchy skin, and when she felt the pain, her hand flew to her arm, nearly knocking her bowl off the table. "Fine! Impatient thing."

Celia summoned the ink back, point made.

"All of that is to say . . ." The bells woven into Lupita's gray hair tinkled merrily as she leaned forward. "There are Rovers in Asura!"

Celia eyed the level of gin in the bottle, then eyed Lupita, wondering if she'd finally figured out how to ingest her liquor by osmosis. She moved the gin bottle to the floor behind them, out of Lupita's reach, and stared into her bowl as her throat closed and her eyes misted.

"Oh, Lupita," Anya whispered.

Lupita had delivered the news as if it were a delicious secret, but bands of Rovers came through Asura all the time. Traveling theater-folk who performed the traditional Commedia Follia, Rovers owned a network of fields scattered across the continent, which they used specifically for their shows. Celia and Anya tried to sneak out every time a troupe visited. Entertaining, because that was their thing, but not enough to warrant such unbridled enthusiasm.

Nothing that meant escape for them.

Oh, Lupita.

"The difference," Lupita continued, as if hearing their crushing disappointment with her bat ears, "is that I know the mother hen of this troupe. We were lovers once upon a time, long before either of you were born. That's a terribly exciting story I might tell you one day. Oh, the passion!"

Celia cursed the true severity of their friend's drinking habit, her thoughts drifting so far away that she almost missed the point.

"Well, anyway, Kitty Kay was reluctantly open to accepting new performers into her troupe when I mentioned that I have two talented friends interested in the lifestyle." Lupita leaned back and heaved out a long, rattling breath. "So. What do you think?"

The spoon on the way to Celia's mouth froze in midair, dripping stew into her lap. Anya's fingers clutched so tight at the table her knuckles paled.

What did they *think?*

Rovers were fiercely tight-knit groups. Impenetrable. Nicknamed Citizens of Everywhere and living apart from regular society, they opened their gates only to sell revelry and illusion. You were born into it, or you stood in the audience — in-between didn't exist. Even "guarded reluctance" to accept new members was a miracle.

Lupita had handed them an opportunity to flee after all, something they'd talked about endlessly, half knowing it would always be a daydream. Aside from inking tattoos, they had no other skills, getting out by ship was impossible because of Anya's stomach, and traveling on foot would never get them away from Asura fast enough.

With a band of Rovers, they'd be fed, clothed, and perfectly disguised. Because Rovers were so separate from conventional society, no one would think to look for two deserters in a troupe.

What did they *think?*

Celia's spoon dropped into her lap.

She finally let herself meet Anya's gaze — ocean blue,

familiar, thrilled and shocked and dancing—then slowly poured a round of juniper gin, her hands shaking as if she'd already had ten shots of the wicked stuff.

"*Dia,*" Anya whispered.

Lupita's muffled voice pushed through the roar in Celia's ears. "Kitty Kay's agreed to meet with you after the premiere to discuss an audition."

Silence.

"When's the premiere?" Anya managed.

"Tonight."

Anya hadn't let go of the table; her fingernails pressed indents into the wood.

This could be it. *Maybe inklings* can *escape the temple. We might not even have to gouge out our eyes to do it.*

All they had to do was convince an impenetrable troupe of artists, led by a passionate hen named Kitty Kay, that they could act, dance, and sing just as well as the people who'd done it their whole lives.

"Damn." Celia slammed back the gin in one go, her voice shaking along with her hands. "I wish there was a deity I could pray to."

Lupita laughed so hard she toppled out of her chair, the bells in her hair jingling all the way.

CHAPTER 4

K̲ITTY KAY'S GROUP CALLED THEMSELVES THE RABBLE MOB of Minos. Though all Rover troupes performed the stock characters and story lines of the traditional Commedia Follia, Celia thought that naming themselves after a creature of hell hinted at something extraordinary.

Lupita approached this with the same carefree air she applied to everything now, but her repeated reminders bumped around in Celia's mind: *As soon as you step into their world tonight, you have nothing to do with tattoos, orders, ink, or Profeta. Remember, you're ordinary orphans looking to escape a perfectly ordinary orphan life.*

Then Lupita added, "Don't mess this up. You won't get another chance like this."

Right. Celia reminded herself that she'd been acting her whole life. She refused to ruin this for Anya.

Lupita donned her best outfit: silver-lined umbrella, a bright teal scarf over her mutilated eyes, a tight black body suit with buckles everywhere. "I'll tuck in every sagging inch if it kills me."

And she'd managed it: everything tucked in, Lupita emerged from her bedroom as beautiful as a vicious moth.

Celia couldn't compete. As the three of them walked out into the night, she fought to straighten her top hat, her suspenders kept falling down, and one of her boot buckles gave her grief, clanging open as soon as she tightened it up around her calf.

She was totally going to ruin this for Anya.

Eventually the few bodies around them turned into many. Native Illinians with their pale, generationally sun-deprived skin; wealthy merchants from Bickland flashing their gold and jeweled teeth that sparkled bright against their tawny beige complexions; robust uniformed sailors from Poclesh, their skin deep-brown and healthy looking, weathered by sun and sea. Everyone soon blended together with a unified lust for entertainment. Shouting, singing, twirling, and bumping along, the bedlam provided good cover.

It also made Celia's heart dance.

Asura's giant port made it a vital international access point for trade, particularly for inland nations like Bickland and Shieha, but it was far from a thriving capital. She'd seen glimpses of the world near the docks: a spectrum of skin colors, languages, customs, and clothing, but people seemed to come, conduct their business, and then travel on, never staying longer than necessary. Maybe it was the gloomy climate, or more likely Profeta's tight hold, but something kept people from settling in Illinia permanently.

Clearly, this Rover troupe didn't have that repellent something.

The vibrant crowd bottlenecked as they approached the Rovers' field. Umbrellas opened when the rain started; from above, the mass of people would look like a painting of jostling dots.

A massive arch over the gates—colorfully decorated with oversize masks of Commedia characters—welcomed them to the field. When Celia first came to a Rover show years before with her mothers, the gate had scared her. So many beady eyes, staring. Then she'd seen the show and had fallen in love with every exaggerated character, and the gate had become one of her favorite parts.

Welcome back, Celia. Come in.

And that night, the masks added a conspiratorial whisper of *Join us.*

They paid the entry fee to a giant on stilts who had a fiery halo looping a foot above her head. The combination of fire, warm beige skin, and tenor cast a bronze glow over her face, obscuring her features but highlighting the deep blue of her eyes so vividly, Celia gasped.

Once inside, the people scattered, seeking out the best view. Tall torches fought against the rain, illuminating the sloping field. The main stage dominated, lit by periwinkle blue and plum purple flames.

A significant number of dignitaries already filled the special section roped off near stage left—mistico and politicians both, including Ruler Vacilando herself, flanked by her bodyguards—so Celia and Anya would aim to put the large crowd between them.

Lupita forged ahead, pushing her way through bodies and

down the slope. Anya grabbed her arm to steer her in the right direction.

A figure jumped in front of Celia, and she shrieked, juggling her umbrella.

He cocked his head to the side, staring at Celia through the tinted lenses of his mask, which was bone white, with a long, pointy beak and beady, too-round eyes.

A plague doctor mask. Creepy as hell and not a stock character of the Commedia Follia.

The darkness of his costume was absolute—tight black leather, a cape of raven feathers, black hat—but he shimmered as if he could capture and harness mist. He didn't look wet, just *shiny*.

Celia's gaze darted to his silver tenor more than once, to reassure herself that he had one. To make absolutely sure he was human.

"Jumpy tonight?" He cocked his head the other way. His voice rumbled, both playful and menacing: playful probably by nature, menacing by virtue of the sinister mask. "There's no need for it, I assure you. We've all been recently fed. There will be no blood price for admission tonight."

He paused dramatically, then tilted his head back and laughed.

Celia caught the scent of cloves and lemon—tangy spice and freshness—as if his beak were actually stuffed with aromatics to protect him from the plague. She pushed out a laugh as her heart settled back in her chest.

Anya scrambled to pull Lupita back, as she'd kept walking, oblivious to the welcome.

"I apologize for the fright," the plague doctor said, inclining his head to them in turn. He annunciated each word perfectly, his deep voice drawing the eyes of everyone close. By design. He lived to be watched. He craved spectacle. Celia imagined a tiny megaphone lodged in his throat, booming out his words without effort. "It's my job to welcome guests who seek the fantastical. But sometimes, I admit, I confess, I get distracted. Carried away. Overexcited. Feverish. Inflamed! When I see such profound beauty . . ." He looked straight at Celia, making her heart unsettle all over again.

Then, in a flash, he had Lupita's hand in his and brought it to his smiling lips, the only visible part of his face. Celia flushed wildly at the feint as the onlookers tittered their amusement at her expense.

"Gorgeous creature." He pressed a kiss to Lupita's wrinkled skin. "I see the wisdom of a thousand moons in you."

She chuckled, and above her eye scarf, her eyebrows danced up and down.

The plague doctor stepped back, clapped his hands, spread his arms wide, and smiled with a whole lot of teeth. "Be prepared for a night of wonder. Fantasy will become reality. Reality will become fantasy. Welcome to the Rabble Mob!"

Everyone scrambled to tuck their umbrellas under their arms, heedless of the rain, so they could clap and cheer. As he bowed, his feathered cape extended outward into two large raven wings beating in a languid rhythm and stirring the damp night air. Then he leaped away into the crowd.

Celia grabbed Anya's arm. "There was someone under that mask."

Anya looked at Celia as if she were addled.

Which she was.

How could she explain it? Every time she'd seen Rovers perform, she'd been caught up in the illusion. They were characters, imagination come to life, not real people. They sold fantasy, and she bought it.

But this time was different. The image of the plague doctor's smiling lips—rising and falling, surging and swelling with his words—burned in her mind. Someone lived under that costume, surrounded by his own tenor of metallic hues just like everyone else.

Someone she could know if they pulled this off.

"Lovely," Lupita mused. "Describe exactly what he looked like."

"A plague doctor with wings," said Anya, practical and succinct to the point of absurdity. "Maybe he's supposed to be Gemello?"

Celia nodded, scanning the crowd. How had he vanished so quickly?

"Maybe," she said. Gemello was the attractive rogue of the Commedia Follia, the disreputable charmer. But if the plague doctor had started with that particular stock character, he'd made it grow wings.

Celia gave up her search and slid over to Lupita's side, taking over his description. "Black as night, with shimmering tears woven into his cloak. Hard everywhere, except where he's soft. Wild and dangerous and playful. You'll yearn for his wings, and he'll take off from under your hand."

She described his act, his persona, and Lupita whispered, "That's better. I can see him perfectly."

If I can draw a picture of the illusion, Celia thought, *maybe I can figure out a way to tuck Anya and me softly into it.*

Just like hiding initials in a swirl of ink.

When the curtain rose, Celia recognized the first act immediately. Two players in identical costumes swept onstage to a chorus of Rabble Mob singers. The character Passion was one person divided into halves: purity and defect, potential and reality. They danced together and laughed, they shoved each other and argued. Always touching, two representing one. Two possible paths—the sinner and the saint—housed in one body.

Rovers normally stayed far away from religion, politics, or opinion. Even their stage language was universal: gibberish sentences as long as they were loud, but sounding *enough* like language to make sense. Exaggerated body movements became punctuation and emphasis. Masks embellished character. No matter what nation they traveled through, the crowds understood.

But the Commedia had originated in Illinia, and Passion's tale was heavily inspired by Profetan lore. Celia supposed that

Passion opened the Asuran show that night to pay homage to Profeta's hulking presence there.

The short play ended with Passion's death, as always. Flanking Passion, a row of angeli beckoned from one side of the stage, a row of diavoli from the other. In every adaptation Celia had ever seen, Passion immediately accepted the embrace of the angels, and then the curtain fell.

But *this* Passion hesitated.

The music had died with her. The afterlife hung silent and heavy.

"Where does she go?" Lupita's breathless words tickled up and down Celia's spine.

Yes, where would she go?

To heaven or hell?

How does her story truly end?

Celia glanced at the mistico and Ruler Vacilando. No doubt they were there as theater lovers—the Commedia was almost as old as their thousand-year-old religion, the regular story lines as benign and universal as the air they all breathed—but how would they react to an *irregular* story line?

Licking fog bloomed over the side of the stage toward Passion.

"Where does she *go*?" Lupita needed her answer.

The fog took Passion without giving one, her uncertain fate disappearing into infinity.

"*Dia* . . ." Anya's fingers had sunk into Celia's arm so deep they touched bone. "To either, neither, or both."

Celia's nerves hummed as she looked around, appraising the crowd's reaction. This new ending to Passion's tale thrilled her. If you still didn't have a clear fate after the Divine's guidance and Diavala's trickery, then all their guidance and trickery didn't matter.

The Rabble Mob had disguised a clever snub to Profeta right in the opening act, and Celia never appreciated theater more.

The curtain fell, and the crowd erupted in cheers, reacting as if to a charming show rather than something skirting close to sacrilege. The mistico and Ruler Vacilando clapped politely, though some head shaking and frowns accompanied their applause. Celia imagined them thinking, *I misunderstood. Surely they didn't do what I think they just did.*

"Lupita," Celia whispered, "your Rovers play dangerous." She spent every act whispering into Lupita's ear, seeking out each performer's illusion and coaxing it to life through words. Through fire, panting chests, flamboyant costumes, music made with voice boxes and stomping feet and clapping hands, and full-faced masks, Celia turned fantasy into reality and reality into fantasy for blind Lupita. Like Passion, each act disguised a subtle defiance to Profeta, something that wouldn't be noticed unless you knew Profetan doctrine intimately.

By the end of the show, the crowd was wild with appreciation, but Celia noted that Ruler Vacilando and some of the mistico had stopped clapping.

Lupita panted hard as she yelled, "Brava! Brava!!"

The performers came onstage for the curtain call, holding

hands to create long, ribbonlike rows of flowing color, bowing through wide smiles.

Celia hooted extra hard for Passion.

But someone lurked in the shadows of the stage. Even from where she stood, Celia could have sworn she smelled cloves and lemon.

The other performers paid no attention to him as he wove through their forms, his pale needle beak threading his darkness through their light. At center stage, he rose above them, hovering and looming, spreading his wings. A flicker of purple flame bloomed near his chest.

The unsuspecting performers still smiled and clapped, congratulating one another and the audience on such a marvelous show.

Lupita must have sensed the fragmented breathing of the people around her, including Celia. "What's happening?" she asked.

With preternatural grace and calm, the threat hovered. Slowly, deliberately, every move calculated, the plague doctor shook his head. The white beak of his mask sliced through the air to the left, to the right, and again. *No. Not good enough. I demand better.*

Every set of lungs around Celia gasped as flames erupted in a blinding flash of purple and blue. They vaulted from the plague doctor's dark chest and blazed around the stage impossibly fast, laying waste to everyone and everything. Performers succumbed to the flames, falling, some disappearing completely.

The crowd surged backwards, crying out in alarm, Celia nearly taken down by the panic.

Just as fast, the plague doctor pulled his power back.

The world settled into some new reality. As one, the crowd straightened and stared, still holding its collective breath inside clamped lungs.

Only one remained unharmed on that stage. His raven wings expanded up and out to a languid beat, as if shaking off ash, before he tucked them back against his darkness. Unhurried, he spread his arms and surveyed the world before him. Then he bowed to a deathly still audience.

He performed the entire finale in silence. He weighed the evidence, he judged, he executed.

All with a smile dancing on his lips.

"Celia!" Lupita hissed. In the stillness, her voice lured the plague doctor's gaze straight to them.

He cocked his head.

A shiver rolled down Celia's spine, invisible fingertips touching each vertebra. The one onstage, staring at her, had wiped everything away. The veil between fantasy and reality seemed stretched impossibly thin, the plague doctor reveling in the confusion his destruction caused. She whispered to Lupita, "The Rabble Mob showed us life—our desires, our fears—and at the end . . ."

It always ended with him.

"Death."

CHAPTER 5

WE CAN'T DO THAT," ANYA MOANED. "NOTHING LIKE IT. Not even close."

The main event had turned into a party. Celia and Anya wove with Lupita through the glamour and revelry, searching for the one who had the power to change their lives. "We can't eat fire," Anya said. "Fly up in the air, dance and tumble, create thumping music with our feet, and make everything look exactly like lust. The three on stilts? Taller than trees but flipping their backflips with no problem. Let's go home, turn in our quills, and let the wrath of the mistico fall. Zuni will probably keep our skulls as pets. It's as good an end as any."

"Since when are you so melodramatic?" Celia shook her head absently, her imagination sprinting in a hundred different directions. "But you're right, copying their show is definitely impossible. It's fine, though, because their show is already being done."

Anya cocked an eyebrow. "Your flask is bone-dry, isn't it?"

Celia blinked in surprise. She'd forgotten about it. "We need to find something different to impress Kitty Kay. I have ideas percolating, dear friend. The hive up here"—she tapped her temple—"is abuzz."

Anya smirked. "Your head's full of bees?"

"Exactly. And usually quite disorganized. But I'm queen tonight."

Anya laughed. "You're in charge for this part. You speak their language."

A couple, holding hands and laughing, blazed passed them, their euphoria nearly knocking Celia over.

Amazing, the switch in the crowd.

It had taken time for everyone to recover from the grand finale. After the plague doctor ended the show with his spectacular reminder of finality and futility, he'd vanished. And somehow, the last thing Celia had seen was his smile, as if he'd etched it into her memory.

No one had dared move. Like mosquitoes in amber, the crowd had waited for a cue. The Mob had trapped them, and only the Mob could release them.

Finally, the performers, including the plague doctor (the flirty, fun version from the beginning of the night), had come out for the true curtain call. That time, the Rabble Mob's bows had been an invitation.

Music soared loud, the audience split the melody with their cheers, and dancing erupted around Celia as if scripted. People pushed past her, rushing the stage, wanting to swing and sway with the creatures who'd stolen their hearts. The plague doctor moved from partner to partner, pressing his black, shimmery, playful danger against anyone who was willing.

And, Celia noted, everyone was more than willing.

Everyone wanted his judgment.

Some of the Mob now milled through the crowd, giving hungry eyes more acrobatics and fire and costume to feast upon. The interactive part of the night—more festival than theater—was alive with levity and cheer.

"Lupita Longoza!" a deep voice called. "I'm over here, you old fool!"

"Kitty!" Lupita exclaimed.

Celia's confident words to Anya moments before vanished like mist. The mind bees she'd hoped to tame squirmed and tripped over one another. Like some cosmic joke, her top hat slid to the left.

Arm in arm in arm, Lupita, Anya, and Celia swiveled toward the sound.

Behind them came, "No, not that way. Over here!"

They swiveled again.

And it went on like that for longer than Celia cared to admit.

Rumbling laughter from the stage pierced her. The plague doctor danced as if he owned the stage, his partner stroking the feathers on his back the way he would pet a kitten. When the plague doctor looked down, fully in control of the long mask, the beak pointed right at Celia, he cocked his head again and nodded, once. *Yeah, I'm laughing at you.*

The confused hive in her head exploded, the bees not only disorganized but full-on panicking. These people had the preternatural grace of fairies, and Celia and Anya had to convince them that they had something to offer? If Celia put on a mask like the plague doctor's, she'd impale whoever came close.

Kitty Kay, when she finally stopped with her hilarious game, materialized in front of them just as the plague doctor had earlier. Her long, orangy-red hair, highlighted with veins of a shocking white, swished against her form like a waterfall. Her sunset-bright orange gown, beaded with diamondlike glass, made the air around her sparkle.

She looked like a phoenix, not a hen.

After she and Lupita had a brief reunion of hugs and cooing, Anya spoke up. "I'm Anya Burtoni. This is Celia Sand."

Kitty Kay's face lit up with a sardonic smile. "A sprite and a changeling! A mouse and a lion! A stump and a sapling!"

Celia stood straighter, cursing that her boots didn't have heels. Stumpy-sprite-mouse might be accurate, but she loathed that it was Kitty Kay's first impression of her.

Kitty Kay grabbed Lupita's arm and threaded it through hers as they huddled under Lupita's umbrella. Kitty had wrinkles on her neck and age spots on her hands, but a regal posture and an unlined face. Her breasts didn't seem to have a problem with overexcited swinging, yet her voice had that underlying breathy rasp of age. Everything about her was so opposite, Celia got faintly dizzy trying to size her up.

Following the ringleader behind the organized pandemonium, Celia and Anya clung to each other. "You *do* have a plan, right?" Anya asked worriedly. The same couple tore past them again, chasing their ecstasy to another spot. A pair of fire-masters tossed flaming bolts between them, casting waves of illumination, then shadow, over awed faces. "These people are . . . different." They'd never seen any Commedia troupe open the field like this after their show, inviting people closer.

It fed Celia's glimmer of an idea even more. If they fumbled their way through this conversation well enough to buy some time, that idea might just grow sparkly enough to become something Rabble Mob–worthy.

"It's okay," Celia said. "We can do this."

They approached a dimly lit wagon set back from the activity in the field. It wasn't as ornate as the others, but it was larger: two stories, extra-wide, ladders crisscrossing the outside, leading from balcony to balcony. A glass dome covered the second floor, providing a view of the stars above, living quarters built to make perpetual life on the road a little more comfortable. There weren't four wagon wheels, but eight. It must've needed at least six horses to pull it.

Anya saw the same thing that Celia did, but she decided to ramble about it. "It must only go in straight lines. Look at how the axles . . ."

Celia almost laughed. Anya could take in contortionists, unearthly costumes, and fire-masters with barely a blink, and it was the engineering of the wagon wheels that unstuck her tongue?

"It's okay," Celia repeated, patting her arm. "Trust me."

Kitty Kay turned a crank so the back stairs descended. She

walked up the cantilevered steps slowly, gripping the handrail. Lupita followed, the stairs wobbling under their movement, her nose an inch from the rump in front of her.

Celia squeezed Anya's hand again. Anya smiled back, and they followed the pair into the wagon.

Calm down, precious bees, the queen's got this under control. Maybe. Hopefully.

Probably not.

Celia straightened her top hat, and it slid to the left.

The inside of the wagon looked eerily similar to the shisha lounge Celia had gotten kicked out of the night before. Fabric, color, flickering light. A green glass hookah peeked out from one corner.

"So." Kitty Kay settled herself into a mass of pillows. "We'll be here for a week and three days minus two."

"Eight days." Anya said, bravely sitting beside Kitty Kay.

"No, not eight days." Kitty Kay threw her a coy smile. "One week and three days minus two."

Celia choked down a startled bark as Lupita laughed. "Stop messing with them, Kitty. Anya is especially literal. But that doesn't mean they don't have exactly what you need."

"Yes—about that. What do I need? Lupe wouldn't give me any clues, no matter how much I tried to coax them out of her."

Celia grabbed a blue-and-gold pillow for something to hold on to and shoved it into her lap. "We're not singers, dancers, acrobats, fire-masters, or diviners." She paused for effect, trying to tame the urge to vomit. "But to tell you what we are would do our act an injustice. It needs to be seen to be believed." *You like the element of surprise, after all.*

Anya nodded, playing along. "We'll reel in your fans so they truly don't know up from down." No one else but Celia would notice that Anya's normally even voice trembled or that the swirl of desire had flushed her cheeks.

Kitty Kay hummed, processing the information.

The wagon swayed under clomping footsteps on the stairs, saving Celia from spewing out more vague words. A performer, painted white with rose-colored lips, poked his head in. "Ah! Vincent!" Kitty Kay proclaimed. "Our famous Palidon!" Vincent froze with his mouth open, mortified. Mimes didn't speak, and he'd been seconds away from breaking character. He snapped his mouth closed and bowed.

Kitty Kay nudged Lupita with her foot. "You could take lessons in decorum from the Palidon."

"What's that supposed to mean?"

"It means you're a loud, crass old prune."

Lupita smiled wide. "Oh, you know I'll be much louder before the night is done. I'm not nearly drunk enough yet."

The Palidon, still in his deep bow, began a slow backwards retreat. His light eyes had fallen to the pillow in Celia's lap, making her realize that she'd wrung it like the neck of an unfortunate chicken. His lips pressed together tight, as if holding back a grin.

"I'll find you after this meeting, Vincent. Go, fill up your dance card. Have fun."

The last remnants of tension left the room on Vincent the Palidon's white coattails as he nodded, swiveled, and left—as quiet as a whisper. Kitty Kay paused to dribble some absinthe down her throat. "Here's what we'll do. For Lupe's sake, for the sake of those treasured years we spent together, I'm willing to give you a chance." With her finger in the air, Kitty Kay shook her head at their exclamations and thank-you's. "I'll give you free rein in the costume house. I'll let you meet the crew and arrange for any props you need. I'll instruct them to help you with their full effort. On our last night—" She paused, swinging her gaze lazily toward Anya. "And when will that be, changeling?"

"On the seventh night plus three minus two." Anya answered, flashing Celia a tense smile.

"Exactly so," Kitty Kay said. "On that night, you'll audition in front of our audience. You'll have to convince me, the crowd, and every member of the Mob that you're the best thing to ever happen to us."

Anya flushed a deeper red. Celia wrung the pillow. *In front of the audience?*

Lupita whooped in delight. "They can do it! Huzzah, my lovelies—"

"One warning, though." Kitty Kay cut off Lupita's celebration, staring straight at Celia. "If you make a fool of me or my people, the Mob will turn on you. The crowd will still get their money's worth. If you fail, the show will go on."

That hovered in the air for a minute. Only Lupita made noise, throwing out some chuckles and juggling them about.

Then Kitty Kay laughed, and beside her, Anya deflated in relief.

A joke. An exaggeration. Over the top was the name of their business. Even the mime had staunchly held on to his mimeness when faced with outsiders.

Celia laughed too. For a minute she'd heard unbridled menace in Kitty Kay's tone.

Still, even as peels of half-drunk laughter boomed from Kitty Kay's red lips, Celia knew that the audience would be the least of their worries. Kitty Kay and her Mob would be much harder to sway.

CHAPTER 6

Bᴇғᴏʀᴇ ᴛʜᴇ sᴜɴ ɢᴀᴠᴇ ᴀɴʏ ᴛʜᴏᴜɢʜᴛ ᴛᴏ ʀɪsɪɴɢ, ᴀ ʜᴀʀᴅ ʀᴀᴘ on Celia's door woke her from a delicious dream starring a shimmering masked performer who'd swallowed a tiny megaphone. She moaned and rolled over. *Come back, plague doctor, come back . . .*

Another hard knock at the door. When Celia didn't answer, Dante barged in right on schedule. He'd made fixing Celia's punctuality his personal mission. He strode over to the window and ripped open the curtains as if they were her eyelids. "Angeli save you, Celia, you'll be late. Get up, up, up." He went to her rickety dresser and began tossing clothes over his shoulder. "Do you always have to choose black?" Pants, blouses, cravats, suspenders, and knickers flew through the air.

Why yes, when the public answered the call for clothing donations, she instinctively grabbed anything roughly her size and black. She waited for Dante to say something about matching the color of her soul, but he was too busy scrutinizing every item in her wardrobe.

A corset hit her face as she sat up. "Stick your nose in someone else's underthings!" she said, flinging the corset back at him. "I'm up."

"Nope." Dante's blond hair matched his pale yellow suit; his bright green eyes matched the decorative accents. Though his outfit was strongly suggestive of leek soup, Dante pulled it off; he'd be handsome in a potato sack. Stupid perfection. Stupid Dante. "I'm dressing you myself and hauling you outside. Get up."

"I'm not letting you *dress* me! Get the hell out of my room!"

He paused from his assessment of her clothing. Stupid crooked smile. "It's not like I haven't seen what you have to offer, Cece."

Dante had been the second one to make Celia's body betray her, and far too recently. Unlike with Zuni, they hadn't stayed friends. They were . . . something else. Remnants of temporary insanity. Foolishly, she'd thought his green eyes danced with a hidden mischief, and for months she'd tried to coax it out. She'd finally realized what it was: a strange brew of ego, apathy, and self-preservation that she didn't have the energy to drink.

She stood up and stomped her foot like a child. "Fine!"

He primped and preened, fluttering around her like a butterfly, tightening this, adjusting that. She glared through it all. "I hate Saturdays" was her only contribution to the conversation he kept trying to start. She and Anya had better things to do than go to worship—even the necessity of sleep had become a terrible inconvenience.

Dante pulled a brush through her hair and straightened out her heavy block of bangs until each hair lay pin-straight and aligned perfectly. "I'll trim your bangs later. You have such beautiful dark eyes, Celia. You shouldn't hide them behind this wall."

She smiled. "That'd be nice, thanks."

His eyebrows knotted into a frown. "Really?"

Celia snorted. "No. Let's go."

Every Saturday was a soul-sucking snooze festival that went on for hours. And hours. And then even more hours. Celia stood in the front row with the other shorties, Anya and Dante behind her so if she dozed off, one of them would catch her if she listed backwards. Thoughts of plague doctors, phoenixes, and the coming audition would have lots of room to roam.

On a raised platform in front of the main temple doors, High Mistico Benedict waited to bless and advise. Unsmiling middling and low mistico flanked him beside cauldrons full of copper kropi and silver virtues, ledger books open to document all proceedings. The mistico's number one job requirement was a love of paperwork.

The Chest Majestic's gilded edges glinted behind them, catching every errant bit of sunlight. As Profeta's most important relic, it held the only supply of Divine ink. The ink stained nothing and was inert most of the time, but it was sentient and alive in a way that creeped Celia out if she thought about it too long. The way it writhed when it sensed that a warm-blooded host was near. The way it could sense the memory of blood on the end of a bird's feather, the only writing implement an inkling could use to control it. Celia had seen and felt the Divine ink only once—the day she put her hands in the Chest Majestic so the ink could enter her bloodstream and make her an inkling forever—and that had been more than enough.

They put the Chest on display every Saturday worship, the only opportunity pilgrims had to bear witness to such an important artifact; otherwise it was in a vault, guarded more fiercely than the nation's treasury.

As Ruler Vacilando arranged herself on her personal balcony, showing as much of her inked skin as the crisp weather allowed, guards opened the main gates. The herd oozed in, prepared to wait their turn for a mistico's attention and a closer view of the Chest Majestic.

To entertain herself, Celia gave each pilgrim some dialogue.

The mousy-looking, worn one: *My dear neighbor, Iggy, is ill. Please, a blessing to unclog the phlegm in her chest? It rattles so. Sounds like she swallowed a frog!* A tattoo telling her to soundproof her walls might grace her arm later.

The snappy business tycoon with gold buckles: *I don't know whether to accept the position as high banker. Could the Divine offer guidance? I'm so important. StrutStrutStrut.* He'd get an image of a coin purse on his chest.

The parents pushing their young teenager forward, smiling and proud: *Here, my Kid is good and strong. They can help in the kitchens or by washing the floors. We welcome a chance to aid in the Divine's work. Thanks for the coin, huzzah!* The youth looked stunned more than scared, and Celia's gut clenched in sympathy. Zuni had probably looked the same a few years back.

As the rain lightened, people shed their heavy cloaks and jackets. Nearly everyone boasted a tattoo; ink made nonbelievers believe, turned half believers into fervent ones. Magic staining their skin meant that the Divine cared for *them*.

Celia searched for her work and glimpsed a tattoo of angel Gaia on the back of a worshiper's neck that looked vaguely familiar. She recognized the bear claw peeking out from under a loose shirtsleeve; she'd been proud of that one.

Another worshiper had a full sleeve of the nine levels of hell wrapped around his upper arm. Working on Anya, it had taken Celia more than a day and a half to complete. The temple had really wanted to drive their message home with him. He'd probably been an interesting soul leading an interesting life, before the ink.

A finger poked her shoulder. She swatted her hand back and smacked Dante's thigh. The stupid firmness of it made her palm sting.

Then she saw the hand mirror: fresh, red around the edges.

Branded on the forearm of Fiona of Asura.

Drab and tired-looking, she held hands with a child on one side and had a sleeping toddler tucked against her other shoulder. She didn't look up from the cobblestones as they moved slowly forward, her heavy eyes half closed.

The order had been specific about her vanity, yet this Fiona didn't look like she even knew the word.

A breeze pushed Fiona's hair shawl down around her shoulders. She struggled to right it, dropping her child's hand in her haste. But not before Celia saw the green-and-yellow bruise, the same colors as Dante's leek-soup suit, wrapping her neck like a scarf.

Whoever put that mark on her neck had large, strong hands. The imprints were so well-defined that Celia knew exactly where each finger had pressed in trying to choke life out.

She froze.

Only her eyes moved, tracking Fiona as she shuffled along. The tattoo Celia had given Fiona told her not to leave her partner. And there her partner was, walking beside her with a large, meaty, possessive hand on her lower back.

Every tattoo was meant to guide or alter behavior, of course. Profeta was powerful because people believed that the ink came from their deity and that their deity knew them intimately.

For years, Celia and Anya tried to find the source of the Divine orders they inked. If they were the Divine's messengers, they thought it was their right to know how the orders came to be. Sneaking around the temple had become a full-time hobby for them, at least two years' long, searching for the link between the Divine, the High Mistico ordained to execute her will, and the people. They'd expected a seer, perhaps. Or a heavily guarded scrying bowl. A secret chapel where the embodiment of the Divine lived. At one point Celia had been convinced that the huge statue of her was alive, truly seeing in six directions through stone, reporting somehow by magic. But what had they discovered?

Bureaucracy.

Mistico lived and worked all over the country. They listened, watched, and counseled. Their various reports, logs, and letters came to the temple in Asura. Lupita had said it felt like compassionate due diligence, not *spying*.

High Mistico Benedict alone was in charge of writing Divine orders, so ultimately, only he knew whether he received inspiration from a deity or a report, although their scientific conclusion was that Divine commands were nothing more than the High Mistico's nonsense.

But it still affected the choices of those who believed, and in the case of a thin inkling line around a tiny six-year-old ankle or a hand mirror on Fiona of Asura, it could ruin lives.

Celia was one of the messengers. She was part of the poison. It revolted her to see the evidence of her role walk right past her on tired legs.

They needed out. Enough of being a part of the biggest hoax in Illinia.

Their act needed to be so spectacular, the Mob couldn't say no.

Celia's bees were finally buzzing in unison. Nothing was more spectacular than the power of the ink.

Celia and Anya couldn't expose their magic, but they would use it.

They'd play like Diavala and be tricksters all the way.

CHAPTER 7

Z UNI LED CELIA AND ANYA THROUGH THE LABYRINTHINE crypts via a dozen shortcuts, twisting and turning with practiced ease, not even bothering to light a lamp. A week had passed too quickly somehow, the reality of what they were determined to do affecting how time turned. Seven days ago, Celia had whispered to Anya, "I have an idea . . ." Six days ago, Anya had whispered back, "And then . . ." Three days ago, they whispered together, "Perfect."

Each night, Celia had told endless stories to Wallis and the fleas. About magical forests, wicked deeds, misunderstood love. Protection. Friendship. She'd whispered, "Sometimes what looks like betrayal is actually the biggest sacrifice." She hoped that Wallis would understand, one day, why she couldn't pull them into an uncertain life on the run. What an impossible decision it had been.

And so many whispers with Zuni.

Time had caught up to them. Only moments before, Celia and Anya had inked their last Divine tattoo. It was a fitting end.

The band enlisting a new mistico was one of the few symbolic tattoos ingrained in the dogma, with no room for personal artistry. Anya inked a heavy black cuff all the way around Celia's upper arm.

This new mistico, Alesso Kazan, was to leave their shoe-repair business and bind themself to Profeta. The temple wanted them to serve.

Anya didn't close the thick band. As she and Celia always did, she left a hair's length between the beginning and the end. It was always their riskiest move.

Celia noticed. Her lips trembled ever so slightly as she held Anya's eyes. Risking this *now*, when they were so close to escape, seemed like tempting fate. But she nodded.

The mistico's band was similar to the tattoos that summoned children to become inklings. If only the slim bands around their own ankles, appearing in the night when they were six, painful and scary, hadn't been shackled so tight. If there'd been a flaw, a chink, maybe things would have been different. Maybe their parents would have seen.

As Mistico Tranki inspected Anya's work, Celia tilted her body against the lantern's light, the tiny, blasphemous gap hidden in shadows. She stopped her trembling by sheer force of will, their habit of protecting each other as instinctual as breathing. The mistico didn't notice the gap. They never did. For all their keen senses in searching for dissent, this was heresy of such magnitude, it was unfathomable to them.

Anya had given Alesso Kazan a way out—a sliver, a crack—should they want to slip through it.

A crack of light appeared as Zuni opened the back door, and

they slipped through. "They'll kill you eventually, Zuni," Celia said, trying one more time to convince her to come. "You don't belong here."

"I belong exactly here. I'll be okay. No one else knows how I preserve the skulls so well. I'm the best. The only."

Damn, had she always been so arrogant? Celia nearly fainted with appreciation.

"I'll look out for Wallis, don't worry," Zuni said. "I'll even look after Dante." Then she had the gall to *wink*. Who did that at a farewell?

Celia flung her arms around Zuni's neck and didn't want to let go.

"I'll miss you," Zuni whispered.

Anya nudged between them. She whispered in Zuni's ear, pulling Celia away. "Only Zuni knows what's best for Zuni. Accept her choice, Cece. We have to go."

With a lingering look, Zuni disappeared, swallowed up by the stone of the temple. Celia stared at the door. *I'll find so many feathers for you, Zuni. So many feathers. Every bird in the world is at risk for my plucking.* It became Celia's sad mantra as she and Anya made their way through the cemetery, crouching low, ears pricked up.

With no money left to hire a gondola, they zigzagged through the cobblestoned streets and over the bridges of Asura. The Rover field was desolate when they arrived. Celia peered through the locked gate to the long row of colorful wagons, seeking signs of life—a fire, people milling—but nothing moved. Anya led the way around a few buildings to the next block, then the next, until they found a tree leaning over the fence.

Celia's belt buckle came undone as she dropped to the ground on the other side, but she didn't bother tightening it. She didn't straighten her hat.

Anya rapped her knuckles against the door to the large wagon where they'd talked with Kitty Kay. When no one answered, she used the crank to lower the stairs. They were about to ascend when everything erupted.

Three young people jumped out.

One after another, flipping left, right, and straight over their heads, surrounding them. Their tenors moved as wildly as their bodies along three different spectrums, They, She, and He. Their skin tones were an array of pale white, soft beige, and deep reddish-brown, hinting at Illinian, Bicklandian, and Shiehan heritage. But they all wore the same black clothing—a loose blouse over a long wrap skirt adorned with silver clips—so similar in style to mistico that Celia cried out in alarm, thinking they'd walked straight into a trap.

"How'd you get in?"

"What do you want?"

"Your hat is crooked."

"Your buckle's undone."

"Are they frozen?"

The trio circled. Not in an intimidating way, but as if they'd discovered a pair of new creatures to examine under a magnifying glass.

"My name is Anya Burtoni. This is Celia Sand. Kitty Kay knows us."

The one with warm beige skin and a mane of white hair in a thousand tiny braids frowned as she circled. "The Intruder and the Interloper. Yes."

The cut settled like a burr under Celia's skin. "Kitty Kay invited us," she said. "We're ready to audition tonight, but we need to get the costumes together and our set done."

The white-haired one's full lips twitched into a smile and she shrugged with exaggerated disregard. "That shouldn't be a problem. If a few weeks of dress rehearsal isn't enough, one day is plenty."

Anya put a steadying arm around Celia's waist, sensing a brewing eruption. "So can we talk to Kitty Kay?"

A nod sent her tiny braids into a free fall over her shoulders. "You can talk to her, but she won't talk back."

Enough. Celia threw her hands up to the sky. "And what does that mean?" Anya's hand squeezed Celia's waist, telling her to rein in her frustration. This was their one chance.

The trio stopped circling. The white-haired one, obviously spokesperson for the group, smiled even wider, the two small silver rings pierced through the edges of her lower lip stretching apart like cymbals about to clash. "You don't know how things work around here, Intruder Anya Burtoni and Interloper Celia

Sand, and with only one day, I'll bet it'll stay that way." When her smile fell away, the rings in her lower lip settled like fangs.

"But!" She clapped. "Kitty Kay told us to help, so help we will. I'm Lilac, that's Caspian, and the quiet one is Sky."

Sky, the pale, quiet one, had a shaved head, except for a trail of long yellow hair leading to a high ponytail. They whooped so loudly at the introduction, it rattled through Celia's brain; then they did a backflip as easily as if they were part grasshopper. These three were probably the stilt walkers Anya had admired.

"The rest of the camp won't wake until well after noon." As Lilac strode away, she whispered to Sky, "One day is better. At least when they implode, the aftershock will be small."

Caspian cartwheeled ahead—his long black hair rippling free and loose—moving so fast his skirt didn't have time to get confused with all the upside down.

Lilac, Caspian, and Sky helped them prepare their act while the shadow of the temple loomed in their peripheral vision.

At one point in the blur, Lupita found them, smiling out from under her bright teal eye scarf. "I'll be right there, front and center. If you get nervous, shout out 'Hollyberry Jam!' and I'll feign heart failure in the most spectacular fashion to give you a diversion." She laughed, adjusting Anya's white feather boa into disarray, then patted Celia's shoulders before hobbling away. The sun went down, and the torches lit up. The gates opened, and people streamed in, the sound of their collective delight swelling loud.

Backstage, Celia and Anya, their masks disguising their faces, but not their trepidation, stood like two boulders in a fast-moving river as performers swooshed past.

Celia forced her words out in a low whisper. "If this works and we get away, how hard do you think they'll look for us?"

"Hard." Anya could comfort with her bluntness or slice with it. "But we're not running from a divinity. All we have to do is outrun a bunch of self-righteous people in robes."

Profeta was so finely tuned, everyone had a part to play: cogs on a perfect wheel, rolling along as a self-sustaining automaton. The ink kept the people in line, made believers flock to the temple. It was the fuel, and Celia and Anya would cut off a sliver of the source by disappearing. "True. But those robes won't let two rogue inklings set a precedent."

Stone-faced, Anya stared at Celia. "Sometimes I wish you'd tell your pissy bees to shut up. I'm trying so hard to be optimistic here."

One of the performers swooshing around them stopped to examine their trembling forms. Lilac. Maybe Celia's horrid mask distorted her view, but for a moment this strange theater creature looked like a regular person. Her eyes, nearly the same shade of deep blue as Anya's, lulled Celia with familiarity.

"You'll be fine," Lilac said. "If you fall on your ass, it's not like we'll eat you." Celia had no idea if Lilac's words were a light joke or a dark threat. The plague doctor had mentioned a blood price. "If you do okay, you'll have nowhere to go but up." She smiled at them both, the rings in her lips shining. "Or, in our case, west. Out of gloomy Illinia and toward the high plateaus of Kinallen. You can actually see the sky there. The stars! You should see the stars . . ."

Celia exhaled hard after Lilac left them, swept away again by the moving color and costume. Stars. Sunlight. Another world.

"So." What else could she say?

"So," Anya replied.

They fell into a hug. Celia's horns got in the way, but they made it work.

Celia wanted to say something poetic and meaningful. Something like, *Hey, this is the last part of a game we started playing when we were six. No, ten, at our final inkling test. Together. Always.* They'd passed their final inkling trial because of a loophole; they never should have been inklings, despite the thin bands around their ankles.

But instead she said only what she had to. "Remember, your quill nub is small enough to swallow. If you have to, don't you dare hesitate, Anny."

Anya swallowed, as if the small slice of quill were already on her tongue. "Let's do this."

INTERLUDE

That night, Celia Sand and Anya Burtoni tuck themselves behind a veil.

A darkened stage. No torches, gas lamps, or candles. Complete blackness, impossible to peel back.

Illumination appears around a pale figure dressed all in white. She moves through the crowd with angelic grace. People crane their necks trying to get a better view. As she walks, the radiance grows to encompass more and more of the audience, bringing them into the light with her.

"She walks among us. She's one of us," the people murmur. But for all her pristine appearance, veins of black lace her dress. This seems significant, but the crowd doesn't know why.

Then the torches lining the stage spring to life, extending the angel's world even further.

A horror lurks onstage. Under a tall domed glass container—a bell jar that should have held treasure—stands a hideous devil. The devil is everything the angel is not: sharp like obsidian, jagged and evil.

Gasps settle. They're relieved that she's trapped.

Thick, curled horns loop from her head. The beast's face is a hideous mix of fur, teeth, and beady eyes. Those

eyes never leave the angel—tracking her every movement. The beast stands coiled as if ready to spring.

The angel leaps onto a stool, hovering over the
crowd, and speaks, telling them a short tale of how that
devil has haunted her for years. It's strange to their ears,
to hear the angel speak their language. Commedia's universal tongue of nonsense is gone, and instead, this one
speaks *sense*.

"Invisible, but somehow always there," she says, tapping her temple. "Knowing my thoughts, weighing me
down."

A few people in the crowd understand. *Yes, that's
exactly what it feels like,* they think.

"I trapped her, but she haunts me still. The weight
may be off my back, but she's still in my head. Always! See
how she watches me, waiting for weakness!" She points
to the devil, her long, loose sleeves fluttering, exposing
her bare arms. "But I've learned to make a game of this
curse. Otherwise I will go mad."

She jumps from the stool. "Let me show you."

As she weaves through the crowd once again, people
part for her. Something is coming.

As the angel addresses the crowd, the devil moves for
the first time. A shower of red lights dance around her
and glint off the bell jar.

Then tiny blue shimmers. Then deep burgundy.

The devil makes those colors appear, but why?

The devil cocks her head to the side and, in a flourish, produces a paintbrush from nothing, writing one word on the side of her glass prison in harsh strokes, mirrored toward the crowd: *Clementina.*

She cocks her head to the other side and writes another name: *Lazzaro.*

The black paint drips down the glass.

There's some clapping and cheering, but not everyone understands the significance. This isn't the Commedia Follia they know: the players aren't interacting; there's no language-like gibberish between them, no exaggerated body movements to showcase emotion.

The people look between the angel and the devil, trying to figure out the game. They seek out the few mistico in the crowd, wondering how they're reacting.

The angel makes sure to touch every corner of the crowd, asking for names, colors, secrets, and then the creature behind the glass immediately reacts.

There's no way the devil onstage can hear any instruction.

A ripple of understanding spreads among the people.

The devil is reading the angel's mind.

In the belly of the crowd, someone says, "Tell her my birthday," and they whisper it to the angel. Even as the angel nods, the devil is already writing: 22 Markon, 14. No one else in the crowd had heard, and it's an impossible date to guess, but the audience member gasps and nods, confirming it with wide eyes.

A few remain skeptical, thinking the show is rigged. The angel seeks them out, asking open-ended questions: "What would you have my devil do?"

The devil attempts, poorly, to stand on her hands. The devil ties a knot in her tail. The devil butts her head against the glass.

The crowd laughs at the creature's desperation. The orders come faster, become stranger. People clamor to be the one chosen to suggest another trick. A few cynics go to absurd lengths to uncover how the illusion works. They inspect the angel's costume, certain that something must be hidden in those long, loose sleeves. They circle the devil's glass, examine the stage, seek patterns in the lights or in the sky.

Even the mistico talk among themselves, wondering at this new act.

Still, the devil performs with barely a hesitation: She writes the musical notation for a child's lullaby. She turns counterclockwise five times, then stomps her feet, then bares her teeth, then bends over and wiggles her behind to the crowd. She writes the names of the dead. She acts like a dozen animals, real and imagined.

Whatever the angel knows, the devil knows too.

Then the angel finds her way to a wailing child, determined to sway everyone in the crowd. "Do you want a turn?" she asks kindly. "Tell me your favorite color, dearest."

Onstage, the devil stands with her head down, breathing hard. For the first time, her beady eyes are not on her captor.

The child points to the devil and blubbers, "You're making her cry."

Faced with an inconsolable child, the angel appears flustered.

The devil snaps her head up, squares her shoulders, and swipes a clawed hand under her coal-black eyes to wipe away stray tears.

"No!" The child shrieks at the angel. "Don't tell her not to cry. Just stop being mean."

The people look again at the black veins in the angel's dress.

They look at a devil who wept: under her glass cage smeared with black paint, exhausted from dancing to their whims.

They're confused. Everything seems backwards.

"Did we get it wrong, and the child is right?"

"Is the true devil among us?"

"Should we free that poor beast?"

This new act—The Devil in the Bell Jar—confuses and thrills them.

That's when the veil goes sideways into chaos.

CHAPTER 8

Celia's costume had two significant components: slivers of mirrors under the thick brow so she could see down without bowing her head, and black fishnet glovettes to disguise the thin lines of ink swirling on her skin.

When Anya, moving through the crowd, swiped down her arm with that suspiciously long fingernail—her disguised quill—Celia had stopped whatever she was doing. A loop to turn around. Arrows to jump or bend. For specific words and names, Celia had easily deciphered the crooked scrawl. Anya had scratched into her arm without looking—concentrating more on commanding the ink to return to her at exactly the right time—but her letters, numbers, and symbols had still pushed together in a meaningful way.

Celia had had no time to doubt. No time to think. She'd seen and she'd acted, drawing eyes to her so Anya could get to the next command. The hair-thin marks of ink had guided her completely. The ink told her to bow, and Celia bowed. Their underdeveloped code had worked for the basic answers they'd been able to predict: colors, animals, numbers. The rest had been Anya's clear thinking, how well they knew each other, and the culmination of years of practice under the watchful eyes of the mistico.

But somewhere inside her deep layer of concentration, Celia's mind had begun to revolt. Little by little it had curled up into a ball, rocking itself, confused, murmuring something like, *Enough, Enough, Enough . . .*

Celia hadn't even noticed her tears until another vicious slash told her to stop them.

And stop she did, without question, already anticipating her angel's next command.

But nothing came.

The quiet lull made Celia aware of herself again: her tears, the heat in her gut, the ache in her throat.

And the pause also made the world come back, but it was a world she didn't understand. Mouths stretched open, making noises she couldn't hear. Half of them shouted at her, the other half flung words at Anya. The crowd no longer consisted of observers, but was an active, roiling mass.

"What's happening?" Celia's words echoed off the glass. A few people tried to scale the stage to get to her. Scuffles broke out.

Part of the crowd melted toward Anya, enveloping her in their anger, a mistico among them. If they unmasked her . . .

A clear, definitive moment of panic, booming like a struck gong, erupted in Celia's chest when Anya fell to the ground.

"No!" Celia smacked the glass, pounding on it with her scaled hands. "Get up! What's happening?" She tried to push the glass dome over, wedged her fingers under the rim to tip it, but its bulk made it a true prison.

Black took over her line of sight. She registered the feathered wings, the hat. One of the plague doctor's gloved hands gripped an iron hammer, the other gestured to the audience for calm. He glanced over his shoulder, and one beady eye stared at her while his smiling lips said something she couldn't make out.

The glass exploded. Celia ducked against the shards raining down, knocking her mask askew, but inside the tiny mirrors she saw feet scampering in front of her, stepping on the broken glass with hard crunches.

Someone, two someones grabbed her arms and pulled her backwards. She tried to twist away from them, shrieking for Anya and shouting about hollyberry jam.

"Quiet," the plague doctor whispered. "The show goes on."

Celia craned her neck for a glimpse of Anya, of Lupita, of anything that made sense, as two fire-masters took to the stage, working around broken glass that had once housed a devil.

A woeful Palidon and an ever-smiling plague doctor tossed Celia unceremoniously onto a pile of discarded costumes backstage.

"Where's Anya?" Her voice cracked, and she had to repeat herself. "Where's Anya?"

The thick curtain covering a side entryway fluttered, and up near the scaffolding, Lilac poked her head through. A wave of the crowd's roar blew in with her. "I told you not to fall on your ass and you both *literally* did just that." She shook her hovering, disembodied head. "But Marco and Tanith have Distraction Level Red Flame underway."

The plague doctor and the Palidon continued staring at Celia, both eerily still. She scoured her memory for the Palidon's name. "Vincent?" The large black teardrop painted on his cheek stood out, shocking amid all the white. Even his clear eyes matched, as if his pale face paint had leached into his irises. He inclined his head in greeting, his stare unnerving in its clarity.

The sad, soulful clown. The naive fool, always pining for love, never fitting in. Celia had always been drawn to that character. Judging by how terribly she'd messed up their one chance at freedom, maybe she *was* that character. "Palidon's my favorite."

Vincent jerked back slightly, as if the compliment were a blow. Then he launched into a pantomime of indelible gratitude, offering her the invisible still-beating heart from his chest as repayment for the compliment. He said nothing, his facial expression didn't change, but clearly he was pleased.

And Celia appreciated the gesture. It broke through the stalemate of stares, distracting her enough that she could swallow the sobbing gasps threatening to escape from her throat.

The curtain blew open again, this time from the bottom, and Anya worked her way around Lilac's stilts.

Celia held her arms out like a child wanting to be picked up. "I'm sorry . . ."

"It's okay, we'll be okay." Anya crumpled down beside her,

repeating those words, as if trying to convince herself. They laced their fingers together, had a silent *What now?* conversation, and then faced their inquisitors from the bed of costumes.

Since neither the plague doctor nor the Palidon seemed inclined to use their voices, Celia braced herself to hear it from Lilac. *Nice try, but*— or maybe a more to-the-point, *Get out before we throw you out.*

The last thing she expected Lilac to say was "You were fantastic."

"What?" Celia and Anya chorused.

Vincent shrugged so high his ears touched his shoulders.

Through those too-round, too-tinted lenses, the plague doctor stared.

Neither of them looked all that congratulatory, so Celia concentrated on Lilac's assessment: *fantastic.* A shiver coursed through her, and her heart ka-thumped painfully against her ribs.

Anya gripped Celia's hand tighter.

Maybe they hadn't spectacularly messed up. Maybe they were living their escape.

"Sure, the near-riot part was bad," Lilac conceded. "Bad luck, that Kid in the crowd." She paused and shrugged. "But they bought into it completely; they helped the angel beat the devil down. But would a devil cry? Would it look so sad and pathetic? That Kid made them feel like they'd chosen the wrong side. But you made them *feel.* That's what we do."

For the first time, Celia thought that those silver hoops in Lilac's lips didn't look like fangs or harsh cymbals, but like rare jewels.

The plague doctor nodded again, his beak slicing the air. When he'd smashed the glass, he'd acted on the people's wants and turned it into part of the show. *You were right! Of course the devil will be freed!*

As if he hadn't just been super intense, he turned to Vincent and said something about the fire-masters, making an explosion with his hands that rocked through his shoulders and shuddered down his spine. Vincent mimed heavy laughter.

Celia and Anya stared at them.

The plague doctor swept toward the exit, holding Vincent's arm. "We'll find Kitty Kay." The plague doctor's first words to them, and Celia didn't know what they meant.

"What will you say? Can we stay? Does everyone vote?"

He didn't answer.

Lilac shook her head at the curtain as they disappeared behind it. "Don't worry about him. He gets muddled sometimes."

"Who is he?" Someone more important here than just another performer. Someone strange, to smile so brightly while staring at the world from behind a mask of death.

"He's"—Lilac took a while to find the right term—"second-in-command. Kitty Kay's his mum."

After the string of silent noise in her head died down—his grandmother, surely; of all the luck—Celia thought two coherent words:

Damn and *it*.

So preoccupied with convincing the hen, Celia hadn't realized that the hen might have a chick. One who started the show and ended it. One who made Celia's heart race and blurred edges until she doubted they'd ever existed. "What's his name?"

"The plague doctor."

"No—what's his name?"

Lilac frowned, and her deep blue eyes tilted up to the rafters. "Ah! Griffin."

It had taken Lilac forever to remember.

When the party began after the main show, Celia searched for the plague doctor. To unmuddle him, convince him. He held more sway over their fate than she'd thought. She went to the main stage, assuming he'd be there again, dancing, pressing, laughing.

But she kept getting foiled by her newfound popularity; everyone wanted to dance with the devil.

As she spun clumsily around in strangers' arms, the plague doctor's white mask appeared then disappeared. Each time she danced her way to where she'd seen him last, he'd conveniently moved to the other side of the stage. Because it was too obvious to be coincidence, it pissed Celia off in rising degrees.

On the cusp of exploding, she dipped under her dance partner's arm, being careful with the curled horns that seemed hell-bent to get in her way with every spin, and ungracefully rammed into a chest.

"May I cut in, good soul?" the plague doctor boomed, the phantom megaphone back in place in his throat. He didn't wait for Celia's partner to answer. One of his gloved hands lightly pressed into the small of her back while the other barely touched her fingers. Every inch of her skin exploded, and she'd never felt more awkward inside it.

Still, it became the most fluid dance Celia had done all night.

Aside from the white mask he wore, the two were uninterrupted black. No one watching would be able to tell where the devil ended and the plague doctor began.

"You've been avoiding me," she said when she recovered use of her tongue, squinting into the lenses of his mask, looking for a flutter of eyelid to ground herself.

"Oh, most definitely." So loud. Always smiling. Looking around at his ever-present audience.

"Why?"

"Because I needed to think some things, and you distract me."

She couldn't figure out whether that was a compliment or an insult, then realized that she truly shouldn't care. "Our act is good. We'll fix it up, no more glass needs to be smashed."

"Yes. You're talented." They swept along in graceful circles. "I can't argue with that. The crowd lapped you up like kittens with warm, fresh milk."

Celia should have been relieved, but that underlying current of *opposite* still lingered.

"But—"

It was a long-drawn-out *But—*

Celia's heart didn't know what to do with itself. Full stop? Flutter madly? A little of both? And she didn't know if her reaction came from a surge of hope, fear of the plague doctor's *but—*, or fear of the plague doctor himself.

He dipped his head so the tip of his hat touched the heavy brow of her mask, his beak pointing straight down between them. If she'd puckered her lips, she could have planted a kiss on the bridge of his white beak. So aware of himself, he gave her the angle she wanted; though still shadowed behind lenses, his eyes became visible.

He smiled, but his words were tight. "There's something strange about your act. Something different. And not good different."

"We're not bad different, we only want to be Rovers." *You're such a lying liar who lies, Celia Sand.*

"I didn't say it was *you*. I said it was your act."

So, not her, but exactly her. She gritted her teeth and pressed a little closer, as if proximity would force him to make sense.

The line of his jaw flexed as he smiled. "Seer's cards might still save us, I suppose. Though the bigness of this feels too much for the tarot to handle."

"Well, if Kitty Kay wants us, we're staying, Griffin."

At that, he froze. "Yes, she wants you," he said after a pause, "despite my reservations."

Celia almost whooped, and she never whooped. *Freedom! Anya, we did it!*

Then he dazzled her with his opposite smile. The line of his mask drew her gaze down to those delicious lips of his. An infuriating wave of goose bumps rolled over her skin, puckering everything up. "And I'm the plague doctor."

The wild butterflies in her stomach had joined her mind bees, and she laughed, trying to calm her insides down. "Well, we're either Celia and Griffin or the devil and the plague doctor. You decide, but make the right choice: you're either dancing with a person or dancing with the devil."

She named his language Riddlish and vowed to master it.

He tensed, not in an uncertain way, but in a fighting way. Someone fluent in Riddlish wouldn't appreciate being cornered by Riddlish threats.

"Well played, Celia Sand." The plague doctor had either spat out the tiny megaphone or swallowed it, for his words came out as soft as a whisper.

Unexpected enough to startle her.

"We'll have to see how this plays out, won't we? Welcome to the Rabble Mob."

He dropped his hand, inserted his performer's megaphone, and Celia was in another's arms before she could even get her lungs working again.

CHAPTER 9

THE REST OF THE NIGHT PASSED IN A BLUR.

Celia had no time to figure out whether she was celebrating or delirious. She laughed and danced until she ached from foot to throat. She flirted like a devil, giving the people what they craved. She caught glimpses of Anya throughout the night. The angel was as much in demand as the devil.

The gates closed, and the noise died.

In the sudden silence, Celia would have floated away if not for Anya's hand pulling her toward Seer Ostra's wagon. The last hurdle to overcome: Kitty Kay's insistence that Seer consult the tarot.

With each card that she flipped, Seer's countenance became a little less guarded, until eventually her frown softened. Lupita had once shown them a book of fantastical creatures of the world, and Seer Ostra gave Celia a clear impression of a sloth: slow and deliberate, placid and gentle. She wondered if Seer hadn't posed in a tree for the sketch so the artist could get the perfect rendering.

After reading the spread, Seer sat back and folded her large, blunt hands in her lap. "Three of Cups, Page of Cups, Six of

Wands, The World, The Fool, The Chariot, Ace of Pentacles, The Sun . . . I couldn't have organized a more fortuitous spread if I'd planned it out ahead of time." Her gaze took forever to get to Kitty Kay. The lines to see her each night must stretch long not from popularity, but due to slothness. "I can see no ill omen at all."

Good!

But too good? The plague doctor's words buzzed in Celia's head, much harder to dismiss now that the cards were so favorably skewed. *The cards might save us, but this feels too big for tarot to handle.*

Even Seer Ostra had no explanation. "No confusion. The message is as clear as still water." She tilted her head back, as if ramping up for a monster of a sneeze, but wheezy laughter erupted from her wide mouth instead.

Buzz, buzz, buzz, went the plague doctor's message. Not quite *Something enough to be concerned about,* but not quite *Nothing enough to completely ignore,* it became an annoying fly among Celia's bees.

Seer Ostra's card reading felt like lies.

While Seer Ostra, Kitty Kay, and Lupita sank deep into a bottle of wine, Celia grabbed the pile of cards and snuggled into Anya. Bad form, terribly bad form, touching another person's tarot uninvited, but desperate times . . .

She had no idea how to read tarot, but they were cards with pictures, and she understood pictures. She cut the deck three times (that seemed about the right amount) and then pulled one card out.

A black sky background, with lightning striking a stone tower perched on a craggy peak. Flames engulfed the top and poured out the windows, gray smoke billowed, and a golden crown floated through the sky as if it had been knocked off the tower by the lightning.

A message Celia could rally behind. Though she couldn't fathom how two inklings joining a theater troupe could cause such destruction, maybe she could hold it up as something to strive toward. *Huzzah, Profeta falls!*

But Anya's breath caught.

Two figures fell from the tower. Two poor souls, not having much fun at all as they plunged to their deaths.

Celia replaced the card and put the deck back on the table. Anya found something interesting to admire out the window.

That card felt like truth.

When they emerged from Seer's wagon, the Mob had already packed most of the wagons and hitched the horses. Mud licked their boots from the late-night deluge of rain.

Lupita wound an arm around Celia's and Anya's shoulders, pulling them away from Kitty Kay. "I'll miss you." Lupita spoke softly, uncharacteristically crooning. "Maybe, when the time comes that you can fully enjoy your freedom, you'll remember me fondly. I've owed you for all the horrors I put you through before I woke up. With this, perhaps, my debt is paid."

She squeezed their shoulders, smushing them both to her chest. "Wish I could come, but I like my swaying home on the water and my good company too much."

"Gin, you mean," said Celia.

Lupita cackled her way back to the Lupita they knew. "A friend of mine has been dabbling in the art of homing pigeons. Okay, fine, he isn't a friend as much as a neighbor I spy on. His hobby is wonderfully loud and entertaining. I'll extend an olive branch to him and his birds when I get home. Keep your eyes on the skies for little purple messengers."

Celia didn't have the heart to tell Lupita that messenger pigeons flew home, not toward roving caravans and back again.

Vincent gestured for them to join him in front of the main stage. Without his Palidon costume and face paint, he looked like a regular person, despite those crystal-clear eyes, perpetually downturned mouth, and the fact that he still hadn't uttered a word.

Celia spied Sky on their stilts at one side of the main stage, Caspian on the other, and glimpsed a few other faces behind curtains and under floorboards. The rest of the Rabble Mob swarmed around the front, where Lupita, Celia, Anya, and Vincent stood, pressing close together.

Some custom was coming, this time with two little inklings included. Celia held her breath.

"Sastimos futura," Kitty Kay cried.

The Mob responded with a deafening roar, "Sastimos futura!" The assault of sound boomed in Celia's chest.

Vincent smiled down at her as she registered his voice for the first time. "Sastimos futura! Sastimos futura!"

Anya chanted loudest of all. Everyone, including the mime on her arm, pushed fists into the rain and demanded another day, a healthy future, as the main stage came down.

It folded like paper instead of wood: walls disappeared under others, boards hinged back and forth like fingers lacing together, curtains disappeared into cupboards that disappeared into other cupboards, new walls came up. They chanted to their collective future until the stage was completely transformed into the largest wagon of them all, ready to roll away with them through the muck.

"I love that part," Vincent whispered.

Celia nodded, but couldn't answer. She glanced over her shoulder toward the temple, but heavy clouds and darkness obscured most of its massive silhouette. Instead of screaming stones, water torture, and dagger slashes, her thoughts went to Zuni and warm freckles, Wallis and the other fleas snuggled on their cots, Teresia in the kitchen sneaking her honey kisses, even stupid Dante and his stupid, haughty opinions.

She pushed the images away, picturing instead the marble statue of the Divine crushing Diavala and the harsh mistico who used those images to demand allegiance. One last glare-off to bid farewell to everything she hated. "Sastimos futura."

Vincent fished something out of a deep pocket. "We have a gift for you." The Mob continued chanting as Vincent took her wrist. Gently, as if afraid to startle a bird, he looped a slim braided rope around her wrist, then around her pinky finger, before tying it off. It rested right beside her tattered leather bracelet from Salome. She hadn't noticed before, but the same bright purple and blue bracelet graced his own wrist. He did the same for Anya, connecting her pinky to her wrist with a thin road of fabric. "Everyone in the Mob wears one."

He touched the cord on Anya's finger, then followed the trail up to the circle around her wrist. "It tethers us together, and then to the world, so we don't lose ourselves to our own fantasy."

"Beautiful," Anya whispered. She met Celia's eyes, no doubt thinking of the inked line around their ankles. This one was warmer. Not delivered with pain. And they'd chosen it instead of it being forced on them. Anya's earnest look said *Maybe this cancels the other one out, Cece.*

Vincent nodded and shrugged, pink coloring his pale cheeks. "It's not much of a welcome, but then again, we've never really had anyone to welcome before."

Standing apart from the Mob beside the horses, the plague doctor stared at them. He'd chanted nothing.

CHAPTER 10

ONE TRUTH CELIA AND ANYA HAD COMPLETELY FORGOT-ten to take into account?

The reality that to escape by wagon, you had to travel by wagon.

Wagons moved a lot like ships.

They swayed.

They rocked.

They bumped.

They listed.

Anya's stomach did much the same.

Celebrating their escape involved much more retching than Celia had anticipated. Seer Ostra's wagon didn't smell much like old fortuneteller and incense anymore. From the bedroll in the corner, Seer Ostra sighed. Poor thing. Probably cursing her beloved cards for welcoming such terrible, smelly company.

The caravan creaked to a stop, and Anya tripped over herself trying to escape into the night for fresh air.

"We're only an hour in," Seer Ostra said.

Celia's bees began buzzing an alarm, and she launched

herself at Anya's leg, grabbing her before she could reach the door. "Seer?"

"The caravan travels in set blocks of time. Ten hours plus one minus five."

Anya gave up trying to get outside, grabbed a discarded cook pot, and heaved.

"Always?" Celia asked, standing and creeping to the window. Darkness, rain, more darkness, mud. Figures moved farther up the caravan, soggy and misshapen.

"Always."

Someone holding a large umbrella stepped out of the head wagon. Kitty Kay.

The someone next to Kitty juggled a plum and periwinkle flame in his outstretched hand. The plague doctor.

With the plague doctor's light, the formless figures became robes Celia recognized very well, though she'd never seen them so colorful as under the flickering of the plague doctor's fire.

A checkpoint. "Seer, may I please douse your lanterns?" Celia asked. Anya lifted her head from the pot, alarmed by the forced calm in Celia's voice.

A long, burdened sigh rose from the tangle of blankets. "Yes."

Celia moved quickly to the sound of Seer's long *yes*. Anya's chest heaved with her sickness, but her mouth stayed shut. She nodded as Celia blew the last candle out.

Outside, the conversation upped in urgency. Arms waved

around. A beaked face nodded. One mistico reached out, as if to lift the plague doctor's mask, but a leg swiped out and the mistico found himself kissing mud. The smiling plague doctor shrugged, as if to say, *Whoops, I slipped.* Kitty Kay helped the mistico stand, and the plague doctor produced a bright handkerchief from nothing to wipe at his face.

Their thorough ministrations in cleaning off the muddy mistico stretched on, looking suspiciously similar to showtime.

"There's a trapdoor under your feet, devil." Seer Ostra's voice rose over Celia's stuttering heart. "You may hide with my root vegetables if—and only if—the angel gets control of her cursed stomach. I will not spend tomorrow scrubbing vomit off my potatoes."

As soon as the caravan stopped, five hours later, Anya lurched outside for fresh air. Celia, on the other hand, had some trouble controlling her limbs. She and Anya had trembled among those potatoes for an hour, listening to Seer's sonorous snores. Then, when heavy footsteps clomped above their heads and the wagon shook with the mistico's violent search, drowsy Seer had calmly offered sweet buns and a free card reading to the mistico who grilled her about two runaways from the temple. Interestingly, they didn't mention that the runaways were inklings. After the wagon had begun its slow crawl again, Seer yelled "Sastimos futura!" loud and long before falling immediately back to sleep.

Anya and Celia stayed in the cramped cellar. Celia had

wanted, desperately, to look out a window and watch the world outside change, but they were both too busy crying. It had become real as soon as the troupe covered for them—no longer temple property, something *else* now.

Without preamble, she and Anya had been scooped up and cradled.

But what were they, then, except these orphaned, cradled things? For the first time, they could be anything. They had the world.

A world they had no idea about.

After Anya had fallen asleep on her chest, Celia absently thumbed the scars between Anya's fingers. Anya was ten years old when she got her first slashes, punishment for taking too long with a tattoo, just after they'd graduated from fleas to inklings. The flow of blood had felt infinite, the red alarmingly bright as it coated her hand like a glove. The mistico wielded those dagger blades with precision: punishment was necessary, but it couldn't permanently disable. "It's love?" Celia had said to Anya, trying to console her friend as she cried. The mistico used it as an explanation for everything, and it sounded so good.

Seer, a relative stranger letting them roost among her potatoes, looked a lot more like love to Celia than the crisscross of scars they both wore. Or the thoroughly entrenched fear of drowning that Celia suspected caused Anya's motion sickness.

When Celia finally plucked up enough courage to step outside—*no temple, no Asura, everything you've ever known is gone*—Anya looked up from where she was doubled over, almost as green as the grass under her feet. "Damn it, Cece!"

The air smelled different—fresher.

"Hey, don't blame me. You can't move on water, you can't move over land. At least when I throw up, it's a reaction to a little drink, not a reaction to *existing*."

The sounds were different—quieter.

The horizon was different—there actually was one.

Lilac came over and huddled under the wagon's awning with them. "You both look terrible." She rubbed her hands to warm them while Sky and Caspian cartwheeled their way over, flinging mud in all directions.

Acting so normal, as if the entire world hadn't changed. People warmed their hands over fires flickering in ingeniously designed portable containers; every wagon had a large awning to keep away the rain. Though everything was soggy, it wasn't underwater. No canals and gondoliers, no bridges, everything green and lush. Celia bent to adjust her boot buckle, inhaling the fresh air, as if to purge Asura from her lungs. *We did it. We escaped.* Her hands shook hard enough that Anya bent to help her with her buckle.

The Mob cast curious looks their way, but extra smiles, too. Camaraderie rather than suspicion had grown last night. Celia supposed it was fitting that the Rabble Mob would thrill at the idea of harboring runaway kitchen workers or graffiti artists who'd painted mustaches on revered statues.

Sky smirked when they popped up in front of Celia, revealing two deep, adorable dimples. Caspian poked his finger into one, and Sky responded by kissing his forehead. Some long-standing game between them, it seemed. Then Sky kicked into a handstand, their hands squishing deep into the mud. Cas caught their boots without even blinking, supporting Sky as they walked on their hands back and forth in a short line, head down, feet pushing toward their namesake.

Anya leaned over and flicked Sky's ponytail. "If I lived upside down, I'd shave my head completely."

Sky's pale hair flopped from side to side as they shook their head. "Ah, but flipping is so much more dramatic with a mane." They scrambled to their feet, and the trio backflipped together to prove it.

Celia didn't know what to do with any of them. With herself. What was her role here?

Laughter surrounded them in that muddy field: the horses nickered; a few of the older Mob members kicked a ball around playfully, faces flushed.

The plague doctor walked by, clutching his hat against the petering rain. As he passed them, he shook his head in a burdened way. Still, he smiled, the curve of his lips always up even when it might have wanted to go down. A gaggle of Kids ran toward him, screaming something like "Oh-be! Oh-beee!" and became a pestering herd, their whines shrill enough to break glass. Would Wallis's voice sound like that, uninhibited and free? The Rabble Mob had five young ones in the troupe, all named Kid until they chose a name for themselves. Celia wondered if that ever got confusing.

She wondered about a lot of things. Annoyingly, her eyes kept prickling.

Anya took a deep breath and pressed her hands to her stomach, as if verifying that there was nothing left to lose. "Why is the plague doctor still in costume?"

Lilac rolled her eyes. "He's always in costume. 'Selling the illusion,' he calls it. He drives the stage wagon at the front so the people who pass us on the road have the plague doctor to wave at and remember."

Cas shook his head, watching the plague doctor diligently ignore the Kids from between Sky's boots. "He died a year ago."

Celia nodded, like, *Hmm, yes, clearly that makes sense,* and cocked her eyebrow at Anya.

"He didn't use to be . . . *so*—" Cas finished lamely. "Death changed him."

Celia nodded again. *Yes, it would do that.* "So his mask hides decay?"

The trio laughed at her. Naturally.

"He *died*, he's not *dead*," Lilac explained. "He fell, bashed his head, his heart stopped; then something impossible like half an hour later, his heart started again." She paused, watching him with something like pity. "For half an hour he wasn't here. So wherever he was, whatever he saw . . ." Hard to tell whether she shrugged or shivered. "He doesn't talk about it."

"You know," upside-down Sky said, looking over at the spot where the plague doctor and the Kids had turned a corner and disappeared. "I don't even remember what he looks like under that mask anymore."

"Huh," Lilac mused. "Me neither."

"I'm pretty sure he's pretty?" Cas sounded decidedly unsure.

Distracted by something, Anya cocked her head and Celia followed her gaze. As crooked as a hunchback, a figure swayed as if caught in a strong breeze, her long gray robe fluttering. Celia squinted into the shadowed hood, but a heavy mat of long hair as gray as the robe obscured any facial features. Gray hair, but with sharp streaks of white veined through it, and a tenor that looked much like the one that usually surrounded Kitty Kay.

Celia's mouth popped open.

"That's *Kitty Kay?*" Anya said, incredulous.

Lilac's explanation for the costume was no explanation. "Kitty Kay's claws only come out after dark."

Celia gestured up the road. "I need a walk." She felt a burning in her guts, her temples throbbed her heartbeat, her hands wouldn't stop shaking. A few minutes in the middle of a wonderful new life, and she was panicking as if High Mistico Benedict had just walked around the corner.

"Come to our wagon after," Lilac said. "We'll find space for you." The stilt walkers' wagon was the one that looked like the shisha lounge. The biggest, housing the members of the troupe past childhood but not yet into adulthood. Lilac nudged Anya's shoulder. "You can vomit into one of my pots instead."

Trying to calm herself, Celia tucked her umbrella under her arm and left them, walking down the well-worn road, peering over short fences into yards that doubled as tiny farms. Outside the city, people had land enough for gardens, and the lushness of everything took her aback. Her fingers twitched at her sides, wanting every juicy-looking pepper, tomato, and bean she passed. What Teresia could do with fresh ingredients like those!

It took her a while, but eventually her breathing slowed, her temples stopped thumping.

She made her way toward a notice board down the road. Despite the efficiency of the mistico, Celia hadn't really expected to see her face and Anya's on parchment yet, but two familiar faces watched her approach. She leaped into a run and tore the papers down, moving down the short bank at the side of the road for some measure of concealment as she ripped them into confetti.

"Bad luck, about Seer's cards."

She jumped and turned in the same motion, almost gutting the plague doctor with the pointy tip of her umbrella as he stood on the higher ground. *Damn,* she thought, righting herself. *I'll never get used to that.* "Or good luck, depending on how you tilt your head."

"Yes." He nodded. "It's often about how you tilt, isn't it?" He tilted his head, capturing a sideways view of her. Then his gaze moved down, slowly, obviously, to the ripped paper she'd left behind in the damp grass.

He'd managed to lose his herd of Kids, so it was just the two of them and silence. "Er, thanks for helping us at the checkpoint last night," she finally said.

He nodded. "They said you stole something of value."

We did.

Ourselves.

"We didn't do anything wrong."

He took a moment, as if weighing whether to believe her. "We've run into trouble before," he said. "You're not the first to use Seer's cellar." Then he held out his gloved hands, clenched into fists. "I have two things I know you want. Which one first, Celia Sand?" He drew her name out into four distinct notes, turning it into a song.

She gave his gloved right hand a quick tap, and he opened it to reveal a muddy piece of gingerroot.

"Ah! Perfect! We all need Anya to have this, so thank you."

She tapped his other hand, and in his palm rested a sliver of mirror. "This fell out of your mask as we packed," he said.

Stuck in a paralysis that didn't tell her whether to plead ignorance or brush it off as nothing, Celia hesitated a moment too long.

His head cocked the other way, assessing.

She held out her hand, and he dropped the tiny mirror into it. "Thank you." She put the shard in her pocket, casual-like, tucking away a prop. Not at all as if he'd handled a giant clue that could give away their true identity. "Everyone here must know everyone else's routine, right?" she said. "Anya and I are all smoke and mirrors, quite literally." Her light titter sounded much more like a donkey bray. Her mind raced, mapping out exactly where they must be if their hard-fought stint with the troupe was already over. The mistico wouldn't out them as inklings, but a mirror might? Perfect.

He nodded slowly, still smiling infuriatingly. "I'll let you try again." He leaned closer.

So she did. Stuttering through the smoke and mirrors explanation of their act. "With subtle body movements, Anya tells me what to do, but everything's reversed in my mirrors . . ." *Holy angeli, does that even make sense?* "The crowd can't see any connection, but she can spell things out or give me orders with this code we developed. There's a healthy dose of common sense and sleight of hand. We use distraction, so people are looking at me when they should be looking at her—" She cut off her babbling when it skirted too close to the truth.

He shook his head, the dark hair that had escaped his hair tie brushing his shoulders. "You're still lying to me." He sounded honestly put out.

"If you believe so, then why the hell are you still smiling like that?"

Because of her sharp tone, he stepped back, and his smile faltered—something, she already knew, that didn't happen often.

"Sorry," she said. *I'll apologize for my tone, but not the lies. Lies keep everyone, including you, breathing.* "Thanks for the mirror and the ginger. You're right, I want both." She tried to chuckle without sounding like a braying mule. "The mask makes me nervous."

"No one else has a problem with it."

There was a big gap between "tolerating" and "not having a problem with," but she decided to let that go. "If you think we're hiding so much, why are we still here?"

He took a deep breath, his chest expanding so it strained against the black fabric of his trench coat. Even the buttons pooled like midnight. He pushed close enough to share breath. "You're in the Mob now, Celia Sand. It truly isn't a difficult concept."

Unconsciously, she reached to fiddle with Salome's leather bracelet, instead meeting the fabric one Vincent had given her. She remembered her exact thoughts when Lupita had mentioned the miraculous audition: *Rovers are impenetrable. Fiercely tight groups. You're either in or out, there's no in-between.*

But with Salome's leather cord she'd learned that lies protected and truth could slay.

The plague doctor made it sound simple, but her deception was about more than taking off a mask. Her truth would reveal a hidden world, a dangerous one.

She nodded. "Got it."

Another pause. Then, with a deep exhale, the plague doctor pulled back, adjusting his hat and mask. After dipping into a deep pocket, he pressed a beautiful red tomato into her hands before he left her. Walking backwards, spreading his arms as if waiting for her to run into them, he said one last thing. "I'm baffled why you're so keen to make me your enemy. I'm a wonderful actor; if that's the role you cast for me, I'll perform. But it doesn't have to be so."

She heard, *Your move, devil.*

CHAPTER 11

AFTER THAT, THE PLAGUE DOCTOR VISITED HER IN DREAMS and nightmares, both. *Poor choice, Celia . . .*

Anya threw a pillow at her. "If you don't shut up with those moans, I'm petitioning to have you moved back to Seer's."

"I'm nervous about tonight." Partly true. Their designated area in Sabazio was smaller than most standard Rover fields, but it would still hold a crowd. After more than a week of constant travel, the caravan had rolled in late the night before. As soon as the gates had clinked closed behind them, the reality that they'd have to perform in front of real live people again hit Celia like a wave.

"Sure, that's it, Cece." Anya flung another pillow. Thanks to Lilac's ginger teas, Anya's weak stomach had held steady through multiple six-hour blocks of travel, but stopping for an extended period would still be wholly welcome.

A faint tapping on the window a moment later, and Celia hauled herself out of bed. She waved at Vincent, trying to push away the remnants of her latest nightmare, then quickly dressed to meet him. Without effort, Vincent and Celia had become friends. He calmed her like a familiar blanket. Better than absinthe even, because his comfort didn't come with the side effects of nausea and hallucinations. With him, she could start to imagine how the Mob might feel like home.

Celia tore into the paper bag he handed her, the smell emanating from it some heavenly combination of butter, sugar, and anise. "A Sabazian shirran," he said as she mashed it into her mouth. "Anise pastries are practically a religion in this region."

She swallowed, her eyes watering with bliss. "You're the best tour guide, Vincent. But I have a hard time believing that the market was open already. Did you steal this from someone's windowsill?"

He didn't smile or laugh (or answer the question). So much like Zuni, where smiles and laughter were as rare as Illinian sun and would shine even brighter if they ever broke through.

As she devoured the rest of the breakfast roll, they began their slow lap of the field. It wasn't their first walk together. They'd crossed paths in the dawn light a few times since Asura, both seeking peace and solitude to sort out personal tempests. By some unspoken arrangement, they'd decided they may as well be solitary together.

"Georgio told me you're trying a revival of *The Severing of Firassus* tonight," Celia said. She couldn't see how they could make the Palidon fit into the narrative, since *Firassus* was an ancient Commedia civil war story line that usually involved too much sword work and blood for modern tastes.

"Yes. But we've rewritten it so it's less about war and more about fashion. There'll be a lot more costume changes than sword fights."

Georgio, who played the insecure and confused Commedia character Fazzi, was the sweetest person alive—considerate, humble—and brilliantly creative. If anyone could make this new version of *Firassus* work, Georgio could.

Vincent sounded nervous. Celia had never been blessed or cursed with feedback after inking her creations, so she couldn't relate to his creative anxiety.

"I'm sure it'll be great," she said.

The shirran fully devoured, Vincent nodded and took Celia's arm.

Their conversation lulled, as it tended to do, and Celia's thoughts wandered from Vincent's new show to hers and Anya's. On the road it had been easy enough to forget that they had to keep earning their place here by doing a job. A job that happened to hinge on no one discovering how they did it.

Anya had analyzed their debut over and over, tweaking and brainstorming and smoothing out the rough edges. Though Kitty Kay had loved the glass-smashing disaster of their first show in terms of novelty, she'd been clear that it needed to be a one-time thing. The Mob might burst with illusion, lust, and revelry, but they still had to work within the dreary realities of budgets.

Up the stairs of the main stage, pulling the curtain back, Vincent presented her with another Sabazian wonder: a new bell jar. The best she could figure was that somewhere in Sabazio lived a baker forty stories tall who put his people-size cakes under display domes.

As they worked together to polish it to a gleam, the rest of the Mob slowly stirred to life around them. Most had warmly received them—something Celia still had trouble processing—but there were still some side-eyes, particularly from Marco and Tanith, the two fire-masters. To block out their whispers, she told Vincent her theory about the Sabazian baker.

Instead of divulging where the bell jar had truly come from, he gifted her with a small smirk. "I'd love to meet that baker. If you ever see them, be sure to let me know right away."

She played along. "I thought Bickland was *full* of giants. Surely you've met your fair share by now."

Vincent's smirk turned into a crooked smile, his light eyes finding hers. "Oh, I have. But a giant baker? I'm imagining those *cakes*."

Such a small smile, barely there, tickling the corners of his mouth, but spectacular. "Oh my," she heard herself whisper. She dropped her polishing rag and hauled Vincent away by the hand, sitting him in the middle of the grassy field after fetching some supplies.

With a regular old quill, regular ink, and regular paper, Celia sketched him. The familiar movements took her to another place. She bent over her paper, surprised by how much she'd missed her art, looking up only to get the proper slant of Vincent's eyebrows or to remind herself of the angle of his lips when he'd grinned. They'd settled back into their original non-smiling state almost immediately, but she was determined to capture them before the memory faded completely.

As soon as she completed the first portrait, she started a second.

Vincent was a prime sitter. He talked more about his new show, didn't complain when Celia didn't respond. Eventually Anya and Lilac joined them. Nearby, Cas and Sky lounged on a blanket, talking in hushed whispers and enjoying the temporary pause in the rain.

Two younger troupe members huddled together, organizing their newly procured collection of sweets in a lush patch of grass, arguing about whether they should save them for after the premiere.

Georgio rested with their head in the plague doctor's lap. Leaning against a gnarled oak tree, the plague doctor stroked Georgio's wispy brown hair off their brow and sang softly up to the leaves. Celia couldn't hear his voice over the distance, but she imagined the notes dancing from his mouth into the air. A melancholy image, though one of them smiled as he sang. The intimacy of the scene—comfort, solace, calm your nerves, friend—tugged at something deep in Celia: a firm reminder that she was among them but not of them. Not yet.

She held the portraits up for her small audience to inspect. "Reality." She gestured at the first, carefully watching Vincent's reaction: pale hair and eyes, sharp angles, and that slight smile so powerful it should have combusted the paper. He met her eyes.

"And fantasy." The second piece showed him as the Palidon. Infinite sadness. Dark lines and contrast. The image popped off the page more, but in Celia's opinion it wasn't nearly as beautiful as the first. "Both you." She handed them to Vincent with a nervous smile.

After studying them for a beat, frowning, he said, "A moment of weakness, thinking of gigantic cakes" and shook his head. As everyone around them laughed, he tilted his eyes up and looked at Celia from under his light fringe of lashes. The corner of his mouth tilted up just a hair, enough for Celia to see the humor dancing there.

Celia's audience grew slowly. Remy, one of the candy organizers, asked Celia to draw her. Beyond remembering that Remy was a contortionist, Celia didn't know much about her. She'd come from the same Shiehan Rover troupe as Caspian, Grisilda, and Fawn (the siblings who played Passion), and at nine years old, she could already bend in ways that made Celia uneasy.

When Celia handed her the reality portrait—someone entirely made of ribs, wide eyes, dark skin, and short hair—Remy squealed, "It looks like me!"

When Celia handed her the fantasy—a shimmery eel with big, round eyes, swimming its way into a complex knot—she whispered, "It looks just like me" and tucked the second picture to her chest.

For Lilac, reality was long white hair in a thousand teeny braids, laughing eyes, twin crescent moon crinkles in the corners of her full pierced lips. And fantasy was a thick-armed deity holding the sun with no effort at all.

"Fantasy me has three eyes?" Lilac paused, then nodded.

"That's about right. Though I don't know about the roundness of my rump. That's a bit extreme, even for fantasy."

Celia laughed. "You told me to get your best angle."

Too late, Celia noticed the gloomy silence that had fallen. Daytime Kitty Kay swayed in front of her—hunched over, gray robed, long hair obscuring her face, so she looked more like a morel mushroom than a person—ready to have her portraits drawn.

Marco helped Kitty Kay to sitting. So blindingly handsome, Marco reminded Celia too much of Dante, and she'd avoided him as much as possible because of it.

Kitty Kay's body made creaks and moans—like music—as she settled. Even so close, Celia couldn't see her face from behind the gray veil of hair.

Celia looked to Anya for guidance, but Anya offered only a shrug. Lilac, Cas, and Sky hovered, trying to smile reassuringly. The plague doctor lay fast asleep, or feigned it well, with Georgio under the oak tree. Remy contorted her body, sucking on a candy and somehow not choking on it. Peering out from between her legs, Remy held up three fingers and mouthed *Three*, as if Celia would know what to do with that advice.

So Celia sketched the Kitty Kay she'd first met, the nighttime version, all glamorous sunset orange with an undercurrent of danger, and then the silent, hooded figure she transformed into during the day.

To break the awkward silence as Celia worked, Anya called

out, "How about you, Georgio? Want your portrait done? Plague doctor?"

Dia, *no!* The plague doctor was even more confusing than Kitty Kay. Most of the time he was loud, abrasive, and easy to ignore, but other times . . .

A few days earlier Celia had swerved around the back of a wagon, making the Kids and the plague doctor look up from their huddle. He'd paused mid-sentence. "In a rage, great Obi *stomped* on the bakery and—"

She'd frozen, stunned with the realization that when the Kids whined about "Oh-bee," it meant they wanted story time —referring to the Bicklandian folk hero, Obi the Giant.

Six Kids were clustered around him, a masked plague doctor—a macabre friend of death who'd literally seen death himself—as if he were a human-size puppy. The child beside him rested their head on his upper arm, another absently played with the feathers on his cloak.

The scene had been too familiar, reminding her of her fleas. She knew exactly what happened next in the story, thanks to a picture book she'd found at Lupita's: Obi's massive foot would catch on fire from the baker's oven, and he would go on to learn a valuable lesson about the dangers of believing town gossip. The ferocity of her *want* in that moment pinned her in place: she wanted to sit with them, she wanted to finish the story herself, she wanted Wallis and her fleas, she wanted the plague doctor—

"Would you like to join us, Celia?" he'd asked after a beat, before looking down and away.

Yes!

"I—"

The Kids nagged him to continue, but he shushed them, his smile unnaturally tight. Was he embarrassed himself? Or had he seen the moment of undisguised want on her face before she managed to shutter it and was embarrassed for *her*?

"I— I'm not good at stories," she'd garbled out, and practically ran off. If it had been anyone else, she might have joined them, but the sudden awareness of this side of the plague doctor had been far too enticing, too frightening. Too much.

That was it: the plague doctor was altogether too much for Celia. Too much in every possible way and from every possible angle. And Anya *knew* it, so what was she doing calling him over?

Slowly, Georgio stood, stretched their long body like a cat, said something to the plague doctor, and walked over to join them. The plague doctor stayed put, his spine apparently merged with the oak tree, but his huge smile beamed at them from across the distance, watching. Celia's hand shook under the scrutiny.

Swallowing, she held up the picture of glamorous Kitty Kay. "Reality," she croaked. Then the mirror image of the person in front of her: "Fantasy."

Not the right answer. Apparently, not even close. Kitty Kay moaned, long and low, and a few people, Vincent included, shook their heads. Marco helped Kitty Kay stand and led her back to her wagon.

Remy shoved her hand in Celia's face. "Want a candy?"

"Sure, thanks." She took it through eyes blurring with angry tears. If she couldn't even understand Kitty Kay, was there any hope she'd ever fit in with the Mob?

"That wasn't so bad," Lilac said, casual.

"Why were you showing me three fingers, Remy?" Celia asked.

Remy sucked her candy, all casual. "You needed to do three pictures."

Damn everyone for being so casual. Sky flipped up and began walking on their hands again, Cas laughing when they fell over.

"Three?"

Every time Celia had asked Lilac, Vincent, Seer, *anyone*, about Kitty Kay's transformation from night to day, she'd gotten a vague non-answer—"That's how she is," "You'll get used to it," "She takes her show to the extreme. The plague doctor got his madness from somewhere." That last statement had been from Lilac, only a day earlier.

"Yeah." Remy pointed to both sketches. "You did fantasy and fantasy. You didn't draw her as she is at all."

Celia blinked, then flopped backwards, away from everyone's eyes.

"You're good." Remy appeared, her round face and big eyes blocking Celia's view of the gray sky. "Your pictures look a lot like you do: black and white and swirly and sharp, all at the same time."

Celia laughed.

"It's a compliment. I meant they're pretty and you're pretty, Lalita. In a weird way."

The shisha lounge owner had called her Lalita—*fragile bird*—but Celia didn't mind it coming from Remy.

"I can teach you some things, if you want," Celia said, casually waving in the sketchpad's direction.

Remy's eyes got a little bigger, but she shrugged, as if it didn't matter to her either way. "That would be all right."

Celia smiled at her.

After Remy had gone back to her friends, Anya let out the snorts of laughter she'd been holding in with effort. "What is it about you that always attracts fleas, Cece?"

Celia's smile dropped away as though she'd been slapped. She turned to the horizon, where, far away, the temple still squashed inklings and little inklings-in-training.

"Oh, I'm sorry," Anya whispered, cutting off her laughter and flushing red. "I didn't mean—"

"No, no, it's okay." Celia went back to her drawing as Anya kept apologizing. "It's okay, Anny, really." She looked to the horizon again and whispered, "But Remy's a pretzel, not a flea." There was only one of those.

CHAPTER 12

Despite everything, Celia and Anya performed well that first night. Even better the nights after.

The audience fell in love.

The devil stayed the devil, and the angel stayed the angel. The crowd didn't get confused, and no glass shards littered the stage. With every performance, they settled further into their roles. Anya developed an organized system for her interactions with the people, and Celia embellished her responses with short, improvised skits. The back-and-forth between them became more coherent while still being entirely unscripted.

Now the Mob lured people in because of the amazing new devil and angel show, *and* a dedication to fashion that even Mama Treeza, the famous Kinallen designer, would have been proud of. Vincent and Georgio's colorful take on the civil war had people laughing so hard they fell over themselves.

The Mob was definitely not traditional Commedia.

Kitty Kay extended the run in Sabazio by two extra nights. People had bought tickets for the next show as they left the gates, *insisting* the Rabble Mob relieve them of their coin.

As the after-show began on extra night number one, Celia found Anya for their ritual dance. A powerful image, they'd thought, for the people to see the devil in the arms of the angel at show's end.

"There's so much touching," Anya said, shrugging off a lingering hand from her shoulder and smirking. "I'm all in favor of lusting and touching, but this is like living in a giant bubble of heat and sweat and anonymous fiery loins." She shuddered with exaggerated conviction as Celia laughed. *Fiery loins?* Anya wasn't wrong, though, and she had a worse time of it than Celia, having to move through the crowd while Celia was safe onstage.

Celia danced with Remy next, who'd been hovering at the sidelines waiting for Celia to notice her. "I did a self-portrait, like you suggested. It's not very good. It looks nothing like me."

"Sometimes mistakes make the best pictures. Show me after?"

Remy smiled from under her thick layer of face paint. "Thanks, Lalita." Her skintight body suit held a million colors, so dazzling and sparkly under the stage lights, it was like dancing with a little star fallen from the night sky. She darted back to her friends before they realized that their human pyramid wasn't pointy enough.

When someone tapped Celia on the shoulder for another dance, she turned and put her arms out. In her cheater's mirrors under the brow of her mask, she registered the robes first.

"Interesting show." The mistico gripped her waist as she took a reflexive step back. The reach of Profeta spread like tentacles, now twisted around her. Celia forced herself to bow her head in mute greeting and began swaying to the music woodenly.

"Ah, I see. You aren't allowed to break character to speak. Trust me, I know all about rules and protocol." He gestured to his clothing, making a light joke at his own expense, as if Celia had overlooked his profession.

He wasn't local. Though she was blanking on his name, she recognized him from the temple. Which meant he'd followed the troupe from Asura and likely wasn't alone.

Anya! Damn it! The music disguised her labored breathing, and the mask covered her swiveling eyes. Mistico often attended the shows, but they never came onstage! But he made no aggressive move against her, as if he only wanted a dance with a faceless, anonymous member of the Rabble Mob of Minos.

People are always so easy to fool, Celia. Remember, you did it for ten years.

But her body didn't remember, not at that moment.

"I've always appreciated Commedia, but these new directions are quite worrisome." He gripped her tighter, but his tone stayed light. "Passion's tale needs the proper ending. No one should laugh at the idea of war, chaos, and disorder, however innocent the spin. And while I wholeheartedly appreciate the sentiment behind your own show, devil, there is some terrible potential for people to see the wrong message. That final Asuran show made a few of us quite nervous."

He was here about the Mob's *messages* and not because of runaway inklings? Could she trust his idiocy, or was he a good actor himself?

Finally, Anya's white form appeared when the lingering

bodies parted just so. Her mask concealed less than Celia's, so Celia saw the exact moment her lips parted in recognition. After a moment of hesitation she flicked her flingers and tilted her head, signaling to Celia that she'd do some reconnaissance.

Celia inadvertently groaned loud enough for the mistico to lose his stride.

"Oh, I wouldn't worry too much. If the Rabble Mob returns to Asura with us, I'm sure a good discussion will clear all this right up."

Of course, sure, back to Asura we go. She nodded as her bees screamed.

"Something's terribly wrong here," the plague doctor said, slapping his hands on their shoulders as if he'd been part of the conversation from the beginning. And Celia would have been relieved—if she could read him at all, but that damn mask, that damn smile. "The devil promised me a dance tonight. But I've been forgotten!"

The mistico legitimately tittered. Celia had time to think, *We're safe if he says anything like, "I'd never forget . . ."*

"Well, I can't see how anyone could forget *you.*"

And Celia exhaled so fast she almost puffed everyone off the stage.

The plague doctor turned to her, held out his hand, and bowed deep. "May I have this dance, devil?" A whisper for her.

She took his hand.

The plague doctor swept Celia away, saying, "You're welcome. Did you know him, or were his hands wandering?"

"What?"

"Painfully obvious you didn't want that particular dance."

"Right. Yes, his hands were wandering."

The plague doctor didn't look down. The smile stayed on his face. But he pushed their hips together as if he wanted to fuse them.

"You've been avoiding me." His tone argued with his smile.

"Oh, most definitely."

"Why?"

"Because I had to think things, and you distract me." In trying to be clever, Celia heard some annoying truth there.

His lips quirked in a new way, as if trying not to smile a little wider at that.

"So you're clear," she said. "I'm mad at you for not helping me out in the field the other day. It doesn't bother you that your mother was the butt of a joke?"

At that, he laughed loud, pulling sighs from a couple dancing close by. "I think you were the joke there, devil."

She had to find Anya. Didn't have time for his insults. "Well, thanks for the dance." She caught a glimpse of white feathers. "But I have to find my angel."

A low hum reverberated from his chest and into hers like a purr. "You could already have him in your arms."

Her mind darted to Anya's words of fiery loins and lust bubbles. It rankled her that her body insisted on reacting to him the way it did, especially in these rare moments when he seemed to forget the stage. One hard ka-thump in her chest was all she allowed. "Save it. I'm smarter than that."

He tilted his head down enough to give her that perfect angle, the one that showed the outline of his eyes behind his tinted lenses. "Too bad, Celia Sand. Too damn bad."

She growled, her hand on his shoulder tightening into a small claw. "*Dia,* I hate your smile. So. Much."

"Why?" And he set the full shine of it on the couple dancing next to them. Both responded with even louder sighs.

"I have nothing against smiles whatsoever—I happen to like them—but I definitely have a keen distaste for horseshit. Let's call it a function of my upbringing."

After a pause, his only response was a low, "Something we have in common, then. Which is why I'm surprised by all the lies you tell."

She took a deep breath and tried to ignore him, her gaze flitting and fluttering over heads and around bodies.

Kitty Kay's flaming orange dress sparkled like fire against the black velvet curtain backdrop at stage left. It was her usual spot, offering a good view of the dancers, her players and acrobats in the field, and the front door to every private wagon. As performance nights wore on, some audience members tended to confuse lines of propriety; if anyone forgot their manners with her troupe, she didn't hesitate to call on the plague doctor and Ravino, who played the blood-soaked and brutal character Savant. Neither was particularly brawny, but no one, no matter how drunk or out of control, ever argued with them. The two of them, side by side and pointing to the gates, were a decent enough security force.

But instead of a stately overseer exuding a carefree manner, Kitty Kay stood in an uncharacteristic pose of power—feet planted, hips squared, arms crossed—as she stared down her nose at the mistico Celia had danced with. Her lips had disappeared, leaving nothing but a tight line.

The curtain above Kitty Kay fluttered, and Celia found the spot Anya was spying from.

Deftly she plucked a black feather from the back of the plague doctor's costume for Zuni—who'd get quite a collection if Celia ever saw her again—and bowed out of the dance.

"We need a truce," the plague doctor said as she walked away. Unlike the whisper of before, he was back to being the plague doctor, booming his words out, his smile a giant, tantalizing invitation. His new partner was practically drooling on his shoulder. "There's something about you—" He paused. Mask, darkness, judgment, the end of everything. Why did she have such trouble looking away? "I never realized how easy it is for Death to recognize one of his own."

Her first reaction: unmentionably embarrassing. Her second was much more reasonable. *Oh, puh-lease.*

His laugh followed her as she wove through dancing bodies, off the stage, down into the field, and around the back. Anya had climbed the catwalk and was precariously perched right above the conversation Kitty Kay was having with the mistico. "I can't hear a thing," she hissed when Celia joined her. Over the dense music and laughter, there was no way to separate out their words.

The mistico's arms gestured broadly as he spoke, his mouth a blur, with no trace of the composure he'd had with Celia. Kitty Kay waited calmly for a space, then delivered a short response. Beside her, Vincent the Palidon mimed a skit unrelated to the conversation: something about climbing a mountain? But Kitty Kay appeared to be winning the argument, shaking her head and shifting forward with flinty eyes, as if trying to push the mistico off her stage with only her body language.

The mistico, his face flushing red and his sparse hair standing at attention, bowed and excused himself. Vincent pantomimed throwing invisible knives into his back. Only then did Kitty Kay shake out her shoulders, inhale deeply, and resume watching her troupe.

"Interesting," Anya whispered. "That kind of animosity has history."

Yes. Wouldn't most Rovers want to make their lives easier by staying on Profeta's good side?

"Go, go," Anya said, practically pushing Celia down the ladder. "Let's go."

By the time the devil and the angel casually sidled up to Kitty Kay and Vincent, the mistico had multiplied. Now three of them stood glaring from across the stage, no doubt discussing how to best manage the situation from there. Their body language said the conversation wasn't over.

"What do they want?" Anya asked. A pair of dancers bumped

Kitty Kay, and she smiled, shooing them toward center stage with a hearty laugh.

Celia swallowed. Because of the checkpoint, the wanted posters, and their friendship with Lupita, there was no way their connection to the temple remained a secret, but so far, no one had outright broached the subject, only danced around it, as was their way.

"Oh, my dears," Kitty Kay said with her usual theatrical trill. "There's nothing I hate more than the sight of a robe. So stuffed and pompous. A vile stain on the shimmer of the world." Her tone was light, but her words raged as fierce as fire. Celia thought perhaps she was being loud on purpose. Goading, taunting. *Stop it!*

Vincent nodded as she spoke.

"They *demand* that the troupe return to Asura. That there'd been some 'public concerns about our message.'" The smile stayed on Kitty Kay's face, but, like her words, it burned hot as she looked at Celia and Anya. "They've tried something like this before, years ago. Profeta is water seeking out cracks."

Vincent nodded again. Celia hadn't realized that she was toying with Salome's leather bracelet under her gloves until Anya took her hands to quiet them.

At the look on their faces, Kitty Kay's lips appeared again as she smiled. "As much as they like to think they own the world, Profeta has no authority over Rovers. Barring an order from Ruler Vacilando herself, there's nothing they can do. We're headed west, and we'll shake off any residual stench of this country soon enough. As long as you two keep your masks on when you're around the public, you're safe here. You two are bright stars in the Rabble Mob, and the Rabble Mob is family."

We're family. The words sounded like a sweetness, a vow, a comfort. But Celia and Anya had known family before, and their only understanding of the word included the knowledge that it could change. Abruptly. Unexpectedly. You could be wrapped in the soft arms of your mothers one moment and pushed away the next because of a tattoo on your ankle. The only consistent family in their lives was each other.

The two bracelets around Celia's small wrist competed for her very soul: a colorful purple and blue braid that linked her to these strangers and to a wide world she didn't know, and the broken, worn-down leather one from Salome just before she'd been ripped from life on a cruel whim. Which one represented the truth of the world? Which one should she believe?

Perhaps some in-between place existed for people like her. Like the plague doctor. Her eyes found him among the remaining guests, everyone still so eager to press close. He'd seen the afterlife and returned. He said he recognized the scent of death surrounding her.

And then the plague doctor's ridiculous words turned prophetic, for as soon as Celia again locked eyes with the mistico from Asura, he fell to his knees and clutched his head, screaming with the wailing torture of the Touch.

CHAPTER 13

THE SOUND LASTED ONLY A MOMENT. ONE OF THE OTHER MIStico pulled the screaming one behind the curtain as the third poured chloroform on their handy rag. The plague doctor laughed as he herded the remaining guests offstage, staunchly pretending that everything was fine, fine, fine. He must have marveled at the mistico's efficiency. Everyone must have.

Dominic. Long after his screams had quieted and his colleagues removed him from the Rover field, Celia had finally remembered the mistico's name.

Dominic would be the newest entry on the Roll of Saints, forever a part of Profetan history, and with that honor came a final resting place at the temple in Asura.

They'd have to get his body to Zuni so his skull could be added to the crypts. Surely they would have had to deal with this before, a Touched away from the temple, but Celia couldn't imagine the logistics. Wouldn't the body rot? Would they take only his head? Sick to her stomach thinking about it, she couldn't *stop* thinking about it. She thought she'd seen all the horrors of temple life, yet here was a brand-new one. Would she ever be free of that place?

The gates had closed. Most of the Mob had fallen asleep without too much trouble. It was rattling, Kitty Kay had acknowledged, but it really didn't have anything to do with them. The show would go on. "If anything," she'd said, "let's be grateful that the temple now has something better to do with their time than harass us."

No love lost there.

Outside the temple walls, the Touch was rare, but everyone knew what it meant. And witnessing it was no small thing; the plague doctor had had to call scary Ravino over to help him when one couple refused to get up from their prone positions. The people had left with wide eyes and trembles and questions on their lips.

It was hard for anyone to miss Kitty Kay's obvious glee that her problem had taken care of itself *and* given them free publicity.

All night, Celia tried to harness a shred of relief. She and Anya were still well hidden. The mistico had come for a completely different reason than to retrieve rogue inklings. That much was clear from the conversations with Dominic before he'd started screaming.

Anya had called it a "shitty coincidence." But as much as Celia wanted to believe her, it didn't feel like a shitty coincidence. Not at all.

All the next day, Celia tried to embrace Anya's reasoning.

"The Mob knows where we came from, Cece, they aren't

stupid. But they aren't concerned." Anya reached out and adjusted Celia's lizardlike dress. "Let's follow Kitty Kay's lead, get through this last show, and get the hell out of Illinia."

Celia pulled her mask off and let it dangle around her neck, feeling claustrophobic under it. "Can you finish setting up?" She tossed a small handful of glitter, coating the top of Anya's head in sparkles. "I need to do some pacing before the crowd comes in."

Anya huffed, brushing the glitter out so it peppered her lace dress, and smiled. "Fine, but pace enough for both of us."

Celia dashed away, high-fiving Ravino as she passed because they'd somehow gotten into that habit, and swerved away from the main stage to make a round of the Rover field. The knot in her gut stayed tight despite Anya's logic, despite Kitty Kay's reassurances.

All she wanted was a little solitude for her bees to calm down, but someone followed her.

"Walk with me?" Vincent held out his arm, and Celia laced hers through it, snuggling into his side without shame.

As her thoughts roiled, Vincent filled the silence. In his whisper-quiet voice he told her about Tanith's cold (with a surly disposition even new fire sticks couldn't tame). He asked about Lupita and whether she'd sent any pigeons (maybe, but none had made it to them). He joked about Chef Foureta's culinary disasters (Seer's food is *so much* better, you have no idea). He wondered whether Celia missed Asura (hell no, except for Zuni and Wallis, and maybe a tiny bit, she hated to admit, Dante).

He didn't mention the mistico, the temple's concern about the Mob's show, or the Touch. Just as with the rest of the Mob, it was as if it hadn't even happened.

A seamless, soothing conversation—the white noise of a river or the wind—so it was only after making a full round of the field that Celia sensed the offness hidden inside.

"How do you know about Chef Foureta?" she asked, a wave of goose bumps erupting across her skin. She shivered. She gripped his arm a little harder, as if a good hold would equal a simple explanation. He'd overhead her and Anya talking about them. Not a big deal.

Vincent sighed. "I should be happy right now, but . . ." His hand moved down her arm and lightly stroked her fingertips.

"Hey, what's going on?" She stopped walking, seeking his familiar features under his face paint: hardly there eyebrows, pale blue eyes, sharp cheekbones. Her quiet Palidon, whether in costume or not.

He shrugged, a small, sad smile on his rosebud lips. Celia had the sudden urge to run, but his gloved fingers continued dancing with hers, twining, untwining. "Is this bothering you?"

She was about to say no, thinking he meant the caress, when he added, "I hope so."

He laced his fingers through hers, his grip no longer tender. Her shiver turned into a shudder. He pulled their linked hands up between them, as if to bring her bare fingers to his lips. "Such tiny things, to cause me so much trouble."

Vincent said this in the same steady way he said everything.

But with those words they stepped over a line drawn in mud and swept aside a door made of silken fabric; even as everything looked the same, the barrier was breached.

She felt it then: a chill in her bones, shivering its way through the depths of her insides.

Celia's fingers flexed and extended in Vincent's hand, and he examined each one. He met her gaze as he kissed four fingertips in turn, and, as if they didn't belong to her at all, her fingers stopped moving to receive his lips.

She could have asked *How do they cause you trouble? What are you telling me?* But instead she asked the obvious. "Where's Vincent?" Because whoever stood in front of her wore Vincent's face, used his body and his voice, but her Palidon had vanished. This wasn't the friend who'd wrapped her wrist in a bracelet, who'd stolen a sweet bun for her, who'd peacefully walked with her so many mornings.

He didn't answer. He didn't say, *What are you talking about? Vincent's right here, holding your hand like a vice, whispering hisses into your ear.*

He smiled at her instead, slow and steady.

And behind that smile lurked menace.

Celia heard herself whisper, "I don't mean to cause you trouble." She didn't pull away, despite the painful grip. Her lungs breathed in a steady cadence, her heartbeat slowed, her mind closed to everything except that moment.

Her body understood that it was time to lie like she'd never lied before.

Celia and not-Vincent stood together as the heavy clouds wet them with droplets as warm as blood. She took a step toward him at the same time that his free hand moved to cup her cheek. From afar, their meeting would appear tender, like tentative new lovers. Reaching toward want. Struggling against it.

His movements so gentle, his intent so clearly the opposite. "And yet you have. You've caused me trouble at every turn, Inkling."

"Inkling?" Celia's slow heartbeat pounded like dull footsteps. The impossible conversation continued, deceptively calm and reasonable. "I'm the devil of the bell jar. A bright new star in the Rabble Mob."

He shook his head, his black teardrop melting down his face from the rain. "No. I bargained with a true devil once, and you're nothing like him."

Ridiculous words—*I bargained with a devil*—but no part of Celia doubted them. "Only the damned speak with devils."

"Well, you served me for ten years, so I suppose you would know better than most." He sounded faintly amused at her words. "Despite my different skins, I know you recognize me. Let's not play this game."

The image of the Divine's marble statue rose up in Celia's mind. Seeing in all directions, able to watch the world from any angle . . .

From behind anyone's eyes.

And the trickster peeking out from underneath the robes,

seemingly bested by the noble force above, but—perhaps—
that false image was her biggest trick of all.

Celia had never believed in a benevolent deity, but the trickster Diavala . . .

Diavala.

The name caressed its way into Celia and wormed its way
through her like the ink in her bloodstream. The name of whispered screams. *Deee-aaah-vaaah-laaaaah.*

And as it pumped slowly through her veins, she felt it. *Diavala.* Not a question, not a statement.

A truth.

A greeting.

Celia's teeth began slamming together in a furious chatter
when she realized that nothing about Vincent's flickering tenor
had changed. Inside him, making use of his body, was something
that didn't even have a soul of its own. How many other people
had this monstrous thing possessed over the centuries? And—
Celia's throat closed—why didn't anyone speak of it afterward?

Diavala.

Celia crunched her hand into a fist, squeezing Vincent's fingers between hers until each of them paled, trying to pull him
out, find him, bring him back so they could continue their calm
walk and return to a world that made sense.

Not-Vincent's gaze lifted from their clasped hands, searching for something in the distance. She watched her friend that
wasn't her friend blink away the fresh rain, frown as if weighing
his next words, and exhale another sigh.

A slightly crooked grin lit Vincent's face. He wasn't made for smiling so. *Diavala.* "It took centuries to build up my power just so—from creating the stage to managing the puppets—but there's little challenge in it anymore. You sparked my interest, Inkling, that day you signed your initials to a tattoo as if it were art instead of instruction. And you thought you'd gotten away with one . . . and then another, and then another. The ink is mine, I saw them all." A terrible pause as she assessed Celia. "I suppose I was careless. I watched you too long, intrigued by your defiance when I should have doused it. I still *cannot* believe you managed to escape, for however brief a moment. If it hadn't been for that last Asuran show causing such a stir, you might have actually made it farther." She shook her head, falsely chastising herself. "But now, here we are."

The crisp understanding that Celia had brought her here—with those initials she'd thought were so clever, her apologetic kisses to those she inked—stole Celia's breath.

"The thief—and the deity she stole from. I felt it was time we met, Inkling."

Celia's panic found words. "I'll go back to Asura." She could hire a coach in Sabazio. No, she didn't have any money. The horses. She didn't know how to ride one, but she'd bonded with a silver dapple on the road. How hard could it be if the horse was on your side? "You'll have your inkling back. You'll get your justice."

Diavala stared at her, nodding slightly. "The noble sacrifice. But no, I don't work in the currency of mercy. If it was that easy for you to put things right, I would have simply allowed Profeta to dole out justice for me." She clicked her tongue, as if scolding a child. "I followed you *personally,* Inkling."

Celia shook her head slowly. Denying the truth, the danger, the threat. If this thing inside Vincent was truly Diavala, Celia had not only brought the force of the temple—zealots in robes, guards and rules and death—down on the Mob, but also brought the mastermind behind it all.

"You've been . . . inside Vincent . . . this whole time?" Celia could barely utter the question. It made such little sense, seemed so ridiculous to put those words together.

"No. I was using Dominic until last night."

Last night, when Mistico Dominic had fallen screaming to the stage, unable to handle the contents of his own mind. Celia stifled the absurd urge to giggle. All this time spent thinking the Touch was a byproduct of years of fanaticism, too much contact with ink, or one of a dozen other theories, only to find out that the Touch was *literal.*

The names logged on the Roll of Saints were Diavala's trail, the rows of skulls in the crypts her mementos.

Diavala saw her connecting the dots. "Madness is an unfortunate side effect of my transfer, but I saw an opportunity to attach more publicity to the Mob, and I took it." She said this with a casual dismissal, but there was calculation there. To what end?

Celia's words were clipped, stuttering their way out of her throat. "What do you want from me?"

"Well, that's the wonderful irony. After watching how the people respond to your show, I realize that you've handed me quite an opportunity. I want you to continue. *Be* the bright star of the Rabble Mob—but better. Shine so bright that people all over Illinia and beyond talk of the devil in the bell jar. With this troupe, this show, you've handed me the perfect platform to finally stretch Profeta beyond Illinia's borders."

Celia saw what Diavala saw then. How their show pushed thoughts of devils and angels to the forefront of people's minds, reminding them of the afterlife, their mortality. The more hideous and scary the devil in the bell jar, the greater the opportunity to present the Divine as safe harbor. Other Commedia stories told the same tale, but this one was new, fresh, exciting, interactive.

She wanted their Devil in the Bell Jar act to spread propaganda.

Just like Kitty Kay, thrilling at the idea of exposure.

Then Diavala cocked Vincent's head from side to side, stretched and tilted it back, and a soft moan pushed its way out. "This one is quite different from the ones I normally use. He fights so hard." She gave these words to the sky and the fresh rain. "How annoying."

Celia clamped her lips against the sob about to burst out. The ominous whisper cracked her unnatural calm like a lightning bolt. "Is he okay?"

Diavala chuckled, a shushing sound like sandpaper grazing smooth wood. "'Is he okay?' How charming and plebeian."

But Vincent's tenor still flickered; he lived, somewhere, and Celia tried to hold on to that.

Her bees stirred, but slowly, as if the hive had filled with smoke as they slept. Their wings hummed *Diavala, Diavala, Diavala.* If Diavala controlled Vincent, what could she make him do? Celia imagined him walking himself off a cliff, jumping into a fire, in front of charging horses, in a raging river, and in each imagining he did it with a smile on his face.

The worst image of all: the quiet Palidon wailing in pain, howling with fury, tearing out his hair and screaming for reprieve. When Diavala was done with him, she'd leave her signature when she left his body behind.

Diavala looked away and mused, "Little Wallis, under High Mistico Benedict's watchful eye and stone fist, they're not dead *yet,* are they?"

Yet.

A thousand memories of holding that flea in her arms rushed over Celia, so real she heard the thrum of Wallis's fluttering heartbeat and smelled the scent of their warm, fluffy hair as it tickled against her neck when Celia tucked them in. *You tell stories almost as good as my papa used to, Celia,* Wallis would murmur. And they'd snuggle into their pillow with a contented smile on their face.

"And," Diavala continued, "I've always wondered what it would be like to see the world through Anya's filter. So practical and clever . . ." She paused and looked directly at Celia. "Such an interestingly high threshold for pain, and so terribly afraid of only one thing: water. Anya—she isn't dead yet, either."

Celia's knees gave out, and she knelt in the damp grass at Vincent's feet, moaning or crying or both.

With a few key words, Diavala had made it clear that her leverage extended beyond Vincent's life to everyone Celia loved. She heard their screams, saw their blood, their skulls.

"I'll do it," Celia whispered. "Of course I will. I'll keep acting."

"You'll do more than act, Inkling. Under your bell jar, you will convince people that you *are* a devil. You will make them talk about you, not just in passing, not whimsically, but out of true fear."

I'll do it. I'll do it. Whatever you want.

Vincent's pale hand reached down to her. "Time's wasting, don't take too long to recover. Polish your mirrors, practice your twitches with Anya, do whatever else it is you do to manipulate that crowd, and make it *more.* You have tonight to prove to me how motivated you are to make me happy."

And Celia took his hand, too stunned to recoil from the cold touch, and stood, meeting Vincent's light blue gaze with the understanding that it wasn't Vincent she looked at.

A tiny thing nudged at Celia. A protection she could bargain for, laughably small considering who stood in front of her, but something that might make a difference for Vincent and the troupe. "Are the mistico truly concerned about the Mob's messages—or was that you?" If she could get their daggers away, their rigid vigilance about all things Profeta . . . "I can't do my act if they shut down the show."

Diavala smirked, close to laughter but stopping herself at the cusp of it. "I see how desperately you want reassurances. You really must work on your game face. But it's a fair point. You will do better with some room to roam. And I've already taken care of it. Or rather, Mistico Dominic took care of it before he fell into sainthood. They will no longer bother the troupe."

Part of Celia couldn't believe the turn in the conversation. As if they were about to lay out the Imp tiles and have a round and were clarifying the rules before they began. She swept off her mask from where it dangled around her neck and put it to her chest as if it were her top hat. With one foot back, she dipped in a deep bow. "I'm honored to finally meet you, Diavala." She tried to sound strong, but her voice shook and her teeth kept chattering and her words were a breathy whisper.

A wide smile overtook Vincent's face, the one Diavala had tried so hard to hold back. Diavala mirrored her and bowed. "Yes. Diavala. You can call me that. Or call me what everyone else does: your Divine. There is only me. I am—and always have been—either, neither, or both, depending on how you tilt your head."

ACT 2

INTERLUDE

The people of Sabazio stream into their Rover field. They're riding a weeklong high, many of them on their second, third, or fourth show. Most of the town is under a spell. The world consists of either color and fire and dreams or the breathless anticipation of it.

They've seen Rover shows before. A few times a year, their field fills. The Commedia represents the whole of humanity: the infinite struggles, the triumphs, the despair. But the Rabble Mob of Minos takes it all and puts it directly in your pocket.

The blur between fantasy and reality happens as soon as they push through the gates. They step on tiptoe to press coins into a stilt walker's palm, and the moment their heels settle back into the grass, the world is different.

A pair of fire-masters juggle the flames of the underworld between them.

The stilt walkers lope about, tall enough to touch the heavens.

The plague doctor pulls them in with his brazen words and whispered promises. They lean closer when he purrs. Their hearts break when he moves on.

The lights of the stage beckon. The gorgeous figure in flaming orange—the clever conductor—stands at the sideline, watching everything.

The curtain rises.

When Passion fights for the afterlife she desires, the audience shares her struggle. When the Commander squashes his servants underfoot, they all rise against him together. Poor Fazzi, confused. His hands flap through the air; he randomly leaps, frightened by his own nose, the sky, the ground under his feet. His mask has huge eyes, wondering at everything. So funny. So terribly relatable.

Tanza talks the most, dominating the stage. His nonsense sentences are loud, his body movements louder, the context clear. He's giant, walking, talking charisma. He swaggers, leading with his chest. *Surely, no one is more intelligent, more handsome, more everything, than I?* And they wholeheartedly agree that at least *he* believes this is true.

The crowd loves these familiar characters, but they yearn for the devil in the bell jar. No one can agree who she is. Most see a servant, someone commanded. But others see a master: a pretense of captivity, a clever manipulation. Still others wonder, *Is there more to this story?*

"I heard a mistico was Touched last night, there on that very stage."

"Surely part of their act."

"That would be blatant heresy. And here they still are."

"I was at the show last night. I saw it with my own eyes. It's true."

"Does it mean something?"

"What could it mean?"

"What does it mean?"

The torches go out for the finale. This is the last night the Sabazian crowd has to unlock the secret of this novel new character.

The angel walks among them, regal and fine, telling them she's tamed the beast.

But when the torches spring to life onstage that night, the beast looks anything but tame. She paces and flails. She shakes her head as if tearing it out of cobwebs.

Her gaze used to focus on the angel with single-minded abandon, but on this night she's distracted by another figure in white: the sad Palidon.

The Palidon stays at the sidelines. His black skullcap sits crooked across his forehead, one of the large buttons on his loose shirt is missing, the ink-black teardrop under his eye is smudged.

And, absurd for a Palidon, he smiles.

The crowd needs closure. They murmur, confused: the show has changed, something's different. What does the Palidon have to do with this? How can the sad clown be *happy*?

They sense there's more to the show than what's in front of their eyes, and they'll understand it only when they decipher the Devil in the Bell Jar.

Whatever the true story is, it's important.

Last night, even the Divine herself had been there.

CHAPTER 14

THE FOUR TENETS OF PROFETA KEPT CLAMORING FOR ATTEN-tion in Celia's mind as she performed that night. With one con-versation, all of Profetan lore notched itself into place. Instead of a table with four rickety legs, Profeta became a coherent, ongoing story.

The tale Celia had told her mothers the night before she'd started her life at the temple—the tale everyone believed—was only partially right. The true story began the same way, but took a darker turn.

Everything had begun a thousand years ago with the Chest Majestic and the very special ink inside. So black, it sucked away all light. So glossy and smooth, it appeared more solid than liq-uid. Only one child could use it, and when people pilgrimaged to see her, she gave them guidance through her pictures. The ink and the child were gifts from the angels themselves, and the tattoos—personal, intimate, and freely given—became a comfort.

But the gifts also made this child a target. It didn't matter whether she'd been merely exceptional or something truly godly, her story ended when she'd been killed by some of the very people she'd tried to help.

I bargained with a true devil once.

She'd returned from death, but she was changed. She was a thief, stealing and using other people's bodies. And however the magic worked, she couldn't control the ink anymore, for technically, it wasn't in *her* blood. She had no body of her own, no blood.

When she told her story, no one had believed her. They'd labeled her Diavala, a heretic, and flogged her to death with a nine-tailed whip representing the nine levels of hell.

There were never two beings, Divine and Diavala. There'd only ever been one.

And there they were.

Perhaps she'd started out good, but for all her desire to help, her own people had killed her twice. It was enough to change anyone from philanthropist to manipulator. It was clear that she held some grudges.

She'd been drowned, much like inkling water torture.

Then flogged. The *Book of Profeta* used a dozen pages to describe the welts on her back in detail. Slits that had opened her insides to the outside. Which, if she'd lived, would have formed deep scars, much like the pale lines scarring Celia's body in hidden places, the result of her dagger punishments.

A mirror of her experiences, inflicted on the ones she must resent most: the inklings who could manipulate the ink as she no longer could. The inklings she was forced to rely on to spread her messages.

Inklings, mistico, the temple, Profeta . . . a flash of words to describe so much, hundreds of years for it to actually build. Miracles, deceptions, alliances, sorrow, all logged in the *Book of Profeta* but the truth of it lost to history.

Now Celia began to understand everything that hadn't made sense about Profeta. With endless patience, using endless anonymous faces, the Divine had built up an entire religion over centuries. She'd trained the first inklings as her servants, recruited mistico to manage the flock. Tricked her way through hundreds of years, to the point where the puppets managed themselves. The fourth tenet — the Return — must be some distant dream for when Diavala could break the devil's curse on her and control her ink again.

Celia saw one thing with crystal clarity: Profetan history followed *one* creature with different faces — from benevolent giver to desperate thief to hidden puppetmaster — and now Celia and Anya were the twisted puppetmaster's new toys.

The curtain fell to hide the bell jar. Clevanta the Bold and Poor Fazzi lifted the jar, freeing the devil while the other performers gathered onstage for the curtain call. "Are you all right, Lalita?" Georgio's Fazzi mask, with its saucer-wide eyes and sticking-up hair, made their inquiry all the more pointed.

Celia ignored them, trying to push her way past. She felt exactly like the perpetually shocked expression of Georgio's mask. They wrapped a strong arm around her shoulder and tried to lead her to the front of the stage. "Calm down, dear."

But no. Vincent's pale form appeared at stage left; he nudged

Kitty Kay's arm and whispered something, his expression care-fully arranged in his normal Palidon gloom, and they both set their eyes on her. Kitty Kay cleared her throat, saying, "That was a little *odd*, Celia."

"It was odd," he agreed.

With Kitty Kay frowning in Celia's direction, she missed the fresh smile on Vincent's rosebud lips.

"But what did you think? Was it good enough? Will people talk about it?" The first words Celia had uttered since she'd greeted Diavala with a bow rushed out in a torrent. And they kept coming, the only thing keeping tears at bay. How awful, to talk to Vincent but *not*. And no one knew he was even miss-ing. "I tried for wild and untamed. Casting doubt on the bell jar itself. Maybe it's cracked, maybe one day it won't hold me. All eyes on the devil, right?"

Diavala nodded, Vincent's light eyes piercing her. "You built on something special."

"What are you two even talking about?" Kitty Kay flicked her fingers, shooing Celia away. "Get in your position for curtain."

Celia grabbed Kitty Kay's hand instead, her thoughts flying so fast her mouth couldn't keep up. "If I had more time under the bell jar, if I could be on the playbill for Malidora . . ."

Won't be enough. How do I get them to love me? Hate me? Fear me?

Anya appeared at her side as the other performers assembled. "Let's go, Cece." She had questions. Celia saw them, ignored them, tightened her grip on Kitty Kay's hand.

The plague doctor appeared on the far side of the stage, ready to make his entrance. The curtain stirred as Caspian and Sky grabbed the thick ropes. Most of the Mob stared at their little assembly, motioning for them to come. *Get it together! You need to be here!*

I need more. Something bigger.

Anya wouldn't stop tugging. "Come *on*, Cece!"

"NO!" Celia took one step back, still holding on to Kitty Kay's hand. Kitty Kay never participated in the first curtain call, so they remained offstage. Even Vincent had stepped into position. "For goodness sake, just lift the curtain without me."

"Lift the curtain without her." Kitty Kay was so red Celia thought she might explode. Vincent smiled even wider, and Kitty Kay shot daggers at him for contributing to Celia's instability. Didn't she see how strange it was for him to be smiling?

Anya huffed out an impatient grunt and left her there, throwing her hands in the air. "What is *wrong* with you?"

The curtain rose, the crowd cheered.

The plague doctor threaded his way through the Mob's celebration. Slow, deliberate. The crowd hushed.

For every other curtain call in Sabazio, he'd made his way to Celia's side before rendering his verdict with blue and purple fire. A way of teasing her with proximity, for he knew she was extraordinarily curious about his magic fire. That night, he couldn't find her. His meandering route through the mob of smiling performers took longer. At one point he even looked over his shoulder.

The crowd had quieted when he'd first emerged, but Celia's soul prickled with the noiseless sound of their unease. They'd noticed his slight discomposure. The finale was ever so slightly longer than perfectly timed.

The plague doctor rose and tossed his flames. Trapdoors swallowed up some of the performers, others collapsed, others skittered like spiders up into the rafters.

Only the plague doctor and darkness remained. He dusted himself off. Usually, the crowd was entirely silent, but their unease had turned to whispering. The plague doctor cocked his head, as if he heard the whispers too.

Celia looked up at Vincent, perched in the rafters, and pointed at her chest. *Do you hear that? They're asking for me.*

He shook his head and nudged his chin, telling her what she already knew: it wasn't good enough, she had to do more.

Celia needed to give the crowd something truly unexpected.

She let go of Kitty Kay's hand, her fingers throbbing as blood rushed back. She pulled down her mask, crouched like a frog, and slowly, soundlessly, crept toward the middle of the stage, well behind where the plague doctor stood. She didn't want to be seen, she wanted the *possibility* of her to be seen. She wanted people to think they saw her devil horns—maybe, perhaps.

The whispers grew louder as the plague doctor bowed. That night, the finality of death wasn't final, because something moved behind him.

Celia thumped the bottom of her bell jar with a flat palm, once, twice, then scraped her fingernails against the floorboards.

As one, the crowd froze. If she hadn't wanted their concentration so desperately, the immediate silencing of all those whispers would have freaked her out.

The plague doctor looked over his shoulder again, inadvertently helping Celia's ruse that Death wasn't alone on that stage.

When the curtain dropped again, he turned on her. "What are you doing?"

Slipping the devil into the famous finale, so she *was the last thing they thought of, that's what.*

But Celia was already up and striding toward Kitty Kay again. With the second, true curtain call, Celia still didn't go onstage to take her bows, despite how hard Kitty Kay tried to wrestle her there.

The roar of the crowd was earsplitting.

"Give me at least twenty minutes under the bell jar each night. I want to close out every show. I will not be dancing afterward, and I want to be on the playbill. Front and center."

Anya looked apoplectic, along with Kitty Kay, the plague doctor, and, if Celia was being honest, most of the Mob. Breaking your own script was fine, but not taking over someone else's. And the Mob didn't have a "front and center" on their posters and playbills. They were a Mob.

Kitty Kay's frown deepened. Vincent's smile widened.

"You have to admit, I'm onto something," she said, pointing to the curtain, where, just behind the thick velvet, the crowd chanted for the devil in the bell jar.

CHAPTER 15

ALL BUT DRAGGING CELIA AND ANYA TO THEIR WAGON BY
their ears, Kitty Kay proceeded to give them the lecture of a
lifetime. With a jabbing finger, grand arm flaps, a flushed face,
and no punctuation to her sentences, she schooled them on
respect, Rover etiquette, and basic manners. Anya might have
been on the receiving end of the tirade by default, but for most
of it she threw her own glare-daggers at Celia and nodded at
everything that poured from Kitty Kay's mouth.

Celia shrank by degrees. "I'm sorry," she said for the tenth
time. Anya tapped her foot impatiently, waiting for what Celia
should have said next: *It won't happen again, I got carried away.*

Kitty Kay clapped her hands once. "You'll apologize to the
plague doctor for *commandeering* his finale." She clapped again,
making sharp points to her list of demands. "You'll do whatever
he needs from you to fix it." Clap. "You'll apologize to *everyone*."
Clap. "You'll forget about this 'front and center' nonsense." Clap.
"You'll *never* change the show under our noses again." Clap.
"When you're done apologizing to everyone, you'll apologize
to everyone *again*." Clap. Clap. Clap.

Kitty Kay took a few deep breaths, her gaze flicking between
Celia and Anya like a pendulum. "Good. Now that that's settled,

we have fifteen days plus four minus five of travel before we reach Malidora. That's how long you have to smooth out these changes and incorporate them into the show properly."

Anya's mouth popped open. "Pardon me?"

"*Properly*. As in, consulting with others who are affected. Finding someone who will sacrifice some of their stage time to your increase. Filling everyone in on a loose script so they don't look like fools." Kitty Kay straightened her hair and smoothed out her dress, her shoulders rolled back to rigid, her stage smile appearing. "You're right, you're onto something. The crowd is multiplying like black flies on bloat. After the last two nights of excitement, I wouldn't be surprised if all of Sabazio packs up and follows our caravan to Malidora."

Kitty Kay might have regained her calm, but Anya hadn't. Kitty Kay patted her on the shoulder, misunderstanding her flushed face for excitement. "Show business isn't about shrugging away fame, is it? So long as you understand you're in a troupe, not solo performers."

"Understood." Celia nudged Anya to respond.

"Understood," Anya said through her teeth.

"Perfect! This *is* exciting then, isn't it?" And Kitty Kay swept out of the wagon with a flourish.

Celia exhaled hard and turned to Anya. "I have a good reason—"

"I *hate* that act, Cece. We're supposed to blend and fade, not pop and bang. I can't think of *any* good reason . . ."

Anya kept talking as Celia pulled her upstairs. They huddled in a corner of the second floor, the domed glass separating them from the lights and sounds of the party in the field below. Marco and Tanith had upped their fire game, juggling at least a dozen bolts between them. Tanith shone with fevered determination, the remnants of her illness unwilling to leave her. Lilac, Cas, and Sky hovered above the crowd on their stilts, nearly at eye level with Celia and Anya. The plague doctor danced onstage, commanding it, looking extra bold and loud and slightly out of control. Celia wasn't looking forward to apologizing to him.

The Palidon performed for a small pack of onlookers, his white morphing into various shades of yellow from the torchlight. His pantomime involved shoulder-wracking sobs, digging himself an invisible hole with an invisible shovel, and then lying in it. Just before the crowd swallowed him, he gestured for someone to join him in his grave.

"So? Talk. Go. I can't wait to hear what you have to say."

Celia's eyes prickled with hot tears as Anya stared at her, arms crossed. Anya expected her to talk ego, adventure, and fun, or maybe to apologize for a drunken error in judgment.

How could she explain this unexplainable thing?

She started with "Vincent is not-Vincent."

Made her way to "It was never about outrunning robes."

Got to "Remember when we thought the Divine didn't exist?"

Until eventually she ended at "Turns out, she's the biggest trickster of all."

Anya's anger melted into laughter.

Then, before disappearing completely, it changed into something that sounded like pain. Celia wanted Anya to reject the story, tell her—firmly and absolutely—that she'd finally lost her mind to madness.

Instead, her analytical mind latched on to words like *immortal, bodiless, cunning.* "But what does she *want* from us?"

Celia explained that Diavala wanted them to be a strange kind of missionary, hardening belief about the afterlife, making people fear the devils of hell anew so more turned to Profeta for comfort and guidance.

Before Celia even finished, Anya was shaking her head. "No. There's something else. This is just one show inside just one troupe. A small reach, even if we became exceedingly popular. It could never be grand enough to push Profeta across borders."

Celia almost didn't say it, her guilt too strong. "She saw my initials, Anny," she whispered. Diavala had come for revenge; now she was seizing an opportunity. The worst-case scenario was that she'd be entertained for a while before she punished Celia. Best-case scenario? It worked, they traveled through neighboring nations, and Profeta spread.

It would either be a short game or a very, very long one.

Anya exhaled. Nodded. The final piece of the puzzle—motivation—in place. "I see." Anya's gaze wandered to all the recognizable costumes and masks below. Slowly, angry Anya was emerging. It didn't happen often, as levelheaded as she was most of the time, because she saved it up for the important stuff. The tips of her ears had already turned red. Her voice had thickened.

It was as if Anya's emotional repertoire didn't include fear; where fear should be, rage always burned instead, and it burned white-hot. "One word from Diavala, and all these people will be snuffed out," she said.

"No. No, Anny. No. Look. I thought about it. She can only do what her host would do. She's bound to playing the roles of the people she uses." In this case, Vincent.

Anya stared. Ground her teeth. "She's obviously found effective ways to make it work, Cece. Zuni has the most secure job in all of Illinia."

Celia clicked her tongue impatiently. "Anya, think about it: no one knows she exists in this form. Diavala has had to manipulate for every ounce of her power because she's *invisible*.

"Profeta is ancient, right?" Celia went on. "Built around solid walls her followers believe without question. Her religion sustains itself. According to Profeta, harboring temple runaways isn't execution-worthy. Diavala can't hop into a mistico and order kills that make no sense; she *needs* those foundational walls to stay strong. She won't break her own rules, so as long as we play within them, the Mob will be safe. No, don't—"

Anya had started shaking her head halfway through Celia's reasoning.

"I'm right."

"Even if she doesn't use Profeta to do her killing," Anya said, "she could use Vincent's hands." The red of her ears had crept down to the rest of her face. She looked flushed and feverish, ready to explode.

The image of Vincent the quiet Palidon stained red with someone else's blood chilled Celia all over again. "No. I thought about that, too. I don't think she can kill, Anny. Another reason she needs mistico. First of all, having murderers in Illinia is bad for image, and she's all about order. Ruler Vacilando's hard line on crime and vice was from a Divine order *you inked,* remember? Diavala wouldn't want to stamp it out and then turn around and contribute to it."

The look on Anya's face said that she was about to argue, and yes, that was the flimsier of the two arguments, so Celia cut her off with the big one before she could get a word in.

"But the proof lies with someone we know: Lupita is a *giant* loose end. She lived Profeta for years, knows everything there is to know about the temple, yet she still breathes despite being the one person who could poke holes in it all. *If* Diavala could kill, she would have tied up that loose end without a second thought. Lupita's alive only because she found the narrowest of loopholes in Profeta's rules and slid right through."

The moment stretched on as Anya thought through Celia's logic.

Anya talked it out further, sliding everything into the proper compartments: "Lupita was calm and sane when she poked her eyes out. If Diavala had Touched her after she'd already been cast out in disgrace, Lupita would have been marked as a saint. Excommunicating someone saintly would only make Profeta look stupid. You're right, she *has* to stay within her own framework."

For someone who wanted unparalleled control, Lupita must be a lingering sore spot for Diavala. Good thing their tutor had faded to the background of life, a bottle of gin in hand.

"So okay, look," Celia said, trying to refocus. "The mistico are her execution squad, but they're gone for now. As long as the troupe doesn't blatantly break any rules of Profeta to bring them swarming back, the troupe will stay safe from those daggers. As long as we do everything Diavala says, she won't have any reason to leave Vincent, and he'll be safe from the Touch for a while. She wants a show, let's give her a show."

"So you're saying we should just go ahead and push more people toward the temple, hoping she stays entertained."

Celia nodded, but Anya didn't seem to notice. She'd stood and begun pacing. "She pulled a Tanza," Anya muttered.

Tanza. The arrogant ass. Always plotting and planning, always taken down by the weight of his hubris.

"Why reveal herself to you?" Anya said. "Every villain goes out when they start to monologue. And it didn't even occur to her that we're using ink to do our show? She called it 'mirrors and twitches'? Oh, she has the weakness of ego. You're right, Cece, we have an opportunity here."

Oh shit no. "No, no, no, that's not what I meant!"

In the field below, Vincent raised a hand from his invisible grave and rose, the crowd around him parting enough so Celia could see who he'd called over. He pulled Remy under his arm, and they bowed together.

Thinking they could find a home with the Rabble Mob had been such a naive dream. It was impossible to escape Profeta.

Celia swallowed the heat that had risen in her throat. "We have no power right now. None. This is different from sneaking around the temple and fooling mistico."

Still pacing, faster now, Anya said, "Kitty Kay needs to know. This thing is inside *her family.*"

"No! The one thing keeping Vincent safe right now is the status quo. We can't do anything to jeopardize his mind, Anny!"

"We need to get in contact with Lupita."

"And how do you suppose we do that? Even if she could see our messages, what could she do from Asura?"

"Dante would help."

"Anya, *Dia,* stop! Help with *what?*"

"He might be able to talk to some of the other inklings—"

"And what? Have you completely forgotten the past ten years? Because I haven't. We were *always* alone, Anny. We did little things, *tiny* things, and even those tiny things scared everyone away from us. Do you really think that if they've been too terrified to sneak out for a drink one night, they'll be eager to take on an immortal trickster deity? What is *wrong* with you?" Anya was ready to leap into the giant's maw and drag everyone in with her. What was happening here? *Anya* was supposed to be the practical, thoughtful one, not her!

Anya had stopped pacing. Her fists, balled up at her sides, looked ready to smash glass. "Even before we knew she was real, we hated her. For years we've seen how she meddles in lives, how the ink strips away choice. How it hurts, influences, manipulates! Doing what she wants goes against everything we are." She made a point of glancing at Celia's hands: Celia was twisting Salome's bracelet in circles, wearing a red, raw path around her wrist. "I am *not* okay with that." Tears of frustration rimmed her deep blue eyes.

"I'm not okay with it either, but if we get anyone else involved right now, her boots will stomp down hard. We can't risk it." Celia swallowed and added, "Not yet. Not until we figure out how to save Vincent."

Celia looked over at the Palidon again, Remy laughing as she performed a handstand on his shoulders. The troupe loved Vincent. Quiet and unassuming, included in everything.

Always there, always watching.

If you wanted to hide in plain sight and keep tabs on two inklings, he was the perfect host.

Vincent made a point of looking toward the wagon where Celia and Anya were, then turned to look at Remy. *You consider this one a little sister, don't you, Inkling?*

And Celia thought, *No, Diavala isn't anything like Tanza at all. Because at the end of everything, Tanza is hopelessly dumb.*

CHAPTER 16

TWO WEEKS OF TRAVEL WOULD GET THEM TO MALIDORA. TWO weeks of thinking, planning, and stress. Diavala had a sense of humor, revealing herself just before the long road trip.

The nights and days soon blurred together in endless turns of six-hour blocks of travel. Celia and Anya rode on the front carriage with the plague doctor, helping him sell the fantasy in their devil and angel costumes, Celia now sporting extra heavy chains around her neck, wrists, and ankles. If Kitty Kay could have found a way to manage it, Celia had no doubt she would have been leading the procession from under her bell jar.

Foolishly shrieking and wailing whenever they passed another wagon, Celia bumped between their shoulders like a Kid's ball in a game of hot potato, the rattling of chains scraping her eardrums raw. The angel and the plague doctor only inclined their heads calmly. *We're on our way, Malidora. Come, see this spectacle.*

Stabbing unease tangoed up and down Celia's spine; she knew her every action and reaction was being tallied and assessed. If she didn't yell loud enough or rattle hard enough, or if one person didn't look up with piqued interest, the hovering threat could become a repercussion. To Vincent. To anyone in the troupe. To friends at the temple. In a hundred different ways. Celia cursed the scope of her imagination and made the biggest spectacle possible from the seat of a slow-moving wagon.

At one stop she'd checked on the carriages following them from Sabazio, counting and then recounting their numbers, wanting more. When one of the older fans spotted her lurking behind a wagon wheel, tallying the people with her clawed hands, rattling chains, and monstrous mask, his heart had nearly given out. But a couple of days later, when Celia checked again, there were two new wagons following the group. Kitty Kay had been right: their notoriety was spreading like a disease, and Celia helped it along with every breath. She had to.

Her noise was balanced by the plague doctor's uncharacteristic quiet, and when Celia shifted her concentration enough to notice, she felt it getting bigger the longer they traveled. Her apology for commandeering his finale had been genuine, except in the next breath she'd informed him that she'd do it all over again in Malidora.

"Interesting," he'd said quietly. Smiling, of course. But, funny thing, she was starting to understand his unchanging smiles. This version—where it felt as if he were looking deep inside her and seeing her too clearly—was the one she had the hardest time with. It made her stutter and ramble.

"Anya and I have dreamed of performing like this since we were little. I just need everything to be perfect."

He'd nodded, as though that made sense. Then, three hours

later, he'd felt the need to tell her, "Don't worry. I won't stand in the way of your ambition."

What did that even *mean* three hours later?

From fierce intensity to carefree flirtation, his presence poked at her raw edges. They circled each other like sword-masters about to duel, superficial conversations somehow always feeling like anything but.

The weather set the general mood. Typical of Illinia, when it decided to rain, it let loose in earnest for days at a time, going from light rain to heavy and back again in a miserable cycle. Though the seats at the head wagon were covered, that didn't help when the rain and wind decided to pummel them sideways.

Between the assault of rain, the heat radiating from Anya—still smoldering about Diavala and taking every free opportunity to unload on Celia about it—the fire licking at her from the plague doctor, and the manic fear that took hold whenever she thought of Vincent and Diavala, Celia was in one of the nine circles of hell. As a fun bonus, her new view at the head of the caravan made it easier to see the shrines to the Divine in front yards or by fence lines. Four-faced, six-eyed mini-statues, stone carvings with lightning bolts honoring Ascension and Return, and everywhere the phrase Inktrava sel Immorti: Always listen to the ink.

The plague doctor shifted toward her. Again. He'd be in her lap soon enough.

His thigh kept pushing against hers. His smile was of the

everyone loves it blinding variety. He'd clearly bathed in made-for-Celia pheromones that morning, basking like a lizard on a rock as he drove the wagon, using his honey to lure Celia in.

She'd always liked honey.

Damn it!

Celia ground her teeth, actively refusing to be charmed. She might not know what to do about Diavala, but this was something she could handle.

Instead of leaning away from him again, she let the next big bounce of the wagon take her closer. Her thigh pressed hard against his from knee to hip, and she slotted her arm under his as if they were puzzle pieces sliding together. Now his arm was a captive of her chains as well. When she tilted her head toward him, her exposed lips under her mask pointed at the long line of his jaw. Her words fluttered against skin. "Is this what you're after?"

She reveled in the moment when his body tensed; he hadn't expected her to play offense.

"Whatever satisfies you, devil." His voice was soft and deep, soothing and calm. But his smile didn't know what to do with itself.

Celia's fingertips grazed the leather of his pants, down and up in one sweeping stroke, with the jingling of chains tracing the trail until she found an open clasp of his trench coat. She notched her thumb into it and cupped the plane of his hip. Two could play at his game. She didn't move her lips from near his ear. "It might work for you onstage, to offer heaven and then snatch it away. But I'm not your audience, plague doctor. Remember that. I didn't pay an admission fee; I don't leave when the gates close."

Her body was alight, but her words came from someone else: sure and strong, as soft, deep, soothing, and calm as his. They swayed together to the motion of the carriage as one body, the rain pattering above and misting them from the sides. She resisted, barely, the urge to pull the chains around him so they were trapped together.

Celia whispered, "If you want to dance with *me,* I'll expect you to finish what you start."

They rolled over a deep rut, and the wagon lurched. Her hand clasped his hip tighter. Her lips rolled closer. With her free hand, she pulled her beast mask down so it hung against her chest like a macabre necklace. "And I'll expect you maskless, *Griffin,* so ask yourself if you're ready for that particular dance." Her gaze roamed along his neck, and she had to quell the absurd desire to search for the source of the clove and lemon scent with her lips.

Her mind had seized on an opportunity to scare him into backing off, using his plague doctor shield against him. But her heart pounded in a way that was incongruent with her threat . . . as if it truly wanted his submission. Every point of contact with him burned through her costume despite the cool damp.

Retreat, retreat. Under her hand, his hip flexed as he shifted.

She waited for him to pull away, to realize that his exasperating game with her was over. She waited for the win.

But he didn't pull away.

Instead, the plague doctor tilted toward the damp *Book of Profeta* in Anya's lap and pushed his words right over Celia's head. "I assumed you two weren't believers."

"We're not," Anya mumbled. "There's nothing else to read, and some of the stories are actually pretty good."

Where Celia was determined to amass numbers, perfect the show, and please Diavala, Anya spent her free time analyzing every word of the *Book of Profeta*, the version in her hands relieved of its duty as a plant stand in Kitty Kay's wagon.

"The ink is a parasite. A subtle poison," Anya had hissed at their last stop. "If we could access the Chest Majestic, smash it, burn the filth inside, all Diavala's power would die with *us*. *We'd* be her last batch of inklings, and a thousand-year reign would end. Look, the Chest is said to be indestructible, but I bet that's yet another Profetan lie. In order to be called indestructible, someone, at some point, must have tried to destroy it." Anya had stabbed her finger at the tattered, water-stained book. "There must be something in here. A story we can look at through a new lens." Anya's single-mindedness was becoming alarming. "If only I could rip the ink from my veins," she'd muttered. "Dangling, dripping, bleeding out in black and red . . ."

When Celia had reached into the Chest Majestic all those years ago and submerged her hands in the ink, it had startled her that it felt so normal. Cool and creamy, like milk. Then a mild tingling as it soaked through her skin and wound its way into her bloodstream, like coming into a warm room after a crisp night. But when she lifted her hands out, they'd repulsed her. Thick, viscous strings of black dribbled on her skin: moving too slowly, congealing into globs too quickly. Instinct had made her try to flick it off, but not a drop of it let go, so determined was it to finish its course and merge with her blood.

She understood Anya's disgust, but she couldn't get over that central fact: the ink was in *their* blood. *They* were the poisoned ones. This was their fight, and it was an impossible one. Impossible to smash the heavily fortified and guarded Chest Majestic unless the mistico miraculously decided to help them. Impossible to fight back at all. Diavala was too powerful, her institution too strong—but Celia had lost the ability to reason with Anya about it days ago.

Stuck there, with no help in sight coming from her friend, wrapped around a plague doctor but determined that he would be the one to pull away, Celia stared at the horses. From the corner of her eye she caught Anya shaking her head and casting her a frown—*What the hell are you doing?*

Fantastic question. Trying to call him out on his bullshit had only highlighted her own.

Every muscle the plague doctor possessed was tight with tension—his leg, his waist, his face—but he acted as if Celia weren't curled around him at all.

And just like that, she knew she wouldn't win.

Still, as the seconds turned to minutes and the minutes stretched on, she realized that maybe he wouldn't win either. The bumps in the muddy road didn't loosen the strain in his muscles, but bunched them up more. And as he coiled, she did too. They tightened together like snakes determined to choke each other.

She didn't need to use those chains after all.

One of his hands had moved to hers at his hip, but not to pull it away.

They passed another notice board with two familiar faces front and center. "There you are again." The plague doctor forced a chuckle, and it rumbled down his chest and fell into her clutching hand. "So popular, you two."

She would have flushed deeper if she wasn't already mighty warm. *Retreat. Retreat!*

The moment the Mob had protected their new members coming through the checkpoint, those notices were made redundant. When Marco had raised his concerns, Kitty Kay's words to him and the troupe had been, amidst heavy peels of laughter, "Since when does the Mob care about the outside world? We have our own!"

And Celia knew that the plague doctor agreed. Whatever crime they believed Celia and Anya might be guilty of or caused them to flee the temple, the Mob's moral compass swung independently from the rest of the world.

No one had dwelled on the Touched mistico in Sabazio. They'd flitted by it so quickly, Celia had to wonder what other kinds of things Citizens of Everywhere routinely saw. Only the plague doctor and Vincent had acted strangely since Sabazio, both for entirely different reasons.

The plague doctor cleared his throat. "Kitty Kay has you on the playbill now. Milloni and Ravino rode ahead to plaster posters all over Malidora that have your ghastly faces on them." He gripped two sets of reins loosely in his free hand, driving the eight horses pulling the wagon in a way that made it look easier than breathing. "The whispers are turning to roars. The rumor is the Rabble Mob have found a way to harness some rare magic. That we're entertainers, but *more*." He hooked a boot around Celia's ankle and pressed his calf along the top of her shin. "Interesting, that everyone is picking up on the *more* you two bring to the show, isn't it?"

Anya mumbled something unintelligible. Celia nodded, her breath clamped inside tight lungs.

She didn't fight him when he casually worked her thumb out of the buttonhole of his jacket. Or when he cupped her hand from behind and splayed her fingers against his chest, holding her palm flat so she felt his heart beating under his skin. A little fast. Like hers.

With a little more room to move, he pointed his mask at Celia, angling his face in front of her so she couldn't escape the hint of his eyes behind those dark lenses.

She didn't fight him, but damn, she should have.

She watched his lips form slow, low, deliberate words— "Your pupils have swallowed your irises, little devil"—then transform into the full force of his wide, confident, unwavering smile.

"Damn it, you're infuriating!" she said. As she tried to untangle herself from the plague doctor, she expected him to laugh in victory. But the only sound he made was a warm, melting hum that flowed through the length of him and into the places where they still touched.

She straightened her hair before pulling her mask on, trying to snatch back the last strands of her dignity, then shuffled closer to Anya.

Anya calmly flipped a page of the book and said, "That was entertaining," without even looking up.

"Hate you too," Celia grumbled.

Anya shrugged. "I'd bet anything his pupils are even bigger, Cece."

"True," the plague doctor said. "It's quite irritating."

Celia wanted to jump off the wagon onto the beautiful silver dapple in front of her and leave them both behind.

Many excruciating minutes later, the plague doctor slowed the wagon to a halt for the next scheduled stop and leaped over the side, leaving them without a word.

The ruts in the muddy road were full of water, streaming like rivers. The sky wasn't its usual Illinian gray, but a violent shade of indigo, the seamless cloud cover deciding to match their moods. Tree branches in the surrounding countryside creaked and groaned, protesting against the wind.

The burst of movement as people emerged from the dozen

different wagons was immediate, loud, and over almost as soon as it had begun. The rain pounded too hard to linger outside, so it was a mad dash for everyone to congregate inside with their friends for a meal.

Celia and Anya were the only ones who stayed out in the misery. With the *Book of Profeta* tucked under her arm, Anya wrung out her long hair like a sodden rag. The rain pounded down on the awning above them like a meat tenderizer as they waited for Seer Ostra, sloth and travel cook, to finish preparing everyone's lunch, so they could run around handing them out. Celia's apologies to the troupe had taken the form of mending Georgio's many costumes, playing Imp tiles with Ravino, hammering nails into wobbly floor planks so Caspian and Sky could frolic instead of work, teaching Remy to draw, and handing out Seer's meals. Anya had helped with some of it.

"I can't handle this anymore," Anya said. Drenched and shivering, her dress more dampened gray than white, she pointedly looked from Celia to Vincent's wagon and back again, her fuse burning dreadfully low. Time on the road had done nothing but make her *wet* and determined to push back against Diavala, every turn of the wagon's wheels toward Malidora cinching her frustration tighter. "I'm going inside, and you're dealing with lunches alone today." Anya leaned in so they were almost cheek to cheek. "You can do it. *It'll be fine.*" She delivered a quick peck to Celia's nose to soften the razor's edge of her words before sloshing away.

The gnaw in Celia's stomach wrenched itself into a knot.

There was the real issue: not the plague doctor's simmering, not the incessant rain, not Anya's preferred reading material.

Celia had avoided Vincent for days, leaving Anya to deliver his meals, but that didn't mean she'd been unaware of his presence. After the night Diavala had revealed herself, where menace dripped from every word, so obviously not-Vincent, Diavala had retreated. In every aspect, Vincent remained mostly the same — quiet, watchful, serene — going about his business as if nothing were amiss.

But Celia noted his sleep-deprived, shadowed eyes, the way he sometimes abruptly stopped and looked around as if he needed to get his bearings, the way he gently traced his purple and blue bracelet from finger to wrist, lost in thought.

"He needs a vacation or something," Remy had remarked.

Celia could have sunk into the ground from the weight of her shame. It wasn't right that she ignored her friend, no matter how terrified she was that Diavala might steal the conversation.

Vincent's wagon was snakelike, with an accordion bend in the middle. The dark and deserted main living area led to the sleeping areas, partitioned off with curtains, making a long hallway.

Or a tunnel.

Or a throat.

"Vincent?" She knew where his space was, had visited this wagon often to draw with Remy or play tiles with Vincent, but she whispered as she walked, holding her mask in front of her as if the horns could defend her. How had Anya done this so often?

"Vincent?" She left a trail of water behind her like the slime trail of a slug.

She took a steadying breath before wrapping her fingers around the thick curtain to his private room.

"Vincent?"

He sat cross-legged on his cot, one candle illuminating the comfortable space, holding a small framed picture in his hands. Celia had seen only a few tintypes in her life. Tenors didn't translate to photographs, so people used them only as keepsakes of family and close friends. Unless you knew the subjects well, the captured images were too vague to mean much. As if dress, facial features, and body type were enough to illuminate the soul of a person.

"I brought lunch for you." Celia placed the plate on his small side table with an abundance of care.

"You're soaked, Lalita." He grabbed one of his blankets and tossed it at her. She juggled her mask to catch it.

Again, stupidly, "Vincent?"

She wrapped the blanket around her shoulders and sat down opposite him, examining his face and searching every dip and line for evidence of the *other*. Even without his white face paint he looked ghostly, his light eyes blending into pale skin, everything leached of color.

Is it you, Diavala? Can you hear everything? Celia stared hard into Vincent's eyes, cursing that there wasn't more light. She needed proof—a dull, darkened gaze, a flicker of malice, some tangible evil and otherness—it had to be there. She needed to see it.

She didn't.

"I didn't grow up in this Rover troupe," he said, showing her the tintype. "We mix and mingle, right? Otherwise we'd be a frightening group, all interbred and strange." He chuckled in his melancholy way. "Well, I suppose we're strange anyway, but strang*er*."

He pointed to himself, a young Vincent, maybe ten or eleven, surrounded by a gaggle of siblings and three smiling adults standing behind their rowdiness. Only a few of the children aimed themselves forward, most ignoring the formality of a portrait session.

"We did this before splintering. All of us over ten years old were sent to different Rover bands." It sounded like Vincent, the conversation innocent enough to be with him.

So Diavala hadn't lied. She took residence *with* someone. Two souls in one body. But did that mean Diavala was allowing this conversation? *Where are you right now, Diavala?*

"Is that why you've been so—withdrawn—lately?" Her heart boomed in her chest. "You miss them?" She swallowed and leaned forward.

"No, just feeling nostalgic. Looking backwards is always laced with a bit of regret, isn't it?" He smiled his sad smile, sounding like an elder at the end of his life rather than a young person on the cusp of experience.

That scared her.

He sighed and put the picture down. "I have been feeling different the past few days, though. It's like I'm vibrating on the inside. A struck tuning fork covered in flesh and skin."

She startled back. "Your bones are humming?"

Humming bones. *It's all games, darling. It's all lies. You lose when your bones hum from the inside.* The fair-haired mistico, with her rotten breath and manic eyes.

Celia's very first lesson after she'd arrived at the temple — and now she finally understood it. The humming bones happened under Diavala's possession. The Touch was a product of unpossession: inevitable, terrible. At the hands of the mistico's training: final.

Vincent misunderstood her reaction and shrugged it off, embarrassed. "It's nothing. I'm just tired."

It wasn't nothing. Finding the cure for the Touch was everything. Celia was prepared to dance with Diavala as long as possible just to make sure Vincent survived without losing his mind.

"When did it start? Sabazio?"

He startled at her quick questioning. "No. When we were already on the road. Or maybe I just didn't notice it. It was so subtle at first, but it's . . . growing." He shook his head, like *that sounds so stupid.*

Then a shudder raced through his shoulders, out of control and sudden. With a quiet groan, his crystal eyes flicked up and caught hers. Her heart stopped.

She swallowed. Inhaled. Leaned backwards. "Diavala?" she whispered.

"The devil's work? Maybe something like that, Lalita." It still sounded like Vincent, the endearment soft on his lips.

But then he smiled again, not sadly. Far too many teeth gleamed. Celia wanted to run.

One moment Vincent, the next Diavala. The other lingered just under the surface. Nothing changed in Vincent's tone or tenor, or in his eyes. He remained her doomed Palidon.

Celia needed to gather information. Be a miser hoarding coin, a farmer reaping harvest, a child collecting bugs. A goal to keep her from screaming. From crumpling. From running.

If she could examine her collection later, maybe something in it would be useful.

"I'm curious—" Celia started.

Diavala nodded. "Of course you are."

Celia swallowed. "Did you feel it?" She swallowed again. "The Flogging?" She thumbed the tracks of scars between her fingers before forcing herself to clasp her hands tight in her lap.

Diavala boomed a hearty laugh, so toxic and strange coming from Vincent's mouth that Celia thought she'd be sick. "My history is ancient, Inkling. Why waste your breath on a question like that?"

But it hovered between them, the acknowledgment that something had gone wrong in Diavala's lengthy story. And with it, the acknowledgment that she'd been Divine once, trying to help people with the ink. That they're repaid her by drowning her. She'd fought to return, bargaining away her own power over the ink. They'd repaid her again by flogging her new mortal body to death. *Her pivotal moments are of death and torture, of something good twisted into something bad.* Celia's gut clenched. When exactly, on that long road, had she turned cruel? When did her mission become one of power instead of altruism?

She'd been invisible since. Anonymous. Stealing body after body. Taking away choice and free will, punishing all descendents of those who'd wronged her in a subtle game only she knew about.

Celia lifted the hem of her dress, exposing the hairline tattoo that labeled her an inkling. Without knowing why, she whispered, "Do you miss this?" Such an intimate betrayal, to awaken the ink's power in the mortal realm and then lose the ability to use it.

"I can follow the ink wherever it goes. I miss nothing." But despite how hardened the statement was, Celia knew the lie of it. Diavala did miss things; otherwise she would have discovered Celia's and Anya's temporary manipulations with the ink long ago.

Diavala exhaled and broke eye contact.

And because she looked away, because it was the first time she'd been anything other than wholly confident in her words, Celia noted them.

Diavala saw her noting them.

Vincent's eyebrows knotted in confusion. He glanced around his room as if he didn't remember getting there. Maybe he didn't.

"What were you saying?" he asked.

With shaking fingers, Celia folded Vincent's now-soaked blanket and gave him a light hug that turned into a hard hug. She yearned to reach into his throat, find the thread of Diavala's essence, pinch it between her fingers and pull it out and wind it around a spool and use it to sew a new, dry blanket for Vincent to replace the one she'd made damp. With the embrace, she said, *I'm so sorry about your humming bones, Vincent. I'm doing what she wants. I promise this is for you.* But her words answered, "Only that the show always goes on."

"As long as you bring me more believers, Celia." Diavala.

This was a madness she couldn't handle.

Laughter burned its way out of Celia's throat. But as she laughed, Diavala's last word echoed . . . *Celia, Celia, Celia* . . . For the first time, Diavala had said it without rancor.

"Or," Diavala said, "it will end with your friend Zuni weeping as ash falls from her pyres, coating her like snow. Don't forget what you need to do here. Everything in your world extends only as far as my patience."

Tipping her head in a minute bow, Celia choked back all the things she wanted to scream and heard herself say, "I'm focused, Diavala."

"Why so obsessed with the devil, Lalita?" Vincent shifted on his bedroll and, with a frown, reached to pick up the family portrait again, tracing the faces of his old family.

Enough.

Her mind told her to go back, continue the conversation. Her feet moved in the opposite direction. She ran out of the wagon and away, no destination in mind except distance. "Did you win your tile game?" Caspian called after her as he trotted off to clean dishes. Anya must have told a white lie to keep people away.

"Nah." Celia forced a laugh. "My opponent is too good!" She darted behind the head wagon, her laughter transforming to retching. How could Anya still believe they could overcome something that ruled the religion of the land, that precious few knew the truth about, that couldn't die, and that wore the face of a friend?

But even as she emptied her stomach, her skin on fire and her insides buzzing, she thought about Diavala's pause, her quick retreat, almost as if she needed to collect herself. A moment where Celia had seen something new in the devil herself.

Weakness.

CHAPTER 17

DESPITE WAGON-TO-MAIN-STAGE ORIGAMI, THE UNDERBELLY of the head wagon stayed constant. In the dark crawlspace underneath, amid a labyrinth created by stacks of boxes and props, Celia sat where the wooden slats above her pressed together and wouldn't betray her hiding spot. The fleeing-from-the-conversation-with-Diavala tumble of her stomach wouldn't settle.

After lighting a candle and putting it on a crate next to her, she lifted her sodden skirt and stared at the bare expanse of skin on her upper thigh. At the temple, it had been her favorite body part for inking Divine orders: a large enough space to accommodate the design, it didn't require too much contortion, and she could use either hand.

Zuni . . .

Celia imagined inking a message—on her thigh to Zuni's. Something sweet first. A message only Zuni would understand: a collage of all the feathers Celia had ever found for her. Then questions: *Are you sleeping okay? How are our favorite skulls—Bruno? Jasmyna? Saccharine?*

Divine tattoos were always inked one-to-one—they'd been taught that the image had to be drawn exactly how and where it would appear on the receiver's body. But with Diavala's bravado ringing so false, it was foolish to assume that was exactly how the ink worked. Celia couldn't stop thinking about the question posed by Wallis's stressed-out friend weeks ago: Can the image change size when we send it to the receiver's body? At the time, Celia had brushed it off as the lament of an overwhelmed apprentice, but now?

If everything they'd been taught served Diavala's purposes, it was possible that they knew little about the ink's true capabilities.

Then she imagined inking a plea: *Tell me what to do, Zuni. I have no idea.*

I can't see more death. I refuse to cause it.

But what if Anya was right? What if there was a chance to take Diavala's power away? Use her ink in a way she didn't expect? Their entire act depended on a loophole. Celia's existence as an inkling was because of one, and it was clear now that Diavala didn't have as much power over the ink as she let on. Could they find a loophole big enough to pull Diavala herself through it?

The twinkling candle on the crate beside her kept her company as her heartbeat counted out the seconds. She couldn't ink Zuni without putting her at risk, and even if she did, Zuni couldn't respond. But Celia pretended, tracing the images and words she wanted to say with her fingernail on her leg, trying to find comfort. Trying to assuage her crippling fear.

The sounds of the Mob got louder above her: people shouting

exclamations as they enjoyed the rest of their break; laughter and footsteps; some muttering about her. The rain had lightened enough for them to head outside and stretch their legs, and she wondered if Vincent was among them. The bangs, exclamations, and giggles piled on top of one another, threatening to crush her under their weight.

Someone opened the hatch leading to her hiding spot. With a quick lick of her thumb and forefinger, she pressed the wick and extinguished the candle. She expected Remy, who excelled at finding her when she didn't want to be found, but the steps landed too gently.

Celia watched the plague doctor make his way through the maze of items, hunching so his hat didn't knock against the low ceiling. A small purple flame hovered an inch above his outstretched palm, lighting his way. He strode with purpose toward the opposite corner of the basement room.

If she tried to hide herself better, she'd definitely knock something over. If she called out to let him know where she was . . . he would know where she was.

So she let him rustle around and go about his business (muttering constantly in some personal version of Riddlish), waiting for him to leave. She peered down at where her leg would be — if she could see it — as if she could touch Zuni with the intensity of her stare. Or tell Wallis and the other fleas a bedtime story. Or even see Dante, stupid crooked smile and all.

Celia learned the hard way that the plague doctor could throw his voice. The muttering hadn't changed volume, he still sounded a safe distance away, but the purple flame in his hand turned the corner to reveal Celia.

"Privacy!" she shrieked, shifting and dropping her skirt.

He held his hands out at his sides in a gesture of peace, one hand absently tossing his purple flame so it flitted up and down like a feather, but he didn't leave. "What are you doing?" His head cocked to the left.

Despite covering herself, she'd assumed an awkward pose, both of her hands pressed against one thigh. "What the hell are *you* doing?"

"I live here."

"Well, so do I, smart-ass."

His shoulders went tight, as if holding in laughter; the bobbing flame froze. "No. I meant, I live *here*."

"Here," she said, deadpan. "In storage." All this time she'd assumed he slept in the same wagon as Kitty Kay. She'd thought it vaguely weird, but since everything about the Mob was vaguely weird, she'd accepted it.

"Well, over there." He tossed a spark of purple flame over a rack of costumes in the far corner. "So you're in my bedroom, in the dark, with your skirt up around your waist. Why — exactly?"

Coupled with her already madly thumping heart, blood rushed to her face so fast she saw stars. She grabbed for a smart comeback, but it eluded her. She grabbed her candle instead. "I didn't know you slept here. I'll leave."

"No, no, no. I insist you stay. This is the best spot to conduct nefarious plots of any kind." He paused significantly. "Or whatever else you might have been doing under your skirt."

She flushed deeper. Everything an opportunity for innuendo with him.

Although, now that he'd mentioned it, that wasn't the *worst* idea.

But instead of retreating to the hatch, he grabbed a crate and sat opposite her. Close. With his elbows on his thighs, he made the sparrow-size flame hop from one palm to the other. With every jump, his mask flashed periwinkle or plum.

Celia watched it dance. "Are you trying to hypnotize me?"

The plague doctor didn't respond.

Until he did. "Let's have a conversation."

Those words meant that this couldn't possibly go well for her. "All right. Tell me how you make your fire."

His lips quirked into an even wider smile, but it was tight, painful-looking. "A secret for a secret?"

Trap. "I don't have time for your games. If this is about my little . . . our . . . thing . . . driving the wagon . . ."

"Our dance?" he offered.

She nodded. "It was stupid, and I didn't mean—"

"I'm not surprised we fit together so well." His tone still said *irritating.*

She smoothed her skirt with clenched fists and made to stand, but she stopped when his smile stumbled, then fell away completely.

"Let's try five minutes, Celia." He pressed his hands together and extinguished the sparrow. "We can do this."

Flushed and embarrassed as she was, being pitched into abrupt darkness didn't calm her. Her heart moved to her collarbone and expanded, hot and huge, trying to force its way into her throat.

He'd blended into dust and shadows. "My purple and blue flame is made from a spectacular but harmless combustion of a common powder mined in Kinallen. The place where the land is so high, so flat, you can reach up and touch the stars. It's only magical for people who yearn to see magic."

Rustling met her ears, distant and close at the same time because the boom of her heartbeat had overtaken the world. He reached through the darkness and opened her palm. "Rub your hands together, then open them quickly."

If he'd dropped something in, Celia couldn't feel it. Only the warmth of his hand cupping hers from underneath.

He guided her motions—taking both hands, pressing them together lightly, back and forth, then opening—and out of nothing burst a tiny purple flame. With the slightest pressure from his movements leading her, the flame bobbed. "Create movement in the air, slight and small."

Mesmerized by the light, wondering again if the plague doctor could hypnotize, she took over the movements. The flame responded to every subtle shift, as if held by an invisible string. She raised her hands in front of her at eye level, trying to give the bouncing flame a rhythm. If she thought about it, she lost control. It became more a matter of willing the flame where she wanted it to go, and the subconscious movements of her body did the rest.

"Whatever you do, don't sneeze."

A bark of a laugh erupted out of her. The flame shot the small distance toward the plague doctor, but he snatched it from the air before it hit him.

The renewed darkness swallowed them, but not before she caught a glimpse of the face of the maskless plague doctor sitting in front of her.

"Or laugh." His rumbling chuckle was nothing like his megaphone laugh. "Are you disappointed it's not true magic?"

"No. I'm disappointed that I didn't notice you'd taken off your mask." Celia had never spoken such an understatement in her life. Nothing of his image had coalesced. Her bees erupted, their chaos absolute. They fought to stretch the glimpse out longer, pulling and tugging at the gossamer threads of impossibility.

"Well, the plague doctor doesn't give away his secrets. Especially ones that steal from his allure."

"But Griffin does?"

A slight pause. "I suppose so." He exhaled slowly and shifted. "I don't tend to give him much thought."

Why? she wanted to ask. *Where did Griffin go?*

Only more subtle rustling as an answer, her ears coming alive with the sound of movements she couldn't see. "Quite a few years ago, there was an actor in the Mob named Stash. He played Gemello in the main show, and he only spoke while performing. It was as if his tongue worked only in front of a crowd. 'Is Stash short for mustache?' I'd tease him. And he'd smile and nod, like, 'Whatever you say, infant.' I followed him around like a puppy, waiting for him to talk to me."

He paused for so long, Celia wondered if the story ended there. The darkness suddenly felt like his protection, warm and thick, heavy and soft. "And?"

The maskless plague doctor in the dark stayed silent for a long time. He cleared his throat. Shifted. Leaned closer so the air around her got warmer. She imagined his lips hovering inches from hers in the darkness: waiting, unsmiling, true.

When he spoke again, she didn't hear a trace of a smile in his words. "This standoff with you isn't as much fun as I remember the one with Stash being."

He put his hand on her thigh gently. Even for the plague doctor, it was too intimate a touch. With it, he told her he knew something was wrong. "I just wanted to say . . ." He paused. Inhaled. "Seeing death is hard for me too."

Celia pulled away as if he'd transformed into a snake. "What? How did you—" How could he possibly know her fear?

"If that's what it was like for you, no wonder you needed to run away. I never imagined the taking of a life could be so . . . *routine.*"

The mistico in Sabazio. The plague doctor thought she was

acting strange because of the trauma of watching Mistico Dominic die. And he was right, but it was so much more. "I—" She swallowed. "I don't—"

All her usual instincts when someone touched too close to truth—denial, flippancy, misdirection—abandoned her. They'd entered a quiet moment of parley, impossible to fight.

If what Lilac had said was true, if he'd died and gone somewhere *other* before coming back, he'd know better than anyone whether that *other* was something to fear.

He might know where Salome was. Where her mothers were. Where so many souls Celia loved had gone.

What might happen to Vincent if they failed.

"What's it like?" Celia could barely ask the question, didn't know if she wanted the answer. Everyone knew the plague doctor didn't talk about it. But he had touched the inevitability they all traveled toward—the one she was terrified Vincent would be shoved into much too early because of her.

"I described it out loud once. Alone. To see if I could." He hesitated, clasped his hands together, close to her, warm but no longer touching her. "It felt all wrong. And now those words are out there, floating around where they don't belong. They don't belong here, Celia."

"If it was wonderful, you'd talk about it, wouldn't you?" she whispered, so glad he couldn't see the buildup of tears in her eyes.

The ache in her throat had grown.

He answered her by not answering. "I hope one day you feel

safe here." The sobering tone of his voice, smileless, maskless, ripped a tiny fissure in her heart. For the first time, he sounded completely sincere. What in devil's hell was she supposed to do with *that*?

When she didn't respond, the ache too overbearing, he took his whisper with him as he left, his warmth pulling away at the last possible moment. She heard him don his mask, clear his throat, and leave her behind in the darkness. Another *Your move, Celia*, but this time she didn't hear a sharp edge at all.

She heard an invitation. Maybe the same one he'd repeated from the beginning.

CHAPTER 18

FANS AT THE ROVER GATES IN MALIDORA GREETED THEM AS they approached. The plague doctor had to pull the stage wagon, and therefore the entire caravan, to a halt. He shouted instructions for the unruly crowd to move out of the way and persuaded a drunk to come down from his perch atop the arched gate lined with oversize Commedia masks, where he'd been swinging a bottle and singing a bawdy folk song about one of the Commander's conquests.

"It wasn't like this in Sabazio," Anya whispered from the corner of her smiling mouth as she waved. It was a good thing—exactly what Diavala wanted—so it felt ominous.

Someone began playing a banjo; more voices sang. The plague doctor shook his head as he clicked his tongue and flicked the reins to get the horses moving again. "No, it was not," he said. Slow, measured, pleased but perplexed.

Cheers, song, some hushed awe, and hundreds of sets of eyes followed the chained devil, triumphant angel, and plague doctor overseer as they led the Rabble Mob of Minos caravan into the field.

Milloni and Ravino, who had ridden ahead to put up posters around the city and prep the field, directed them in, directed the fans to stay out, and shouted what sounded like the same warnings they'd been shouting for days. Milloni, sweat dripping profusely from their bald head, bellowed a hearty laugh as a soul dressed like their character, the Commander, took up the song the gate rider had been singing. "I'm getting too old for this!" they shouted at the plague doctor as the wagon passed, good-natured and lovely but looking too worn down for the *beginning* of a run.

As soon as they were all safely inside, Kitty Kay called Milloni and Ravino to her for an explanation. The gears in Anya's head spun out of control as they listened in on the conversation. Celia saw it on her face, felt it in Anya's grip on her upper arm. They'd known that the Mob's fame was spreading—the glass-smashing finale in Asura, the mistico's dramatic death in Sabazio, and the thematic changes to the content of the show had all stoked rumors and fueled gossip—the evidence in advanced ticket sales and in the herd of followers who'd been trailing the caravan in greater and greater numbers. But Ravino explained that the public response was actually bordering on fever, far more widespread than they'd thought. "There was a riot in Quantoro a few nights ago. A local theater group put on their annual Commedia Revel but weren't prepared for the crowds. It spilled into the streets and got out of control."

"Quantoro isn't even along any of our routes," Kitty Kay said. "Surely that had nothing to do with us."

"It had everything to do with us," Milloni said, still glistening from the effort of keeping the crowd back, patting a rag across their brow. "We heard the story from someone who'd been there, passing through Quantoro on his way here. And he wasn't the only one taking a trip to our next advertised destination. People from all over Illinia are—" Milloni looked to Ravino.

"Pilgrimaging?" Ravino offered.

Milloni nodded. "Pilgrimaging to see us. We shared a pint with him and his friends, trading conspiracy theories about the meaning of the New Commedia."

"They didn't know we were part of the troupe." Ravino's perpetually frowning face twitched into a smile that showed too-pointy teeth in a too-large mouth, making Scary Ravino look even scarier. He nudged Milloni, almost knocking the smaller performer over. "Good thing, right? We barely made it out of there alive as it was!"

Anya's grip tightened as Milloni said, "This 'New Commedia' strongly centers on the Devil in the Bell Jar. People think it's canon in the making. They're treating it like a puzzle to solve."

Celia and Anya hadn't noticed that Marco had joined them as they eavesdropped until he asked, "What is it about you that's speaking to them?" If he didn't sound so confused, it might have been a compliment.

"Okay, whatever you're thinking"—Celia said to Anya, leading her away from Marco—"my answer is *maybe*." The chink in Diavala's armor had been tiny, maybe imagined, but Celia couldn't ignore it.

"This changes things, Cece. We have a stage. We're talking

and people are *listening*. Imagine all the things we could say." Her dark blue eyes gleamed with possibilities, all the frustration of the past days melting into determination. "We did this every day." Anya was practically vibrating. "We inked Divine tattoos meant to convey one message, but we always put another message underneath. This is the same subtle art, but to a much wider audience." She pulled Celia into a hug and whispered, "We've been practicing for *exactly this* our entire lives."

Maybe they could think about pushing back against Diavala, Celia thought, but Vincent was their priority. They needed to go on a little field trip for him first.

The next day, as the Mob prepared for their first night on the Malidoran stage, Celia found Anya in the glass dome of their wagon with some unfamiliar, ragged costumes bunched in her arms like grim bouquets of wilted flowers. Though the crowd at the gates was already chanting and singing, there was still a bit of a wait before night fell and those gates opened.

Kitty Kay oversaw the preparations from behind her veil of gray hair, quiet and reaperlike, ensuring that there would be no repeat of Quantoro-type riots under her watch.

Vincent and a few others were heaving the bell jar onto a newly built podium, raising the viewing angle so the devil could be seen from anywhere. Grisilda and Fawn, Passion's two halves, added alterations to the hems of each other's dresses to match the pattern of Anya's. The angel in the crowd would now have twin bodyguards, Kitty Kay insisting on protection for the one who roamed through the crowd, just in case the touching got out of control. As of that night as well, Cas, Sky, and Lilac would be at the edges of the crowd on their stilts, perched lookouts for "problems and perverts," as Sky had so succinctly put it.

Celia's eyes burned with the effort of holding back tears as she changed into the costume Anya offered her. A regular thing now—this pressure behind her eyes from lack of sleep and moving this way and that way and thinking in circles. Below, Vincent wiped his brow and shook his head at something Remy asked. Celia seemed hell-bent to find him wherever he was at any given moment. So aware of him, she swore in her more burned-out moments that she could *hear* his humming bones following her, haunting her, getting louder. Diavala skulked in the background and watched through Vincent's eyes. Yet her steady presence couldn't be ignored. In the weeks since Sabazio, Vincent had lost weight and paled; every time Celia looked at him, he appeared fainter, vanishing by degrees.

Checking the Roll of Saints wouldn't *help* him, precisely, but it could give them information on the Touch, something to go on. It was the only thing they could think to do for him.

The Roll of Saints was an organic document in which the mistico logged everyone who had experienced the Touch. Celia and Anya knew about it from Zuni, who'd seen the original a few times: every skull on her shelf was an entry.

It wasn't a holy relic like the Chest Majestic, but rather a practical bookkeeping item, a binding contract that the families of the Touched would be financially taken care of by Profeta.

Each temple would have a fairly up-to-date copy, but it wouldn't be easy to check.

Many years ago, while the plague ran rampant through Illinia, a pair of con artist siblings had taken advantage of the chaos and had falsified entries. A quick way to get a lot of free money, a scandal that saw them both executed in the temple's main square when the scam was discovered. It was one of Zuni's favorite stories.

Since then, the Roll had been for mistico only.

Hand in hand, dressed as the regal Salantia, a Commedia character with witchlike powers, and the bedraggled Cont, a servant, Celia and Anya quickly became intimate with the streets of Malidora. It was a large city, almost as big as Asura. By the count on the notice board near the city limits, it housed seventeen Profetan temples. Dozens, if not hundreds, of mistico.

But everything about the city felt foreign. The buildings sat on brick foundations at ground level instead of on stilts and piles to avoid floodwater, and they had front porches instead of high balconies. Roads and alleys crisscrossed without being interrupted by canals and bridges. Carriages pulled by a range of animals—horses, goats, even the occasional rickshaw powered by human muscle for hire—crowded the streets. The people roamed in larger packs, their dress less opulent than the richer port city of Asura but more colorful, a rainbow sea of scarves, coats, and hats.

Celia's and Anya's thick face paint, disguising their features into the gnarled witch and her dimwitted servant, was over the top, but they needed to be labeled frenetic fans of the Commedia. Their alter egos of Devil and Angel stared at them from Rabble Mob posters pinned to every lamppost and wall, their other alter egos of Wanted by the Profetan Temple filling any blank spaces between. They couldn't walk a block without seeing their faces looking back at them.

A couple of Commedia fans tried to bond with them. "Can't wait for the show!" one said, clutching at Anya's arm. With a slight paunch of middle age and rough hands from work, he proudly wore a purple and blue ribbon in his hair, a token from the plague doctor he must have picked up at a previous show. His eyes went wide and wild, and he giggled between his words. "We came from Sabazio for this. The Mob is creating *new* Commedia, but no one can figure it out!"

His companion knocked his arm and gave him an exasperated grunt. "Shod a horse, Fallan. I keep telling you that stuff wasn't staged." She turned a much more sober gaze toward the disguised inklings. "This oaf doesn't get it." She knocked him again, and Anya took the opportunity to peel her arm away. "The Mob plays around but they don't *play around*, right?" she added, stomping her feet absently as her friend concentrated on staying upright.

"No, I think he's right," Anya said. "We're watching" —she paused long enough for Fallan to lean forward, then she laughed and playfully nudged him, her acting skills fully tapped—"*revolution*."

Since the pair didn't seem inclined to let them pass, Celia huffed out her question. "We're looking for the Viaggia temple?"

Fallan blinked, as if he didn't understand her words, then nodded so enthusiastically that he almost lost his head. "Sure, sure. We were headed to the Rosso Pesta pub, but we could join you. Where are we now?" He swiveled around, getting his bearings, bumping into a group of rowdies who looked as if they'd drunk the taps dry at the Rosso Pesta. "The closest temple is the Viaggia site, right, Pia?"

Pia rolled her eyes.

Celia desperately grabbed Anya's other arm as Fallan swept her away. Company wasn't what they'd had in mind when they set out, but if it would hurry them to where they needed to be, all the better. Celia held her other arm out for Pia and forced a smile, and the four of them marched off together.

With each block, their herd grew exponentially. Many sported ribbons similar to Fallan's or cheap mask replicas of their favorite Commedia characters. Celia's and Anya's painted faces no longer looked out of place.

Pia assessed the growing crowd. "*Revolution . . .*" She tasted the word on her tongue. "I like that."

Celia nodded, trying to ignore the ridiculousness of leading a procession of Rabble Mob rabble toward a temple. A few had spontaneously erupted into song, dancing their way down the dim street. A group of young adults piggybacked one another in a ruckus game where they tried to knock other pairs over. Tenors of a hundred varieties flickered, as unique as the people attached to them, but with dominant hues that allowed for common identities.

"So you're following the Mob as well?" Pia asked.

"Something like that. You know."

Pia's thick eyebrows knotted—no, she didn't know at all—but she squeezed Celia's arm again and smiled. They'd bonded over a shared love of Commedia and the Divine—what more was there to ask of a chance meeting of strangers?

A miniature version of the marble Divine besting Diavala greeted them as they rounded the next corner. The white statue, set into the recess of a red gabled roof, was the only indication of a place of worship. The whiteness of the statue gleamed against the deep crimson of the building.

As they approached, Pia stared at the statue with a wistful look, her steps lengthening. "Sometimes I worry, you know? Fallan has three tattoos already, so what do I make of her silence with me? Am I not important enough?"

The longing in Pia's voice took Celia by surprise. "It only means your decisions are entirely yours, Pia." It was one thing to understand that Profeta was everywhere, another thing to hear people wish there were still more of it. By Pia's metric, someone as tattooed as Ruler Vacilando was enviable.

"But what if I'm making all the wrong choices?"

"What does that even mean? Wrong or right when it comes to *your* life? Don't you know yourself best?" Celia was pushing too much, she knew. A true believer heading to a temple wouldn't talk this way.

Good thing Pia considered herself a philosopher. "Maybe *wrong* isn't the proper word. Mistakes, then."

Celia laughed. "All the ink in the world won't keep people from making mistakes, Pia. Those three tattoos on Fallan might have stopped him from making three mistakes, only to see him make three more."

"Perhaps it's a matter of degree." Pia looked ahead at Fallan fondly. "He wanted to adopt a child, years ago. That was his first tattoo. Fool would have ruined his life, and perhaps the child's, if he'd gone through with it."

Celia stopped walking, swallowing a lump. "How do you know it would have ruined his life? Or the child's? Maybe they needed each other."

With a dismissive wave, Pia grunted and pulled Celia along. "Then he wouldn't have gotten a Divine tattoo, now would he?"

Such sound logic, if you believed in an omniscient, altruistic deity. "Okay. You win." Celia ground her teeth as her imagination spun out images of happy parent Fallan and happy adopted orphan. Maybe it would have been wonderful. Maybe it would have been a mistake. Either way, he should have made the choice for himself.

Instead, he was following a theater troupe around in a drunken haze.

Pia's smile faltered as they climbed the stone steps toward the entrance, a hooded figure with a battered Gemello mask holding the door open for them. "I'm just saying it would be nice to know that the Divine thought of me."

Anya had already begun to pull Fallan inside when he hesitated, tucking his ribbon in his pocket before he went in. Others had removed their masks. Celia's and Anya's face paint was a calculated risk they hoped would cast them as wayward devotees rather than disrespectful hooligans.

All conversation halted as they crossed the threshold into the Viaggia temple. Compared with the noise the group had made outside, the silence fell as if at a funeral. Some wrote messages to the Divine on parchment; others approached the mistico for advice or hushed blessings. Pia made her way toward Fallan as he stared at a stained glass imagining of the Divine's Return: smiling, bowing crowds overcome with emotion at a human-shaped spark of white, orange, and yellow lightning.

Anya had managed to corner three mistico, their lips tight as they assessed the out-of-place costumes in their holy house, but they all held their tongues against quips, listening intently to the questions Anya whispered. Celia heard her begin without preamble: "My cousin Dimdam of Asura told me that the High Mistico has resigned. Can this possibly be true?"

Celia snorted—*Cousin Dimdam, how gossipy you are*—but she knew that Anya had it under control.

She made sure the other mistico were occupied—the crowd had become a blessing—and pulled up her hood. She would stick to the shadows.

Celia casually weaved around lingering bodies, stopping to nod or bow in deference, one hand pressed to her heart, the rote gestures flooding back. Her heart drummed loud in her ears.

Access to the Roll would be severely limited. A private room, most likely.

She circled the nave. On pretense of admiring some iconic paintings, she rounded the altar at the apse.

Behind a curtain at the apse's stage right, Celia found a door.

Opening it a Celia-size crack, dropping the curtain, taming its flutter, she stepped away, not having to pretend that her boot buckle needed tightening. She bent, she buckled, she scanned for robes. Anya had four mistico occupied in full conversation now, but she managed to signal Celia.

A message hastily scrawled in ink, written on her wrist right under the noses of four mistico, as they'd done countless times before at the temple. As they did onstage every night. *Careful*, had faded from Celia's skin before she finished whisking herself behind the curtain and through the partially opened door.

Hope for Vincent pushed her onward. Anyone might have seen her sneak through that door, and Anya couldn't hold the mistico's attention much longer. Celia's heart thumped as if it would give out.

The room was lined with bookshelves, and on an oak desk amid haphazard stacks of parchment was a locked glass box with a thin, leather-bound volume inside.

Dates. Names. Hope.

Celia blew her bangs off her sweaty forehead as she pulled on the tiny gold lock and stuck one of her hair clips in the keyhole. She'd never picked a lock before and had no idea what she was doing.

A quick snap of air movement told her that someone had come in behind her. She swiveled, thinking, *Please be Anya.*

It wasn't Anya, but the person who'd held the door open for them as they entered the temple. Celia couldn't believe she hadn't recognized him before, even with the ratty Gemello mask. The posture, the jawline, the errant curls of hair at his nape, the silvery shades of his tenor. She made a quick decision and jabbed her finger at the lock. The plague doctor and his expert sleight of hand may as well be useful.

He understood what she needed. The moment after his slim gloved fingers touched the hair clip, the lock fell into his palm. She lifted the top of the glass case as he swept silently away to listen at the door.

Anya's previous warning rang loud: *Leave it exactly as you found it. They'll notice.* Oh, what irony it would be if Celia were caught tampering with the Roll and met her end at a public execution. As if all she wanted was money.

The ledger was arranged by date of affliction, with meticulous columns of data on every individual. She ignored everything in the distant past and began her search fifty years earlier—people who may still be alive—her fingers sweeping down each page. There weren't as many entries as she'd imagined: about one a year, punctuated with the occasional cluster. Each one, a whole person before Diavala had possessed them. Each one, Touched when she'd left.

Celia needed one name.

One name without a date of death.

That person would prove it was possible to survive the Touch, and perhaps even be able to reveal *how*. Even just one name meant hope.

A warning message came from Anya. Celia hid her arm from the plague doctor's line of sight.

Every Touched mistico had a date of death exactly three days after affliction. The few names with different professions had a range of death dates, anywhere from one day to many weeks, depending on how quickly the temple could deal with the problem.

Another note from Anya. *Out!*

The plague doctor whispered a hoarse word, the first sound he'd made since following her into the room. "Time . . ." *It's running out.*

A few pages left. She went quicker down the line, looking only for a blank space in the columns marked Date and Method of Death.

Hurry. One name. No time.

The plague doctor rushed over and tried to pull the book from her hands, but Celia blocked him with her body, flipping pages, scanning. *Just one name . . .*

Her finger landed on Halcyon Ronnea of Wisteria Township. Touched three years ago. No date of death, only: "Symptoms disappeared."

She heard the voices—not approaching, but *there*, behind

the curtain and cracked door—seconds before the plague doctor finally won their personal war, hastily placing the book back on its pedestal and fitting the glass lid on top.

On the wrong page. And without the lock.

The mistico who came in uttered an alarmed "What are you doing in here?" at the same moment that every bone in the plague doctor's body deflated. A loose arm flung out, capsizing a stack of books. As his boneless body tried to catch them, he juggled through a cascade of apologies and knocked over the glass case, the lid smashing as it met the floor. The Roll of Saints was next, knocked behind the desk. The character Gemello made enough noise for ten people.

Celia had backed away, her gaze darting between the quickly recovering mistico and the plague doctor's transparent act. There was no way out of the room unless they bowled the mistico down, and that became more impossible as each new body pushed its way in, drawn by the ruckus.

Slurred "Sorrys" competed with shouts of outrage as the mistico assessed the situation. Two shrieked and swept over to the Roll, picking it up tenderly and inspecting it for damage. One mistico had already left to summon officers. Another advanced slowly toward Celia, giving the-plague-doctor-as-Gemello cagey looks as he tried to help the mistico with the Roll. "I think I saw a page fall out. Is the spine damaged? What happens if you can't find that page?" The plague doctor was a wild card no one wanted to play; Celia, on the other hand . . .

Celia's mind spun as she muttered excuses. She'd give herself up willingly, end this game with Diavala, and face the temple's justice, but she knew others would join her if she reneged on their agreement. She had to get out of there.

"Do you realize how much trouble you're in?" The mistico's chastisement was almost endearing, it was so misplaced. "This isn't the place to bring your poor choices, young one. Officers are on their way."

The plague doctor popped up beside them, his Gemello mask crooked but his smile wide. "Are you sure your ledger is accurate?" he slurred, gesturing to the floor where the mistico huddled, searching for wayward pages. "I thought I saw Great-Grandfather Kharin's name, and *trust me,* he was no saint . . ."

Unsure how to answer, the mistico glanced to her colleagues, then took one step toward Celia and the plague doctor, flustered. "It's not your concern—"

Celia grabbed his hand, and they pushed past, the plague doctor giving the mistico a hip bump for good measure, nudging her off balance.

It wasn't a graceful exit: they swam through confused bodies, dodged angry mistico, ducked and feinted. Anya jumped in front of two mistico, cutting off their pursuit. "What sort of chaos is this?" she shouted over the other shouts. "Oh, my— look, it's happening!"

Celia and the plague doctor pushed through the front doors and ran. She didn't know how to lose him and didn't have the time to try. Anya had jumped into diversion mode, and Celia had to deliver some ink for it. As they ran, Celia took out her quill, snapped it down to its nub to disguise its length and shape, and sketched on her arm without looking. It didn't have to be much of an image, but it *did* have to be hidden from the plague doctor.

Nothing about the night had worked the way they'd planned.

But Celia had found one name that offered hope for Vincent, and Anya could boldly lie better than anyone.

They swerved into an alley, and Celia almost collapsed. "So you followed us." She panted, trying to catch her breath, not winded from running as much as from the concentration it took to hold the ink in place on Anya's arm. It needed to last on Anya as long as possible without being permanent, and because they mostly concentrated on quick disappearances, the skill of holding an image was a novel one. She leaned against the brick building in the alleyway for support, concentrating on pausing the ink in limbo—not allowing it to go into Anya permanently, yet not pulling it back.

Voices coming up the street made both of them press into the shadows. Pia, Fallan, and a few other Mob fans swept by: "You wanted extra excitement tonight, Fallan. Stop griping at me; I didn't know they'd cause a scene." Pia's tone sounded equal parts amused and haughty.

The plague doctor pushed off from the wall and checked around the corner. His Gemello mask didn't suit him right then, despite what a good player he was. Gemello, the endearing, easygoing rascal, would never flex his hands into fists, stand so rigid, or start a sentence ten times only to cut himself off. He watched Celia expectantly, waiting for an explanation.

The seconds turned to minutes. Enough time passed that Celia worried their distraction had backfired. Instead of being momentarily distracted by the fresh tattoo on Anya's arm, maybe the mistico had found a reason to detain her. Anya was supposed to dart away before any heavy questions began.

The minutes turned to more minutes. *Come on, Anny, I can't hold it much longer.* She thought she might pass out from the concentration; her vision swam.

Turning the corner into their agreed-upon meeting place, Anya launched herself at Celia, knocking any remaining breath out of her. With relief, Celia pulled back the last thread of ink she'd been desperately clutching.

"Anyone?" Anya asked. Then she noticed the presence beside her and drew back.

Feeling as if she'd run a marathon, Celia waved a hand vaguely. "It's just the plague doctor."

Anya's mouth popped open, her features rearranging themselves into hard lines and thin lips. "You followed us!"

Unbothered by her outrage, the plague doctor in the Gemello mask finally found his words, aiming them at Celia calmly. "Why do you hoard feathers?"

Whatever she'd expected him to say, it wasn't that. She

blinked. "They're for a friend who loves birds but never sees them."

"Ah! You *can* speak truths." He exhaled, as if puffing away stray cobwebs from his face. "I was really beginning to worry it was a medical condition."

They had one more thing to do that night. Celia hoped she wouldn't pass out before it was done. How long could you function on adrenaline alone, exactly? She must be breaking records. "Here's another truth for you, plague doctor: I'm glad your nimble fingers are here. We need to break into an apothecary."

With only the slightest hesitation the plague doctor turned and strode to the main street, gesturing for them to follow. He tossed his usual smile over his shoulder, his lips now pairing nicely with his roguish mask. "Ah, now *that* is some mischief I understand."

He knew something was wrong and he knew she kept secrets, but it was as if he imagined some minor tribulation and had every faith in an eventual win. Just like that, he'd hopped onboard her ship without realizing that the deck was rotted.

That time, his smile almost killed her.

CHAPTER 19

THEY RETURNED TOO LATE TO SCALE THE FENCE AND DISSOLVE into the bustle of the Mob's final preparations. Anya led the way through to the main gate, pushing a path to the front through the assembled crowd.

The stilt walker at the gate leaned down and turned the color of her name when she recognized the people under the makeup. "Are you *kidding* me?" Lilac hissed. "Kitty Kay is *screaming* for your heads right now!" She called for Ravino, and he used his murderous Savant persona, covered in blood and grinning as if he'd thoroughly enjoyed eating those children, to keep the crowd at bay while the three of them squeezed through the gates.

A few outraged shouts of "queue jumpers!" and "they didn't pay!" rose up from the crowd.

Ravino bellowed right back. "The first of the blood offerings tonight, but not the last!" As he outlined the criteria for getting devoured by the hungry maw of the Rabble Mob of Minos, Celia, Anya, and the plague doctor flew toward their wagons to change. Ravino's stalling, while a prime effort, wouldn't last long; he wasn't accustomed to monologuing.

Kitty Kay intercepted the plague doctor by throwing his mask and some colorful words at him. Grisilda and Fawn, hands linked, ready to open the night as Passion, herded Anya toward her new position in their act, Remy and her friend trailing behind with Anya's angel dress.

Celia darted toward the main stage, where she would wait, out of sight, until the end.

The Palidon waited for her by the back entry to the stage. "You went into Malidora." Vincent's mouth might have said those words, but Celia's clenched stomach told her it wasn't Vincent saying them.

Georgio launched themself past where Celia had stopped, tossed her costume at her, and continued on up the stairs. "Half an hour, tops." They'd sweated through their costume already, dark crescents smiling under their arms. "Here." They doubled back a moment later with a wet cloth, their wide-eyed Fazzi mask dangling from their ears.

And then Celia and Diavala were alone.

"We went to stir up some interest in the show." Celia tried to steady herself with the rhythmic removal of her makeup. *Wipe in small circles,* Remy had told her. *It doesn't hurt as much.*

"Did you."

She balanced Diavala's monotone, emotionless words with overenthusiasm. "We led a parade!"

A long pause.

Small circles, change direction, more small circles. Her makeup had started off yellow and red, but now it stained the cloth a cockroach brown. The crowd's chanting had increased to a dull roar as Ravino's story wound down.

Diavala took the devil dress from Celia's hands, deftly undoing the clasps that Celia's shaking, tired fingers couldn't manage. Lifting the dress over Celia's head and pulling it down, she smoothed the tulle, positioned the forked tail, adjusted the slimy scales on Celia's shoulders.

The silence felt poisoned. Acrid, like a festering sore.

While Diavala fastened the long line of clasps at Celia's spine — *snap, snap, snap* — cool fingers brushed her skin.

"You seem to forget how well I know you, Inkling. Always going left when others are content to go right. Your shock is wearing off. You're coming to terms with this new reality. I don't know why you went into Malidora, but it's clear that your infuriating wiggling is returning. And so I have a gift for you."

"No, that's okay, I don't need any gifts." Celia's thoughts galloped in opposite directions.

The clasps took forever — *snap, snap, snap* — but as the last one snapped with finality, Diavala turned Celia around and put her hands, Vincent's hands, on Celia's shoulders. Celia felt her breath, Vincent's breath. She saw Vincent's face. His flickering tenor in silvers and golds radiated around his body, a thing so taken for granted, but such absolute proof of life, of a soul. And Diavala had none.

"It's something to focus you until we travel on and cross into Kinallen." Diavala pushed a stack of pale cream letters, bunched together and bound with twine, into Celia's clawed hands.

Celia recognized the thick paper. She'd handled hundreds of them. She'd inked according to the words on them.

Divine orders for new tattoos.

She undid the twine and flipped through the names gracing the front of the letters. One for every member of the Mob.

As if Diavala had known that Celia would eventually fall out of line.

"But I am focused. I—" *I won't stain what I love with what I hate.* "I—" *I don't have time. We're finally figuring you out. We have to plan . . .*

"You'll do them. Every single one. I'll be watching." So quiet and serious, Diavala sounded like a concerned parent. "You blame Profeta for your misery—the mistico, me—but one day soon, Inkling, you'll realize that people aren't worth all this effort."

Diavala retreated, and Vincent returned. With his hands still on her shoulders, Celia felt the change from tension to relaxation, then back to tension of a new sort. He looked down at Celia. "You don't even have your mask on!" Then his features arranged themselves into a deep frown. "Or did I already say that?"

Celia wrapped her arms around his waist, clasping the orders in tight fists, and pressed her cheek to his chest. "You're breaking my heart, Vincent," she whimpered.

He seemed to be trying to wind time backwards. A hand on the back of her head, gentle, holding her close. A *shhhh* of comfort. An awkward chuckle with a joke about absinthe delirium.

A whispered confession. "I don't know what I did to break your heart, Lalita. But I'm sorry."

She nodded into his chest. Wrapped her arms around him tighter. Fit herself between his arms. His hands stroked her hair in short, tender sweeps. And they stood together.

One crying.

One sighing.

Both confused.

That premiere night in Malidora, the devil had a full hour under the bell jar. The acts leading up to it had changed too—shifts in tone and theme—as if the effects of the sinister menace caged onstage had seeped into the Mob's collective consciousness.

"That was *fabulous!*" Kitty Kay grabbed Celia where she huddled backstage, away from the dancing and celebration. "With that one hairline crack in the bell jar, a few in the audience *bolted away*, Celia. They're losing all perspective!"

Kitty Kay shone with pride, patting Celia on the head. "But they'll be back." She winked and waltzed away to revel with the others.

Ah, the goal of every player—to con their audience so completely, Celia thought as she snuck to her wagon after her special curtain call. A few people caught a glimpse of her, a devil escaped and slinking through the shadows. "I swear I saw her horns!" "What are they keeping from us?" "She can sneak through the cracks . . ." Their loud, attention-grabbing intrigue forced her to take such a circuitous route that she'd sweated through her costume by the time she lost them.

Celia snorted. Losing perspective indeed.

But that meant their show was working exactly as they needed it to. In the wagon, Celia uncrumpled the Divine orders and ripped into the first few, waiting for Anya to be done with her new part of the show: paranoid dancing, looking over her shoulder as if waiting for something to take its revenge, flirting through distraction, her bodyguard Passion hovering close and on alert.

"They're normal," Celia muttered, exhaling hard. She'd expected the orders from Diavala to be decidedly not-normal: eyeball tattoos or full-faced masks of ink. Her instinctual response was to burn them, rip them into pieces and toss them back at Diavala like confetti. But Vincent would receive the Touch, then someone else, then someone else . . .

When Anya finally found her, Celia had worked herself into a full rage. "Diavala's threatening the rest of the Mob now, not just Vincent. She's *gloating* about the power she has over us."

Anya read through the first few orders and inhaled sharply, hissing through her perfect teeth. Through a gap in the window curtains Anya's gaze drifted to Lilac. Like a rope connected her, Lilac looked up at the same moment and smiled, her lip rings catching stray rays of torchlight and making her smile that much brighter.

Diavala was staking a claim to their skin. "Screw her," Celia said. "I kept thinking we have nothing, no bargaining power, but we have so much more room to maneuver than I thought. This stack of orders"—she grabbed the papers violently and crumpled them in a tight fist all over again—"is so we stay in line. She's reminding us to be scared of her. But it also shows some desperation."

Anya arched an eyebrow and tilted her head as her eyes slowly brightened. "She's trying to shorten the leash."

Exactly. If Diavala was trying to pull them in tighter, it meant they were tugging in the right direction.

"We have to do them, but we'll design them our way," Celia said. The stack of orders felt hot in her hand. "And we can test the ink's boundaries, experiment with her connection to it." *I miss nothing*, Diavala had said. But they already knew she did, so what other loopholes could they find?

Their biggest problem was time: inklings got significant breaks between orders because the work weakened them, depending on the complexity of the tattoo. More ink meant a longer recovery. They were, quite literally, giving part of themselves away. Once, Celia had done two full sleeves connected by a design along the collarbone—three days of intricate work—and she'd been incoherent for a week. Celia wondered what they'd look like after doing two dozen permanent designs without pause.

An aggravatingly clever diversion—this would keep them very busy indeed.

As if reading her mind, Anya said, "We just have to be organized about it."

As the reality of inking tattoos on the troupe sunk in, Celia barked out a laugh. She put her face in her hands, trying to calm down. For weeks she'd felt every emotion imaginable, and her body tingled from it.

The trip into Malidora had still been worth it. If Halcyon Ronnea could survive Diavala's Touch, Vincent could too, and if they needed it, they had a drug that would lessen Vincent's suffering until they could find Halcyon and get answers from them.

"We need to get the Kids away from this," Celia said, peeking out between her fingers, her face smushed in her hands and her words slurred. "Maybe Gil and Millie can take them to visit another troupe until this calms down. I'll suggest it to Kitty Kay." Gil and Millie were the most elderly of the Mob, the resident authorities on traditional story lines and continuity, but they hadn't performed for years, and the "New Commedia" had been making their role fairly redundant of late.

Anya looked out the window, her eyes unfocused as she admired some horizon beyond the loud theater grounds around them. "We're going to take her world from her, Cece, just like she's done for generations." Still determined to burn everything down. "The people are right. This is canon in the making."

Already planning the design of the first tattoo, all Celia could think was, *The Mob will survive this. Vincent will survive this. Only their skin will suffer.*

CHAPTER 20

CELIA AND ANYA BEGAN WITH SEER OSTRA'S ORDER THE next morning. Away from the troupe, sitting together on a blanket on the pretense of mending costumes, Anya kept a lookout over Celia's shoulder while Celia prepared to ink.

"Get it over with," Anya said, pulling one of Passion's huge dresses into her lap. She stabbed the needle into the hemline without even looking at what she was doing. "The first one will be the hardest for them to accept."

Seer's note was simple: *She will not find the future in a stack of cards.* The image was to be on her chest, to show what her heart was supposed to turn away from.

If Celia had been isolated at the temple, she would have understood it as a clear order against reading tarot. She might have imagined someone addicted to the point of ruining her family, wealth, morality, or health.

But now she knew that every message was nothing more than a ruse. A ploy. A game.

A random dance to entertain.

Because Celia now knew Seer Ostra well, it made her furious.

More furious. She already hated the idea of etching onto so much beautiful skin without permission.

As Anya continued stabbing the innocent dress, Celia unbuttoned her blouse and began to draw on her chest, muttering through her anger. "Take away someone's livelihood, her life. Wouldn't it be hilarious to see how a sloth navigates the world without the one thing she loves?" She pushed the quill harder into her skin to get a thicker line. "Ouch, shit."

She used as few lines as possible to form the picture while still making it as beautiful as she could: a difficult thing to do when drawing the Devil tarot card.

Years of experimenting had taught her how to fulfill an order and keep it ambiguous at the same time. Celia didn't know people's circumstances, so she'd tried to stay broad while addressing the heart of the order. Fiona Jenoah's mirror tattoo — *Family is everything* — gave no tangible instruction. She could have chosen to see it as a rallying call to take her children far away from the threat in her life.

Dante had seen it. "You leave too much room for misinterpretation!" he'd hissed at her more than once. To which Celia had always thought, *Well, why do we bother with art at all? Why don't we ink a blunt line of text on their foreheads?*

Just as they took the opportunity to leave a tiny gap in the upper-arm bands enlisting new mistico, Celia and Anya had always incorporated ambiguity into their work. No one but Dante had ever called them out on it, but it had always been there.

Seer Ostra had told Celia that the Devil card related to bond-age, addiction, and materialism. ("It looks like you under your bell jar, doesn't it?") Celia fulfilled the order with the image. No mistico inspecting her tattoo could argue that it wasn't a clear message against tarot reading.

But.

When Seer Ostra looked down, she'd see the Devil reversed, which represented detachment, breaking free, and a reclaiming of power.

She glanced up for Anya's feedback. "Perfect. Now let's hope we're not the last ones to arrive for Seer's show."

Celia sent the image to Seer, concentrating on allowing more ink to funnel away so that it—hopefully—appeared slightly larger than she'd drawn. The experiment would either work or it wouldn't. Then she buttoned her blouse and pulled her cloak tight as Anya quickly collected the blanket and costumes.

In the distance, Seer's alarm rang loud with yips and excla-mations as the image began forming on her skin. People quickly emerged from their wagons to see what all the noise was about.

Seer reacted to the tugging pain, but also to the picture itself. "It's the Devil tarot!" she cried, stretching out every word in her sloth-speak. "The most o-min-ous por-tent!"

"Are they *all* going to be this loud?" Anya mumbled as they approached.

"Relax, Seer," Celia whispered to herself. "Once you see it, you'll love it."

A formidable crowd had formed around Seer's wagon, everyone watching her pace.

"No one in the troupe has ever been inked by the Divine before," Lilac whispered out of the corner of her mouth when they joined her. "This is an earthshattering freak-out from placid Seer." Her brow furrowed with her frown, and Celia could see the trail Lilac was ready to amble down. *What will we do without our card reader? What does this mean for the Mob?* Lilac looked at each face in the crowd, her frown deepening. *If Seer needs guidance, do others too?*

More murmurs started, and Celia saw the beginning curls of doubt licking through the foggy air, yet these people didn't believe in much beyond the edge of their glorious stage. She knew none of them were believers, but could this be what turned them into such? It happened all the time. So deviously manipulative: the only true magic in the world, and how long can anyone ignore magic staining their body, staring at them? Everyone yearned to give it meaning. With the transfer complete, Celia let the ink go so it became permanent.

Anya cleared her throat. "But, Seer. Don't the cards mean something different when they're upside down?" *Yes. Move it along, Anya. Perfect.*

"But it's right side up!" she wailed. "Why would this happen to me? Why now?"

"It's only right side up to us." Remy caught on first, clever thing! She walked toward Seer, sucking on one of her candies, and bent herself in half so she saw it upside down, her head beside her feet. Celia willed it to happen: *See what you need to see.*

Seer paused, moved her gaze to her half-open blouse, and stared at the image on her fuzzy chest: a slightly larger one than Celia had drawn on herself. A few people lost interest and went back into their wagons when her pause stretched on and on.

When Seer finally looked up, her smile was as bright as the sun. "The Devil reversed!"

Celia met Vincent's eyes and nodded. *Pull the leash as tight as you want, Diavala, and we'll always pull back. We know the practical boundaries of Profeta even better than you do.*

Beside her, Anya glared and muttered something similar, but also completely different. "Your own rules will choke you until we choke you ourselves."

Vincent mimed a round of applause.

Celia and Anya tried to avoid everyone for the rest of the day, waiting for the shock to settle before inking the next tattoo.

But daytime Kitty Kay, silent and ominous, was peculiarly active. She appeared at their side when they collected their lunch, watched from across the field as they rehearsed, even entered their wagon and stood there, staring through her hair, as they tried to nap.

Celia's skin crawled. She twisted Salome's bracelet into knots, traced the Mob bracelet from finger to wrist and back again. For hours, she lived an unsettling preface. As Anya walked by on her way to change, Kitty Kay trailed behind her like a shadow. Anya kept up a one-sided conversation, but Celia saw the cracks in her fake composure. Their eyes met, and Anya shrugged. *Well, looks like she's onto us.*

As soon as the sun set and Kitty Kay transformed into the glamorous phoenix, she pointed at them with a long finger. Under her usual nighttime composure lurked obvious, simmering anger.

Come.

It was their audition all over again. In their wagon, after Kitty Kay had kicked everyone else out, Celia collapsed into a pile of pillows, pulled one into her lap, and started wringing it. Anya bravely sat right beside Kitty Kay, her spine locked, her face set as her mind whirred. Kitty Kay poured drinks, her fake smile intimidatingly large. Only Lupita was missing.

"This has gone too far." Kitty Kay had no hidden menace in her voice; it was bared like fangs. No preamble. No pleasantries. "Time for truth."

Anya began explaining.

Kitty Kay held up a hand, cutting her off, the rolling boil of her anger perilously close to spilling over. "Lupita plays a drunken fool well, but we go back so many years, I know her better than she knows herself. I've known since the beginning what you were and what I encouraged the Mob to accept."

A thick silence fell. Anya's mouth opened and closed as she tried to form words around this revelation. Celia's mind bees buzzed in a confused mess.

With her gaze flicking between Celia and Anya, Kitty Kay continued. "I assume Lupita never told you when our love affair ended in a broken heap. At exactly the moment she abandoned me for a tattoo around her arm. She saw sense eventually, but it cost her much. It cost me much. But it will *not* cost my troupe."

Anya tried talking again, only to be quickly silenced. For someone who'd demanded truth from them, Kitty Kay was reluctant to relinquish the floor. A burst of wholly inappropriate laughter tried to worm its way out of Celia's throat.

"My hatred for the cult runs deep. Smuggling two inklings out of Asura was a small revolt. Or let's call it revenge. Me cackling with glee at fooling the thing that had stolen my own rapture, my happily ever after. I accepted the risk on behalf of everyone here, never imagining it would truly endanger anyone.

"What I'm *not* willing to accept, right now, is a revenge so bitter on my tongue. I thought it a small rebellion. But with Seer's skin stained with what I hate so fiercely, it's become bigger. Now *we* must become bigger."

But all Celia could think was, *She doesn't understand. The villain isn't a herd of mistico in robes. They're pawns as much as we are. They get the Touch. They're used too.* She managed a croaked, "But she's real. Diavala is real. And she's here."

Anya nodded ferociously.

Kitty Kay's eyes widened. Then her lips pressed together hard and her eyes narrowed. For a brief moment her determined face didn't know what to do with itself.

When they told her about Vincent, Kitty Kay's eyes misted and she slammed back her drink. When they told her that the intention of the show was to help spread Profeta to neighboring countries, she brought out the hookah.

But when it was all said and done, Kitty Kay leaned forward. With a trembling hand she straightened Celia's top hat, she cupped Anya's flushed cheek. Tender gestures disguising fierce resolve.

"Diavala may be real, but so am I. You will finish the orders, brush away your insufferable isolation, and then we will plan, Inklings. Nobody comes into my troupe uninvited. No one. Now it's even more personal."

Dropping her hand, Kitty Kay assessed Celia and Anya both. "You realize there's no way we're making it out of this with our lives, right?"

Blunt.

Harsh.

True.

They nodded.

"So let's agree to do as much damage as possible before we go."

As the phoenix rose to her full splendor, Celia was blinded by a vicious, revenge-seeking red.

And for the first time, instead of the thought of help frightening her, she liked it.

CHAPTER 21

WHEN LILAC'S TATTOO APPEARED AFTER THE SHOW THAT evening, Kitty Kay had called the Mob together to address what looked to be the beginning of a trend. "This is nothing but a play of desperation, my lovelies!" she announced through a wicked smile, making sure that her gaze lingered extra long on Vincent's woeful face. "The mistico have always been wary of innovation, but rest assured—we break no laws here, we practice no blatant blasphemy in our shows—you are doing nothing wrong."

Ever polite, Georgio pressed their Fazzi mask to their chest and dipped into a bow, nearly poking themself in the eye with the long nose of their mask. "But please, Kitty Kay, what if the Divine is actually speaking to Seer and Lilac with these messages? Shouldn't they listen?"

It seemed as if Kitty Kay had to fight the urge to roll her eyes. Anya gifted Celia with a smirk. *Dia, she is our people, isn't she?*

"That's fair enough, Georgio," Kitty Kay said. "But remember, we've had the luxury of seeing with our own eyes that most of the world has much more sense." She paused. "I will never tell you what to believe. Your mind is your own. I only want to point out that you needn't worry about retribution from the institution." She nodded to Seer Ostra and Lilac. "But ask yourself if you want to listen to a deity whose institution deals in retribution."

Anya nearly swooned.

Kitty Kay clapped her hands and held them above her head. "Now, let's concentrate on making the rest of our stay in Malidora a memorable one!" Her hands formed fists. "Sastimos futura!"

And the Mob had chanted back, then dispersed, the matter settled.

Everyone looked appeased by Kitty Kay's logic: it solidly connected the visiting mistico, their concerns about the show's message, and the tattoos.

The runaways they'd taken in from the temple were a separate matter entirely.

Since then, Lilac's blouse had hung open in front, inviting eyes. Most orders were intended to cast doubt on their livelihoods, as if Diavala aimed to sow discontent, but Lilac's went further and was far more intimate: her order spoke of childhood trauma and the need to aggressively confront it.

Diavala must have stolen knowledge from Vincent to know these details of Lilac's past, and that level of invasion infuriated Anya. She'd spent a lot of time perfecting Lilac's design: at the dipping notch in Lilac's neck now rested a lotus-shaped pendant with crossed swords etched into the face, tracing the length of her collarbone like a necklace.

"My strength and beauty come from my muddy roots," Lilac had confided when Celia asked what she thought it meant. Lilac's cheeks flushed crimson, both embarrassed and proud. The swords were battle-ready, but the lotus softened the sharp edges, and Lilac had chosen to find the peaceful and pure alternate meaning.

"They're exactly what you've been teaching me, Lalita," Remy said a few days later. "Art is art is art. The heart makes the meaning." Such a clever, clever thing. She'd hollered with glee when her tattoo had come: an ornate tangle of ivy around a book, unfurling at one end to welcome the sun. Her order had implied that she should study more and bend less. She decided it meant she should bend more and maybe study, too, and she'd immediately arranged herself into a back bridge to practice her sums.

With only a tiny bit of guidance, it was easy for the Mob to grasp the nuances Celia and Anya tried to convey in the pictures. It filled their hears to bursting to see people they cared about find their own meaning in the art rather than the discord Diavala had intended.

But by the time they reached the bottom of the stack after six days of inking—pausing only for nightly dances under the bell jar or the occasional nap—Celia's body was in full-on revolt. Anya was faring better; after three days it became clear they couldn't *both* become incapacitated, so Celia had begun sacrificing her ink for all the designs. Either Anya inked on Celia, or Celia inked on herself. One of them had to keep presence of mind, especially the one who roamed the audience on a nightly basis and was at risk to be plucked by greedy hands who wanted a piece of an angel for themselves.

Anya had given Celia updates on the troupe's reaction to the wave of tattoos; on Gil's, Millie's, and the Kids' road trip adventure to another troupe; on Kitty Kay's opinions and their ongoing planning; on Diavala's eerie calm through it all. But at some point Celia stopped listening. The ink swirled around, overtaking everything. The real world didn't exist anymore except in shards of occasional lucidity.

The plague doctor had always known that the storm swirled around Celia. After every tattoo, he'd nod at her or give her a lingering, too-long gaze. A thick, invisible chain, ghost remnants of the chains she wore while traveling, seemed to wrap from his waist to hers, hell-bent on pulling them together. Once, when she passed him, he put his hand out as if to summon more of his magic fire, so she slowed her stride to watch. Instead, his fingertips grazed her wrist before moving down to her hand. An unconscious gesture, as his smile had faltered like an earthquake. "Marco's is particularly beautiful," he'd said of the fire-master's new flame tattoo. "It's too bad I won't get one." Then he stuffed his traitorous hands in his pockets and walked away, the sad lilt in his voice confusing Celia for days after.

To him, they were a puzzle to be solved. *This storm is made of ink,* she imagined the plague doctor thinking, *and Celia brandishes a quill.*

Lilac pressed a cloth smelling of rotten wood to Celia's forehead to bring down her fever and spoon-fed her a disgusting mushroom concoction. Both pushed heat from her core out of her skin. Celia glistened, but the medicines kept her temperature below the cusp of emergency. She felt stretched out and ragged, like a threadbare nightgown washed too many times.

"Sleep. I'll check back soon," Lilac said before leaving her.

Yes, sleep. After the last order was done.

The plague doctor's. She'd endlessly shuffled it to the bottom of the stack, his words haunting her. Why had be been so positive there wouldn't be one for him?

She couldn't put it off any longer. Forcing herself to muster the last reserves of her energy, Celia read his card. She blinked, refocused, and tried again.

Nope.

Then: laughter.

Then: laughter with some crying.

Then: some sound so alarming Anya blew in with a look of wild fright on her face, her top hat askew in a way that didn't look right on her.

Celia tossed the order in the air, lay back, and stared at the candle beside her pillow. Anya scrambled for the plague doctor's card as it fluttered through the air like a damaged butterfly.

"Don't bother," Celia whispered.

Always, Divine orders were the same: the message at the top of the card, often followed by specifics about size or location.

But the plague doctor had been right; there was no message for him at all.

His cream-colored card remained blank except for three words at the bottom.

Don't bother, Inkling.

"What does that mean?" Anya whispered.

Celia kept making that terrible noise: part sob, part laughter. After Celia had convinced everyone in the troupe that the Divine's ink meant nothing, Diavala could turn it around and still make it mean everything.

When she singled out one person for a most intimate and personal mindscrew.

"There's a trap here." Anya stared hard at the card, as if she might be able to spring it.

"Absolutely."

Diavala had told them to do "every single one," and Anya clearly had one in her hand for the plague doctor. If Diavala didn't want ink on him, he shouldn't have gotten a card.

"But I don't know what it is!"

"Me neither." Celia stared into the candle's orange flame. It was still a Divine order for the plague doctor. They needed to choose between listening to the words on the card or doing something about the existence of the card itself. Neither option was truly safe. And if this was a trap, they may as well go with the more satisfying option and avoid othering the plague doctor when he already lived at the fringe.

"*Don't bother* is different from *Don't,* isn't it, Anny?" Celia asked. A blank card was different from getting none at all.

"It is." Anya's hard exhale made the candle dance. "But this could be a bad idea."

How nice to have Kitty Kay around for a tiebreaking vote. How nice that she agreed with Celia. "We're a unit," Kitty Kay said. "I won't let her splinter us with her games."

So Celia went to fetch some ink and a needle and a plague doctor.

CHAPTER 22

ANYA SCURRIED AFTER CELIA, REPEATING "BAD IDEA" SO often it transformed from two little words into a whole new land. Bad idea, badidea, Badidea.

Celia kissed Anya on the cheek. "You keep planning with Kitty Kay," she whispered. "We're so close." In truth, she only vaguely understood their percolating plan because she'd been in an exhausted stupor for days, but they seemed pretty confident.

Once this was over with, maybe Celia could actually help.

She grabbed the plague doctor's hand and yanked him down the road for privacy, reveling in the new world of Badidea. So in contrast to black, inky darkness, Badidea was a colorful quilt, a new frontier, a realm of upside down.

A place where they could push back against the ink by filling in a blank all on their own. The plague doctor had received an order, and she would most definitely bother.

Part of her wished she could have tattooed him in secret, as she'd done everyone else, but since he firmly believed he wouldn't receive a Divine tattoo and she didn't know the reasons for his certainty, receiving one might make him even more suspicious. She had to approach it from a different angle.

Plus, as Anya had pointed out, this offered the delicious

opportunity to test for another loophole. They already knew that Diavala couldn't see temporary ink transfers, so when, exactly, did she see the permanent ones?

"Anya, keep track of the time!" she called as they walked away. "If I'm not back in an hour or two, ask this one how I tasted."

And, oh, she laughed for a good long while after that.

"You're in a good mood tonight." The plague doctor matched her delirium, skipping along next to her as if they were off to a fabulous party.

She tilted her face toward him, the dimming twilight tingeing his bone-white mask an ashy gray. "This smile"—she waved her hand dramatically by her lips—"is horseshit of the tallest order!"

He turned up the radiance on his own horseshit smile, nodding, skipping along. "I know. Any minute now you'll pass out under the weight of it."

"And then . . . you feast!"

"Oh, I don't know. You're little. Not much more than an appetizer. I'd probably carry you back to camp and tuck you into bed. I'd press a cloth to your forehead and pretend there was hope." He leaned toward her conspiratorially. "You see, a plague doctor isn't much of a doctor at all. We're the ones left behind after all the real doctors leave. We tally the dead. We hold hands and stand sentry at bedsides. When the rest of the world flees, we become the unfortunate mask of any remaining humanity."

Celia reared to a stop. Her smile fell to the ground.

"What?" he asked. His smile twitched, as if it wanted to join hers in the mud at their feet.

"That's sort of beautiful," she said, studying his mask with new eyes: the white sleekness of it, the birdlike angles, the dark contrast of the lenses.

After a moment he looked away. "I've always thought so."

Without shame, she took in the rest of him with the same intensity. He embodied conflict—hard beak and soft feathers, straight spine and curled hair, strong shoulders and vulnerable lips—but maybe those opposites were his bookends. He shifted his weight from foot to foot, so slightly she wouldn't have noticed if she hadn't been watching so closely. At his side, his fingers twitched. He glanced up the street for no particular reason.

He had a hundred tells, companions to the twitches of his never-ending smile. They were both liars, but where she lied with words, he lied with his body. The part she'd never seen before was that, like her, he didn't enjoy it. His tells said, *I don't want to. Not all the time.*

"There you are," she whispered.

The bump on his neck dipped up and down with a swallow even as he made a grand show of looking around for whoever she was talking to. Now that she'd seen his lies so clearly, she couldn't unsee them. They stacked—one on top of the next— like kindling on a fire.

Surprisingly easily, Celia picked her smile up off the ground before resuming the walk. Maybe, like her, he wanted to stop lying but had simply forgotten how.

The lights of the Rover field disappeared behind them as they turned a corner. Someone peeked through his front window, his tenor shining out like a faint lantern in the deep night, and promptly screamed at the sight of a plague doctor sauntering down his street. This section of Illinia had been particularly affected by the last plague, and that good soul was aged enough that perhaps he remembered.

Celia nudged her chin at where the figure had clamped his curtains shut. "You should tell him you're humanity's unfortunate face."

"Alas, it's my burden to be misunderstood."

Celia cheeks hurt from smiling. She went on her tiptoes and slapped her hands on the plague doctor's shoulders for leverage. In Badidea, he didn't scare her at all. There in Badidea, she understood him perfectly. "You, plague doctor slash Griffin Kay slash judge, jury, and executioner, *thrive* on misunderstanding." Her wide smile battled with his. "It helps you hide."

"Ah." He nodded. "I wear my costume to hide from a world I can't handle. Yes. I've heard that theory, many times. Sorry to say, you're not being original."

She didn't speak again for a long time. Only smiled as he smiled. He made a move to keep walking, as if the conversation were over.

"You know what's unoriginal?" She stopped him again,

pushing his beak down with one hand, seizing the angle that proved his eyes existed behind the goggles. "Your constant smile is unoriginal. Pretending you possess only one emotion is unoriginal." She smiled wider, her entire face alight. "I don't think you hide from the world. I think you see it and understand it and love it."

He cocked his head. "But . . ."

"But you try too damn hard." His smile faltered. Still, Bad-idea had room only for truth. "You try too hard for mystery and adoration. You try too damn hard to sell the illusion that everything is wonderful and fun."

One long moment passed — a moment where Celia thought he might have heard her — before he laughed in her face. "I see why we don't know how to handle each other. You think I try too hard, and I've never met anyone like you — who doesn't genuinely try at all."

He pushed closer, nudged his beak between them, stared her down. Still, he chuckled, but nothing had ever sounded so patently hollow and false. "I've seen sparks of personality in you, Celia Sand. Onstage. When we went into Malidora. When I particularly annoy you or scare you or pull you. When you're with Anya. But you're the one who hides. You extinguish every spark before it has time to catch fire. Tonight, when you grabbed my hand and led me away from camp, I thought, *Finally, she wakes!* And tell me *that's* not losing at life, tell me *that's* not trying too hard, when tonight is the first time in weeks, months, *years* maybe, that you've passionately grabbed something you want instead of hiding from it."

Celia sputtered, trying to work her shock into a glare of outrage. "Your ego is *gigantic*. I'm not, and have never been, like one of your fans, all fawning and desperate. I don't passionately want you."

He didn't shake his head or step back. Breathing hard, he waited for her to look at him. Then he delivered a one-word truth. "Liar."

Everything inside her shook, but she held his gaze, hating the necessity of blinking.

He cocked his head, assessing her. Gently, softening out, he put his hands on her upper arms. "But I meant something bigger. I may try too hard, but that's infinitely better than living as a terrified observer, extinguishing everything before it has a chance to burn."

Badidea had turned on her. Sunk its claws deep. Through her half-crazed delirium, she nearly shouted him down, wanting to beat him with words like *temple, manipulation, mistico, lies, Diavala,* until he understood why she extinguished sparks—so a raging fire didn't consume her and everyone around her.

Panting breaths of sustained rage permeated the air. Since Badidea was such a strange place, she didn't know if their showdown had illuminated more truths between them or built a final, impenetrable wall. She didn't know whether the tightness in her gut tasted like shame or triumph.

His hands clenched and unclenched at his sides in a manic beat. "I'm so tired of this particular dance. It's time to talk to me."

"But that's the trouble! I don't know who the hell you are!" She laughed and put her hands on his chest to push him away. But she did no pushing.

His smile had vanished again. Bolstered by the power of Badidea, Celia placed her hand on the beak of his mask and waited for a second to see whether *Whoops, he'd slip*.

He didn't.

So close, she felt him give his permission, though he spoke no words, didn't nod.

The plague doctor's hat fell away as she pulled off his mask.

"Hi, Celia." Griffin's eyes met hers for less than a moment before he turned his face away, his shoulders as tight as glass. For once, he awaited a verdict instead of delivering it. So close, so quiet, so still.

Cas had called him pretty, but he was more. His nose was a little on the long side and he had a jagged scar running toward one of his eyebrows. His eyes, as dark as midnight and just as deep, swallowed the world and then spat it back out. His black wavy hair, unruly, revolted against being tied back, thick strands of it drifting across his neck, ears, cheek.

On the left side of his face, tiny black stars stretched from his temple to the muscle in his sharp jawline. The constellation Leonus, nine stars strong.

Under the plague doctor mask lived Celia's personal dagger: sharp and cutting and crafted for her.

"Damn." It came out as a squeak. Lifting his mask was the worst idea she'd ever had. "Hi, Griffin."

Her fingers fluttered close to the constellation, but she didn't touch it. The feeling of his skin under her fingertips might make her explode; the little air between them was already heat-wave heavy. "When did you get this?" She'd thought no one in the troupe had received a tattoo before she and Anya had come along, and she wondered if someone she knew had done it.

"I did it a few years ago."

Her hand stopped fluttering as he looked at her. For the span of heartbeats they stared.

"You did it." If he'd done it himself in the old way Ruler Luca the Ninth had banned generations ago, the subtle constellation under her lingering fingertips was heresy of the worst kind, every tiny star a twinkling death if a mistico ever had reason to look through records.

This proof of defiance against what she hated made her bees curl up and purr. Why would he do it? What did it mean for him?

Now that their eyes had met, they had some trouble letting go. The line of his jaw continued its flexing, making the biggest star, Revanen, move in a spastic beat. He smiled again, but this was a smile in name only: an upward slant of lips saying nothing of happiness. "You're either my end or my beginning, Celia. I still have no idea how to tilt my head with you."

Later, she wouldn't remember whether she'd said her next words out loud or if they'd stalled on her tongue: *This feels like a beginning.*

Her breath hitched. "I'm a fairly skilled artist, and I came armed with a needle, ink, and a flame. You're convinced you won't get a tattoo like the others in the troupe, and I don't think you should be left out." Given what graced his face already, tattooing him in the old ways was not as novel a notion as she'd thought setting out. Her gaze went to his lips, waiting for his stage smile to return like a window slamming shut.

He didn't turn away. He didn't smile or reach for his mask. He inhaled all the air of Badidea into his lungs and held it there. "Well, that's terribly disappointing." He let the air out regretfully, slowly, his chest collapsing under the clasps of his jacket. "Of all the things I thought you wanted from this walk, that didn't even make my list."

Celia would have loved to see that list.

He locked eyes with her, dark on dark.

The silence stretched. She watched his new lips intensely. These real ones could give her clues, about him, his thoughts. She imagined the string of questions running through his mind: *Is this a test? A gift? Why does she need this? Why would she do this? Why and why and why?*

But all he asked was a simple, "This is the spark you grabbed on to tonight?"

"Yes," she breathed.

He nodded and leaned in, bringing those new, secret lips

even closer. His eyes, his brow, his scar, his constellation, her dagger. "Then let's start a fire."

Celia sat cross-legged on the patch of damp grass they'd found between some buildings and stared at the calf in front of her. *His* calf. Not much, only one leg exposed from the knee down, and certainly nothing as exciting as finally seeing his face, but enough to make her flush red, as if he'd stripped down naked for her.

Through all the touching that came with being in the Rabble Mob—strangers dancing in his arms, flirtations, and fantasy—his costume had always covered him head to foot. The darkness wrapped around him as if even his shadow wanted to stay as close to him as possible.

Now she got the top and the bottom of him at once.

Her bees screamed at her: *Can't back down now!*

She screamed back: *I've never gotten permission before! I don't think I expected him to say yes!*

The bees cuddled up again and purred: *Bare skin, bare skin . . .*

"Everything okay down there?"

Nope. She reached her free hand out and ran her fingers over her canvas. They both inhaled sharply at the warm contact, and his calf quivered slightly under her touch. She traced the ridge of angled muscle, then swept around to his shin.

Whatever had happened between them now felt more like a truce than a stalemate. It needed delicate hands, or it would shatter.

Holding his leg, she made the mistake of glancing up. The long line of him stretched out in the grass, his feathered cloak pressed tight to his spine like a blanket. With his head turned away, curls of dark hair lapped against the nape of his neck with the soft breeze, offering her a glimpse of yet more skin. She smelled cloves, but whether the scent wafted down to them from someone's baking or clung to him, she didn't know.

The design was already completed, lingering patiently on her calf until she sent it to his. Celia had often had to wait for mistico to inspect her work, sometimes for hours, and she knew that as long as the ink had a host body, it was content.

But her current subject wasn't.

He shifted to cross his arms under his head like a pillow. "This isn't nearly as uncomfortable as I remember," he said. "Doesn't feel like you're poking into me at all, in fact." The quiver in his leg when she'd touched him had moved into his voice.

Celia inhaled. Checked her borrowed pocket watch for the precise time. Cursed herself for forgetting alcohol. And commanded the ink to Griffin.

Through burning tears that she didn't understand, she watched the image form on his calf. She'd never watched her work bloom on another person before. Not like this, from start to finish. She'd drawn parts of it in the old style, with more pokes and stabs to disguise her usual sweeping lines, so that it would feel more like receiving a traditional tattoo than a

Divine one, and she was so close that she saw his every twitch of discomfort.

And for the first time, her art wouldn't be anonymous.

Though she was still an inkling fulfilling an order, everything about this one was different.

When it was done — an hour or ten days later — she checked the time again, put her face in her hands, shaking, and severed the ties, giving it to him fully. "It's finished."

She didn't have the courage to watch his reaction, but she heard his intake of breath. Then a bark of laughter. "What the hell?" More laughter. Not the particularly good kind. "I expected a feather or a flame, not my own face!"

Covering most of his calf, stretching from ankle to the back of the knee, the plague doctor mask tattoo stared with dark, beady-eyed intensity. The lines lay perfectly crisp except where necessary shadows smoothed them out. Sinister and ethereal, it was easily the most beautiful tattoo she'd ever done, Celia thought.

"It's not your face, Griffin."

He laughed again. "For someone who thinks my ego is gigantic, you just fed it."

"Stop." She looked at him, contorted in a sitting position as he examined the mask, and didn't speak again until his eyes met hers. "It's important to you, but it's not you."

He dropped his gaze back to his leg. Just as before, when she'd traced his constellation without touching it, his fingers danced over the image. There was no blood, but his skin was a vicious, angry red from all her pokes and jabs, raw enough that it didn't look suspicious. His gaze moved from his discarded mask to Celia's face, the stone walls of the buildings around them, and back to his calf. He'd interpret the art however he wanted—if he thought it was a little too on point, so be it—but Celia had tried to give him something special. Freedom from some of his lies. A reminder that the plague doctor was a public image, not the sum of him.

The last thing she remembered him saying was a growled, "And you call *me* infuriating."

But also, maybe a bit later—or did she imagine it?—a whispered "It's beautiful . . ." which sounded a lot like *Thank you.*

CHAPTER 23

THE LAND OF BADIDEA SPIRITED CELIA AWAY FOR ANOTHER two full days and nights. Anya and Kitty Kay called it "inking a mountain of orders," the rest of the Mob called it fever, but Celia knew. Her memories had melted into a kaleidoscope, but she remembered entering Badidea with the plague doctor, then dallying there with Griffin, even if she remembered little after.

Kitty Kay wouldn't allow Celia to be ill any longer. She came into their wagon just before sunrise and sat at Celia's feet, wringing her hands and whispering a lecture. The devil had performed each night, but Kitty Kay spoke of mania and mistakes. "Get it fully together by tonight's show, Celia. We need to get everything under control again." For the first time, Kitty Kay sounded more panicked than thrilled. The crowds had ballooned, fights had broken out when they'd had to limit entrance, and every inn and hostel in Malidora was booked to capacity. "We're walking a precarious tightrope between perfection and chaos."

With Kitty Kay so invested, their plans to fight back against Diavala had come together and hardened. Ironically, part of their goal now aligned with Diavala's: make sure everyone was paying attention.

After the run ended in Malidora, the Mob would continue on toward Kinallen as Diavala wanted, amassing fervent followers along the way. The planned route included a strategic swing through Wisteria Township so they could learn how Halcyon Ronnea had survived the Touch.

Then, when the whole of Illinia was watching them, listening hard to what they had to say, and they could protect Vincent from Diavala's wrath, they would expose the lie of the ink.

The seed of the idea had been born after their very first show. The manic crowd, the confused blur between fantasy and reality, the smashed glass. How the people had turned against the angel and had wanted, had *needed*, to free the manipulated devil trapped in the bell jar.

For their grand finale, they would flip what the crowd saw again, with one significant alteration: instead of hiding how they performed their act, Celia and Anya would let the world see it.

That would become the new canon—a trickster who cons you into thinking she's angelic and pure; a lonely, trapped fool robbed of free will; and all that manipulation because of tattooed orders. The ink was *not* divine.

Tattoos would be the star of that show.

They didn't expect to live long enough to see the fruit, but if the roots were deep and strong enough, if the people truly equated the Rabble Mob with truth and illumination, they hoped the message of corruption and control would spread from one stage all the way to the consciousness of a nation.

Celia would have been the first to deny it, but it actually felt *possible.*

Lecture completed, Kitty Kay swept out of the wagon that morning, muttering under her breath and a bit more stressed out than Celia found reassuring. A little predawn light shone, the borderline between nighttime Kitty Kay and daytime Kitty Kay. Still in a Badidea-tinged world of unclear thinking, Celia tiptoed around sleeping bodies and roused Anya. With a finger to her lips and a *shhhh,* Celia whispered, "Let's watch the phoenix combust."

But when they emerged, Anya wiping her eyes and yawning, Kitty Kay had already vanished. Dumbly, Celia stared at the fog lying low over the Rover field, wondering where it hid its secrets.

"She lives!" Vincent called, emerging from the shadows, dressed and made up as the Palidon, though their show was hours away. "I'm glad to see you fully lucid again. I've been waiting to commend you both on your work."

Not Vincent.

Diavala linked her arms under theirs without question, taking one on each side. Anya's sleepiness had vanished, her eyes as wide as moons. Her gaze raked over Celia, head to foot, as if assessing her fitness for the impending conversation and how much she should allow Celia to say. With tight lips and frown, she settled on, *Let me do all the talking.*

Celia tried to match her strides to Vincent's and Anya's long-legged ones, loping beside them with ridiculously huge steps as they sauntered.

"Impressive work with the commands, Inklings. Every tattoo fulfills the order. Yet none of these people have taken the order to heart."

"They took it to heart—only their own, not yours," Anya answered.

Diavala showed no reaction. "Putting the Rabble Mob aside for a moment, did it ever occur to you that people accept my ink because they need to?"

"They accept it because they don't know anything else," Anya said. "And because they're scared."

"Isn't damnation something to fear?" It seemed that Diavala wanted to speak philosophy that morning.

Celia eyed her and Anya warily as they walked, feeling that this particular conversation would go as well as rams fighting during rutting season.

"Imagine," Diavala said. "Someone has a choice to make—flee the temple or don't, ink the orders or don't, walk with me or don't—and they know, with absolute certainty, that their choice hides a right path and a wrong one. One leads to heaven and the other to the pits of hell. If something like a little picture nudged them in the right direction, how can you say that's not a blessing?"

Anya clenched her teeth. "If it worked like that, it would be a blessing, yes. But it *doesn't*. The picture leading them is random, not a nudge in any right direction. It's a whim of yours, *not* a path toward heaven or hell. It's meaningless. It's manipulative. You take away their choice, their free will."

"Human stupidity is infinite. Why is choice lauded as something so wonderful? People *want* to be guided: it's reassuring and calming, it settles the chaos inside. That's why it's never mattered *how* people respond to the ink, as long as they do."

Settles the chaos inside . . . Diavala held her fist between two large black buttons on Vincent's Palidon costume, animating her words with a gesture, and Celia had to admit she heard something appealing there.

But Anya was laughing. Hard. "You're saying your deception is *noble?*"

"It's a kindness, yes. My ink puts tortured minds at ease."

"You'll never convince us that faith is better than choice."

"Oh, don't say never, Anya. It's such a final, absolute stance, and only the biggest fools deal in black and white." Diavala clicked her tongue; then her gaze caught something over her shoulder.

Her gaze went to Celia. "You should stop toying with that plague doctor of yours. Vincent's been getting such an aggravating earful." Across the field, the plague doctor inclined his head in a long-distance greeting as he sauntered toward Seer Ostra's wagon for his breakfast. "You've stirred up quite a tempest inside him, something I find regrettably relatable."

"I'm not about to chat romance with you," Celia said. The plague doctor saw only Celia, Anya, and Vincent in that field, but as the seconds ticked on, something slowed his strides. He watched them more closely, his head tilting as he puzzled it out.

Diavala sighed and dropped her head in defeat, a gesture human enough to startle Celia and Anya both. "It was a confession of the heart, Inklings. A part of me wanted this to go a different way. This dance with you began as a charming comedy, but with the black staining Griffin Kay's calf, it's leaped into the pits of tragedy."

Sensing that something bad was coming a moment before Celia did, Anya dropped Vincent's arm and shoved her way to Celia's side, clutching her free arm with both hands.

Diavala leaned in closer, the gleam of Vincent's pale eyes lighting her next words on fire. "I truly, *truly* can't suffer my ink being so bastardized."

Time halted. Anya's grip got tighter. "Bastardized?" she said. "The card clearly had Griffin Kay's name on it; he was due a Divine tattoo. All we did was fill in the blanks."

But Anya's argument didn't matter.

They'd gambled and they'd lost.

"It's gone!" Vincent stepped back, his mouth slightly open, eyes wide as he looked between Anya and Celia. And a smile, not Diavala's menacing one, but Vincent's pure one, began to twitch at the corners of his lips. Celia's lips started to follow them, lured by the sheer joy of a burden lifted. "My bones are quiet again!"

At the very climax of his smile, it crashed.

He crashed.

To his knees, hands covering his face, a howling scream cutting through the air between them.

Anya dropped too, struggling to pry his hands away from his face. "Oh no, no, no . . ."

It was Anya's desperate whispers that made it real, her choking sobs. Celia took a reflexive step back, shaking her head. *This isn't happening.* The plague doctor ran at full speed toward them, his raven cloak flapping behind him as if he was trying to take flight. His shouts sounded like harsh caws, and Celia could make no sense of them.

"Celia!" Anya's hands cupped the sides of Vincent's face as he tried to wrench free, smearing his black teardrop. His body was tight, ready to run. His screams mixed with sobs.

And then, another scream. High-pitched. Unfamiliar.

Daytime Kitty Kay, the unspeaking reaper, let out an ear-piercing shriek of alarm, a hundred distorted sounds following on the heels of it. For Kitty Kay to lurch out of character so hard and so fast pulled the Mob out of their wagons as if the world burned.

Marco and the plague doctor ripped Anya away from Vincent when she wouldn't let him go.

Between shredding his voice box with unearthly screams, Vincent moaned as if his soul were on fire and mumbled nonsense exclamations. No one could calm him. Head in his hands, ripping at his pale hair, he paced and rocked and cried. By degrees, his Palidon costume broke with him. White and black fabric hung in tatters; his makeup bled. Vincent's symphony played the familiar notes of the Touch.

Collective shock and grief pinned most people in place. Balancing out the stillness, Kitty Kay, moaning, pacing back and forth, Remy beside her. Between Kitty Kay's hunchbacked form and Remy's full-body shivers, it wasn't clear who held up whom. Remy glanced up, tears making her face shine, and met Celia's eyes. A silent plea of *Help him!* over Kitty Kay's guttural noise.

I'm sorry. I can't. Not with this.

"There's so much pain, so much," Vincent moaned and sobbed. "I'd like the humming back, please? Lilies and snowdrops. No, no, no . . ."

The cluster of people around him grew. Eyes widened. As they tried to string his nonsense together, they realized that this was more than a little drunkenness, more than being upset.

They bore witness to a fissure. A stretching apart.

And with no mistico around to silence it, his torture went on for hours.

Vincent met no one's eyes and responded to no questions, too lost in the torment pulling him under. Lilac made him a tea that might have steadied his nerves, if this had anything to do with nerves, but he flung it to the ground with an angry shout. Marco tried to get some warmed rum into him; Vincent only tightened his lips and turned away. His skin gleamed with sweat, his eyes shone with fever, his hands trembled, and his knuckles threatened to break through his pale skin.

The plague doctor pulled Vincent's hands from the roots of his hair, wrapped his arms around his shoulders, and rocked with him in the grass. "Shhh . . . Vincent."

Celia met Anya's gaze, her eyes red-rimmed and swollen, and said a hundred things without words. *What have we done?* screamed the loudest. Repeated, repeated. *What have we done?* Every one of Kitty Kay's moans echoed it. *What have we done?*

"They killed me," Vincent whimpered. "They pushed me under the water and held me there. I tried to help—they killed me."

"Who did?" the plague doctor asked.

"He liked me at first. But I tried to escape him." He laughed: a poisonous, lecherous sound. "He didn't like me then. Only he could push you out. And he pushed me, hard and fast. A thousand years later, and he still pushes me out."

"Who does?" the plague doctor asked again, more urgently.

One of the diavoli, Celia thought. *This was the bargain with the devil Diavala told me about.* She took a long swig from her flask.

For the first time in hours, Vincent looked up. At Celia. "The true prison is here," he whispered. "But at least he left me my toy to play with, in a way. And I'll play with the blackness forever . . ."

Just as Diavala had used Vincent's memories to become a convincing copy of him, some of Diavala's memories had strayed to Vincent. The rambling story he told was so similar to Celia's: loneliness, trying to escape, bound by a powerlessness so absolute it was a looming, inescapable shadow.

Diavala had reproduced her origin story over and over again through inklings. A thousand years ago, this had started.

"You want to go back?" Celia's voice cracked. It sounded as though Diavala wanted to find her way back to the afterlife but couldn't get there.

Vincent grabbed his head again, bending over and moaning. "Stop it. Stop talking! My bones hummed, my skeleton sang, but everything's so quiet now." Everyone was soaked from the rain, and Vincent shivered as if he'd never know warmth again.

He screamed about ink. About drowning. About nine-tailed whips.

He fought anyone who tried to comfort him.

When he began viciously scraping at his skin, ripping and tearing and drawing blood, the plague doctor tied his hands together. He cradled Vincent's head in his lap even as Vincent snapped at the plague doctor's fingers with his teeth.

"She actually can't do this very often." Anya's words trembled as she fought to make sense of everything. "She wouldn't want her whole flock to go mad."

For the first time in her life Celia loathed Anya's practicality. "Well, won't that comfort Vincent?" she screamed.

Anya stepped back, glared, then grabbed at Celia's drink. "*This* isn't helping. It never helps, Cece!"

A sob pushed out of Celia's throat, burning in its intensity, as Anya flung the flask. It hit the outside wall of the wagon and flopped into the mud.

They stared at it. And listened. The screams carried better in a field than in a temple, with no stones to swallow their sound.

The plague doctor pulled Celia aside. He grabbed her shoulders, pressed his beak down between them, and growled at her. "*This* is the storm, Celia Sand, and did your cursed silence help?"

Everything in Celia's body shriveled. "It is. And it's my fault." She staggered away from him and thought of Lupita. How smart she'd been to get rid of her sight, how lovely it must be to live at the bottom of a bottle. Lupita knew exactly how to blur the jagged edges of reality so they didn't cut.

Celia put her face in her hands and mourned her soft-spoken Palidon.

At the temple, Celia had put her initials on some tattoos, marking them as hers instead of *hers,* and it had been like waving a flag under Diavala's nose. Diavala had noticed her, but Vincent was the first to truly suffer for it, and now Celia didn't even know where Diavala was.

Who Diavala was.

INTERLUDE

The sign on the Rover gates that night reads CLOSED.

The crowd waiting outside doesn't appreciate that. Not after investing so much time and effort for this spectacle they'd been promised.

When it looks as if a riot will knock the gates down, a new sign is added: CLOSED DUE TO TRAGEDY.

Still not good enough.

Finally, one of the fire-masters adds a disclaimer: WARNING: THE DEVIL HAS ESCAPED THE BELL JAR.

The people of Malidora now understand.

From the now-infamous Rabble Mob of Minos, that message makes sense.

The people don't disperse quietly to nurse their disappointment.

They hear the screams and moans rising from behind the gates, and they flee.

CHAPTER 24

THE CHLOROFORM THEY'D STOLEN FROM THE APOTHECARY IN
Malidora numbed Vincent long enough for Lilac to brew a
strong tonic of jipep seeds and pour it down his throat. An evil
weed that grew in barbed clumps, it induced a barren, void-
like sleep. It was the preferred poison for fairy-tale villains, and
Celia had never heard of anyone vile enough in real life to use
or abuse it. Not even Profeta.

Lilac had swept out of Vincent's room in tears. "I'm worried about dosage! I don't know what I'm doing." Then she was
gone, seeking rest with the other exhausted, red-eyed members
of the troupe. The Mob had taken short shifts watching over
Vincent, everyone wanting to help, no one strong enough to
do it for long. Seer Ostra had changed him out of his shredded
Palidon costume and into a clean shirt and pants in the time it
normally took her to don one earring.

Celia foolishly thought she'd outlast them all. She rested her
cheek against Vincent's stomach and looked up at his face: blu-
ish pallor to his skin, tight swell of his lips, sharp juts of his hol-
lowed cheekbones.

"Hold on," she whispered. "It'll be okay."

His heartbeats ka-thumped with decades in between.

Celia almost fell asleep between those ka-thumps, each one tapping her back to full consciousness like a clock tick.

"We wrecked her."

Celia recoiled at Vincent's words, his voice hoarse. She bolted to the curtain to get Lilac, but more hoarse words stopped her. "She was so good, before." He hadn't opened his eyes, his lips barely moved, and despite the gravelly crackles in his voice, he spoke with a measure of lucidity that shouldn't coexist with the Touch. Something in the jipep seeds had steadied him, even as he swam through a void. One tear formed in the corner of one closed eye, hanging on, refusing to let go.

Celia went back to him, grabbing his hand and leaning in close. "You have to be strong, Vincent. There's someone who can help you."

His whimper tugged the tear loose. "We didn't deserve her when she was good, but we deserve everything she gives us now."

She followed the tear from his eye to his cheek, until it fell to the blanket. Then another, then another. Nothing she said could make them stop. Everything he said made her tremble. His heartbeats ticked on, counting down.

Celia fled like a coward shortly after Georgio came to check on him.

When she found Anya, she learned that the timeline of their plan had moved up. Vincent's screams had proven Diavala's instability. Even trying their best not to anger her hadn't kept Vincent safe in the end.

As the plague doctor approached Celia and Anya where they paced a rut in front of Vincent's wagon, Celia's stomach churned. "We have no choice, Cece," Anya reminded her. "We need more help."

Celia nodded. "I know." She still felt like throwing up.

The plan to flip the show would have to happen much sooner than they'd expected, before Diavala had a chance to move against them again. They needed someone to fill the void after they were gone and lead the troupe through the dangerous aftermath. The plague doctor already suspected the storm that swirled around Celia; now it was time to arm him for facing it.

But if dealing with Diavala had been complicated before, it was even more so now that they didn't know where she was. If she caught even a whiff of their scheme, it was over.

Celia's infuriating bees whispered, *If she's inside Kitty Kay, it's over already.*

And if she's inside the plague doctor, she's about to get a giant clue.

Celia swallowed; she hadn't forgotten that the plague doctor rendered verdicts for a living.

Dozens of times onstage, she'd been overtaken with the rest of the Mob by his final, jubilant destruction. *Not good enough,* he silently declared over and over again. Part of the show, an invitation for revelers to return, a hint of danger to make them question the line between fantasy and reality.

It felt fated that he should pass judgment on all her lies.

As Anya slipped away into Vincent's wagon to join Georgio

and make sure that Vincent stayed dosed, Celia tried to match the plague doctor's smile. "Ah, plague doctor, brace yourself."

"For what?"

"I'm going to use words to tell the truth instead of twisting it. You want a spark? I found one I'm chasing straight to hell."

He nodded, then led her away with the kind of slow, measured walk that was the silence before thunder. "It's a wonderful thing that you're finally ready to remove your mask," he said. Tight words, tight smile. He tilted his head to the clouds and bellowed, "Finally, she's ready!" Then he chuckled in a way that ripped into her and burned her from the inside out. "But I need a good, deep drink and a whole lot of shisha before I'll be able to hear you without wanting to strangle you. So away we go."

Celia found herself sitting on the plague doctor's cot in the crawlspace under the stage. His bedroom gave no hint of the chaotic jumble stacked outside the fabric panels that separated his space from the rest. A neat tower of books rested in a corner. A lantern. A hairbrush and a toothbrush on a small dresser. Sparse and undecorated, as if the plague doctor led a perfectly mundane existence.

Until you noted the velvet pouch, cinched tight and sparkling, hinting at the magic of his purple and blue flame. Or the garment rack, where black leather and feathers competed for space, pressed together close, as if nature demanded that they exist together. Or the map tacked to the far wall, with indecipherable notes and arrows pointing to places Celia couldn't even pronounce. The neighboring country of Kinallen, a small green space on the map, drew her gaze. It had been her and Anya's promised land for years; a fairy-tale place starring in every daydream. Profeta remained a fringe religion outside Illinia, but with the way the Mob's popularity had grown—devils, angels, and strange, unexplainable occurrences at the forefront of everyone's mind—Celia now believed there was a real chance that Diavala's plan to spread the ink further could work. If they took Mob fever to Kinallen, if ink began staining skin . . . Kinallen had always seemed impossibly far, but there it was, only a few finger spaces west of where they were. The border now felt woefully arbitrary.

Good thing they were stealing that plan from Diavala's fingertips.

It was Griffin, not the plague doctor, who sat in front of her, a hookah between them, at home in the middle of his nest. It shocked her all over again to see him without a beak and beady eyes. She'd begun to believe she'd made Badidea up. She stared at the constellation near his eyes as she tried to muster the courage to speak.

But he spoke first. "How did you become an inkling in the first place if you're not a believer? I thought it was impossible unless you proved your loyalty in some mystical, foolproof way."

She sucked in a breath, her secret flung out into the heavy air. Just. Like. That. His words swirled around them with the passionate red of the shisha smoke.

"How long have you known?" she asked.

"Since Asura. How . . ." He paused to chew on his anger while Celia sputtered. "How is this surprising to you?"

"Because you didn't say anything!"

He pinched the bridge of his nose, as if dealing with her were a unique brand of torture. "You're admitting it now only because I'm taking your choice away. For weeks I've given you every reason imaginable to trust me. To trust the troupe. Honest question: Is your opinion of us that low, or is your opinion of yourself that high?"

She swallowed and almost threw up. This wasn't how she'd expected the conversation to go. Again. But perhaps this would be easier.

"Well, it's impossible to be an inkling unless you pass a special test." Not a denial, not an admission. A political response that acknowledged the truth without dipping into details: she shouldn't have passed, she'd wormed her way through a loophole.

"Onstage, how do you make the ink fade?"

So he knew that, too. Kitty Kay hadn't known until they'd told her. Even Diavala herself hadn't yet pieced together how they did their show. But, Celia supposed, a born-and-bred illusionist with curiosity must have a keen advantage. She bit back her question and said, "Another impossibility."

He took another drag from the pipe and puffed the smoke out in a thin stream. As it rose in tendrils, it tinted the world red. "This isn't starting well."

A smile lit her lips, as sharp as shattered glass. Diavala had bested her again. Confessing, talking truths without fear, was an impossible thing for her to do on a good day. But now she found herself in the strange predicament where she couldn't, even though she wanted to.

Diavala could very well be on the other side of the gates, in one of the dozens of mistico, in one of the hundreds of fans, in one of the thousands of fervent believers who invented miracles to compliment the ink staining their body. But Diavala could also be within the troupe.

She could be sitting across from her.

So Celia had to walk another tightrope: tell enough truth so he had his answers and could lead his people when Kitty Kay could not, but not enough to reveal anything of their true plan.

"I'm going to start with the most important thing." She inhaled. "Anya and I *had* to execute those Divine orders for the Mob. If mistico interrogate you about them or about us, you need to make sure that everyone pleads total ignorance. *Of course* no one knew about the two stupid runaways, let alone that we were inklings."

"But no one really responded to the messages. How do we explain that?"

She waved a hand in dismissal. "Mind games. It doesn't matter *how* people respond as long as they do. There is no *right* way. All Profeta wants are followers, *worshipers*."

She stared at him deeply, needing him to hear her. "Do you understand? Sooner or later, mistico will descend. You have to lead your people through the maze of temple bureaucracy by pretending you know nothing about us. Whatever you say about the ink doesn't matter, but about our presence here, *that* will have to be the performance of a lifetime."

Not at all alarmed about anything she'd voiced, Griffin nodded. "Tell me the rest."

"The rest is big and horrible."

Though Vincent's screams had stopped, the sounds had crept under floorboards and through the walls of the wagon, the memory of them tickling along their spines.

"The rest will explain what's happening with our friend." Griffin's sentence sliced through the smoky air. "I need it."

Celia started with Fiona's bruise and the fresh tragedy that had haunted Celia for the past few days, of Fallan's lost chance to have a child. Why Celia and Anya hated the ink. Why they'd run away.

And she told the plague doctor about Vincent. About Diavala using his body. About the true danger.

Griffin had closed his eyes for her story, swallowing the new information and filling in the gaps between what he'd known before, but his eyes opened now and pierced her. "We have a shitload more problems than mistico who ask questions."

His blunt assessment almost made her laugh. He still didn't know the half of it.

Then, with hard swallows and a bit of shisha, she told him about inking her initials in her work. In stutters and stops, the confession fell. "I did this unprecedented thing . . . She took notice. All of this . . . because of me. She wants to use the Mob's fame — the Devil in the Bell Jar's fame — as a steppingstone to take Profeta outside of Illinia."

Griffin listened. He listened some more. She could read nothing in his body language — whether he believed her or not, whether he wanted to run or tell everyone, whether he hated her or pitied her or was only thinking of Vincent. He didn't even react upon hearing that his own mother was tangled up with them.

Immobilized in silence, she waited for him to process everything. Waited for his verdict.

He put his hand on her thigh. She would have liked it if it hadn't felt like a confrontation. He smiled his smile, and she had a fleeting moment where she doubted who was sitting across from her. "That's not everything. Tell me what you're plotting from here."

A sob hitched in Celia's throat, and she had to look away. Back to lies. "There's nothing we can do. The show has to continue as normal."

Griffin clenched his jaw, grinding his teeth. Exactly as Anya always did when she knew Celia was lying.

"Damn it," he hissed. "Even when I understand why you keep secrets, I don't understand it."

Celia forced herself to look at him. Her eyes blurred with salty water.

After being motionless for so long, his movement startled her. She flinched back, expecting a strike, if not with hands, then words. *How can you ask me to trust you after all these lies?* But he leaned forward to cup his hands around her neck. Pushing his hands into her hair, he pulled her close so they sat scrunched angry forehead to scrunched angry forehead. "You keep ignoring the fact that there's only one person here who isn't on your side, compared with the many who are. And it's always been so. From the moment you stepped onto our stage in Asura, it was your stage too."

His thumbs stroked gentle lines on her throat. The warmth of his hands pulsed down the front of her and the back, spilling over like water, settling in a deep blush. Everywhere. But she didn't know whether it was lust or fear. The fever rose in his eyes too, some deep want balanced with a loathing for it. He pulled back just enough, his face filling the entire frame of her vision.

After wanting it for so long, she cursed that he'd taken off his mask. The plague doctor held allure as a fantasy, but the reality of Griffin pulled her in real ways that fantasy couldn't compete with. Her personal dagger.

His gaze, still blazing with a fury she loved and hated at the same time, went from her lips to her eyes. His touch was so out of sync with the look on his face, she didn't know whether to move closer or pull away.

The two of them existed in frozen time, the air between them pulling and pushing. Their chests moved too fast for people at rest. His dark gaze roamed her face in a slow dance, always, always returning to her lips, as if they were the treasure at the end of the trail. A treasure he either wanted to bury and burn or savor and save.

He spoke *we,* he spoke *us.*

Us—her biggest fear—because the more alone you are, the less you have to lose.

And losing was inevitable.

His gaze met hers and held on tight. As dark as bitter coffee, his eyes swallowed her. His exhale, hot and hard, fluttered against her hair. So lost in the darkness of his eyes, the feeling of his hands on her neck, she barely heard his whisper, "Just when I think you're my beginning, I find out you're my end."

CHAPTER 25

THE FANS RETURNED IN NUMBERS AT DAWN. THE SCREAMS emanating from behind the gates had died — the devil was contained again — and their feverish lust for the show burst past all reason. They ripped apart the CLOSED sign themselves, as if they were doing the Mob a favor.

Eerily calm, the plague doctor informed them — hovering over them with his wings outstretched and surrounded by purple fire — that they would get one final show and then they would leave peacefully.

Or, instead of passing judgment on the show, he would judge *them*.

They clapped and cheered and pressed their hands over their hearts, Pia and Fallan included. For a moment Celia thought a mass swoon might happen.

But the plague doctor's announcement caused a ripple of confusion to spread through the Mob.

Wait, we're performing?

The show continues?

But what about Vincent?

Celia and Anya broke off their whispered planning as Marco, Ravino, and a few others called for an explanation. The plague doctor glanced over, offering Celia his sharp, beaked profile, and even in its melancholy Celia's heart ka-thumped. Diavala had called him ruined. If so, his ruin matched hers.

It felt real for the first time, that this night would be the end of everything she and Anya might have found with the Mob.

Marco put the Mob's spreading frustration to succinct words as the plague doctor approached: "We can't go on as if everything's fine."

"Oh, I'm sure we would all agree that nothing's *fine.*" The plague doctor swept a grand arm toward the gates, then toward the wagon where Vincent lay, drugged. "But unless we want a full-scale riot, we can't remain closed, and unless we want to squash hundreds of people under our wheels, we can't leave. Malidora's *demanding* that we take the stage."

"Kitty Kay won't agree to this," Marco said, and most of the people around him nodded.

"Diavala was irritated about your initials, about your escape, about your dally into Malidora," Kitty Kay had said to Celia the night before. "But she didn't get *angry* until you used the ink in a way she didn't like. She knows you have power. Remember that. Tomorrow night, onstage, when you're pushing toward the end and it feels like what you're doing won't make a difference, remember her fear." Matching Vincent's slow breathing, she'd hugged herself, closed her eyes. "Take strength from that. She hurt Vincent because she's *terrified* that you'll find a way of using her own ink against her."

Kitty Kay had opened her eyes, met Celia's gaze, and viciously hissed, *"As she should be."*

As she should be.

At Marco's words, a big part of Celia wondered if Kitty Kay's revenge red would lift the shroud of her leftover act and her daytime persona would fall away like a moth-eaten cloak she'd worn too long.

But Kitty Kay remained her same reaper-gray self. Their staunchest ally, their most aggressive partner, would be around only when night fell.

"Kitty Kay isn't available to make this decision, so you know it falls to me," the plague doctor said, wearing a new smile now—a wild one edged with desperation.

Ravino wrapped his arm around Milloni's shoulders and they backed away a step.

"Maybe we should vote," Ravino offered.

"No. One final show is a necessary compromise."

"This is madness." Marco clenched his fists, red with frustration. "You're too stubborn for your own good."

The plague doctor laughed. "Well, you're not wrong."

"This is just like the time with the cat," Marco muttered, then looked up at Celia and Anya. "I bet the plague doctor never told you how he died?"

All they knew was that he'd fallen. Celia liked to imagine the plague doctor scaling balconies to save someone from a fire or jumping from a runaway wagon with a Kid in his arms.

Marco continued. "He tried to rescue a stranded cat and fell out of the damn tree."

Anya snorted and laughed. A few others joined her, momentarily slicing through the tension. The plague doctor didn't laugh. Neither did Celia.

Anya stopped abruptly. "Seriously?"

The plague doctor bowed low. "I *did* save the cat." He bowed exactly as Diavala had bowed to Celia that first night. Or he bowed the way everyone bowed. It could mean everything, it could mean nothing. "See? There's madness all around. It's inescapable."

Inescapable madness that someone close had a skeleton ringing like a struck tuning fork. They felt the beginning of the end. Maybe, whoever's bones sang now was lying low, trying to survive. Maybe they'd curled in on themselves, determined not to anger the beast lurking within them, stretching their time out like taffy, holding on.

Fear was a powerful silencer.

And if you already knew what death looked like, all the more reason to dread it.

By that point, most of the Mob had grudgingly accepted the plague doctor's decision, the stately bow and talk of the world's madness diffusing their fight. Vincent was as safe as possible, what harm could come from one more show? But Marco sighed and looked toward the gates. "Maybe we can reason with them—"

"No, Marco." The plague doctor's voice, so deep and final, was like hitting bedrock. "Don't bother."

The plague doctor looked at Celia while delivering those words.

Pinned in place, her stomach churning violently, Celia might have ignored the coincidence—she desperately wanted to—but beside her, Anya inhaled sharply.

A whimper clamored its way out of Celia's throat. Had she expected that the devil wouldn't play dirty? *Only one person here isn't on your side; I can't suffer my ink being so bastardized; a personal tempest I find regrettably relatable . . .*

The Divine order of *don't bother* had been a poke from Diavala. The biggest hint of all.

Don't bother. I'll be using this one next.

It hadn't been a mindscrew for the plague doctor after all. It had been one for her.

Anya's expression—soft-eyed and heartbroken on Celia's behalf—stabbed like a blade. Celia pressed her palms to her stomach, then against her eyes, unsure which would betray her first. "All right, everyone, just shut up." *Take control.* Diavala might suspect something, but she didn't *know*. Their plan could still work. The rest of the Mob could be free, *if* the show continued at least one more night. Celia thought the plague doctor had been lobbying as an ally, but apparently not. Still, for the moment, both their wishes lined up.

If Anya didn't stop looking at her with such a crestfallen expression, Celia was going to scream.

Marco raised an eyebrow to the clouds. "Did you just tell me to shut up?"

"Simmer down until nightfall," Celia answered, "and then you can confirm everything with Kitty Kay."

Marco blinked. Then, when he couldn't poke a hole in her simple logic, his face rearranged itself into its previous scowl. Celia walked away, leaving him to his muttering.

It took a second, and then, behind her, the plague doctor began laughing. That long, terrible laugh of lost control, of the floor caving in. Celia was almost tempted to join him.

Or the plague doctor's bones sang, and it was Diavala laughing, full of glee that her plan was working so well and everything was a disaster.

Anya spent the day saying goodbye to the friends she'd made.

Celia should have joined her, but instead she sat drawing. Alone. She understood pictures because they could be anything, mean anything. Maybe a teardrop today could be rain tomorrow. Or even something good: a fresh pear or a cheery mandolin. And maybe, one day, something so lovely it breaks your heart: paisley on your child's dress the day they whisper their name for the first time.

Pictures stayed the same but changed with you. They were the past, the present, the future, all at once.

When the plague doctor approached, Celia didn't look up through the blur of pale blue smoke around her. "The shisha's sad too," he said.

"Ah, finally someone understands the shisha's moods like I do." She kept drawing, the lantern flickering with the soft breeze.

The plague doctor's plague-doctor smile loomed, ready for his crowd. When he made to sit down, Celia waved him away. "Go away, plague doctor. It's almost showtime, and I'm sure you have things to do."

This particular section of field was separated from the rest by a steep slope, its isolation precisely why Celia had chosen it, but he still made a big show of looking over his shoulder before he took his mask off. "You're endlessly stubborn," he said.

She gestured to where Griffin had dropped his creepy, soulless mask. "You know I have no interest in him."

He removed his hat and his gloves and his winged jacket, too. Celia didn't know whether to sigh or scream that he wasn't leaving.

His hands looked as if they could form a fist and demolish something or catch a butterfly without harming it. As he swept his coat off, a sliver of skin peeked at her from above his well-fitted pants. His loose shirt opened enough to show an inviting V of chest.

It infuriated Celia that he could make her flush so easily. *I shouldn't have any interest in you, either.* She settled on a combination of sigh and scream, and she assessed him as he sat on the grass in front of her, adjusting his shirt and endlessly fidgeting. "You know you're far from naked right now, right?" she asked.

It took a moment, but then he laughed. "There you go, doing that thing. I hate being so disarmed." Funny, he used the same word Celia would have. Her butterflies responded. So did her bees. *Enough! Shut up!* she chastised. *You don't even know if that's him!*

She began another sketch. Her body was uncomfortably *there*. She'd wanted to disappear, not be so aware of her lungs and her heartbeat, her skin and her lips. She didn't trust anything anymore.

A splat of salty water spoiled the picture, and she ripped it out of the book.

"If you have nothing important to say, how about telling me what Kitty Kay really looks like?" The pile of discarded half sketches beside her fluttered in the breeze. "And don't say 'As she does,' or 'Like herself.'"

He sifted through her drawings, then leaned over and tapped the top paper of the sketchpad in her lap. "This."

Celia almost flung the sketchbook in his face. "It's blank."

"Yes."

With measured words and clenched teeth, Celia tried to respond reasonably. "So your mother has three sides: night, day, and nothing."

He shook his head. "Not nothing, no, but she hasn't had a clear reality for years. Her character was Lilliana, based around the phoenix: death to rebirth and back again. At some point it took over. No one knows what she looks like anymore, but it's there, somewhere — her third side. It has to be, right?"

"No, Griffin. Maybe she's broken."

Everyone's breaking was inevitable. Shouldn't he, above all, understand that best? Instead of responding, he adjusted his shirt for the hundredth time. A surge of pity rose up for him, and Celia wondered if ten years from then he wouldn't be the same as his mother: the mask fused to his face, all feathers and talons with nothing left of Griffin underneath.

"Doesn't it bother you that no one knows what *you* look like anymore?"

He blinked, tilting his head up as if confessing to the clouds. "Well—it *didn't*." The words he left out hung in the air. *Maybe it does now.*

He helped himself to a swig of rum from her flask, his jaw working as if chewing a brick of stale bread instead of drinking liquid. "I know what you're trying to do." He looked at her. Took another drink. "You got a little too honest with me. Putting a wall back up between us is safer, isn't it, *Lalita?*"

Falling from his lips for the first time, her endearing nickname sounded like the slur it was. *Fragile Bird.* Something so easily broken it demanded pity. In that moment, she hated him. If there'd been nothing between them, Diavala might not have been interested and he might have stayed safe. He tilted his head to the left, innocently, sweetly, and she wanted to claw that beautiful tattoo right off his face.

She took her rage out on a fresh blank page. He watched her draw, quiet again, so that she heard the roar of blood in her ears.

Until the stutter in his breath told her he recognized what her hands were drawing.

She looked from the drawing to his lips, searching for a quiver in the smile . . . and there it was. For someone who pulled eyes to him onstage every night, he had little idea how to handle being seen.

Bolstered, Celia kept going with the sketch. He leaned in to watch, so close to her they were nearly cheek to cheek. His unruly hair brushed against her skin, making her quill stagger like a drunken fool.

When she finished the portrait, he stared down at it, his face hidden behind his hair. Because she'd aimed to disarm him, she didn't expect a whispered confession: "You're good at finding him." As if he were lost and she held the only map. "Me," he amended.

She'd drawn Griffin in profile to get the Leonus constellation right. No smile on his lips, no trace of plague doctor at all. He gazed off the page at something in the distance. Whatever his dark eyes saw, he wanted to swallow it, his expression one of awe and anticipation.

If she'd held her portrait up beside him, it would have been a mirror image. No bullshit in either likeness. Raw. The face on the page looking into the distance: anticipating, wanting.

The face in front of her looked at her the same way.

They watched each other. The only plague doctor nearby was the tattoo on his calf.

It was too much that he understood her. And too much that he liked her anyway, despite what he understood.

"No," she said. "Don't. You're not allowed to do that." *This is torture, go away!*

"Tell me what you're planning for tonight so I can *help*." He grabbed her hand, making her drop her quill, and his fingers lingered on her wrist. The way he'd taken her hand after she'd inked Marco's tattoo. As Vincent had done before becoming Diavala.

She yanked her hand away. "You *know* I can't tell you anything more when Diavala can win any conversation with one well-placed lie."

Or with touches, confessions, intimacy.

"The problem isn't her lies. I'm asking how you plan to fight something immortal alone!" Griffin's voice shook hard. "Her win *is* bloody inevitable, Celia!"

She slammed her hands to his chest to get him out of her face. As if that hadn't occurred to her! "Stop it! I'm playing your game exactly how you want. Stop threatening me!"

Griffin balked, his shock stretching his next words out like a soft lullaby. "Threatening you?"

Then his dark eyes narrowed, swallowing her as always, but this time, spitting her out. His new understanding of their conversation created something harder, firmer, a tangible thing between them as large as a mountain. "You hear me threatening you." He shifted backwards, giving the mountain between them the space it needed.

She met his gaze.

He shook his head slowly, disbelief etched into every line on his face. "If someone who's not me comes inside me, Celia Sand, you'll be the first to see it. You'll see it even before I do."

Which might have been true, but it wasn't what she needed to hear right then. "Can't you stop with the Riddlish and say, 'No, my bones aren't humming'?"

He raised his hand with an overabundance of care, as if afraid of startling a bird, and tucked her hair behind her ear. She needed to read it as condescending, but all she saw was a tender, infinitely sad resignation. "No," he whispered.

No, his bones weren't humming, or No, he couldn't stop with Riddlish?

His lips did that thing, that thing where they waited. Waited for her. But Celia's stomach felt hollow, every butterfly inside lying dead in an unmoving pile. He took her hand, fitting her palm inside his with the fluid grace of an underwater dance. Then, watching her face for her reaction, slowly moved it under his shirt. Her palm met his hip: taught, smooth, warm.

"Let yourself trust me, Celia."

Her butterflies stirred, telling her *This doesn't feel like a lie.* The long grass swayed. The lantern flickered. With her palm against his skin, she felt the slight movement in his hips as he shifted, knew what he would do before he did it. Wanted it.

He moved closer, pushing his fingers under her hair and pulling her in. So close, his lips grazed against hers, a hint of cloves and lemon, softness creating lightning.

Languishing underwater, their gazes pulled up at the same time and met, dark on dark. "We don't feel like a lie." She whispered it against his lips.

But she didn't claim them.

She wouldn't remember how long she hesitated—whether they were pressed together, breathing with exaggerated calm, lips hovering and waiting, fingers on skin, for a second or for a year—only that it was too long.

The spell broke.

Griffin pulled away, cleared his throat, and stood. "You know, you're so good at seeing." With sadness, he gazed down at his portrait. "You're so good at peeling back something to its core and finding its meaning. But you're terrible, *terrible* at listening."

She crumpled the picture and flung it at him. It fell to the damp grass at his feet. "There's nothing in the world worth hearing. Everything is lies heaped on lies. Don't give me your shit, plague doctor. Your mask is the biggest lie of all, and look how quickly you reach for it."

He hesitated before tugging it down over his face. "Point taken."

Then he nudged the discarded portrait with his boot. "But you keep that. Since it can't speak, you'll never have to listen at all." He walked away, mumbling about how much he hated Malidora, how much he hated rain and lies that poured like rain.

Celia grabbed at the drawing and threw it back at him with a scream. "No, *you* keep it! So you can remember who you're trying so hard to forget."

A few paces away, he stopped and took deep, steadying breaths. Head bent, hands opening and closing at his sides matching the rhythm of his lungs.

Celia swiped at the tears under her eyes and glared at him when he turned around. She'd push him away a hundred times if she had to. The risk to her heart, to their plan, just wasn't worth it.

He didn't demand more answers from her. He crouched beside her and tilted his mask away so he could press his lips to her ear.

He left her with a whispered "Sastimos futura."

Despite how much the Mob chanted it, she'd never known those words to pass the plague doctor's lips.

ACT 3

CHAPTER 26

THE ENTIRE MOB STOOD PRESSED TOGETHER BACKSTAGE AS the crowd streamed into the field. No plague doctor greeted them to make their lungs sigh or their hearts stutter, no haloed specters on stilts took their payment.

Kitty Kay stood on the narrow catwalk over the stage so the players had no choice but to look up at her. "As you can tell from the thunder in the field, things have changed. This has stretched beyond a mere Rover show. Somehow what we've done here has swelled past our gates and leached into the very soil of Illinia. I know you want to help Vincent. The truth is that to help him, we must first find a way to outrun our fame."

She took a deep breath and scanned her Mob, memorizing each face, saying her silent goodbyes. "I implore you: Get through tonight. Get through tomorrow. Then the next day. Help each other and help Vincent. Hopefully, soon, Malidora will be a speck in our past.

"We know what the angel has had to deal with already, and now the entire crowd is a wildfire. You *must* stay in view of each other at all times."

A boom of cheers erupted from behind the thick curtain, proving the crowd's volatility.

But that crowd would be the very thing that would protect the Mob from Diavala's Touch. If anyone fell to the Touch that night, the entirety of the Mob would be canonized. With how rare the Touch was in the general public and considering the way the show had already grown, gossip would explode — but it would center around the Mob itself. That was the last thing Diavala would want, to take attention away from Profeta and focus it on the Mob. Celia had to keep reminding herself of this because the alternative — that Diavala would hop in and out of heads and leave mass madness behind — was unbearable.

Finding loopholes was Celia's favorite thing, except when they hurt so much.

Kitty Kay swept down from the catwalk and into the middle of the cluster. "Take care of one another. Remember, we're family."

The echo of Kitty Kay's earlier words hummed: *You never know, Inklings. Maybe we'll be able to meet them in Kinallen. Victorious.* Celia clenched her fists to hold on to them, as if they could escape through her fingers like grains of sand.

The Mob scattered into formation. After that night, they'd be safe from Profeta, and Diavala would have no use for them.

Celia's bees hummed their sad, low lament. *Except Griffin, except Griffin . . .*

And then she put her head down and prepared to transform into the devil of the bell jar one last time.

Celia had never looked into the crowd while she performed, her concentration had had to be absolute, but that night her gaze, unbidden, kept moving to the people below her.

Caspian, Sky, and Lilac walked the periphery on their stilts. With their bird's-eye views, they took stock of Anya's movement through the masses, looking out for trouble. The Devil in the Bell Jar was the one and only act, involving the entire Mob.

Bennetravo, Celia read on her arm.

A staple request. Celia forced her lead feet to move in the lively dance, bumping into the glass on purpose because the crowd always loved being reminded that the devil was imprisoned. The hairline cracks spiderwebbed even more.

Seer Ostra stood near her wagon at the back. Marco and his fire-master partner, Tanith, performed at the sidelines. A handful of Commedia Follia character players—with their outlandish costumes and colorful masks—peppered the crowd. She saw Tanza, Savant, Gemello, Divo, Fazzi... Everyone was staying visible.

Celia's show had adapted to evoke the image of blood in a dozen ways. She pressed both palms to the cracked glass—smearing the red paint she'd written with earlier, her body coated with shimmering reds of glitter—and waited for another order.

Soon, she kept repeating to herself. *Almost time.*

When Anya signaled, Celia would give up. Look as pitiful as possible. Defeated. It would have been a nice touch to have a Kid point at the shattered devil and say, *You're making her cry! You don't have to be mean!* But, onward. They couldn't rely on a child to point out the fallacy this time, so they'd have to make it stronger themselves. Once the crowd pitied her again, a black tattoo would appear on her arm and she would take off her glovette and show it to them. She would point at the angel, and then she would perform the order. And another, and another. For as long as they tolerated it, she would show them that her ridiculous actions were based on inked commands. Ink equals manipulation. Ink equals bondage. Ink equals tyranny.

That would be it for both of them. They would be done dancing.

They had to hope the message would be enough to spread through the audience, surge into Malidora, and crest in Asura. The Devil in the Bell Jar: the greatest Commedia ever performed, because it would take down a temple.

In the belly of the audience, the plague doctor pushed his way toward Lilac. He shook his head, his hands making a string of exclamations Celia couldn't decipher. Lilac wasn't nearly so animated in her body, stuck high on her stilt legs, but she nodded and her mouth moved with blistering efficiency.

Anya stood as still as stone, her twin bodyguards making space around her.

The crowd had changed, no longer held in thrall, but raging impatiently against the pause. A few people waved fists in

Celia's direction, angry that the show had stopped. Angry at being ignored. Kitty Kay had moved down to the grass, enacting her regal version of damage control as she put her hands out in peace to the people who clustered around her. She glanced at Celia, and sharp shards of desperation pierced through the distance.

Celia had thought that Anya was giving her time to catch her breath after dancing the bennetravo, but it was more.

Some order had been commanded, but the devil wasn't responding.

Just as that night with Vincent when Diavala first revealed herself, Celia's body reacted in a way that prepared for a fight. Her bees rallied into formation. The fresh certainty that she'd missed something huge kept her company under the bell jar. She had no idea what that huge something was, but it caressed her shoulders, whispered in her ear, slunk up her spine.

This was Diavala's work; otherwise Anya's hesitation wouldn't be so pronounced, the plague doctor and Lilac wouldn't be arguing, Kitty Kay wouldn't be panicking. Anya didn't *want* to ink whatever demand had come from the crowd.

But the crowd required it.

What did we miss, Anny? Celia nodded. *Whatever it is, the devil has to do it.*

Anya nodded back.

The sting began on Celia's forearm. She watched Anya draw it, impressed with her manipulation. She made it look as if she were holding her arms tight against a chill, giving no indication that one long fingernail existed or that it scratched into her skin.

In the cheater's mirrors under the brow of her devil mask, Celia read her arm.

And knew what she'd missed.

No! She flushed, as red as her paint and glitter.

Diavala had managed to whisper a suggestion into someone's ear, knowing it had the ability to sink them all whether Celia did it or not.

Mask off, was the command.

Mask off.

Her gaze bounced up to the plague doctor, now at the side of the stage, balanced on the balls of his feet, ready to leap into a run. He pointed at the audience, shouted more words she couldn't hear, but she understood his Riddlish then. *Pay attention, Inkling! This is going sideways on you!*

The last order made its way through the crowd. "Mask off!" they shouted, passing it on. "She can't ignore a command!"

A line of the plague doctor's purple fire lapped around her, unsolicited. She had no idea what it was meant to accomplish. Where Griffin might try for diversion, Diavala would want to add to the chaos.

Before long, the entire crowd yelled and waved their fists at her. "Mask off! Mask off!"

If Celia ignored the order, she knew with certainty that the crowd would riot. They nudged close to it already.

The angel and devil act had always been a little too real, disbelief suspended so far that people forgot they were at a show. The Mob had become so popular because of this *more* they'd brought to their act. Their effect on the masses was what gave their plan the possibility of success.

But now it would be the very thing to trap everyone.

Cas and Sky battled to stay on their stilts as people turned on them. Tanith and Marco enacted Distraction Level Red Flame but were being yelled at with equal measure. Seer Ostra and some of the other players had their hands up in deference, backing away, looking wildly around for help.

It came down to a few dozen people at the mercy of an angry six hundred. Celia and Anya had thought the crowd could be protection, but they'd been so eager to cause mayhem of their own, they'd forgotten the one solid rule of the business—don't lose control.

And unveiling someone wanted by the temple wasn't on the playbill.

Diavala didn't need her mistico after all. The Touch wasn't her only weapon. She'd found a way to unmask their con just moments before they'd been set to reveal her ink and unmask her. She'd turned their own crowd against them first.

Quaking, trying to steady her breathing, Celia deliberately exaggerated her movements so the people would understand that the last request was coming. She produced her paintbrush again with as much flourish as she could. She waited, building up the performance, buying time so Anya could work her way out of the heart of the crowd. Once Celia took off her mask, it would be confirmed, irrevocably, that the devil under the bell jar was a true devil after all—a criminal worth a thousand posters, whose crime, ominously and mysteriously, remained secret. It wouldn't take long for them to unmask Anya after that.

Diavala had bided her time, watching patiently, knowing she had a failsafe against any inkling shenanigans.

A subtle move with the cut of a dagger's blade.

The inklings had escaped the temple, the devil had escaped the bell jar once already. Both times Celia had thought they'd managed it because they were lucky and cunning and good.

She saw the whole truth then.

And under the bell jar, the devil took off her mask.

It didn't take long for people to realize where they'd seen her face. Celia had seen it herself. Every street corner in Malidora showed either the wanted criminal or the devil in a bell jar; her two identities, one or the other, pasted all over town.

Now merged, front and center.

She couldn't hear their reactions clearly—the shouts and exclamations had been muted to her for the whole act—but she saw shock and outrage plastered on hundreds of faces. The exact reaction she'd wanted when they revealed Divine ink, but now for the wrong reason.

Every show they'd done since Asura had added kindling. A spark in the crowd had ignited after they heard the screams behind the gates. The plague doctor's mini-spectacle had stoked the fire higher. Then they'd gotten more riled up with Anya's pause. Frenzy to frenzy to frenzy, and now, justice in their hands.

Anya and her Passion bodyguards were almost at the stage, pockets of people trying to halt their progress until they were drawn to other movement: Caspian, trying to get to Sky's side; Ravino trying to assert his blood-soaked authority. The crowd surged this way and that, confused about where to aim their attention but knowing it needed to be aimed.

Celia turned toward the white-masked plague doctor as he leaped into a run toward her. Ready to smash her out of the bell jar as he did that first night. Could he summon carpentry tools as well as purple fire? Where *had* he gotten that hammer?

Absurd. Hilarious.

If he freed her after this particular unmasking, he'd directly link the Mob to their heresy.

She shook her head imperceptibly. *Calm down, dagger. You've read the crowd, you know this is going wrong. But look at me.*

She mouthed, *protect and lead,* and held the plague doctor's gaze as if he were still the plague doctor. Steady. Begging. Pleading.

One last chance to be wrong.

Now was the time to make sure the Mob claimed complete ignorance. Diavala may have forced Celia's identity out in the open, but the Mob might still be able to wriggle free if their leader guided them well.

It took one infinitely stretched-out second, and then the

plague doctor turned from her toward the audience. Asking for an explanation for their distress, she assumed, as she watched hundreds of people give it to him with the force of a tidal wave.

Celia stood straighter, her heart thudding against her ribs.

One giant of a reveler near the front of the stage brandished a wrinkled wanted poster he'd kept on him, doing his due diligence. An officer of the law, maybe.

The plague doctor gave him a giant shrug, as big as the baker forty stories tall in Sabazio, and nodded. The officer enlisted some helpers, and they advanced on her after the plague doctor waved them up.

Such a small thing under the bell jar, needing so much muscle to detain her.

Well, she *had* made it pretty far from Asura. Who knew what other tricks this devil held in reserve?

As they lifted the glass, Celia kept her eyes on the plague doctor.

He spoke in clipped, angry bursts. "We live in a small world—isolated, even as we roam—we had no idea we were harboring a fugitive."

The opposite of what Diavala would say—she'd want them all roped together.

Oh, thank mercy. Celia pressed her hands to her stomach, the butterflies threatening to burst out. He met her gaze, and his glare would have shattered the glass around her if the people hadn't already lifted it off.

He did a lot of yelling, most directed at the Mob. "Lead the people out." "Refunds." "Apologies." And a not-so-subtle "We will cooperate fully, of course," through his teeth, as if he were infinitely pissed at this turn of events. Still, it boomed as a firm order to every set of ears in the Mob. *Cooperate fully. Cooperate. Listen to me.*

He met her gaze as he gave a solid hiss of "We trusted you" when the giant officer and the mistico were sure to hear. "All this time."

And she finally heard him.

You're not the storm, Celia. I'm with you, as I've always been.

But because she was so manipulative and devious, she didn't apologize. Of course she didn't. She glanced over her shoulder at the officer who'd bound her hands, saying, "Dumb of them, wasn't it?"

She shrugged at the plague doctor, hiding a wave of relief behind a mask of resolve. One consolation to the show's end was how well he understood her; he'd taken on the role she'd cast for him without flinching.

The plague doctor growled, turned away, legitimately pissed at her, as he should be. It brought her back to the reality closing in. Instead of safety for his people, Celia had tightened the chains even more. So focused on outmaneuvering Diavala, they'd forgotten about the mistico still hunting for two runaway inklings.

"I have to get this under control." The plague doctor said it straight to her with the familiar tilt of his head to the left, then disappeared into the crowd before the officer could argue.

Not how we wanted this to go, Anny, she thought when she glimpsed Anya in white lace struggling against her own captors. *But at least we didn't help her take the poison to Kinallen. A victory.*

Celia shrugged away from the officer, determined to walk on her own. Head high, proud, arrogant, she pushed herself into a new character—the cold, manipulative deviant. The Mob could still be safe if they did this right.

CHAPTER 27

HOPE, PANIC, HOPE, PANIC.

Celia didn't know how to be anxious when she didn't know exactly what to be anxious about.

Officer Nero Ferrara was the type of person who didn't know the meaning of the term *off-duty*. "I don't think I like you," Celia said. She had no idea why he'd even come to the show in the first place, since *fun* also didn't appear to be anywhere in his vocabulary. His tenor was an unusual combination of bronze and silver hues, each as dull and muted as he seemed to be.

He snorted. "I'll survive."

The crowd had been disbanded with force when more officers and then mistico had descended. The gates were locked, this time not to keep others out, but to hold the Mob in. Celia had been taken backstage, the curtains drawn shut, and sequestered with Nero. It had gone deathly silent outside, and Celia knew little about what had happened in the three hours since the abrupt end to the show.

At one point she'd heard Marco yelling that no one knew anything. That they'd been deceived by Lalita. He used her nickname, as if she'd given them an alias to cover her identity and dupe them all. Infinitely smart of him to follow the plague doctor's lead. She urged him to yell louder, savoring his bellowed outrage because everyone, all the way to the streets of Malidora, would hear it.

Later, a scuffle between one of the officers and the plague doctor had pushed through the curtains. He'd still had his mask on, yelling a number—"Twenty! Only twenty!" as if it were the most important number in the universe—as the officer tried to catch him. He'd danced away and leaped back out into the fray, but not before shouting it once more at Celia: "Only twenty of us!"

There were twenty-nine in the Mob. He didn't want them going after Gil, Millie, and the Kids. And a couple of others who had managed to sneak away? Another consolation, then, that not everyone would be swept up in this net. But where was Anya? Kitty Kay? Celia expected her allies to be keeping her company.

Celia would have loved to pace, as that had become a hobby of hers even more pronounced than shisha and absinthe of late, but her bound ankles made it impossible. "What's the plan, then?" She felt with her bounded hands along the crate she sat on, hoping for a miracle sharp nail to appear. "Are we road-tripping back to Asura together? Because that would be a riot. You're so much fun." She was close to spilling her insides into her lap.

Nero raked his hands through his short brown hair, and it stayed up, standing at attention. She wondered if he came from Bickland, for he had nearly the same shade of tawny beige skin as Lilac and was big all over too. Celia tried to ignore the fact that those huge hands could snap her neck like a twig, should they be so inclined. "What drama," he muttered.

"I have to pee." When she tried to stand, Nero kicked an abandoned top hat over to her with one tree trunk leg.

She pushed her fingernail into her palm so hard it drew blood, but she managed to hold in her scream. "Damn it!" She squirmed like a worm against her bound hands and feet. "In case you missed it, you're about ten times my size and could break my entire body with one flex of your big toe, Nero, so why the hell do I need to be tied up like this?"

He ignored her comment, but asked, curious, "You must have known this could only end one way?"

"We fooled the Rabble Mob for weeks; it was the crowd who surprised us." Lying used to be so easy for her, and now, when she needed her skills the most, she could feel them slipping away, gossamer thin.

He snorted again.

Asshole.

"Yours and Anya Burtoni's faces were everywhere. Stop trying to claim that no one here knew anything." Nero appraised her with a long look, cracking his knuckles. Of course he had an annoying habit like that. Then he pulled his shirt out of his trousers and lifted it, showing her the inked image of a salamander perched on his brown abs as if sunning itself on rocks. "This appeared when I was eighteen."

"Pretty. And what universal wisdom did a salamander give you?"

He ignored her sarcasm. "One spring when I was young, the pond near our house was overrun with yellow and brown salamanders. My siblings and I spent months catching and playing with them. I left home as an angry sixteen-year-old, but the ink told me to go back. A month later, my mother died."

A touching story, so Celia tried to be reasonable. "I don't think you're stupid, so I won't point out that you could have found significant meaning in anything that showed up on your rock abs. You wanted to go home. The ink gave you an excuse."

He nodded and, for the first time, smiled at her. It shaved a decade off his face, and she wondered if he wasn't closer to her in age than she'd first thought. "Maybe that's true. But if it hadn't been precisely a salamander at precisely that time in my life, I wouldn't have had a chance to say goodbye to my mother. The ink tells us what we want to hear; I'm glad I listened."

It settles the chaos inside. Some of Diavala's words intruded, Nero unintentionally giving them life. "A charming story of utter coincidence," Celia said, squirming more, infinitely annoyed at her bladder because mentioning having to pee made her aware that it might be a good idea.

Nero stood and went to the curtain separating backstage from the front. He poked his head out and growled some nonsense to himself. When he turned back, his face held the deepest frown she'd ever seen. "When my captain is done rounding up the Rovers, she'll want to have a conversation. And while I don't have any loyalty to you, I'll give you a warning you should take to heart: she's not as personable as me, certainly not as patient, and you'd be smart to not hand *her* any bullshit, because she can sift through it better than anyone I've ever known."

Celia swallowed, but managed, "Aw, you do like me."

His deep brown eyes drilled into her but were slightly less crinkled in the corners.

"Sorry I ruined your night," she said.

He cracked his knuckles, went back to the curtain, and peered out again. "I never got my card reading. It's the only reason I came."

"Well, let me tell you something about that. It's horseshit. Like the ink, like the temple, like our lives. Like everything in the world."

Nero stared at her with a blank expression. "You don't believe that."

"Oh, I do." Celia put her head down and stared at the floor.

At least, she used to.

Nero hadn't lied about Captain Andras. She was a vaguely human-shaped shard of obsidian.

"The Rovers have all been questioned," she barked at Nero, tapping her toes with her long baton as she paced, accentuating every word. A jagged tattoo crept up both sides of her neck, ringing its way deep into her hairline like a chokehold of ink, and Celia would have bet her life that Captain Andras hadn't tilted sideways to see a different message.

"We're escorting Celia Sand back to Asura so she can face Profeta's judgment." No mention of Anya or anyone else, so Celia took a moment to daydream a cartwheel.

Then the captain shoved her baton in Celia's face. "The beaked young thing who looks like death is going to be a big pain in my ass, and you put that thorn there. I don't like thorns."

No.

That sounded as if everyone would come with them. Her mental cartwheel stopped mid-spin, leaving her tilted all wrong. Celia smelled the tang of copper, saw the wet, glistening end of the baton. Was that fresh blood on it? Plague-doctor-being-a-pain-in-her-ass blood? How hard and how many times would you have to hit flesh with a baton to draw blood? "I hope it was worth it, Celia Sand. Your extra-special heresy will deserve such extra-special treatment, I can't even imagine." Her eyes glimmered as if she'd already tried, very hard, to imagine, and had enjoyed every moment.

As she loudly complained to Nero about the logistics of travel, a group of her officers came in, muscling Anya and Kitty Kay into the chairs beside Celia. They were both bound, but where Kitty Kay looked angry and discomposed, Anya was tattered to the point of ruin. A still-bleeding scrape wept blood down her cheek before getting soaked up by a gag, which looked to be made of her own previously white dress. From the way her ocean-blue eyes blazed, Celia knew she'd brought that chaos on herself.

The rush of blood to her head made Celia's eyes burn, and Nero stared at her hard, peeling back her reaction layer by layer. She made herself shrug with indifference and nodded to Kitty Kay. "But these people aren't guilty of anything except stupidity. We conned the whole troupe. They didn't know what we ran from."

Kitty Kay stared straight ahead, jaw clenching. "No, that's not entirely true. *I* knew. I covered for you and diverted the Mob's questions. You're not that clever, devil. I did all the heavy lifting for you." She stared at the ink on Captain Andras's neck when she spat out, "I hate Profeta so much that my shield was impenetrable."

Pretending this was news, Celia arranged her face into anger at the insult, then confusion, then grudging admiration. "Well then," she mused. "I'd thank you, but given the circumstances . . ." She gestured at their captivity.

Anya threw in a violent, muffled scream of frustration, but in her case, she wasn't acting.

Nero raised a dubious eyebrow and crossed his arms but said nothing at their little exhibition. Didn't even snort his opinion again.

"I have no idea what's going on here." Captain Andras said, looking between Celia, Anya, and Kitty Kay as if she expected one of them to tell her. "Fortunately, it's not up to me to figure it out. *Un*fortunately, your mask came off on my turf, and I have orders to return you to those who own you. *Un*fortunately, I've been instructed to bring an entire freak show along too. What were you even doing here, Ferrara?" A barked insult, not a legitimate question, so Nero didn't bother responding.

Who was issuing these orders?

The curtains fluttered, and two people entered. When the lamplight illuminated their faces, Celia moaned. Beside her, Anya sucked in a breath.

The first mistico was one from Sabazio, who'd been there to confront Kitty Kay about the Mob's message but had ended up having to slit the throat of a Touched colleague instead. "Nice to see you again, Solemn Mistico Aurelio," Kitty Kay said, her tone saying the very opposite.

The second mistico stepped forward. Iron-gray eyes peeled back the layers of Kitty Kay's forced calm as he'd done countless times before. A slight smile lit High Mistico Benedict's lips when he looked between Celia and Anya.

They understood Diavala's greeting. *Hello again, Inklings.*

High Mistico Benedict cleared his throat. "On Ruler Vacilando's order, you're to return to Asura with us."

Mistico Aurelio fumbled in his satchel, wordlessly producing a letter with Ruler Vacilando's seal, holding it up for Kitty Kay to read. She promptly turned her head away. Even amid the tumble of her emotions, Celia appreciated that.

High Mistico Benedict's lips twitched again into something resembling a smile, if a smile had fangs laced with venom. Every line on his face etched deeper.

Celia's bees nudged her. *This is not coincidence. This is calculated.*

Panic started overtaking her senses. Red and bright. Hot and fierce.

This is a culmination.

Cold sweat dotted Celia's forehead as she battled through not pissing herself. Captain Andras left with Aurelio, and now only Celia, Kitty Kay, and a rigid, mostly clueless Nero remained.

Along with the High Mistico himself, who'd come all the way from Asura.

Celia's panic became a monstrous force; she felt ten times bigger yet antlike at the same time. And then a wide smile — so bright it felt like something held back for a lifetime — took over High Mistico Benedict's face.

Diavala set the brightness of that smile on Celia and Anya. "Of all the things to overlook in your scheming, Inklings, to forget that my temple has been looking for you for weeks was woefully stupid." The way she smiled, so knowing and sure.

Thrilled.

Culmination, Celia's bees said again.

As if Diavala had always intended to end up exactly there, backstage with runaway inklings, using High Mistico Benedict's body.

As if she'd had centuries to set up that moment.

Anny, we missed so much more than I thought. Looks like we missed it all.

Some tears tracked their way through the blood on Anya's cheek, making streams. Her nostrils flared and her chest heaved, silent fear compared with Celia's.

Celia found that she couldn't stop laughing and babbling. Maybe if she kept talking, she could pretend this was still a matter of revenge. "Too bad we screwed you out of Kinallen and Bickland. Shame your plan for the devil in a bell jar didn't amount to anything."

Kitty Kay tried to shush her.

Nero didn't seem to be trying too hard to sort out the conversation. He'd been tasked with managing a mad performer, and now she spoke true madness. He cracked his knuckles in a rhythmic beat, glancing between Celia, Anya, Kitty Kay, and Benedict, as if wondering who would bite him first.

Celia traced Diavala's route backwards, body by body, from the temple all the way to that moment. Diavala had tracked them down using Mistico Dominic. It must not have been too difficult, given their connection with Lupita and the loud chaos of the Rover show in Asura. She'd caught up with them, watched them perform in Sabazio from a distance, been intrigued, seen an opportunity. She must have used Dominic to maneuver Benedict into place. Perhaps the initial message to Benedict had been: watch the Mob, don't move in, something's coming. Anything Dominic had told Benedict would have felt bigger as soon as he'd been Touched. Then Diavala had possessed Vincent, and all the while Benedict had listened, lurked, watched, convenient and close already, for Diavala to be able to hop into him when she was done with Vincent.

Diavala was a sheepdog, manipulating a herd. What else had

she maneuvered into place using Dominic and Benedict these past weeks? After birthing and grooming an entire religion for centuries, it felt as if Profeta was Diavala's concerto to play, she needed only to strike the right key.

Kitty Kay tried to talk over Celia's shaking and tears, still rigid in her stance that the rest of the Mob had nothing to do with the runaways. In the corner, Nero shifted from foot to foot, uncomfortable, and since he didn't know what was going on, Celia kept looking at him, hoping to latch on to some of his blissful ignorance. High Mistico Benedict waved him away when he noticed their eye contact. Nero didn't argue and was gone before Celia could beg him to stay.

Diavala crouched into a squat so she was eye level with Celia and Anya. Side by side, hands tied behind their backs, chests panting, they stared at the face of the gray-eyed monster who'd plagued their life at the temple and now hid a new monster inside. Kitty Kay and Nero had faded, and it was just the three of them: the deity and the inklings who stole from her.

"How could I pass up an opportunity like the one you handed me?" Diavala dug her thumb into the wound, tortured them by drawing it out, smiling all the while.

What did we hand you?

A predator watching its dinner. "And to reach such astronomical fame in a matter of weeks!"

Diavala had wanted them on that stage for *this*. But what was *this*?

Anya hiccupped and gasped around her gag, choking. Celia had frozen like a rabbit, all her previous babble spent.

"Now," Diavala said. "You can make sure my Return is unforgettable."

Immediately the room rushed back. Kitty Kay slumped forward in her chair as if her guts had fallen out. Her vibrant red hair veiled her face so she was half-daytime, half-nighttime Kitty Kay. Stuck. Either, neither, or both. Still, even as her body showed defeat, she mumbled that the Mob had had nothing to do with any of this.

Anya met Celia's eyes and whimpered, a sound so foreign coming from her that it tore Celia open.

"Your Return." Celia's voice cracked and wobbled. The logic snapped together quickly. Perfectly set up. Horribly perfect.

As the Divine, she was invisible yet revered, unknown yet among them. If the manipulation and games were becoming too dull, what would she want?

She'd want a true face.

A deity walking among the people would only solidify their adoration. She could erupt from the shadows and truly reign. With Ruler Vacilando bowing to her, Diavala would control the treasury, the army. She could take Profeta into other nations personally: a Divine in the flesh rather than carved in stone. She'd tried it before and had failed on a spectacular level—been flogged for it, retreated—but she'd had centuries to make sure she didn't err again.

All the dogma about the Return of the Divine already existed; she'd needed only the perfect blend of timing and circumstance.

And they'd handed it to her.

"Ruler Vacilando received her prophetic tattoo a few days ago," Diavala said. With Ruler Vacilando's fresh tattoo—the Divine walking among the people again, a lightning bolt— the fourth tenet of Profeta had been heralded. The countdown would soon be complete.

"All of Illinia will know that you stole the ink—"

You did steal the ink, Celia's bees pointed out.

"They will know you tried to subvert Divine messages—"

You did subvert messages.

"Then you tried to spread your influence to the masses—"

Your dominion of the stage leached into the streets.

"You're more than a devil in a bell jar, Celia. You're the new face of Diavala herself."

You're Diavala, her bees confirmed.

"How could the Divine *not* return, exactly now, under exactly these circumstances, to stop such heresy?"

You're Diavala, her bees hummed. *She will be crowned the Divine.*

"And I've found the perfect body," Diavala continued. As High Mistico Benedict, Diavala straightened to full height, towering over them. "I already have all of Profeta's mistico behind me. The lore that foretold the Return is engrained. I have the ruler of Illinia ready to welcome me. Once the Divine is unveiled in

Asura, belief will only harden. And spread. I'll take Profeta into Bickland and Kinallen myself. I never needed you for that. Your show was only an opening act for mine." She shook her head in pity; then her eyes glinted. "There hasn't been this much excitement in *hundreds* of years. Everyone is watching."

And when High Mistico Benedict cleared his throat, a rough exclamation point to everything Diavala had just laid out, Celia's bladder decided it had had enough.

CHAPTER 28

THIS ISN'T OVER YET." KITTY KAY STAUNCHLY RETRIEVED HER revenge red as officers and mistico assembled her Rovers in the field. She gave her family ferocity to look upon: a defiant chin, a proud spine, glittering orange like fire under the lanterns' light. Celia and Anya were the only ones close enough to see her hands shake. The Mob had been officially charged with just one crime so far—willfully spreading heterodoxy—but it was enough to get them all back to Asura. Ample time for more charges—and punishments—to be laid down.

"We'll figure this out," Anya whispered, her voice hoarse. They'd finally ungagged her when it looked as if she would choke to death on the hem of her own dress. "I have an idea."

Most of the Mob seemed confused more than scared; they pressed together and whispered, looked around for guidance. The plague doctor stood apart from the rest, flanked by three officers. His shirt was ripped, and his raven cloak had lost a wing, errant feathers occasionally tugged away by the breeze. Even from far away, his breathing looked irregular, his chest heaving too much considering that he stood still. Marco didn't try to hide his rage as he engaged in a tug of war with one of the mistico. Only those two were bound, as were Celia, Anya, and Kitty Kay.

In whispers, Kitty Kay told them this would still all work out because it had to. "Damn her for coming into my troupe. No matter what happens, my family will never be the same after this; it needs to be worth the loss. Get your spunk back, both of you. Harness your rage. We will still have a stage; we can still do some damage. This *isn't* over yet."

"I have an idea," Anya whispered again, her eyes closed as she imagined the color and shape of this phantom new idea.

High Mistico Benedict had summoned Nero back to their side as he organized the officers and mistico for the cumbersome trip back to the temple. Celia recognized some of the mistico from Asura. Others were new, called to the scene from the smaller temples in Malidora, she presumed. Every single one made sure to glare at her. Diavala herself had tried to advance her scheming under their watch, and they didn't look likely to forgive that.

Celia soon noticed how their anger pointed almost exclusively at her. For the most part, they glanced over Anya and Kitty Kay. That was encouraging. Maybe all hope wasn't lost after all.

"Where's Remy?" Celia couldn't find her. Her absence was glaring, but Celia didn't know what to make of it.

Then, through the din of conversation and orders, Celia heard a sound. A hoarse cough. A shout.

A whisper of "Oh no . . ." from Anya.

That one shout turned into a stream of words, growing louder. A sea of dark robes and colorful dresses turned toward the approaching sound as every conversation stopped.

The sudden silence amplified the lone voice.

Celia tried to shout, but the words got stuck. Large hands clamped around her wrists to keep her from running toward the sound.

It was Remy who emerged from behind a back wagon first. Out of breath, flapping her arms, a wild look on her face. "I'm trying!" Her hands went to her short hair, her gaze darting around looking for someone. She landed on Lilac and lurched toward her, oblivious to the officer who grabbed her arm and held her back. "He wouldn't take it anymore. He was awake, and he threw it on Seer's vegetables, and I don't know where you keep the chloroform! I couldn't make him stay put!"

The officer forced her to her knees even as she kept yelling and apologizing, and the image of such a tiny young person muscled around by a large, unwelcome person shook the Mob free from its compliance. Ravino went to tip the scales in Remy's favor; Grisilda and Fawn harnessed their practice as bodyguards and pushed their way to the front of the Mob, linking arms. The plague doctor shouted for calm and acquiescence even as he struggled against the officers holding him.

Anya twisted against Nero's grip, Celia twisting with her. As he fought to hold on to both of them, they fell to the ground. He stepped on their bound wrists, one pair under each boot, not hard enough to crush, but more than enough to pin them. And together, Celia and Anya watched Kitty Kay, free of Nero's grasp, run down the slope awkwardly, her hair streaming behind her, and tumble down, hard, when she tripped, all the while crying out terrible ululations. Shaking, shattering, she struggled to get up.

Celia and Anya were sideways on the ground when Marco temporarily won his tug-of-war and took off, his captors giving chase. He didn't run toward Remy, but toward Vincent, who'd just staggered around the corner.

"Oh no," Anya moaned again.

Kitty Kay's ululations peaked as a mistico grabbed her.

Celia pressed her face into the wet grass.

It had been too long—hours—since Vincent had been dosed. The jipep seeds had loosened their hold. Vincent's tortured shouts were summoning his own execution. The plague doctor's resistance grew more urgent. Had he told Remy to hide with Vincent in Seer's cellar, thinking they both might be safe there? He twisted and bucked, no longer appealing for calm. Captain Andras bashed the back of his knee, and he folded.

"I feel these things!" Vincent yelled, then added a guttural moan mixed with a scream. "So quiet but so loud! From working alone on a hill to the clutches of a devil to hundreds of years looking at the world through someone else's eyes . . ." Pale and gaunt, his clear eyes reddened, his sharp jaw even sharper, he was a shredded version of the friend Celia had walked with.

He didn't struggle when a mistico grabbed him. "You need

to understand! These humming bones tell the truth!" he said over his shoulder to the mistico, who was soaking a rag.

"She's so desperately lonely," he said to the mistico in front of him as she brought the dagger up.

Marco was taken down and pinned, mere paces away, but Vincent didn't acknowledge his shouts.

Celia called up the memory of Vincent's perfect smile, as rare as diamonds, as warm as a fire. How his eyes had danced at their stupid joke about giant cakes. How he'd sat so still and patiently, indulging her when she'd wanted to draw him. How he'd suspiciously lost nearly every game of Imp tiles after it became clear that she was a sore loser.

She remembered when he'd welcomed her with a bracelet. A simple gesture. The best moment of her life.

Just before the chloro-soaked rag pressed against his face, he laughed and said to the sky, "This is probably for the best."

"No!" Marco shouted. An officer slammed his baton down, the crack as Marco's nose broke sounding like a thunderclap. The Mob was made of heaving shoulders, rocking backs, and bowed heads. Collective shock and grief pinned most people in place.

They'd found that one name on the Roll of Saints—proof that someone had been Touched and lived—but it hadn't mattered at all. For Halycon Ronnea's name, they'd gotten the Divine orders. They'd pushed every boundary to define the ink's capabilities, but had ultimately pushed too far and pissed Diavala off. Their effort had cost them Vincent, not helped him.

The dark tinted lenses of the plague doctor's mask found Celia, and they shared a moment of surreal pain. Something un-understandable.

A quick conversation of exclamation points.

A question mark.

A period.

My fault. My fault. I'm sorry.

Celia remembered things.

Like the day Lupita had gouged her eyes out. Lots of blood, quickly bandaged, and Celia's detached thought, *Hope this works.*

Like how nice it had been to be able to say goodbye to Salome before she'd been taken away—because one day's warning had been such an unexpected luxury. *Play tiles with me,* Salome had said. She knew better than to waste time running. So on Salome's last day among the living, they'd played a few hands of Imp tiles and pretended it wasn't her last day.

"It's all right, Cece," Anya said. Her eyes were so blue. "Look at me. Don't look up."

Celia was lying sideways.

So instead of a V, they cut a >.

And there was death.

Anya kept whispering, "Cece, look at me. Look at me, Cece." Her voice fluxed like waves. And even after Celia met her eyes, she kept whispering it, "Cece, Cece. It's all right, look at me. Be strong." Her lips scrunched in a peculiar way in an effort to say those words over her own crying. Her eyes bled tears.

The sobs reached a crescendo together. Loud wails mixed

with screams. Kitty Kay's heartbreaking cries tempered with soul-racking moans. So loud, their grief. So overwhelming.

And Celia had no idea how to join them.

Celia had grown so desensitized, she'd forgotten how the rest of the world grieved.

She understood then why the Palidon always wore the black teardrop under his eye.

Because his breaking was inevitable. Like everyone's breaking was inevitable.

But the Palidon was the only one brave enough to acknowledge it.

CHAPTER 29

THEY TOOK ANYA AWAY FROM HER. CELIA ROCKED INSIDE the dank prison coach, bumping along, leading the disgraced Rovers back toward Asura with her giant shadow, Nero. If not for the one small barred window facing the rear, it would have been travel by coffin. With her hands on the bars of the window, Celia scanned the procession behind her. The Rabble Mob's caravan of wagons moved under a heavy guard of Ruler Vacilando's officers and mistico alike, another dark carriage like hers near the back. Perhaps Anya was there with her own shadow—iron-eyed with humming bones.

Celia's knuckles turned white on the bars.

They traveled almost constantly, so Nero let Celia stand and pace and look out the window. The two of them had been alone for days, quarantined from the rest of the group.

Every once in a while Celia asked him, "Where's the angel?" *Where did you go, Anya?*

He'd go statue instead of answering, but she kept trying.

"What happened to the angel?" Anya must have lost her quill fingernail, otherwise she would have used it a hundred times by then. Sketching the outline of her idea, shading in contours, adding dimension. The last thing Anya said to her before they'd been pulled apart was a fierce, "Make your peace with it, Cece!" If what Kitty Kay had said was right and they did have a stage in Asura, Anya had found a brilliant way of using it. She wasn't done fighting yet.

But the image of Anya whispering, *Be strong, look at me,* while sobbing was the one Celia had circling around in her mind.

Where are you, Anny?

Finally Nero answered. "I don't owe you answers, Inkling."

So he'd put it together: not regular runaways, but *inkling* runaways. Celia's teeth ground into nubs, hating that he had to be so clever.

And damn it, she hated that title even more. Spouted from lips that knew nothing about her life, as if she were a petulant child and should have accepted the honor bestowed on her when her mothers abandoned her.

"If anyone calls me Inkling ever again," she said through her teeth, "I'm flying at their face with my fists."

He arched an eyebrow. "This is a long trip, and it will be a lot worse for you if you insist on snapping at your jailer."

She snorted but otherwise ignored him, pressing her face to the bars. The Illinian countryside rolled by. People stood at the roadside and watched them pass. Huddled under umbrellas, families clutched one another close. Celia wanted to ask them what they thought was happening. What did they see in a pack of famous Rovers guarded by Profetan mistico?

Celia got an answer, of sorts, from a loud group that had

set up a temporary camp by the road, passing the time with drink as they waited for the procession to roll by. "There she is!" one bellowed, pointing at Celia's face in the window. Their friend dropped his flask in the ditch and rifled through his pockets, eventually whipping out two crumpled papers: her wanted poster and the Mob's advertising. The people shoved at one another, all wanting confirmation for themselves. Celia grasped for something to say—"Don't believe what they tell you!" or "It's not what it looks like!" or "These people did nothing!"—but the first rock hit her arm as she reached out, stinging furiously and unexpectedly.

They trotted beside her coach for a long time, chucking pebbles, aiming for the window she'd now retreated from, making a game of it, until Nero interceded and yelled at them.

She rubbed the red welt on her arm. So much anger aimed at her already, and they didn't even have the whole story. The rumors were obviously flourishing, but Celia had no doubt that the true reason the temple had spent so much time and effort on her capture would stay a secret until the bitter end.

More dramatic that way. More of a spectacle.

A stroke of genius, to directly link the Mob to the Return. The connection would come together seamlessly. Instead of the Return being a grand but distant thing, the people would be intimately affected. *I saw their show! My parents told me about the Devil in the Bell Jar. I still have my playbill. I wasn't fooled; I knew something was wrong. Their show was too different, too strange, the messages too mixed up.*

To think, all that time we were watching Diavala . . .

Hundreds of people followed behind the prison coaches and Rabble Mob wagons. The crowd had transformed from audience to players in the greatest show of all, and they knew the grand finale would be in Asura, even if they had no idea what it would look like.

It felt like a funeral march. They all traveled by coffin.

"I hate this."

As long as Celia hated, she had something.

"Is your arm okay?" Nero cracked his knuckles as he stood near the window, long after the rock throwers had dispersed.

"Not at all. But should my jailer really care?"

"I—" Nero started his sentence ten times before landing on what he wanted to say. "I don't understand what's going on here." He sat beside her on the floor, folding his giant legs under him with supreme effort.

Simple words, becoming a doorway. So Celia walked through and told him everything. What did it matter if he knew all her secrets?

It passed the time, anyway. And like a masochist, Celia went into explicit detail as she described the sections about the Flogging in the *Book of Profeta*. They were now a primer for her final moments, and they didn't promise to be pretty ones. She was scared of the pain, more scared of losing herself to it. Most of her story was awful, but she saw no reason to spare Nero the ending.

When she finished, she waited for his reaction.

Nero gifted her with a succinct, "Now *that* is some horseshit, Inkling, but I appreciate the effort."

She sighed. "Yeah. I wouldn't believe it either." She almost thanked him for listening, since it was already more than she'd get in Asura.

Whenever the carriage stopped, Nero bound her. Inevitably, Captain Andras made her rounds. Celia and Nero were stop one, a head count of everyone in the troupe was step two, and if they were close to a town, hiring a messenger to send into Asura with their location and various directives was step three.

"Where's the angel in all this?" Celia asked, staring as the door slammed shut on them again.

Nero put his finger to his lips. "Quiet," he whispered, so low she could barely hear him.

Something unusual lingered in Nero's tight line of a mouth. He never backed away from eye contact. An imperceptible difference in his demeanor Celia hadn't noticed until then.

She decided to try again. "Where's Anya, Nero?"

Before he could answer, Remy's hissed whisper of "Lalita-aaaaa" sprang up from under her feet. Hiding below the frame of the carriage? Celia flopped down ungracefully and pressed her lips to the floorboards.

"Go away!" she hissed with as much heat as she could. "The captain is doing the head count!" How had Remy escaped?

"And your friend is under guard," Nero added, falling back on his old routine of enforcer. He even crossed his tree-trunk arms as he talked to the air, as if Remy could see his authority through dusty wood.

Celia put her lips to the floor. "Go away!" Was that crunching gravel under bloodred boots she heard in the distance?

"I drew a picture for you." Remy shoved it through the cracks between the wood right under Celia's grimy nose. Celia grabbed the paper with her teeth and yanked it through the floor, ripping part of it, cursing, and silently begging Nero not to turn back into a complete jackass.

But alas, he did. "Shit!" he said, and in a flash of agile movement that belied his size, he had the door unlocked and open. Remy held Celia's gaze and didn't cry out, despite being dragged into the carriage by the scruff of the neck like a wolf pup. Celia had the terrible impression being captured had been her plan all along.

"A prisoner can't pass another prisoner notes," Nero said, stating the obvious. "How did you even get out?"

"I'm bendy," Remy said, proceeding to demonstrate how she might have slithered through an opening too small and awkward for anyone else.

"She's a child, Nero!" Now Celia definitely heard crunching gravel, getting louder. "I've been teaching her to draw." She tried to squirm her way to sitting but owing to her bound hands, she ended up flat on her stomach with a half-ripped piece of paper beside her. "It's probably an eel. We liked drawing eels. In knots. It's an eel or something, right, Remy?"

"It *is* an eel, Lalita! And it's my best one yet. I needed to show you." Clever, stupid thing made her wide eyes even wider, and her voice crept an octave higher than normal. She winced against Nero's hand at her collar, though Celia could tell it wasn't a tight grip. "I'm sorry, Officer," Remy whimpered.

Nero rolled his eyes and pulled her back out of the carriage. "Nice try. Bend your way back to your people quickly and don't make me regret this. Don't let the captain see you, and *don't* try this again, because I won't be nice the second time. I'll give you to her myself."

She darted away like a grasshopper. In the time it took for Nero to close and relock the door, Celia had time to shuffle over to the paper, lick it up, and start chewing.

"Oh, for goodness sake." Nero yanked it out of her mouth. He tossed it aside like the decoy it was, hoisted Celia to her feet, and proceeded to give her a not-so-gentle pat-down. "Hands. Mouth. Lift your tongue." He ran his big hands through her hair as if she might have slid a blade in like a barrette.

"She's a child," Celia repeated when he didn't find anything. "And she's so proud of her knotted eels."

When he unfolded the paper, cringing against the saliva coating half of it, he stared at it for a long time, searching for meaning. Eventually, he sighed. "It's a nice eel. You're a good teacher." He folded it and put it in his back pocket.

Then he bent over and grabbed the sliver of a quill nub that Celia had kicked under his bench as he'd pulled her to her feet.

Her clever, bendy old shadow bested by her clever, giant new one.

"Sorry." He stuffed it in a deep pocket, sounding as if he meant it a little.

Damn it. She really needed to keep hating him.

She needed that quill even more. Celia and Anya had tried to ink with other implements—a needle, a fork—but only feathers dipped in the ink of the Chest Majestic channeled the ink in inkling veins—a truth that hadn't been so inconvenient until then. Where had Remy even gotten it? Sneaky, perfect little thing, she'd probably nicked it from Celia's stuff while the mistico were rounding everyone up.

"We have a long time together, Officer Nero. I can teach you how to draw knotted eels."

He appraised her, kept right on being his clever self, but eventually nodded. "Tell you what: don't do anything stupid to force my hand, and I won't toss it out the window. Yet."

"Deal."

But a few days later Celia did something stupid. She ended up on her stomach again, her face pressed hard on the wooden boards, a boulder of muscle and knee shoved into her spine.

Worst pickpocket in history. Nero had been sleeping, and her fingers hadn't even grazed his pocket before she kissed the floor.

"Where's the angel?" she yelled. "Where is she?" She didn't know if it was physically possible for her to die without Anya nearby. She kept yelling it until he slapped a hand over her mouth, and then she yelled it some more until it turned into a whimper.

He leaned down. "You're shouting your weakness for everyone to hear, and trust me, they're listening."

Nero tossed the quill nub out the window after she'd done that stupid thing, delivering on his promise.

It took a few more days, but eventually Celia's bees went dormant, colors disappeared into gray clouds, and time lost meaning.

She'd scraped at corners only to get broken nails and splinters. Nero had no weapon on him she could fantasize about stealing. The iron bars didn't change shape under her grip.

She dreamed about that long-lost quill nub—the sliver of hope it had offered. How could they keep fighting without their only weapon?

Ripped, stained, and smelling like the rest of the carriage, her costume dress hung in tatters. Nero had taken pity on her and demanded a scratchy wool blanket. She'd wrapped it around her torso like a high-waisted sarong at first. Then like a shawl. Then around her legs. It covered only one-third of her body at a time. She lived her new life two-thirds cold.

Celia learned to like the plank floor the most. The air seemed lighter down there. Or heavier. She spent more time lying prone and less by the window. More jostling to the rhythm of the cart and less time picking at the wooden slats. More time with her eyes closed than open.

Her existence melted into days and days of random stories.

"A rat used to come by the crypts," she whispered. To Nero, to herself, to no one. "Zuni made a deal with it. She named him Squire and declared him to be a civilized rat. She told him if he could keep it a secret and not tell his rat buddies, and of course stay away from the corpses, she'd put out a bit of good food and fresh water for him every day. He never caused trouble, and she fed him for three years before he died." A pause in her whispers. "We always thought Squire was the smart one, but it was Zuni."

"Why?" Nero asked.

"She made the rat forget he was a rat."

Nero gave her another blanket, and she lived one-third cold.

On the floor, Celia kept talking, trying to block out the squeaks and squeals of the carriage, Nero's regular breathing and knuckle cracking, and the silence of outside. "I'm sorry," she said to Anya. "I shouldn't have pulled you through that loophole with me six years ago."

"I'm sorry," she said to Griffin, "that you'll die again. That's not fair, for someone to have to do it twice."

"I'm sorry," she said to Remy, "that you had to see so much blood so early."

Her biggest apology went to her Palidon. So big it wouldn't fit in the carriage if she voiced it. *I'm sorry, Vincent. If my story had ended when it should have, yours wouldn't have ended in Malidora.*

She wept until she had no tears left.

Later, she asked Nero, "How can you believe that a salamander told you to return home and say goodbye to your mother, but you can't believe that the true devil is disguised in robes?"

"Stop making fun of my salamander." His lips quirked again in his now-familiar wry way.

He sat on the bench while she lay on the floor, and they stared at each other for entertainment. Her stories went limp. Her mind dried.

Out of nowhere, Nero told her the answer to the question she'd needed since Malidora. "Anya Burtoni's in the black carriage at the back with High Mistico Benedict and Solemn Mistico Aurelio."

For the first time in days, Celia became unlimp. She hoisted herself to her elbows and stared at him.

"But you're the prize, Inkling Celia Sand. It's all about the devil in the bell jar." Nero shifted on the bench, his knuckle cracking reaching absurd proportions. "I suppose the good news for you is that the more attention the devil gets, the less falls to your angel."

It felt like a clue, a nudge. She cocked her head, assessing the tells she was somewhat of an expert on by then. He cracked his knuckles and wouldn't meet her eyes.

Interesting. And she had nothing but time to unravel that mystery. She lay back down. "Thanks, Nero."

CHAPTER 30

THE CARRIAGE DOOR OPENED AND CLOSED. CELIA'S EYELIDS fluttered open, then closed.

Someone nudged her foot. "Visitor." If it was Captain Andras, Nero would have tied her up. If it was anyone in the troupe, he wouldn't have called them a visitor.

"This trip has been fantastic, but alas, it's at an end," Diavala said with Mistico Benedict's gravelly voice.

This wasn't the first time Diavala had come in to gloat. She loved the sound of her cold, authoritative new voice.

Nero cracked his knuckles. He lived on some perpetual fence now—a knuckle-cracking, fidgety guard, thinking things—unable to choose which yard to leap into. He'd listened to her horseshit story. He'd heard every conversation between Celia and the High Mistico-who-seemed-like-something-else. He'd asked Celia questions, trying to sort through the haze, but sometimes his voice had stopped working halfway.

"Celia Sand. Sit up." Sounded like Diavala had been asking for a while.

Celia forced her spine to uncurl, and sat.

"Ah, you don't look good, Inkling. There's no glimmer of hope around you now."

"You win."

"Almost." She sat forward and laced her fingers together in her lap. "You cut a straight path through the field for me, but you have to finish the harvest."

"No thanks. Not interested."

Celia started to lie back down, ready to return to her hard bed of wooden planks, but Diavala said one more thing.

"I see you're lacking in motivation, which won't do. I don't want a fragile bird onstage accepting that nine-tailed whip. I want fire and rage. The louder you shout, the more devilish the devil looks, the better for my haloed coming. So I'll give you this: if you can find your motivation to passionately hate me again and put on a good show of it, then you can be the first to die." She laughed with cheerful choir bells in her voice. "Maybe I do work in the currency of mercy, after all."

Diavala needed Celia's cooperation.

Celia knew something like this would come, thanks to Nero's nudge — *"You're the prize, Celia Sand. It's all about the devil in the bell jar."* She also knew she could trust exactly nothing coming from Diavala's mouth, and no bargain she made for Anya and the Mob would ever be honored unless it suited Diavala.

But Celia found that she still had it in her to hate something. She hated how much Diavala's words appealed to her. Irrevocably selfish, she began a string of daydreams where she went first and didn't have to watch Anya, Griffin, Remy, Kitty Kay, Lilac . . .

"I won't help you." Her voice cracked, giving away how much she wanted to if it meant an earlier death.

Celia held Nero's gaze through the conversation. "I won't help you." She sounded firmer that time. Good. "They'll see me as nothing but what I am, the Mob as nothing but what they are. There was never any evil. You'll be executing a group of people for the petty crime of hiding a young runaway from the temple or for expanding their art or some other flimsy thing. Your haloed coming won't be able to rise above those bloodstains. You've always tried to convince the people of your benevolence, but what kind of altruistic deity would do that? The people will see the truth eventually. You think flogging me will solidify your hold, but you'll only be sowing the seeds of doubt. The reaping *will* come. It's just too bad I won't be around to see it."

Diavala cocked her head to the right. "It's true, the people will judge. I've experienced it before. But before you give a blanket no as your answer, think for a moment about what you might be able to accomplish as a fiery scapegoat. With a strong enough scapegoat, someone to shoulder all the blame, the people might be inclined to see the Mob—Anya even—as deserving of mercy. If so, I wouldn't overrule them."

Celia trembled and clenched her hands into fists. Diavala offered her hope, but she had a way of twisting everything around to her own ends.

"You know this is the end for you," Diavala said softly. "Why wouldn't you do everything in your power to draw eyes away from the people you love? You might be the only one fated to die in Asura, depending on how well you perform. This has always been between you and me, Inkling. I really take no issue with these colorful souls. They're only here to keep you inspired."

The noise of the people who'd followed the caravan, always a background murmur, roared louder as High Mistico Benedict swung the carriage door open, stepped out, and swung it closed behind him. They always got so excited with movement.

Nero stared out the window at the crowd, his face soft for a moment, before he shook his head and cracked his knuckles and paced—one large step back and forth for him, crossing from one side of the carriage to the other—like a pendulum.

"If you had a quill right now," he said abruptly, "what would you do with it?"

The truth popped out of her mouth before she could choke it back. "I'd ink messages to Anya."

"What kind of messages?"

"A picture of a salamander, maybe. Whatever I thought she needed to hear."

"And Anya would do the same for you?"

"Yes."

He nodded, as if that made perfect sense. She thought he might ask something like *And what would you need to see, Celia?* but Captain Andras had returned and was gesturing for him to lead the prisoner out.

Instead of pushing Celia forward, he hopped out of the carriage and walked away. "I need a break."

Nero's conscience screaming so loudly didn't make Celia feel all that great. Still, it was some consolation to know she hadn't imagined the strange bond growing between them.

Captain Andras seemed unbothered by her officer's dissent. She bound Celia's hands in front of her, and Celia scrambled out of the carriage ungracefully, her gaze lingering on the spot where Nero had disappeared near the back of the long line of wagons.

The crowd of strangers drew Celia's gaze. Hundreds of them, pressing together behind an iron fence and a giant gate, eyes wide open. People who'd decided that being there—right there in that empty field—was more important than attending to their regular lives.

Though there were no lit torches burning purple and blue, no haloed stilt walkers or welcoming plague doctors, Celia recognized it as the same Rover field where they'd auditioned so many weeks before. Where the devil's bell jar was born and then smashed. Where Vincent had given her a bracelet and she'd found a home.

High Mistico Benedict walked with authority to where everyone could see him, Captain Andras muscling Celia along behind. The people cried out, craned their necks, surged forward, and threatened to knock down the gates. They were like those ultra-devoted fans of the Rabble Mob, like Fallan and Pia

—the ones who went to every show and dressed as their favorite characters—but louder, and so many more of them.

They were there to catch the swirling rumors. To settle the frenetic energy. They wanted the truth; they knew it was big.

For the most part, High Mistico Benedict ignored them with an exaggerated aloofness that only made them crave his attention more. Since all the other mistico deferred to him, since he so clearly had the devil of the bell jar under his thumb, it was no stretch to understand that he was the leader. And he reveled in their cheers and cries, tossing significant looks at Celia to make sure she noted their interest.

Their adoration was for Profeta and for *him,* as the one who'd personally captured the heretics. Diavala had taken all the Mob's fame and shifted it directly onto High Mistico Benedict's shoulders.

And now she was giving the people a small glimpse before the true unveiling at the temple.

"This is either a procession of the faces you can still try to save," Diavala said to Celia in a low whisper, "or the order in which they'll be executed in front of the masses for my Return."

As officers led the Mob out, Celia barely recognized them. Gaunt and thin, with scrapes on their faces, matted hair, and ripped, stained clothing, they looked nothing like the bright, shining stars of the Rabble Mob.

They looked broken.

The crowd, unsure about them, didn't cheer. Celia suspected that many had been ardent fans—some would surely have been at the last Malidoran show—but they were at a new show now. The Mob had deceived them with tricks and illusion, had affronted their morals by going against temple justice and harboring fugitives. The Mob had taken it too far, and until the truth was fully illuminated, they guarded their hearts against sympathy.

Cas and Sky walked out first in their natural pairing, holding hands. Celia realized that she'd never seen them apart. They breathed and lived together, and they would stop breathing and not live together. They looked so much smaller without their stilts. Cas didn't front flip; Sky didn't mime punting him in the rear; neither walked on their hands.

They nodded at her as they passed. Cas attempted a weak smile. Sky held their linked hands to the clouds and gave a blessing, *Sastimos futura,* as if it were still a possibility. Small defiances, trying to save their dignity.

They'd be the first to die.

Even from a distance, Celia could have counted Remy's ribs. Remy locked eyes with her Lalita and didn't let go. There was no accusation in them, only determination. Even after all she'd seen in Malidora—her desperation to help Vincent, a front-row view of his sharp, bloody end—it was as if she still believed that Celia wouldn't let her down.

She'd be the third to die.

Marco and his partner fire-master, Tanith. As soon as his raging eyes locked on Celia, he shouted, "This isn't over!" and earned a baton thump to his gut. He straightened and continued his march, his footsteps staking hard claims to the mud under his boots.

Seer Ostra, garish in her style, had unbuttoned the top clasps of her blouse so the Devil tarot peeked out at the world. A small rebellion from the sloth herself.

Though they weren't bound, none of them left the line. The rain poured down on them, washing them out. Limp hair got limper. Beaten-up fabric clung to beaten-up bodies.

The plague doctor was next, wearing his one-winged cloak of shiny raven feathers over tight leather—darkness with hints of starlit sparkles. Or rain. Or tears. His plague doctor smile was big and brazen, and he turned his gaze to everyone he could. As he passed a mistico, she flung her hand out and knocked his mask and hat away. "Face them," she hissed. She knocked his smile away, too.

The Mob sucked in a collective breath and stopped walking.

A few people in the crowd looked away, as if ashamed for him. Embarrassed. Marco, of all people, let out a dangerous sounding howl on his behalf.

Griffin stared at his mask, lying on the grass. He looked up at the mistico who'd exposed him. A few places in line behind him, Kitty Kay warned him not to do anything stupid. Those words made the mistico take a step backwards, as if she hadn't quite thought her move through.

Slowly, the maskless plague doctor inclined his head, his curls sweeping across his brow, a dangerous smile playing at the corners of his lips. He maintained eye contact with the mistico as the smile bloomed back to full size. "I'm astounded at your boldness, Solemn Mistico," he said, loud enough so his words rang out across the field. "Most people are more subtle when they're trying to get me naked."

Someone gasped, another someone giggled.

Caught in a spell of the ink gracing his face and his words, the mistico only stared as Griffin scooped up his mask, tucked it under his arm, then gestured for the Mob to keep moving. With the same huge smile, loud words, and confident body, he showed everyone that he was still the plague doctor, even without his mask.

"Arrogant ass," Diavala muttered. She hadn't missed how many people now wanted a longer look at him rather than the bald one in drab robes.

Griffin tilted his head to the left, offering Celia his Leonus constellation, and he pressed a hand to his hip, reminding her of the warm skin underneath.

Her heart ka-thumped, as always. If only she'd listened to it sooner, those last moments with him could have been so different: leaning into his arms, trusting him as he deserved, answering the pull of him. But instead she'd let paranoia put a wedge between them.

Only then did Celia realize that Kitty Kay had spoken. At midday.

Kitty Kay wore her sparkly orange nighttime dress, but tattered and stained, it hardly looked like the same garment. Her red hair seemed more gray than usual for the nighttime version, but more red than usual for the daytime version, and it was pulled back in a tidy bun, not one strand of it hiding her face. She wore no makeup, her age lines showing, and her eyes looked smaller. She held hands with Ravino and Georgio as they walked single file, and her gaze scanned up and down the line of Rovers, taking in every detail of their dress, their bodies, their expressions. She leaned back to whisper something to Ravino, while giving wide-eyed Georgio's hand a reassuring squeeze.

All those weeks ago, it had been Lupita who told Celia what Kitty Kay's true self was. Not gray-robed reaper. Not even night-time phoenix.

Mother hen.

And as her gaze continued to assess the state of her family, she included Celia. Their gazes locked, and she lifted her hand to the sky.

"Sastimos futura," Celia whispered back. Her voice cracked. She'd never seen anyone so beautiful as the real Kitty Kay.

At the end of the line, separated from the rest, were Anya and Lilac.

Celia didn't realize that she'd lurched forward until Captain Andras grabbed her by the shoulders, delivered a swift punch to her side, and hauled her back. She blinked hard, her vision swimming. "Anny."

Celia tried to pull away from Andras's tight grip. "Anya!" Why wouldn't she look? What had they done to her? Lilac walked beside her, arm in arm, watching her intently, occasionally whispering a quick question or reassurance. Anya appeared thinner but not emaciated, so her motion sickness must have been more or less under control despite the constant travel. By all accounts, Anya appeared her usual self—composed, calm—but given the circumstances, it had to be forced. She'd amassed an anger so volcanic since they'd left the temple, it couldn't just vanish.

Captain Andras leaned over Celia. "I'd love if you made trouble."

"Screw you!" Celia yelled in the captain's face. "You think I care about your shit? You think you're bloody relevant to me?" Celia turned away. "Anya!"

Nero appeared but lingered back. "Why isn't she talking?" Celia yelled. "What didn't you tell me, Nero? Anny! *Dia*, look at me!"

She finally did. Infinite pools of deep blue found Celia. Those same eyes had soothed her for ten years, reminding her over and over again that life was more than absinthe and shisha and despair—that freedom and love could exist even alongside fear and sorrow.

"She was ever so loud," Diavala said. "Sowing discord among the other prisoners, trying to hatch plans under my nose. When I caught her trying to bribe an officer into delivering a message to you, I had to do *something*."

Anya held Celia's gaze as her lips moved for the first time. But no sound came out. She put both her hands to her throat.

And Anya *shrugged,* with a crooked smile tickling at the edges of her mouth. *No big deal, Cece. I'm fine.*

"You took her tongue." Celia was shocked that she wasn't more shocked. Hate, dormant for weeks, now flooded her, lighting every bit of her skin on fire, her body suddenly engorged with it. It was so big it smothered her shouts, closed her throat.

"No." Diavala laughed, as if the idea were absurd. "I couldn't risk having her starve. You'd be no good to me at all if she died." So the idea was absurd only because Diavala didn't want to lose her leverage, not because it would be cruel and inhumane. "I simply told her if she uttered one word, about anything, to anyone, I would force you to watch us kill one — or more — of your friends. We have a lot of spares. And she's been blessedly silent ever since. You two are a perfect package; threaten one with a knife, and the other bends in half trying to take the knife herself."

This new hate tasted as bitter as bile, as caustic as acid. Captain Andras pressed the dagger to Celia's throat when she tried to push forward again. Celia ignored it and held Anya's gaze.

Then Anya made a point of tracing the purple and blue bracelet around her wrist, reminding Celia to focus. Without words, she signaled the same thing to Celia that Kitty Kay had said to the plague doctor. *Don't do anything stupid.*

Celia reached out with her bound hands, trying to grab Anya's pinky. She filled in the silence with what she thought Anya would say. *You look like shit. Always such a mess.* Or maybe *Here I am, Cece. You're not alone.*

Nero was right. Anya was Celia's weakness.

And her strength.

"Together," Celia whispered, choking on the word. At least they would go together.

Then she felt a familiar heat on her wrist. Her heart jumped and stuttered, knowing what it meant without knowing what it meant. Careful not to move suddenly, she looked down, tilted her tied wrists, and saw . . .

Ink.

One tiny dot on her skin, like a blemish or mole, but one that had never been there before.

Her head wanted to snap back to Anya, but she forced it to move in a natural scan.

Toward the line of Mob members. Down the length, holding every set of tired, sunken eyes along the way. Past every guard. Panning over the fevered crowd, who reveled in getting an intimate glimpse of Profetan justice.

To Anya, whose forearms were tucked against her chest, hands hidden. Behind Celia, keeping back, Nero was so obviously trying not to be obvious about averting his gaze that it was obviously obvious that's exactly what he was doing.

So he was a trickster too, pretending to throw Remy's delivered quill nub out the window. She decided not to be too pissed that it had taken him this long to decide what to do with it.

The devil looked at the angel, and the angel stared back.

Celia listened to that one dot of ink from Anya, and heard *We fight, Cece. We use the ink against Diavala.*

She doesn't control it, we do.

Remember.

Celia pressed her thumb over the tiny splotch on her wrist. It couldn't deliver safety, couldn't save them from death or madness, but it held a sliver of power. It promised havoc and mayhem before the end.

Onstage, offstage, the Mob lived knowing that the show went on until the last curtain fell. Seer Ostra and Remy, Georgio and Ravino, Caspian and Sky—all the way down the line, they held her gaze, and she heard each of them say *You're not alone.* She met Marco's gaze across the distance, his stomping boots, his angry eyes: *This isn't the end.* She looked at the maskless plague doctor, who'd been dealt a blow and gracefully turned it into an attack: *Tilt your head a different way.* And Kitty Kay—not a gray reaper, not an orange phoenix, but a mother hen to them all, her true form finally shining through—*My family will never be the same after this. We have to make sure it's worth the loss.*

Celia went back to Anya: *We'll use her own ink against her.*

Finally Celia heard it all.

Diavala turned to her and loomed as the parade came to an end, saying, "So what do you think? Be Diavala and try to save them or continue to wallow in useless despair. That's your choice."

Celia twisted away from Captain Andras with such a violent jerk that she ended up on the ground. "I'll need my costume and mask mended. You'll have the devil you want."

She yelled at Diavala, kicked at her, pushed for undignified with everything she had. As Celia screamed and flailed, she remembered the Tower tarot card she'd pulled so long ago. Two poor idiots falling to their death, the cause of so much destruction.

We're about to be pushed out of the tower, Anny, but we're burning the place down first.

High Mistico Benedict put his hands out, appealing to the crowd for calm. As Captain Andras hauled Celia away, one of the onlookers lobbed a handful of mud in her direction. And, like a perfectly choreographed dance, the jeering began.

The Divine Returned, against Diavala in a bell jar.

Until they used the loopholes to flip everything right-side up.

Nine tails of a whip would strike her down, but Celia and Anya would die so spectacularly, they would take the devil with them, immortal or not.

CHAPTER 31

AS THEY MADE THEIR WAY THROUGH ASURA'S STREETS
toward the temple in the final leg of the journey, Celia thought
of their final inkling test. Over and over, her mind tossed it
around. Designed to weed out the worst, only the purest ten-
year-olds survived it.

Celia shouldn't have survived.

But what had always been her hidden shame might end up
serving her well.

The test itself was a well-guarded secret disguised with
vague language—sever ties to your old life, prove yourself
—otherwise, more parents would ignore the tattoos that told
them to donate their children.

At least Celia hoped they would.

Celia and Anya went through four years of training. Lupita
taught them about art—form and function and interpretation
—and about Profeta, this and that and whatever. Celia and
Anya had each other, linked pinkies since the beginning, and
that made sense even when little else did.

After four years to the day, all the six-year-olds-now-ten-
year-olds stood in a lavish room together in front of Ruler Vacilando herself.

The room didn't matter; even the nerves Celia had felt for the test disappeared. She had never seen Ruler Vacilando that close. She marveled at the intricacies of her tattoos, how they claimed her body bit by bit, no space wasted. She'd thought time would have dulled some to gray, but each one shouted in vivid black. *Beautiful,* she thought. *She's a canvas.* For the first time, the ink made some sense to her. It decorated and drew the eye. It told stories.

"Focus!" Anya hissed her favorite word, low and quiet, and stomped on Celia's toe for good measure.

The children pressed around her. Some trembled, some smiled, but no one knew what the final inkling test actually entailed. For a year Celia had tried to bribe, blackmail, or con the secret from the older inklings, but they hadn't survived that long by being gullible.

All she knew was that very few of them would pass and become full-fledged inklings. In the group that preceded them, only six out of a few dozen had moved on.

Ruler Vacilando began a short speech of congratulations: for making it so far in their training and for their dedication. "It is an honor and a privilege to become the Divine's messengers, and as such, she must know that her messengers are steadfast and reliable. Your tutors have already evaluated you on your skills. This test is a measure of character."

That made Celia squirm. Monroe, her perpetually muddy friend who dug in the garden and climbed trees whenever they weren't studying, mouthed *Fail* at her with a crooked smile.

Celia didn't know whether Monroe meant that they expected to fail or if they expected Celia to fail. Probably both.

Ruler Vacilando snapped her fingers, and the mistico began herding their charges—two by two—into adjacent rooms. "For expediency, you take the test together," Mistico Lupita said. "Follow me." Celia's heart soared, glad that Anya would be there to keep her focused.

They followed Mistico Lupita. No windows, no furniture, the room was only ten steps by ten steps. The three of them stood in silence long enough that Celia began to sweat, wondering if the test of character was standing forever without asking any questions or making any comments. If so, she'd surely fail.

The door opened, and the new High Mistico walked in with four guards and two couples. Far too many people for such a small space, but that's not what made her throat close.

Celia barely recognized her mothers: their clothing so fancy, their lips stained red in the style of the rich. They were far removed from the shopkeepers Celia had known. But their smiles were the same: glowing, proud of her.

Ridiculous, a vicious voice in her head whispered.

Those smiles were sharp stabs in her gut. Despite how badly Celia wanted to scream at them, she'd learned to follow Anya's cues. She pushed the urge way down.

The other couple must have been Anya's parents. She shared her father's dark hair and blue eyes, her mother's keen calculation as she appraised the situation.

Everything that happened next flooded together.

Another speech, this time from High Mistico Benedict, centering around the people who'd done their duty and served Profeta by giving their children away. *Ridiculous, ridiculous.* Twin smiles from people she'd loved, who'd pushed her into four years of cold stone, lonely nights, and constant fear. She tried calling up the good times—a cuddle, a laugh—but they'd been harassed out of her, tainted by all that had come after.

Celia realized, with more sharp stabs, that she hated them. She hated their calm smiles and bowed heads. She hated that they didn't push their way to her and scoop her up. *Come to me and scoop me up!*

They loved her, but they loved something else more.

When Mistico Lupita produced a dagger two handspans long, the room tightened.

When she demonstrated how to use it, Celia stopped breathing. A precise, textbook step one and step two, similar to the way Lupita might point out how to use contoured lines to add depth to a picture.

The gilded handle felt warm in Celia's hand, as if it belonged there.

High Mistico Benedict leaned against the wall, picking at his fingernails. Overseeing each test was such a chore. "Kill the people who abandoned you, or die yourself," he said simply.

The room erupted, most of the noise coming from Anya's father. The guards, anonymous, nameless, forced their parents to their knees. Celia's mothers didn't smile anymore, but neither did they fight.

None of it made sense.

Celia looked at Anya, who stared at the dagger in her own hand as if she didn't know what it was, for the first time her thoughts written in a language Celia didn't understand. They'd both assumed that if you failed the test, you'd be released from duty to Profeta, not from *life*. Anya had wanted to fail on purpose.

No wonder the older inklings wouldn't talk about it — their payment for breathing had been to force their family to stop.

"Make your choice," Lupita said. "Kill or die."

"This is outrageous," Anya's father shouted. "We gave our beloved—"

"Do it, Celia," Mama said. Her smile had returned, fringed with tears. She held Mother's hand. "You're part of a bigger story."

Celia trembled like a sapling in a storm. Had they always spoken in code? She understood Anya's father far better. His shouts rang loud, giving words to everything Celia felt. *Deception, crooked, torture, don't make them . . .*

Don't make them.

She stared at her mothers' red lips, so out of place, and thought, *Red suits them.* She tightened her grip on the handle, a jewel on the hilt digging into her palm.

Kill them, or die.

Celia didn't want to die.

"Don't make them!"

"Do it, Celia."

She turned her heart to stone. She blocked out Anya's father and all the sense he made.

Celia made her choice: *Kill. Live.*

It was on her mothers' red lips; they wanted her to pass the test, to live, even at the expense of their own lives.

Maybe this, finally, would fill the gap inside her.

She lifted the dagger to her mama's neck. All it would take was one slash to either side of her throat. Then two more on her mother's. Even a life at the temple was better than no life at all, she reasoned. She could ink people with messages all day, cuddle up with Anya every night. Anya could correct her lines and she could make Anya laugh and they could go on like that, making sense as they always did.

Anya, who was watching her.

When Celia hesitated, her mama panicked. "Come on, darling. It's okay. Be brave."

This was the first time Anya had ever looked to Celia for guidance. Anya mirrored Celia's movement and placed her dagger at her father's throat. She shook so hard it was a miracle she didn't slice his neck up like a turnip for stew. He'd stopped shouting, his tearful eyes pointed up at his child.

But he wasn't crying for *his* neck.

In order for that life Celia wanted, Anya would have to kill too.

Celia imagined blood staining the hand that had held hers

for four years, the pinky that had wrapped around hers the first day. What would happen to those calm, infinite dark blue eyes? Would the spark in them dim or flicker out? Celia loved them exactly as they were.

The world entirely changes when you have an audience made up of someone you love. When you care for their soul more than your own.

She understood her mothers then. For the briefest of moments she understood what it was like to love something so absolutely.

I can do this, but you can't, Anny.

You can't.

A calm settled over Celia as she dropped the dagger. Her tears fell silently, a betrayal from her eyes. "Forget this. Let's go together."

Celia's mothers fully panicked, Anya's father joining them as they shouted. Seemed that everyone, suddenly and fiercely, wanted to die in that room.

Anya nodded, her own silent tears falling. Instead of daggers in their hands, they found each other's pinkies.

High Mistico Benedict left to supervise the next test. Mistico Lupita led them back out to the main room, shutting the door on their parents' ongoing exclamations.

The gilded room was full again with the children Celia had known for four years. It was clear which choice most had made behind their own closed doors. There was so much red: hands, eyes, hearts.

Monroe, smaller than even small Celia, had more than dirt on their face now. A smear of crimson painted their skin, as if they'd tried to rub what they'd seen and done from their eyes. They looked at Celia but didn't see her. They looked at their hands. And saw them. And cried.

They were different tears from Celia's and Anya's: an internal horror versus resigned fear. Though both manifested in salty water, theirs may as well have been made of acid.

Only a few would fail and die with Celia and Anya. Yusef wept silently. Dante was as aloof as ever, rankling Celia. Not even his own impending death could phase him?

Anya squeezed her pinky and, absurdly, laughed.

That's when Celia knew she'd made the right choice. If Anya looked like Monroe, like Cleo, like all the others stained with red, if she couldn't laugh in the face of this stupid place, that would have been a tragedy.

But when everyone was assembled again, the mistico and their daggers didn't move toward Celia, Anya, Yusef, or Dante. Their robed forms surrounded the red, wailing ones. Monroe's face disappeared behind black fabric. Shrieks rose up.

Ruler Vacilando congratulated the graduating class. With each word, a shout was silenced, either from the circle of frightened, bloodstained children or from behind the closed doors.

Celia didn't understand what was happening. The calm that had fallen over her when she dropped the dagger transformed into something big and hot and bursting. Anya pressed her forehead against hers and they squeezed their eyes shut, clamping their hands over each other's ears.

If Celia could wind the spool of her life back to the exact moment when she broke, it wouldn't be when her mothers gave her away or the years of soul-crushing punishments. Or even the instant she realized she was willing to kill her own mothers.

It would be this moment: Anya's hands over her ears, eyes shut tight, that hot, bursting thing trying so hard to get out.

Is everything a lie?

What devil do we serve?

The temple wanted the weakest servants, not the ones who might fight. The apprentices who slit the throats of their families, the ones who chose to keep breathing, *they* were the ones who failed.

No family member left the temple alive on graduation day, their usefulness fully spent. Closing the circle, tying up loose ends.

The test was presented as simple black and white, like ink on pale skin: Are you strong enough to fully devote yourself?

Yes? You'll kill?

Then you're not weak enough to serve. Diavala wanted sheep for her herd: docile, pliable, unaggressive.

Celia would have killed. She should have died for it.

And without Anya, that's how it would have gone.

Celia was a murderer, like Monroe, like Cleo, like all those others, in thought if not in deed. But she'd found a loophole in her love for Anya and survived when she shouldn't have.

She'd lived with that knowledge for six long years. It had eaten away at her core. It had scarred worse than any dagger cut. But now, she realized, it would be her strength.

Playing Diavala onstage wouldn't be an issue. Profeta had made sure of that.

CHAPTER 32

They dumped Celia in her favorite stark cell: the one with the rat hole in the corner so furry nighttime visitors made sure you were too paranoid to sleep. The dungeon in the temple was a short series of small rooms. Solitary confinement before the true punishment of water torture or slashes, so the rogue inkling had time to adequately dread.

There weren't enough cells to hold so many people individually. Celia was placed with Marco and Seer Ostra.

Seer sat on the ground and patted the space beside her, inviting Celia to sit and fall into her bosom, as if Celia were six instead of sixteen. "I'm glad the cards kept this from me," she said. No accusation in her rumbly voice, only acceptance.

Celia's umbrella of *Us* had been dozens strong since the beginning.

We can do it, Anya had inked earlier. *We'll end this nightmare.* She'd spent the last day of travel wearing her quill nub down, telling everyone with disappearing messages what she and Celia would try to do onstage. They hadn't explicitly asked for help, but Celia discovered *Us* was funny like that—they hadn't needed to ask.

Seer nodded, as if hearing Celia's thoughts. "At least we'll do some damage before we meet the afterlife." And a slow smile curled over her face, as though she couldn't wait to get started.

Turned out, revenge red had spread like Marco's fire through the rest of the Mob.

They had an impossible audience. An immortal adversary. Even if they won and were able to convert the people into seeing the ink as manipulation instead of something divine, even if they took down Profeta, even if Celia survived the flogging, Diavala could still exact a desperate revenge through the Touch.

But they would perform one more spectacular show.

The Rabble Mob of Minos would be remembered.

When the door of the cell swung open later that day, Celia tried to blink the hallucination away. When Dante didn't disappear, instinct made her grab the closest person, Marco, and push him out the door. "Get him out of here. Run!"

Off balance, Marco slammed into Dante's chest. Dante put steadying hands on Marco's shoulders, but stared around him at Celia. As if he didn't recognize her.

Maybe he didn't.

Marco sidestepped the stranger he'd barreled into, flushing wildly, and peeked into the hall. He backed away, hands up, as long-robed mistico stepped forward, flanking Dante on all sides like wraiths, barring the hallway completely. Their energy was hard to ignore. It thrummed from their robes down to the floor and touched Celia's bare feet, charring like lightning. Excitement, barely suppressed. They knew the Mob was somehow linked to the prophetic tattoo on Ruler Vacilando's body.

Rhythmic popping drew Celia's gaze; Nero stood right beside High Mistico Benedict at the back of the group, cracking his knuckles, not looking too pleased with his new assignment. Damn. She'd been stuck in close confines with him for so long she'd forgotten how big he was. With the other mistico there for scale, even extra-tall Benedict, Nero looked like an utterly different species.

"Welcome back, Inkling Sand." Despite Dante's wooden voice, he didn't let go of Celia's eyes. It wasn't coincidence that led him to be the one opening the door, but what was it? How much did he know of what was going on? As Celia stared at him, trying to figure it out, an infuriating prickle started up behind her eyes. *I can't believe I actually missed you, you asshole.*

The corner of Dante's mouth twitched—as if he knew exactly what she was thinking. "Tomorrow night, you and the Rabble Mob of Minos will be publicly executed."

Without any warning, Marco punched him in the stomach.

Not much of a punch, considering that Marco was half starved and weak, but Dante staggered back a step. Recovering, Dante shook his head, his gaze now locked on Marco. "Be smart. Fighting like *that* won't work." It was whispered and subtle, too soft for the mistico to hear.

Something passed between Dante and Marco—a magical,

instantaneous shift when they realized they were on the same side — and Celia was surprised that the aftershock didn't rumble through all the cells and down the hallway, knocking everyone over. Anya had contacted more people than Celia had assumed, and Celia was infinitely relieved. She didn't want to die with her friends believing she was evil.

It disoriented Celia, seeing Dante and Marco together. Both so handsome it was barely fair to the rest of the world (despite one's swollen nose). Practical Dante to passionate Marco. As they appraised each other, they seemed to notice something of the same thing.

Dante exhaled a long breath and shook himself off. He glanced at Celia again, this time with a quizzical eye, before stepping back, deferring authority to a few chattering mistico. He'd volunteered himself as bait. A no one tasked with opening the door and being the first body to meet danger if the trouble-makers inside had any fight left in them.

High Mistico Benedict — Diavala — pointed at Seer Ostra. "You first."

"Her first, what?" Celia pressed herself in front to shield Seer, as if they couldn't go right through her.

"Just to get cleaned up," one of the mistico said, holding out a gallant hand to her. Seer moved into the hallway and waited patiently while Diavala offered instructions on how she wanted Seer presented. Seer left with her makeover crew of mistico, asking a very good question in her sloth way: "What . . . do you know . . . of *style*?"

None of the remaining mistico wanted to touch Celia or Marco. They talked among one another, Diavala interjecting her opinions as they examined the pair from top to toe, moaning about the work involved in getting them costumed and presentable for their necessary public death. Seemed that they were the last cell because they were the most work.

Dante raked his gaze over Celia in an all-too-familiar way, taking inventory of her flaws. Her face flushed, and she thought perhaps he deserved another punch to the gut. How great would he look after a month in a prison carriage?

Probably still great. Asshole.

"Sounds like you have something spectacular planned," Dante murmured, so low that Celia made out the words only because she read them on his lips. He pressed his hand to his forearm significantly, indicating the spot where Anya must have messaged him with heretical disappearing ink.

It hit her then, what a big deal it was for Dante to even be there, considering the magnitude of what was going on. Survivalism was Dante's signature style. He never did anything to stand out, neither good nor bad, but walked a line as close to invisible as possible. Even if all he could offer was a familiar face, a word of encouragement, and some confused frowns, the fact that Dante was risking his carefully crafted image and associating himself with their catastrophe made those infuriating eye prickles come back.

She nodded to Dante—hating the way her gut twisted when she thought about the plan—and tried to give him a devious smile. "So spectacular," she whispered. *So damning. So terrible. So necessary.*

Finally, a pair of mistico settled on Marco, who cleared his throat before leaving the cell, his hand grazing Dante's hip as he passed, as if in apology.

Before Celia lost the opportunity, her thoughts scrambled as she tried to grasp something, anything, that she wanted to pass on to one of the only friends who might survive this. The crowd was thinning too fast.

"High Mistico Benedict? Do you remember Halcyon Ronnea of Wisteria Township?" Celia's words rushed together in a near-unintelligible torrent.

"I don't." Diavala's expression didn't even flicker as she gestured to the two remaining mistico to collect her.

But Celia set her jaw and tried to look as if she knew a million things Diavala had overlooked. "You should take better care of your loose ends. Halcyon knows your life from the inside out: every success and every failure of the past thousand years. Every secret. Every weakness and flaw."

Careful not to look at Dante, Celia willed him to take note of Halcyon's name. They'd paid too dearly for it to evaporate into nothing, unused and abandoned. She needed to know that even if they failed that night and Diavala reigned, there was still hope.

High Mistico Benedict's gaze turned steely even as he smiled. "Interesting. If you feel this *Halcyon* is your salvation, it's too bad for you he isn't here."

It took a moment before Celia registered what Diavala had said.

He.

Without a tenor guiding the way, *they* was always the proper address. There was no question that Diavala remembered who Halcyon was.

But she was right: Halcyon wasn't there, so Celia's false posturing evaporated into nothing. Still, *Remember that name, Dante. Tell Lupita, tell Zuni; if this doesn't work, tell anyone who survives.*

Diavala leveled her gaze at Celia, and something softened. "Enough of the past, Celia. Our final dance is all about the future. And here we go."

The mistico herded Celia out of the cell and led her away, and she basked in the resurgent warmth in her veins, the flush of her cheeks, the pounding of her heart.

She loved that Nero nudged her shoulder with his elbow as he fell in line with her—as if they were solid allies. He might not live under the umbrella of *Us* with them, but perhaps his massive meat-cleaver hands held it over their heads. He'd given Anya a quill and she'd gotten her voice back, so she could tell Celia exactly what she needed to hear.

Even if it was horrible. Final. Gruesome.

Celia loved that when she glanced back, Dante nodded and held her eyes. A silent promise. *I'll remember the name.*

The thing she loved most was that all of it together meant she still had some hope.

CHAPTER 33

CELIA HADN'T BEEN TO THE TEMPLE'S MAIN SQUARE IN SO long, she expected it to look foreign, but the same familiar wet cobblestones, torches, and awnings greeted her. The same six-eyed stone statue loomed over it all.

Only one thing differed: on the high, wide platform in front of the main temple doors stood the devil's bell jar. Shiny and clean, but with the same ominous hairline cracks, it was recognizable to anyone who'd seen or heard of their show.

The guards lifted the heavy dome and threw her under it, shuddering when her forked tail grazed a sleeve, blanching when she turned her heavy-browed gaze up at them. On her hands and knees, breathing heavily, Celia waited until they left. Until it was she alone, a cleaned-up devil in a bell jar.

Flogging day for the new Diavala. A Return to the mortal realm for the omniscient Divine.

Celia barked out a laugh, then stood and took out her frustration and rage on the glass. Since she'd first set foot in the temple ten years ago, it had been Diavala's show; Celia had always been a prop. She harnessed every feeling of impotence and misery she'd ever had and pounded against the bell jar, shrieking and screaming for good measure.

The scurrying inklings slowed to watch the devil rage. Celia screamed nonsense at all of them. Possession wasn't as loud and obnoxious as Celia made it look—much more terrifying in its subtlety—but they were lucky enough not to know that.

As the first cracks of morning light began sneaking into the square, the scurrying became more pronounced. Still, the gates remained closed and Celia remained alone on that stage. Unprecedented, to have Saturday worship in the evening, but it was an unprecedented Saturday. The curtain wouldn't rise until nightfall.

In the late afternoon, inklings began lining the sides of the square in rows two or three bodies deep. Dante positioned himself much closer to the stage than he normally did. The space around him seemed emptier without Celia and Anya with him. Smartly, he avoided her gaze. Wallis stood with the other fleas, holding their crossed fingers to their chest and staring at her with none of the same sense of self-preservation as Dante.

Celia stumbled when she saw Zuni standing sentry near the main gates. The crypts were hidden at the opposite side of the temple, but perhaps Anya had asked her to look out for Lupita, help her. Lupita would be too stubborn to stay away, but she just might break from her mourning. Celia pressed her clawed hand to the glass. *I found so many feathers for you, Zuni. So many.*

At least triple the number of guards went to their stations, and peppered among them were the officers who'd escorted the Mob from Malidora. Nero would come out only with High

Mistico Benedict—and Celia wondered briefly how he'd feel when he realized he'd actually been promoted to the Divine's bodyguard.

Captain Andras had become Celia's new shadow, standing beside the bell jar. The whip tucked into her belt flicked its nine tails with every movement, ready to find Celia's back. She smiled with a lot of teeth whenever Celia looked over at her or at the whip on her hip.

Emerging from behind thick doors, Ruler Vacilando assumed her place at her personal balcony, all of her ink on display, including the fresh one prophesizing this event.

"You think the ink staining your body marks you as important," Celia muttered to her, "but you've been used your whole life, and you don't even see it." Ruler Vacilando smiled down at her as if she'd heard, nudging her shoulder in Celia's direction to remind her of the mark there that had heralded this event. Celia hissed, "You're embarrassing yourself."

Celia spent her last day isolated in a swarm. Her gaze found Dante's, Wallis's, and Zuni's, over and over, the only friendly faces among hundreds.

Workers lit the torches as the sun went down.

The stone steps leading to the temple became the path toward the new Rover field. The gates opened for the show. Instead of ticket sellers collecting coin and handing out playbills on their stilts, a gaggle of guards and officers welcomed everyone.

Still, a show.

Lupita was one of the first inside. She groped her way through the crowd, pushing people out of her way, until Zuni took her arm. Lupita wore no eye scarf, either because she'd forgotten or because she wanted to unnerve. Celia leaned toward believing the latter.

No procession of morose lemmings existed that night. The people barreled in, shoving and jostling to get to the front as quickly as possible while still remaining respectful enough not to get kicked out for overexuberance.

It took only half an hour for the square to fill. They packed in and squished together, smaller people on the shoulders of bigger ones. It wouldn't be the regular Saturday worship circulation of bodies as they went to the front to speak with the mistico and then made room for others: tonight the ones lucky enough to get in would stay.

The mistico jostled among themselves too, trying to be close to the wonder that was about to happen.

Perhaps they expected the Divine to float down from the clouds to the stage after the executions. Perhaps they thought that the six-eyed stone statue would break free of its moorings and take a bow. Whatever they believed, they knew the Rabble Mob of Minos had something to do with the Return. Something glorious would happen.

The gates closed, locking out the unlucky thousands who still graced the 180 stone steps. From above, the stream of people must have looked like a long, curled tongue licking its way from the mouth of Asura to the delicious treat at the temple.

Everyone stared at Celia, alone onstage under her bell jar.

Anya, still somewhere backstage with the rest of the Mob, waiting to be ushered in for their part in the script, inked one last clandestine message to Celia: *No matter what happens*—if they failed and the whip came down, if they'd miscalculated again and Celia was flogged as Diavala, if everyone died with her because their terrible, wonderful plan didn't work—*remember I'm holding your hand, Cece.*

Celia inhaled. She would be brave. She wasn't alone.

"I'm ready," she whispered.

The large stone doors leading into the temple creaked open slowly, and every set of lungs in that square stuttered to a stop. Framed in the doorway stood High Mistico Benedict. So tall, his features angular and sharp, with a deep blue robe on instead of the usual black one, he was the perfect figure to command attention. Immaculately put together, back straight, knowing smile. He'd personally orchestrated and overseen it all—of anyone in that square, he knew the most about what the night might bring. He took only two steps before one of the middling mistico fainted. Commotion in the front row of the crowd told Celia that the mistico wasn't the only one.

"Are you kidding me?" Celia muttered.

High Mistico Benedict stepped forward. Alone, so no one could deny who was in charge. Arms wide, so everyone saw a greeting, a welcoming hug. That in itself was extraordinary—a smile on a mistico, a posture of warmth and happiness—and already people reacted with an underwater roar. Nero, newly promoted bodyguard to the High Mistico, stayed well back so as not to intrude in the moment. Cracking his knuckles, his gaze swiveled as if he didn't recognize the world anymore. It seemed to elude him how he'd even gotten there.

As Diavala passed the bell jar, she tilted her head to the right, a slight gesture of acknowledgment to the devil trapped inside. *Hear that, Inkling? Everyone is so excited to meet me.*

To meet *us*, she meant.

It had always been between them.

Oh, and they *were* excited. Celia heard it clearly, a rising wave of sound. If she'd taken all the sound ever made inside the temple walls — conversations, whispers, even the screams of the Touch — and wrapped them up together, even centuries of sound wouldn't compete with this.

Diavala walked to the front of the stage, shushing the incessant roar with uplifted arms. With a commanding voice that flowed to all corners of the square, she set the stage: explaining how a trickster, disguised as an innocent inkling, had escaped the temple with the intention of spreading lies and vice throughout Illinia.

Celia began pacing. Her gait had a slight limp because her knee bothered her from an earlier baton hit, but maybe the people would wonder if it bent the wrong way, like a goat's. Her hands flew around, making unheard exclamations. Her curled horns shimmered with wetness, as if she'd crawled out of a swamp. Her forked tail swished behind her with her steps.

Every once in a while, unpredictable and sudden, she'd slam her hands on the glass, raging against her prison. *Hideous*, she wanted them to say. *She belongs there*, she needed them to think.

For now.

So far, Diavala was doing everything Anya had predicted— providing backstory, setting up the hero, the villain. The show was unfolding as planned.

Soon would come the side characters, the prelude to the main event of the reveal, the flogging, the ultimate triumph.

With perfect dramatic timing, the main temple doors creaked open again. One by one, the members of the Rabble Mob were led out.

The alluring plague doctor was first, the one with the roguish smile and secrets. He'd always begun the show by offering temptation and ended it by passing judgment. Many in the crowd had danced with him, been held in his arms. It had been a rightness and a wrongness at the same time; maybe they'd felt guilty for liking it so much, as Celia had. He stood onstage, legs spread apart, gloved hands clasped in front of him, sweeping his gaze from one side of the crowd to the other, judging them again with a wide, rakish smile on his face.

Despite where he now stood, flanked by two guards and a mistico holding a dagger, Celia knew that most of the crowd would still jump at the chance to dance with him. Those arms would give them the darkness they craved.

He met her gaze—mask to mask—and she remembered

their first dance. They'd started as devil and plague doctor, had made it to Celia and Griffin, and, closing the circle, they were the devil and the smiling plague doctor again.

He stepped forward and bowed twice: once to the audience, and a deeper, longer, fuller bow to the creature under a bell jar. *One more dance, devil.*

The others followed the plague doctor's lead as High Mistico Benedict introduced them—by stage name so they were instantly recognizable—each bowing with their own signature flair. Kitty Kay, in her phoenix orange dress, artfully went up on her toes and reached her hands to the sky, her hair an immaculate red waterfall with one gray streak, looking as if she were off to a regal ball rather than an execution. She didn't bow when she came back to the ground; she nodded to the audience, to Celia, and then put her hand on her heart.

The High Mistico used terms like desertion, aiding and abetting, heresy, and willfully spreading heterodoxy, making it all sound official enough. The subtle subversions the Mob had always put into their shows were twisted into catastrophic proof of dissent.

Assembling in a line at the edge of their new stage, the troupe looked unbothered and perfect, their costumes mended, their masks in place. Despite the guards and mistico muscling them around, they chatted and even laughed. Grisilda and Fawn began practicing some vocal exercises, echoing each other's gibberish scales. Each new member joining them in that line was greeted with hugs and smiles even as High Mistico Benedict named their crimes, justified each execution. Such good players, even Celia couldn't tell whether their casual calm was forced or true.

Anya had guessed that Diavala would build up to the reveal; she'd been waiting too long not to savor this moment to its fullest. Like Tanza, feeding her insatiable ego.

As the Mob was put into position, Celia continued to flail around, as if possessed, under the bell jar. She stole effects from every show she'd ever done: dancing, turning, writing on the glass in weeping black paint. Diavala had even provided her with colored glitter to throw around like a fool. Nothing too absurd for the devil under the bell jar. No commands came from the audience, but Celia didn't need them. Most knew of their show, had already bought into it.

Then the doors to the temple creaked shut behind Marco and Tanith in their sharp black-and-red fire-master suits. Marco glared as he stomped to the front, ready for battle.

Celia's gaze flew to those heavy double doors, not understanding. The audience was assembled, the devil was under the bell jar, the Mob were all onstage, Diavala was finishing off the list of crimes.

Everyone was in position—except Anya.

Diavala came close enough to the bell jar so that no one else could overhear, watching Celia's reaction with undisclosed glee. "Remember, she can live if you play along. This is a gesture of my goodwill."

All those days ago, Nero had called it. Celia had screamed

her weakness and Diavala had listened. She'd split them up and taken a hostage, another fail-safe against any inkling shenanigans onstage.

"Damn it, I hate youuuuuu!" Celia wailed at Diavala, weaving it into her performance.

Diavala acknowledged Celia's rage with a wicked smile.

Celia slapped her palms against the glass as Diavala walked back to the front of the stage.

Another jab on her arm. In her cheater's mirrors, ink bloomed and then disappeared quickly. *Diavala wants you to behave.* And Celia swore she could *hear* Anya hiss it from behind those closed doors.

Don't, Anya inked, and then, irritatingly, dotted a string of exclamation points so Celia didn't misunderstand her. Anya might not have been onstage with them, but that didn't mean she couldn't communicate.

This was it. What they'd intended to do in Malidora, they would do now.

And then, if that wasn't enough, they'd do a little bit more.

Diavala thought she'd bested them, but they'd experimented with her ink in earnest. All those orders for the Mob they'd completed, the trip into Malidora, their act every night. By now they knew every limit and could have mapped out the boundaries like expert cartographers. Being separated like this made the night harder for them, but not impossible.

Not at all.

Celia took a deep breath and took herself back to their first show. Unlike that first night, however, she reached toward pandemonium on purpose.

Her transformation changed abruptly: from angry devil to trapped innocent in a blink.

Celia made herself look small and spent. Her shoulders rocked with exaggerated sobs. She wrote the word—*Why?*—on the glass with her paintbrush. She made deliberate eye contact with the people in the front rows to get them to see her as broken and lost. One couple kept drawing her gaze. Fallan and Pia, holding hands. Fallan's souvenir ribbon was again tied in his hair, with Pia holding its twin in her free hand. Celia took it as a sign of loyalty to the Mob, as if they hadn't made up their minds yet, and bolstered, she performed directly for them.

I may have horns, but do you see the cruelty in this?

The Rabble Mob whispered to themselves now, robust acting cranked up even more, pretending to be confused at the switch. The guards behind each Mob member had to duck wildly gesturing arms. Captain Andras tapped her baton on the glass with angry code—*whatever you're trying to provoke, devil, stop it.*

Celia didn't know how well it was working, but hundreds of faces processed the message.

Diavala reacted to the change with grace disguising her anger. The devil couldn't beg for mercy. The Mob couldn't change the show—their own execution. Celia's gaze didn't move from Diavala, but her insides reached toward the Mob at the side of the stage.

She put a clawed hand over her heart. The signal for pandemonium.

Please, let this work.

INTERLUDE

A dimmed stage. A devil trapped behind glass.

She stole the Divine ink from the temple that bore her. She ran away with it in her veins and conned her way onto a stage. The Devil in the Bell Jar was never a show, but Diavala herself deceiving them and leading them astray. Thankfully, she was caught before a wildfire of chaos consumed the land and they turned away from their beloved Divine.

The devil does ridiculous things under its glass prison. Every gyration of its body is grotesque and ugly. Many in the crowd know how the famed Mob show ends: a triumph of good over evil. They are a part of the good, and tonight will be no different. They always win.

They wait with bated breath to see how this long chapter will end.

Then the devil begins weeping. Pleading with her whole body for them to end her torment.

Tentacles of swirling gray fog spread through the crowd, reaching, caressing them with doubt.

But there should be no doubt. She is Diavala herself —a trickster, a thief—they can't sympathize with her!

They cast covert glances around them, wondering if they're the only ones feeling strange. They look to Ruler Vacilando for cues on how to respond, but she ignores them, intent on the show in front of her. Her hand flutters to her shoulder, absently stroking her Divine ink.

It seems wrong, though, so wrong all of a sudden, that they've broken such a thing. It may be ghastly, but something tugs and roils inside them. They don't want to believe they were part of what put it there. Part of its humiliation.

A few begin to make their way toward the stage. One giant—who, if they thought to ask what hid under his officer's shirt, would show them a tattooed salamander—abandons his post and is the first to move to the front.

Then a blinding flash of purple and blue flames erupts from the stage, startling them, making them jump back. They hadn't expected the rest of the Mob to be part of this. They'd thought the night was about the Devil in the Bell Jar, the final act in a show that began in the Asuran Rover field months ago. They shield their eyes against the unexpected newness of it. They squint toward the stage, waiting for the image to re-form. Their excitement has transformed to nervous anticipation, for whatever is onstage now will be novel. Something deliciously fresh for them to react to.

When the purple and blue flames die down, the devil is gone.

Someone stands there, the beastly mask at her feet. She doesn't look exceptional. Dark hair, dark eyes, pale skin. So small and slight, she seems closer to child than adult, despite how those dark eyes flash with feeling. She looks more frightened than frightening, far from the Diavala they'd imagined. Just a person in a costume.

The people would murmur to one another if they could breathe. Music begins. At first it's nothing more than a low hum, and they think it's their blood singing in their veins. As the volume increases, they realize it's the Mob itself, singing a woeful lament. The volume rises until it's caressing every corner of the temple, perhaps all of Illinia.

How she weeps and tries to escape her prison. Hands on the glass, pushing, pleading.

How beautiful and fragile she looks. How broken.

With her paintbrush—the one she'd used to mark her prison before—she writes *Help me*. The ink drips down the glass like tears.

The Mob sings a moan set to music.

It's beautiful. And so sad.

When a few of the inklings add their voices to the lament, more doubt blooms. A young, raven-haired inkling near the stage leads—no, too young to be an inkling yet, an apprentice—their voice powerful and strong even as they dart nervous glances to the light-eyed High Mistico.

Something stirs among the mistico then, because they see something similar to the final inkling test. A test of loyalty, where a choice must be made.

They look to one another, to the heavens, to their High Mistico. Could this be their test? Perhaps this has all been orchestrated to determine if they are kind and compassionate, if they are merciful and benevolent.

If, now that their Divine is about to manifest for them, they are worthy of her.

What does the Divine want them to do?

The Rabble Mob's act has always included the crowd. Somewhere here is a call to action. They'd all heard stories of a show, once, where the people freed the devil because they'd seen something different.

Maybe this was the difference, right here in front of them.

Their High Mistico still hasn't moved to stop the singing, nor signaled for execution.

A few mistico begin moving forward, as if they have no control over their limbs. The Divine is testing them, and they won't fail her. They believe in her benevolence, and they need to prove it.

The person with the hidden salamander is beside the bell jar, speaking to the one trapped behind glass.

The crowd stirs. More people begin moving. Mob mentality takes over, and then it's no longer about whether they should free her or not, but about who will be the one to do it. They fight for the honor of setting things right, jostling one another. They act on a base human impulse that's impossible to rationalize.

A couple steps forward, one of them raising a blue and purple ribbon above her head like a banner. They will right the wrong. They will free her.

And the one trapped behind glass smiles like the sun. Yes, come to me! We're on the same side! She turns her gaze to the High Mistico and nods at the victory.

He is in no hurry. He doesn't gesture the mistico back or ask Ruler Vacilando to do anything. In fact, when guards grab two members of the Mob, he commands them to stand back.

This fuels the people and the mistico both. He is the leader for this epic day, and he does not stop them.

They made the right choice.

Then everyone goes still.

But every heartbeat speeds up.

A black spiral has appeared on the collarbone of the little thing trapped behind glass. A message in ink.

She looks down at it, awash with new despair. Then she spins around and around in circles, obeying the order.

Moments before, they'd been wholly committed to freeing her, convinced that their Divine wanted them to. The Mob's chorus had urged them on. Inkling voices complimented the show. Ruler Vacilando had only bowed her head in reverence. The High Mistico who'd captured her and brought her to face justice hadn't interceded.

But . . . the ink. What did it mean?

She winces against pain and lifts her shirt, showing her midriff. A black handprint. She presses her hand to the glass at precisely the same angle, doing what she's told.

The person with the salamander on his stomach has stepped back. His gaze swivels away from her and toward the crowd. His huge arm sweeps to them. *Come!* He gestures to the crowd. *Come!* He begs the mistico.

People move their hands to their bodies, touching similar inked commands that they'd accepted and answered.

That they believe in. That they will never doubt.

They know the truth then: if the Divine commands the one trapped, she's supposed to be trapped. The Divine sees all, knows all, and the ink is her way of speaking.

They'd almost made a terrible mistake and failed her test.

The near heresy around them is tangible. It's frightening and exciting to be a part of something so big. Hundreds of people are entirely made of silence and hesitation. Now, no one wants to be the first to move.

They may well be frozen there forever.

A blue and purple ribbon flutters free, swirling in the air with a gust of breeze before settling at the base of the glass dome near the devil's feet. The unmasked devil stares at it.

The High Mistico is onstage again, facing the people, his back to the bell jar. He says, "The devil and her followers still had one trick up their sleeves, trying to lure you into disavowing the ink. I am glad, my people, you're not so easily fooled. Your faith is your greatest strength."

Ruler Vacilando speaks. "Our faith holds true."

Yes, they think. Our faith is strong. The ink is truth. Thank you for saving us from our own folly.

Inktrava sel Immorti. They will always listen to the ink.

And they wait for the Divine to reward their loyalty with her presence.

CHAPTER 34

IT LOOKED LIKE FAILURE.

On the pretense of adjusting her dress, Celia smeared paint to hide the marks on her collarbone and her stomach so no one noticed when they disappeared. Anya had chosen simple designs and visible parts of the body, but as Celia had discovered in Malidora, it was difficult to hold them in place for long. The Mob had sung extra loud, seamlessly working around Anya's unexpected absence, so Anya had known when to ink them.

A loosed ribbon at the base of the bell jar fluttered in Celia's peripheral vision, flashing periwinkle then plum and back again, taunting and teasing her. It looked like failure, but there was always another side, another way to tilt your head.

They'd gotten the crowd to pity her, as planned. They'd gotten the mistico to see something different than a devil under a bell jar, as planned. They were going to free her. Celia and the Mob had cast themselves in the light of good.

Then, the ink.

The people hadn't bought the story Celia and Anya had tried to sell. The people would always believe the ink was pure. Ruler Vacilando had stood and bent herself in half, her forehead on the low wooden banister of her balcony. She may have been perched up high as overseer, but her pose only proved who served whom.

It had been easy to convince the Mob to see the ink in a different way because they saw everything in a different way; the rest of Illinia was a wholly different story. Believers would always be believers. Salamanders would always become significant to those who needed a salamander. Smoke and mirrors couldn't hide the fact that people saw what they wanted to see. How could she and Anya have ever thought to compete with rapture? If they'd tried this in Malidora, they would have surely failed.

As Celia watched the worshipers, their love and reverence shining, a familiar ache rose in her throat. Their Divine was such a lovely thing: a spirit of caring, an invisible hand cupping their cheek. Their mistico were solid pillars upholding a rich, sacred tradition. Their ink was sacred art and substance. If Celia hadn't come to the temple and seen the inner workings, poked around for answers, and gotten disillusioned over the span of years, she knew she'd have been one of them. They weren't stupid or gullible, they knew only the outward face of something she'd seen the putrid guts of. Sometimes she pitied them. More times, she envied them.

Diavala addressed the crowd, then turned to Celia and spoke. Though her words were mostly muted, Celia caught the general idea. *See the masses behind me; they are mine. See how they love the ink. They will never turn away from it. See it, Inkling, how little power you've ever had.*

The ink would always win.

They'd hoped this first part would be enough to illuminate the ink's corruption and make people see the truth. But they'd suspected it wouldn't.

Yes, Celia thought. *We may be rats, Diavala, but we finally realized it.*

The contingency plan lived and twisted in her gut like a worm. Now that its time was coming, Celia couldn't tell whether the worm was excited or agitated or afraid, but it writhed unbearably.

Celia splayed all ten of her fingers against the glass. *Ten. This started when we were ten, Anny.* Then she clenched her hands into tight fists. It was time to close the loophole.

The people's belief *was* their greatest strength, and they would use it.

Here was Celia's final inkling test.

She would become the murderer she'd always known she was.

Blood roared in Celia's ears as Diavala commended the people for holding true. Then Diavala moved close enough to have one last conversation with Celia.

"Nice effort, Inkling," Diavala said, her voice muffled by the glass separating them. That barrier wouldn't be there much longer, and Celia's hands twitched at her sides.

Diavala tsked, enjoying herself. "If you hadn't gotten your friends involved, there might have been hope for them. Alas . . ."

Perfectly on cue, the Mob began singing again, starting

softly, ready to surge, giving the finale a proper musical accompaniment. Diavala arched an eyebrow at the singing Mob, but otherwise gave no outward sign she hadn't expected it. If she were to cast herself as the Divine, she couldn't make it look as though she'd lost control at any juncture of this day. The hymn was more choral chant than war march, nothing alarming.

But Celia was close enough to see every angry twitch on her face.

"Background music will only bring the whip and blades down faster, Inkling," Diavala said. She'd humored them and tolerated one interruption, but this was too much.

"Of course." Celia pressed herself against the glass and stood on her tiptoes, trying to look directly into High Mistico Benedict's light eyes. "I expect nothing less." She wouldn't cower. She refused to bend. But something nagged at her, and this was her last opportunity to settle it. "I know your story: the child whose own people drowned her. The child who returned only to be killed again. Even after all this is over here and you rise as the Divine, immortality sure is a long time. Something terrible is bound to happen to you again."

Diavala's eyes narrowed. "If that's a threat, it's a feeble one."

Celia could barely form the words. *Vincent made it sound like you curse your life.* She was speaking to someone she hated, who wanted to destroy her and would destroy everything she loved, who pushed people around like playthings. Someone she very much needed to destroy.

And yet.

"If you could die again, for good this time, would you?" Celia asked.

Diavala clicked her tongue impatiently. "It's irrelevant. And every action has a cost, Inkling."

"True," Celia said. "But I've decided I feel sorry for you, Diavala. At the end of the day, you're under a bell jar like I am. Yours is bigger—infinite—and far emptier. You created an entire religion, but no one really knows you. Except me." Even though she whispered those last two confessional words, Diavala heard her.

Celia understood abandonment, disappointment, and betrayal. She knew how it rotted you from the inside. Diavala had said to her once that people weren't worth it, nor was investment of hope in them, because they always disappointed you. On particularly bad days, Celia would have agreed—attachments aren't worth it, better not to care—but she'd always had Anya to kick her ass, straighten her out, and prove her wrong. If not for Anya being a light, she might have fallen to darkness too.

The moment paused.

Not a great idea for Celia to reach for empathy, because it had a habit of growing.

Her gaze flicked to Diavala's neck. *High Mistico Benedict's* neck. The place where she would press a dagger. And slice. Diavala would live, that was certain—she would steal another body and perhaps find a way to rise from the ashes left behind in the wake of that night—but High Mistico Benedict wouldn't. Celia couldn't ignore that he still existed in that body, his tenor gleamed at her even then, pulsing along its spectrum.

If Anya said it was the only way to stop more of Profeta's harm, did that absolve Celia of calculated murder?

"Your crowd is expecting you." Jittery, Celia nudged her chin at the people, needing to get this over with before she lost her resolve.

Diavala laced her fingers together and nodded. "The night has barely begun, Inkling, and here you are trying to rush me? With your little attempt at subterfuge, I've barely had time to enjoy the prelude to my homecoming." She paused and stretched her neck, offering Celia another view of her future, the bump bobbing with a swallow in a very human way. Celia's bees reminded her, *You've always been a murderer, in thought if not in deed*, and she steadied herself.

"But you're right," Diavala said. "Now that they've met Diavala under the bell jar, I think it's time everyone met the Divine." Diavala tilted her head to the right. "After the Mob's executions, that is. They're begging for it, with this incessant noise. And when it's just you and me, alone on this stage—Diavala and Divine—the people can get a proper introduction to me while you get a proper introduction to what being flogged to death feels like. It's been a pleasure, Celia Sand."

Diavala gestured to the two mistico behind Caspian and Sky. They nodded, getting their chloroform rags ready. Quiet.

Practical. Quick. Merciful, even. Still, in the end, deliverers of death despite the rapturous prayers on their tongues. Lupita had been an anomaly in the swarm when her conscience had finally overcome her faith.

Diavala presented the first two to die and surveyed the crowd with an air of triumph. A few people waved their fists, proud that they hadn't been fooled by the devil's tricks. Now they were done with the prelude and were ready to leap to the main event: the moment the Divine bested Diavala, once and for all, starting with her minions.

Caspian turned to Sky and whispered something in their ear. They held hands, and their fingers laced together, dancing with intense familiarity—light touch, stroke, caress—their point of contact so small but becoming the biggest thing. Becoming everything.

Let's speed this up even more, Diavala. Now that they'd started the wave of chaos, they had to keep it going. They had to keep Diavala reactive until the bitter end so she didn't have time to see their final move.

If nothing else, chaos would reign that holy night.

Murderer, murderer, her bees whispered. *You finally get your chance to claim your truth.* Celia held her breath, her heart thumping loud and echoing off the glass.

After the stop in the field outside Asura, Celia had maneuvered her way close enough to Griffin to ask him one question. "Would you free me from the bell jar even if I was the devil?"

"I've met the devil, Celia," he'd said, watching Diavala with the burn of Vincent's death still fever-bright in his eyes. "And you're nothing like her." He'd turned back to Celia and aimed those dark eyes at her. "I'll be there, as always."

And there he was.

In the time it took for him to leap into a run toward Captain Andras, she had lifted the baton from her belt. And with a wild look of confusion on her face—a plague doctor swooping down upon her like a carrion bird!—she hesitated long enough for him to grab her baton.

Before Celia had time to duck, the plague doctor smashed the glass bell jar with it, aiming for the hairline crack. The glass rained down on her in splintered shards.

The mistico behind Cas and Sky had frozen, mouths agape, and looked from their chloro rags to High Mistico Benedict to the glass shards littering the stage to the unmasked devil and the very-masked plague doctor—the singing and smiling and dancing plague doctor, because if anything, he's the one who excelled at chaos—and back again.

In shock from the devil's escape from the bell jar, the crowd balked. Mouths hung unappealingly open. Fists that had been waving moments ago hovered in the air, unmoving. A few more guards had moved into the swarm to aid the people who'd passed out.

The Mob began moving as they sang—small movements, like a step forward, a duck, a bend—but all together effectively giving the impression that they weren't contained. They could run. They were thinking about it. Maybe this was the beginning of a mass escape.

Uncertain, the people in the crowd either pushed to get closer or pulled farther away, they either whispered or argued with one another. So much movement and noise, trying to make sense of what was happening, that the entire square bubbled. Guards were breaking up a few fights in the crowd, and inklings and fleas broke formation to press close to friends, thwarting the mistico's attempts to restore order. The escape of the devil in the bell jar had stirred the square like a stew in a giant's cookpot.

Dante, Lupita, and Zuni stood together with Wallis and the fleas, having taken advantage of the mass of movement. A lock of Dante's perfect hair stuck to his forehead from sweat. Not much, but enough that if they survived the night, Celia would have fodder enough to tease him forever. Zuni and Lupita held hands like old friends.

Nero stood at the end of the line, four guards holding him. He'd made himself part of the show when he'd tried to help.

Celia decided she loved his salamander.

The Mob showed no fear. They sang. Held hands. Seer Ostra nudged Caspian and gestured to the tattoo on her chest, starting a ripple that saw every Mob member shift their costume enough to showcase their ink.

Music enveloped all, reaching crescendo. After the quick game of cat-and-mouse between the plague doctor and a livid Captain Andras, he nodded to Celia significantly, then waltzed over to join the Mob, squeezing himself beside Kitty Kay. Red-faced, Captain Andras stomped her way to Diavala to apologize, or explain herself, or demand the plague doctor's head.

As important as Celia was, it took quite a while for the guards to notice her standing so quiet on top of her shattered bell jar amid all the other noise and movement. She'd been freed, but hadn't yet done anything with her freedom.

Except enjoy how seamlessly everyone had gotten into formation.

Guards flanked the sides of the stage, preventing escape; a row of mistico stood behind the row of Mob members, ready with their daggers; and Diavala stood in front with Captain Andras and her nine-tailed whip. The pair were closest to the people, right near the edge of the stage. If that whip came down, those first few rows in the audience were in a splash zone.

When a guard finally had the presence of mind to grab Celia, she shouted, "No! I had nothing to do with that! Don't give me to the High Mistico!" And so they immediately delivered her to her position beside the High Mistico.

As she moved, the fabric of her costume brushed against her raw skin. When they exposed her back for the flogging, they were in for a surprise.

Carefully planned, meticulously designed, Anya had inked a very special Divine tattoo on herself throughout the day, sending it to Celia the moment Diavala was preoccupied with her audience. From one shoulder blade to the other, dipping all the way to Celia's lower back, fire had raged. Her wild gesticulations as the devil in the bell jar had disguised her reactions to the pain, otherwise she would have twitched like a bug and given everything away right there.

Weeks earlier, Diavala had admitted that her powers weren't limitless, and with every Rabble Mob tattoo, Celia and Anya had tested those limits and poked at edges, trying to find the exact shape of Diavala's link to the ink. "See? I can have faith, Cece," Anya had said with a wicked smile. "I have faith that she has no idea how far we're willing to go."

The hidden tattoo was a culmination of every experiment. Anya had transferred the ink from one body part to a different one, she'd channeled more ink so that the image stretched, becoming as large and visible as possible. And, most important, it was still invisible to Diavala. She could see every path the ink took, that much was likely true, but as they'd learned with the plague doctor's "don't bother" tattoo, it wasn't immediate. Anya's theory was that she had to be actively looking.

And why would she search for a Divine tattoo that night, when she was convinced that she'd won?

Just as with Tanza, Diavala's hubris gave her tunnel vision.

She wouldn't see that inklings had all the power until it was too late.

Judgment time was fast approaching. The meaning of the tattoo on Celia's back would ring clear across Illinia.

Hopefully.

Celia felt a jab on her arm. Ink bloomed and then disappeared quickly. A punch from Anya to focus. As if Anya knew exactly when Celia would start worrying.

Captain Andras looked hungry. She uncoupled the whip from her belt.

To the hum of Mob singing, Diavala struggled to find words to match her fury.

It was strangely satisfying to see her floundering. Celia shrugged. "We're performers, and you gave us a stage," she said sweetly. "Did you really not expect us to use it? If we're all going to die anyway, at least we can have the satisfaction of creating a Mob-size smear on your blessed night."

"Everything will settle itself with your flogging. Of that, I'm positive." Diavala took a deep breath. "This looks like disorder now, but when everything is said and done on this night, it will only look like desperation. All this"—she gestured to the neatly assembled rows onstage, now quiet, contained, and watchful—"only proves collusion. You could have saved them if you'd cooperated. Instead, you convinced them that there was hope in fighting back. And every inkling knows that hope doesn't exist here." Leaning in, she whispered a hiss into Celia's ear. "At least when I was flogged, I knew it was a mistake. But you will deserve every strike. Two dozen lives will be lost for nothing, their blood will be on your hands, and *that* will be your only legacy, Inkling."

Captain Andras tenderly stroked the nine tails of leather, trailing them between her long fingers like fluttering ribbons, so eager to take out her anger at the plague doctor's embarrassing baton robbery on Celia's back. "So she goes first, then?"

Diavala nodded. "She goes first. Let her bear the pain of the whip, let her bear the pain of her followers watching it strike."

The crowd wasn't in a rolling boil anymore, but they still simmered, waiting. What had felt like years of chaos had been only minutes, and it was clear that everything was under control again. Justice would be done.

Diavala turned to them and thundered, "Your patience is admirable, your faith even more so. Diavala had more tricks up her sleeves, but all this has only been prelude to the most glorious day in the history of Profeta. Our Divine has finally returned to us!"

The temple doors opened again, and there was an angel.

Anya drifted out, flanked by two mistico.

And she looked like perfection.

And she walked tall and proud.

As she approached Celia, she lifted her mask.

And met Celia's eyes.

"No matter what," she whispered. "Be strong, Cece."

And she tried to smile.

With her arms held aloft, the crowd roared for her.

And Anya took center stage.

CHAPTER 35

EVERYTHING MOVED IN SLOW MOTION, AS IF THE TEMPLE HAD been plunged deep underwater.

Like a puppet testing out its strings, High Mistico Benedict prostrated himself at Anya's feet, jerking and twitching as his tenure serving Diavala came to an end. Whether it was sheer stubbornness, determination, or some lingering command still leading him, he didn't utter a sound for a few seconds.

The harsh noises of the Touch began—the High Mistico was so close to divinity, he was so overcome!—and then they quickly stopped when the closest mistico dragged him away.

Hundreds turned their gazes to the angel in white lace.

She held out her arms. Smiled. Took the time to look at everyone, holding eye contact significantly before moving on. The initial blast of cheers had died. People wept, fell into deep bows, or stretched their arms out as if to touch her. Wails of emotion tore through the new sound of measured prayers from hundreds of mouths. Ruler Vacilando's personal guard were trying to revive her back to her senses, so full was her delirium.

Diavala said nothing. She didn't have to. This moment had been building for weeks, for years, for centuries. Her ink had always spoken for her anyway, and it made sense that she wouldn't bother with such trivial human mundanities as speech. The sea of faces believed that the one dressed as an angel was their Divine. *Look at her,* they seemed to murmur to one another. *She walked among us all this time. She was the one who knew I needed guidance in my marriage, my profession, in dealing with my personal loss.*

Maybe the Divine wasn't what they expected, but still, she seemed to be exactly what they'd expected. Waves of black hair: young and beautiful. A regal countenance: old and wise.

She moved like someone young, but, with a different tilt of her head, deep wisdom in her gaze made her look ancient.

Magic.

Her lace dress so simple yet so elegant, as beautiful as a true angel fallen from the heavens.

The link to the Rabble Mob made perfect sense: from within that very temple the Divine had noted Diavala's new scheme. She'd watched it take shape, then followed her, disguised as another inkling. From the temple to the Illinian countryside, they'd battled.

In the eternal fight between good and evil, there in Asura it would end.

Celia felt their rapture as a tangible thing, wrapping around her like barbwire. As she stared at Anya, her heart thumped in a painfully slow rhythm, as if it knew it had only a thousand beats left and foolishly wanted to stretch out Celia's time.

A message on her arm shocked her like cold water. For a

brief moment she thought Anya was playing some sort of new game, clever thing that she was. A ruse of some kind, maybe trying to spare Celia from the whip in Captain Andras's hand. Profound relief flooded through her and those black dots in her vision became bright, dizzying starbursts.

But Anya's arms were held up to the heavens. No matter how skilled she was with hiding her messages, she'd never perfected doing them without using her hands.

Keep going, the message said.

Celia shook her head, tossing away thick cobwebs, and turned to the Mob. They all stared back at her. Then she found Dante, standing with Lupita and Zuni. It could only have been him, turning forward again after tilting to hide his arms. Dante? Using the ink and breaking a rule so huge? And when had he learned to do it? He nodded at her.

Some, like Remy, Wallis, and Zuni, had the decency to look stricken. The others held no expression save determination. The plague doctor gave Celia another bow. Lupita trembled so terribly it was a miracle she hadn't fallen over. Her swiveling, drowning eyes were aimed in Celia's general direction, trying to pin her down, and her normally smiling mouth had disappeared into a fierce thin line. Kitty Kay looked more phoenix than hen as she nodded, the set of her mouth matching Lupita's.

They all told her to keep going.

"Don't you *dare*," Celia hissed. How *dare* they act as if Anya's disappearance from this show was a wardrobe malfunction around which to improvise? Celia may have dropped her mask, but never had she felt so beastly. Her hands clenched into fists, fire consuming her.

Anya's eyes were closed, and tears streamed down her face. Anya's face, Anya's body, Anya's familiar tenor.

But definitely Diavala's tears. Being seen for the first time in centuries had almost undone her. She opened her deep blue eyes only long enough to look at Celia and twist the knife. "You never even had a chance, Inkling." Anya's lips. Anya's voice.

Celia tried to sink to her knees, but Captain Andras caught her under her arms, holding her up, murmuring consolations in her ear that weren't meant to comfort. *Swift whips, deep and hard, your death will come as quickly as possible, but not quick enough.*

Diavala spoke to the people, starting onstage with her mistico and then going down into the audience. She walked among them, talked to them in small groups. The parallel between this new display and Anya's and Celia's act blazed. There hovered the angel, walking among the people. Onstage stood a defeated devil. Unwittingly, she and Anya had taught Diavala exactly how to work a crowd.

So practical and precise, Anya excelled at planning, at logic. She could take fragments of information and make detailed schematics. Wisps of ideas becoming thick swirls becoming tangible threads. She'd talked it all out for Celia just that morning, sending every detail to Celia's forearm, including contingencies. How could this perfect plan of hers have gone so wrong?

Celia didn't know exactly when her mind betrayed her, but

by the time she realized what she realized, her face was wet and her eyes burned. Captain Andras kept telling her to shut up, as if grief so huge could simply be swallowed back.

With extreme effort, Celia straightened and looked at Anya. It wasn't Anya anymore, but it *was*. "What do I do now?" she whispered to her one true love, hoping she'd hear.

But Celia already knew what Anya would want, and that's what flayed her worse than any whip ever could.

Anya's plan hadn't gone wrong at all: she'd known it would lead here.

Anya wanted Celia to follow through—*Profeta falls, no matter what*—and kill her.

Since Celia had always been so good with lies, it was profoundly strange to see the truth. She lifted her trembling hands —the first sign of her body revolting—to her eyes, trying to block it out.

Such it was, when you saw everything right-side up for the first time. When you stopped tilting your head and didn't like what you saw.

Anya had taken the plan to the end and hadn't brought Celia along.

Celia knew what she had to do next, but not if she could do it. It had been bad enough when it was to be High Mistico Benedict's neck, and now . . .

After having every plan to outplay Diavala go sideways on them, they'd learned that they needed to push further. They both knew, with a sharp insistence, spiked and vicious, that there'd been no turning back the moment they'd plotted murder.

That was the moment of damnation for both of them. *Make peace with it, Cece,* Anya had said.

But this was even worse than damnation. This was the end of Celia's everything.

Celia turned around and threw up all over the devil mask she'd tossed to the ground and kicked away earlier, coating its hideously shiny horns with the wretched depths of her stomach. People watching might have thought it was fear of the whip that reduced her so; they couldn't know that she would have seen the whip as a mercy.

Celia had only one choice to make now: listen to Anya, or let her down.

Returning to the stage, the angelic Divine gave Captain Andras the order she'd been waiting for. "Flog her for her crimes. Her attempt at rule ends with her death. And my rule begins."

In the front row, the splash zone, Pia and Fallan cheered along with everyone else. Celia didn't think they were bad people and didn't doubt their intelligence; their faith was just that strong. They saw something different on that stage than what was actually happening.

And it would always be so.

"Be strong!" Kitty Kay shouted her strength, trying to give it to Celia. And she started singing again. Loud and far her lone voice stretched, demanding this horror of Celia, lifting the curtain on her damnation.

"Yes, be strong," Diavala said as other Mob voices joined Kitty Kay.

Or maybe Anya said it.

Celia would never know, and that was the moment that killed her.

Infuriatingly, some of Vincent's last words echoed, *She's so desperately lonely*, but Celia threw them away. She would waste no effort on pity or regret. She was dead already, and dead she would stay.

"Enough nonsense. Let's get this started, shall we?" Captain Andras muscled Celia around, took her dagger out, and sliced a line up the back of Celia's costume. It peeled away like a second skin.

Looking over her shoulder, Celia met Captain Andras's gaze. "This is bigger than us," Celia said. "I need your dagger."

Captain Andras swept a hand down Celia's back, her fingers tenderly moving around the black image. Celia was reduced to another prop. Another pawn. She hadn't existed for them as a person before, and she didn't now. She was an easel holding up a work of art.

The mistico, lined up so nicely behind Celia, had a wonderful view of the ink on her back. Some openly wept. Some had their heads bowed. A few collapsed to their knees.

So quickly, they reacted. So absolutely without doubt.

Anya had planned it—of course she had—that the meaning of the image would translate perfectly.

Celia turned and showed Ruler Vacilando what they were reacting to.

Diavala didn't understand why Celia was not being whipped. She closed her eyes, and Celia imagined her sifting through Anya's thoughts and memories, pushing aside what she didn't need in search of the one thing she needed now.

What is this new scheme? What image could possibly compete with meeting their Divine in the flesh?

Diavala would know the plan as soon as she found it. She would understand their clever end goal. The realization was coming that her ink had betrayed her.

Celia nodded to the Mob without making eye contact with any of them. Kitty Kay and the plague doctor left the line and went to stand with Diavala.

Anya.

Diavala.

Celia couldn't look at Kitty Kay—that final, horrible song of death still dancing at her lips—but Celia imagined Griffin behind his plague doctor mask: the dark, angry sadness in his eyes, the salty water leaking on his Leonus constellation. Still, he was an excellent actor, and this was the role Anya had cast for him.

"Ah, I see," Diavala said, realization dawning like a sigh. And she opened her eyes and pierced Celia with a rage so absolute it was miracle it didn't shove Celia immediately into the underworld. "Really. You know you can't kill; I made sure of it. And if it was impossible before, how can you do it now, when I wear *this* face? How utterly ignoble and desperate of you to keep trying, Inkling." All she saw was the inkling who'd been some fun now making a last, desperate play. Her rage simmered at the loss of her grand entrance, not because she believed that Celia would do the thing they'd set out to do.

"There was always a fundamental flaw in your test," Celia said, holding out her hand to Captain Andras, who fumbled with the nine-tailed whip she'd tucked back into her belt. For a moment Celia thought, *Thank you, yes please, use it on me before* . . . But the captain held out the leather grip toward Celia, the tails dancing like a waterfall of hair.

Celia recoiled and almost threw up again. "No. I said I need your dagger."

"I've born centuries of inklings," Diavala said. "There is no flaw. You're embarrassing yourself."

But there was a flaw, and Celia and Anya were proof. "*Can't* kill and *won't* kill are very different things," Celia said. "Remember that, after all of this: you're the one who chose us."

By now the crowd's alarm rang loud. With the devil freed and holding her hand out for a dagger and their newly unveiled Divine suddenly looking like a captive, this was taking a turn they didn't understand. How was the devil making demands? And why was everyone listening? Confused guards moved in.

Captain Andras barked orders at the guards to hold steady, Ruler Vacilando stood and flung desperate words at the people to "wait and watch the wonder," and Celia almost laughed, the alliteration so unintentionally poetic it tasted like a poisoned dessert. *Woe to the inklings who cannot escape, but wait and watch the wonder . . .*

Celia's outstretched hand trembled. Violent convulsions took over her body. Her teeth rattled. Still covered in black paint and glitter, and though she'd dropped the mask long ago, her forked tail still swished back and forth with her movements. The scales on her dress were sharp compared with the delicate white lace on Anya's.

They both remained perfectly in character: Diavala and the Divine.

Celia spoke the truth: "I am Diavala. You are the Divine. This is exactly what you wanted."

CHAPTER 36

CELIA COULD HAVE HARNESSED STRENGTH BY IMAGINING SAVing Wallis and the other fleas, in exacting revenge for Vincent, Salome, and so many other deaths, or even in mourning those strange casualties of Profeta: Lupita's eyes, Fiona's neck, Fallan's child. So much despair and manipulation to fuel her hate.

But all she thought of was Anya.

Celia bowed to her—a grand gesture that saw her almost fully prone—deference to an extreme. As she rose, she held her hand out again and asked Captain Andras over her shoulder, "Will you disobey the ink?"

The cold metal of the dagger hit her palm, and Celia wrapped her fingers around the hilt. Captain Andras, now a solid ally.

Diavala shook her head in disappointment at Captain Andras. She swept a dancing hand toward the rows of mistico; the still captive Mob, some on their knees with daggers pointed at them like arrows; the people of Asura. *You still see who's the devil here, don't you?*

Celia trembled. She silently swore. She had to do it.

She looked behind her to mistico. "Will you stop me?"

Stop me!

She asked the same of the guards. "Will any of you stop me?"
Please! Stop me!

Her gaze went up to Ruler Vacilando. "And you? What does the Ruler say?"

Intercede, intercede, intercede . . .

No one moved until Ruler Vacilando nodded. Immediately, Kitty Kay grabbed Anya's shoulders and held her immobile. The people hadn't seen yet, but they listened. They watched. They'd turned to stone, an integral part of the same morbid tableau.

The ink was too strong to argue with. Celia was a slave to it, right to the bitter end.

The rest of the night fell away, and there they were. Celia and Anya, linked pinkies since the beginning, and a true interloper between them.

That was what fed Celia. "I always knew you'd steal her from me," she said through her chattering teeth. "From the moment we met, I knew we were doomed. Such a gift you have, to make children terrified of holding hands and playing and laughing. Right from the beginning, this monster's den taught us that connection and trust are your enemies if you want to keep breathing. I was *six* when I realized that Anya would kill me. It always felt dangerous to love her."

Celia took a step forward, breathing hard. "You think I can't do this, but you forget one crucial thing: we've known this was coming for ten years, and that's plenty of time to say goodbye."

And she looked into Anya's deep blue eyes and finished her goodbye. *I'll always love you, Anny.*

Diavala struggled against Kitty Kay's solid grip. Her slow hatch of understanding had taken some time, but something in Celia's face had finally triggered a long-dormant emotion.

Terror.

She'd seen her future written in black ink. She tried to call to her guards, her mistico, the Ruler, but nothing was as powerful as a Divine tattoo.

Inktrava sel Immorti: Always listen to the ink.

The dagger had to come down.

I'm sorry. Celia held Anya's gaze, hoping she was there somewhere in that deep blue ocean.

A burst of blue and purple flame erupted in the plague doctor's palm, hovering there, flitting and dancing as he acted as gatekeeper between the crowd and the deliverance onstage. He swept the flame behind her, illuminating her back to the masses. "Would any of you go against this command?"

No one moved. No one breathed.

On Celia's back was the Ascension—an image of death everyone recognized, of the Divine leaving the mortal plane—but instead of a lightning bolt representing the transformation, it was a dagger.

And the date.

The day the Divine died, the day Anya died, the day Celia died.

The image of the prophetic Return looked so much like the Ascension, almost as if the Divine had vowed to leave the people twice. And Profeta's story had never continued after the Return—it had always been an image of finality. A countdown: four, three, two, one.

The plague doctor addressed the crowd. "The time of the ink is over." If there was any tremble of uncertainty in his voice, the make-believe megaphone in his throat disguised it. "The Divine has served you faithfully for centuries, but we need to release her. She has given us her final message. She revealed herself because she needed to make sure you heard it. Live on without her. Live well and live passionately. Your destinies are up to you. Sastimos futura."

The trembling blade came up, removed from Celia even though she knew her hand was the little thing holding it. *A shell, just a shell.* Anya didn't exist anymore. She'd died the moment Diavala had taken her over; there'd never been a way for any of them to walk away still breathing that night. Halcyon was a dream. An impossibility.

"Your ink wins, Diavala. As I should have known all along."

As long as it existed, the ink would always win.

"No, wait." And, though nothing had changed in her appearance, Celia knew that Diavala had retreated.

And given her Anya.

More manipulation, to let Anya come through for a moment. Celia almost dropped the blade.

Anya's eyes widened, her body trembled.

"You said no matter what, Anny . . ." Celia whispered it, her voice cracked. She didn't even understand what she was asking.

But of course Anya understood her.

Anya closed her eyes. Her trembling stilled. She didn't beg for her life. "Cece," she whispered, and through supreme effort, Anya fought the creature inside her and grabbed Celia's dagger hand. She wrapped her fingers around Celia's.

Held the dagger with Celia.

Then looped her pinky around Celia's.

Anya had always known it would end this way too.

Then another hand gripped Celia's and Anya's, gnarled and bony, wrinkled skin hanging in loose folds. Three hands gripped the blade, folding over one another to make a wall of fingers strong enough to overcome a trickster.

A cluster of other people pressed closer. Celia saw hands caressing Anya's hair, heard whispers offering strength. The plague doctor made sure that no one crowded close enough to block the people's view. This was still a performance, after all.

Those hands steadied Celia and guided her. And pushed for her.

Like going through butter. Once, twice. Twin slices on either side of the neck. In that perfectly efficient way Lupita had taught her so long ago, Celia closed the loophole.

"I'm sorry." Celia repeated it over and over. Her dagger-less hand went to Anya's cheek and brushed it, to her hair and caressed it. Her gaze followed her fingers, taking inventory of every detail. "I'm sorry." She cupped the back of Anya's head, thinking of Diavala's words, *people aren't worth it*. But they were. Anya was.

Celia choked on her words, laced her fingers into Anya's hair. "I'll see you again."

And she knew it was true.

Everything moved impossibly slowly.

But it was over in a moment.

When Diavala broke through Anya's resolve, she tried to pull the dagger hand away, but the damage was done. Those wrinkled hands on Celia's were a lot stronger than they appeared.

By the time blood spilled, warm and wet, over Celia's hands, the truth was clear to everyone. It was written all over her back.

Inktrava sel Immorti. Always listen to the ink.

That was the signal for pandemonium.

CHAPTER 37

NERO GRABBED CELIA AND TRIED TO HAUL HER OFF THE stage.

Red lingered everywhere.

She tilted her head, trying to make sense of right-side up.

The Rabble Mob, in line at the front of the stage, took their curtain call: holding hands, bowing deep, exclamations from Marco and the plague doctor booming.

Some still sang, if they could through their tears. Crying for Anya. For Vincent. For one another.

For what they'd just done.

Caspian and Sky lifted their linked hands again, and the Mob cut off their song to chant: "Sastimos futura! Sastimos futura!"

The spectacular finale, perfectly choreographed.

Diavala had set up a night to be remembered, and she'd gotten it.

The winged plague doctor, a tiny purple flame hovering near the center of his chest, delivered his final verdict.

For the first time, his judgment became Yes.

This is how it's supposed to end.

The purple and blue flame erupted from his chest, consuming everything onstage in magical fire.

"Sastimos futura!"

To a world without the Divine. Without her guiding ink.

A thousand people screamed and wept, Celia among them.

Ruler Vacilando had descended from her balcony in a mad rush, her cape left behind. She pressed a hand to her tattoos, one after another, mouthing silent words, trying to understand. A mistico grabbed her in an embrace as she ran toward the stage. They clutched each other in a wholly inappropriate way, united in grief, nursing a disappointment so profound a new tapestry would need to be woven for it.

Lupita knelt by Anya's side. Some mistico approached Lupita as if she were half Divine herself. She'd been brave enough to act on the Divine's final, ultimate order when the devilish devil the Divine had enlisted hadn't been able to do it on her own.

The Mob took more bows, ending the show of all shows. Remy bolted into a run, aiming straight for Celia and Nero, tears coursing down her face.

Diavala? Celia thought. With all the death Diavala had already experienced, she wouldn't linger in a dying body. She'd already found a new host. Was it Remy?

Right-side up made no sense at all. Celia didn't know which way to tilt her head.

"Let me go, Nero," she said. The realization that Diavala was still *somewhere* also meant that she was no longer *there*. She was no longer in the body lying on the stage.

Bleeding.

Dying.

Without Celia.

"Let me go, Nero. Let me *go!*" She pushed him away, strong enough in her need to escape the grip of a giant.

She fell to her knees beside Anya and suddenly didn't know what to do. Her hands flew from Anya's neck to her hands to her eyes, landing everywhere, doing nothing. Everything so warm, so red. "Anny, we were supposed to go together. I hate that you did this." With the back of her hand, Celia swiped the tears and snot off her face, smearing the slick wetness of Anya's blood on herself instead. It fell to her lips, the taste of what she'd done. "But you'll wait for me there, right? I won't be long, I won't be long, Anny."

She pushed one hand to Anya's neck to cover the wound. Anya's ocean blue eyes had already dimmed, she gave no Anya-like last words—*Pull yourself together, Cece. You're always such a mess.* Her tenor, familiar enough to Celia to pick it out of a crowd of thousands, flickered painfully, vanishing by degrees.

"I hate that you did this!" Celia screamed. And someone, Lupita, tried to shush her, put an arm around her shoulders, but Celia pushed everyone away. No one else mattered. "Promise you'll wait for me?" and she hooked her bloody pinky around Anya's bloody pinky and squeezed.

Amid all that red—ribbons of it staining the stage, Anya's white lace dress, Celia's hands and knees and soul and heart—were thin veins of black ink. It must have been buried so deep, the ink in her blood, that it ebbed out only when life did.

With a shriek, Celia ripped her dress and dabbed the ink

away, barely able to control her hands, her tears, her wails. She worked with single-minded determination, wiping and dabbing at the tendrils of escaping ink with clumsy, fumbling fingers. "I got it, don't worry," Celia repeated and repeated. "I'm getting it all. Don't worry."

Finally, after ten years, Anya would be free of it.

Celia got every last drop of the black ink off of her love. Anya would have wanted that.

And as the last light of Anya's tenor disappeared, she looked every bit an angel.

CHAPTER 38

W HEN CELIA OPENED HER EYES TO RIGHT-SIDE UP, ZUNI was there. Freckles dotting her nose, fingers lacing together under her chin, a fierce non-smile on her flawless face.

"I collected so many feathers for you," Celia whispered.

Lupita elbowed Zuni out of the way. They both peered at Celia as if she were about to explode. Or disintegrate.

"Pretty scarf," Celia said. Fresh teal, patterned with cheery paisley swirls. Or teardrops.

"Done," Lupita whispered. "Done."

"How drunk are you?" *How drunk am I?* "Are you my angels?" *Or my devils?*

It took a long time for her to realize that she was neither drunk nor dead. A long time to see impossible as possible.

She put her hand over her heart and felt for it—the ka-thumping—and it tapped there, under her fingertips.

Lupita batted her hand away. "Smarten up, idiot child. If you're dead, then I'm dead, and that would make this night-mare decidedly unworth it."

"Who else is dead, then?" Did she even want to know whose bodies Zuni had burned? Whose skulls she'd cleaned with her rats or beetles or acids? She looked around for the first time and realized she was in the temple infirmary. Unbound, with no mistico or physicians hovering.

Celia doubted her aliveness all over again.

Zuni tenderly stroked Celia's forehead. "You've put me out of work." Something like a smile passed over her face, but Celia couldn't be sure, for she'd never seen Zuni smile.

"Did that really happen?" Celia asked. She meant, *Did I really do that?*

Zuni's face softened so much it hurt. Celia closed her eyes and wished she hadn't asked.

"It's what she wanted," Zuni said, sounding far away, as if she spoke to Celia through glass, her forever bell jar.

"Where's Diavala?" Celia heard herself say. Whose bones hummed now? "We need to find Halcyon. He's the final link to destroying her. We need to get to Wisteria . . ."

To Celia's ongoing rambling, Lupita grumbled and growled, muttering that maybe they should put her under again. Apparently Celia had been unconscious for a few days, held there by one of Lilac's teas as a mercy. Celia eventually fell silent; many more ka-thumps passed.

Zuni spoke to her in a hushed voice, as if Celia were a fragile thing and noise would shatter her. She said things like "vanished," "chaos," "fracturing," but not much of it made sense to Celia. She tried to feel her bones; did they vibrate inside her, or were they silent the way bones should be?

"Sorry about this," Zuni said. Her hand floated down to Celia's collarbone, and she lightly traced the tattooed spiral there. "Dante had to make it permanent because it was part of the show." She trailed away. *It's Divine canon,* Celia heard. *Your skin is forever part of the spectacle.*

Sorry was a ridiculous word.

Celia shuddered and lifted the bottom of her shirt. A tattoo of a hand branded her stomach, the insides swirling in an abstract pattern, sharp and soft at the same time. Zuni didn't mention the one on her back. Celia vowed she'd never look at it. Her last gift from Anya; the one that ended the world she knew. She had three permanent reminders of the ugliness they'd orchestrated onstage.

They were quiet long enough that whatever drug was winding its way through Celia's veins had time to pull her back into dreamless sleep.

A good place, with no red stains. No black ink.

Anya was there. Waiting for her.

"He's not the peacock he used to be, Celia," Lupita said later of Dante, her new best friend. Then she chuckled. "Well, maybe it helps that I can't see his strutting anymore."

Dante was the one who had told Lupita to help with what everyone knew Celia wouldn't be able to do. Without Dante and Zuni being her eyes, Lupita wouldn't have known what was happening. "He cares for you in the strangest way," Lupita mused, chuckling. "As if you're a black adder he's determined to tame."

Save Celia from it, Dante had said.

Celia began to tremble all over again. She'd never get her body under control. The ka-thumps were there. Was that enough? Celia had been the one holding the dagger. Lupita had saved her from nothing. If she tilted her head the wrong way, the right way, she saw it. It consumed her.

"I'm sorry you had to do that, Lupita." Tears burned Celia's eyes, and she couldn't meet Lupita's blind gaze, even from behind the happy teal scarf.

Lupita leaned over, the bells in her hair jingling. "It was a way of righting my wrongs. You always said you didn't kill so you could save Anya, but I've always known it wasn't in you to do it. Dante knew too. The temple got it backward: the ones who didn't kill were the stronger. You understood this, even when you didn't understand it."

It sounded familiar. As if she'd had the same thought, once, forever ago. Celia still didn't fully understand it, but the way Zuni and Lupita looked at her, it was as if they believed she'd have time to figure it out.

"Where's Diavala?"

Lupita laughed in a strange way: half happy, half devastated. "No one believes she exists anymore. She lost all her power with two cuts of a knife. Everyone believed in her Return so absolutely that when her beautiful new body died, she died too. There's no way she can come back from this. Half the temple has already disappeared, trying to make sense of a world where the Divine has left them. It's a mess out there. An absolute disaster. But everyone's safe from the poison."

"But where is she?" *I took away her power, her consolation prize, her toy. She'll need her revenge.*

And, more important, *Celia* needed revenge.

Zuni squeezed her hand. "It's so quiet, Cece." Zuni said this as though they thought Diavala was truly gone. Could it be possible?

Ruler Vacilando would have to make her own decisions about the nation now. The mistico weren't a threat anymore, not even the iron-eyed one who'd haunted Celia for ten years. He was now just a cleaned skull on a shelf.

Their Divine had been freed from her servitude.

And it was quiet.

Profeta had fallen, no matter what.

CHAPTER 39

IN AN IRONY OF IRONIES, RULER VACILANDO COMMANDED THE blind, perpetually drunk, half-mad excommunicated mistico to restore order to the Asuran temple.

Lupita had spun her a story of how she'd seen this coming years ago. She'd taken out her eyes because she couldn't bear it. But from losing everything comes strength. Not everyone would have been brave enough to kill their Divine, even if it was by the Divine's own order. Lupita had been meditating alone on this inevitability for years.

Her isolation had had nothing to do with gin and absinthe and loss of faith, or so she told anyone who would listen.

The mistico remaining at the temple still reeled from their shock. They aimlessly wandered the halls, crying, screaming. So deep was their grief, it sounded much like the Touch, except it had a pulse: it settled with sleep and occasionally stilled with conversation. Despite how much Lupita loathed the temple, Celia came across her with a comforting arm wrapped around another mistico as he sat, despondent, in a dark hallway. Lupita knew exactly what it felt like to lose your Divine.

The Mob had been so convincing with their final show that it couldn't have been anything but preplanned and then staged with precision. The Mob were new heroes, suffering for their Divine, then carrying out her last order like martyrs. The mistico understood that their Divine cared for them, but she'd needed to leave. Her message, words from her own mouth that night, had been one of hope and a new era dawning.

That era would begin by shattering the Chest Majestic in her honor. A way of thanking her for centuries of guidance. A way of saying, *We'll be fine without you. Be free.*

Lupita believed that Diavala had gotten it wrong; she'd never been immortal. That a millennia ago she'd been tricked too. That the ink had tethered her to the land of the living, and once they destroyed the Chest Majestic and the bond was severed, she'd return to the afterlife she'd lost before.

That she would truly be dead.

Celia stayed at the sidelines and watched Lupita, Dante, and the Rabble Mob close out an era. The main square was packed again with inklings, mistico, guards, and other workers of the temple. No one lined up in a structured way. Ruler Vacilando didn't perch in her balcony, but stood near the back. Rank didn't exist anymore. They all just needed to say goodbye to someone they loved.

Nero smashed the Chest with a sledgehammer as big as his head (making it look as light as a feather), and Marco set it aflame. Kitty Kay's gaze found Celia's and she nodded. *We did it.*

The Chest burned, inky black smoke rising from it as the crowd looked on.

Besides Zuni, none of them would even be unemployed.

Lupita gave a rousing speech. Not even slurred. She'd left her green fairy and juniper gin at home. She announced that the infrastructure of the Profetan temple would still be used in the Divine's memory.

Hesitant cheers rose up.

Ruler Vacilando had decreed it, so funding would continue and donations would still be accepted. The temple would be an orphanage. Housing for the homeless. A place to receive hot meals.

The cheers got louder. A few people smiled, imagining the future. They turned their faces to the statue of their Divine with a look of pure rapture.

The plague doctor popped up beside Celia at the side of the stage. "Bloody *hell*," she said, and paused to restart her heart. *Come back, ka-thumps. Come back.* She resisted the urge to punch him, but barely.

He wound his arm under hers, pulled her close, his beak between them, and whispered into her hair, "You've been avoiding me."

"Oh, absolutely."

"I wish you wouldn't." He pulled her tighter to his side as they watched the black smoke feed the sky. "It ended as Anya wanted it to."

"Yes, everyone keeps saying that."

A deeply sad chuckle rumbled from his chest, but other than that, he didn't respond.

Celia didn't pay any more attention to the ceremony. She put her hand on his chest and felt his ka-thumps, trying to decide what she felt about them. Everything seemed so muted now. "It snowed once," she said. "When we were about seven or eight? And all of Asura was pushed under this cold, white blanket. I hated how it stung. How it muffled everything but also made everything so loud. The crunching of boots in the snow were like giants munching carrots." *Giant carrots, maybe to make into a giant carrot cake, Vincent?*

If the plague doctor had a question about the relevance of her story, he didn't say anything. He only hugged her closer, as if he knew what she was trying to say. *I'm under a terribly cold blanket.*

The plague doctor exhaled, wrapped her up tighter, keeping her warm. "They'll clean this place up nicely."

There were so many plans being thrown around that Celia could barely keep up. Lilac, Cas, and Sky wanted to be the personal stilt-walking entertainers for the orphaned Kids. Part of Celia thought their ultimate goal was to turn the place into a carnival. Wallis and Remy were circling each other in a strange dance of new friendship where they bonded over their shared exasperation with Celia. Each night for weeks, Celia had fallen asleep with a flea on one side and a pretzel on the other, wondering how she deserved them. Seer Ostra was ready to embrace her retirement and bake a mountain of sweet buns in a real kitchen, which she'd never worked in before. Marco and Dante were ramping up to be . . . something. They'd be great together because their massive egos perfectly balanced each other.

Even Kitty Kay and Lupita had gotten their own happily ever after, decades after they'd lost hope of it ever happening. Wallis had gifted them with a loud, "Eww, gross, find some privacy!" when they'd caught them kissing.

Part of Celia wished she could see the fresh beginnings rise from the ash.

Diavala might be gone.

It looked like she was.

But she might not be. And if Celia ran, Diavala would follow her. The tattoo on her back and the bloodstained bracelets she refused to remove would follow her. Forever tainted, Celia had to take herself far away from these fresh beginnings.

And it scared her to think of what she would turn into, now that Anya was gone. Outwardly, she responded to the bursting of hope around her, but inwardly she felt shriveled and hollow. Something would have to grow in that empty space, and she didn't expect it to be beautiful.

Without Anya being a light, I would have fallen to darkness long ago.

Despite the silence, Celia still saw Diavala everywhere. She was close. Mourning the loophole her dark twin had pulled her through. Waiting. Planning.

Once, Celia had caught a glint of something in Dante's eyes. It was gone by the time he'd turned to say something to Marco.

Then she'd seen it in Remy, who'd insisted on inking herself in the old ways with a matching handprint on her stomach, swirly and sharp, like her Lalita was.

Like the tattoo on her back, this haunting had become part of Celia's payment. Every action had a cost.

She felt the plague doctor's ka-thumps under her hand and held her tears in, distracting herself by pulling his mask up and off. Stupid thing. She wanted Griffin. Or at least she had wanted him before.

"I know what you're planning." Griffin wrapped his fingers around hers and held them at his lips. Did he know? He probably did. He must know all about unfinished business; his own death was the biggest of all. "You should go to Kinallen. You wouldn't believe the stars." His small smile widened, and something stirred in Celia's stomach, a butterfly warmed enough to reawaken. "And when you see *how* they mine that common powder, you'll never want to leave. Your entire world will explode with blue and purple."

More butterflies, rustling faintly. The two of them melted together so no one watching would know where Celia ended and Griffin began, but their lips didn't meet. The smile fell off his face slowly, until he was all serious. "I *do* have to restock my supply of this wicked stuff, so it would make sense if we traveled together . . ." His gaze went from her eyes to her lips and back again.

"Well, that's stupid. Beside me is a dangerous place to be."

Griffin's dark eyes swallowed her. His hands on her back warmed her. His ka-thumps erupted from his chest and pushed right into hers. "Only because you're dangerous, Celia. But I have some ideas about how we can play with that fire."

She flushed at his words, more butterflies woke, and he tilted his head in that familiar way, savoring how he could make her squirm.

But.

To the right.

Angling his Leonus constellation away instead of offering it.

Her heart pounded, trying to bash its way out from behind her ribs.

And then it stopped.

She put her hand on his cheek and tried to tilt him the proper way. *Tilt the right way, Griffin. Damn it.* Such a small thing—the tilt of your head—but it could change everything.

Griffin had told her once, "If someone takes me over, you'll be the first to see it, Celia Sand."

Payment, payment. Everything had a cost.

Griffin frowned at her, at the hand on his face pushing in a way that didn't make sense. It began as a twitch of his eyebrow, cool and questioning. Then she watched every line on his face tense, one by one, in response to what he saw in her expression.

Tension coiled slowly. They were so close, dark to dark, she felt every one of his muscles harden. He closed his eyes and dipped his head, maybe listening to the humming of his bones, hunting for the melody.

She ignored the crowd behind and around them. This was a place of new beginnings.

A place neither of them belonged.

Her mind darted to the name *Halcyon* like an arrow finding its mark.

Surprisingly calm, Celia wound her hand into Griffin's hair, pulling him to her by the vulnerable nape of the neck. Griffin accepted it, trembling. He wrapped his arms around her shoulders, hugging her tight. His breath and loose hair warmed and tickled her skin. All her butterflies had woken now, they were bursting and bashing against her ribs, trying to punch their way out, recognizing the fight wasn't over. *He's ours!* they screamed as they fluttered. *Diavala will not take him, too.*

She pulled away enough to cup Griffin's face with both of her hands and whisper, "Off to Kinallen, then. We will gaze up at those stars, whatever it takes."

Celia kissed the constellation beside Griffin's eye and sealed her vow.

ACKNOWLEDGMENTS

This started as a seed of an idea, and it took years to grow into the book you hold in your hands. There are so many people who helped make this story happen, and I am deeply grateful to every one of them.

To my incredible agent, Daniel Lazar, who continues to amaze me with his dedication and work ethic. I couldn't have asked for a more stalwart champion, and—bonus—you're also a much better therapist than you give yourself credit for. And to Torie Doherty-Munro, who plucked INK out of the slush, fell in love with these characters first, and provides never-ending support in all things great and small.

Huge thank you to my editor, Nicole Sclama, who pushed me to find the best possible version of this story. Your patience, guidance, and enthusiasm have made all the difference in my debut experience, and I am so grateful to have you on my side. Thanks also to Kiffin Steurer, Jessica Handelman, Kaitlin Yang, Diane Varone, Alia Almeida, Anna Ravenelle, John Sellers, Maxine Bartow, and the rest of the team at HMH. Your work remains mostly a mystery to me, but that doesn't mean I don't appreciate it with my whole heart.

Thank you to my early readers, who helped me figure out what this book was about so I could rewrite it: Emily Smejkal, my wonderful sister-in-law, who's read almost everything I've written despite not having slept since 2013. Mary Taranta, a talented writer who needs to put more books out into the world, stat. Dani Sharp Bird, whose insight was so helpful in those early stages. Kimberly Garnick Giarratano, who had more faith than I did that this book would be published. And Jade Hemming, the witchy goddess of my heart, who keeps trying to get me to word sprint even though I'm more of a snail.

To my Pitch Wars mentor, Jessie Devine, who taught me that true revision is painful and wonderful at the same time, and who helped me develop the idea of tenors so the gender representation was as limitless as I could possibly make it. Thanks to Brenda Drake, the Pitch Wars team, and everyone in the PW16 class. I've always been a quiet one in our group, but I appreciate all the support and commiseration that continues to this day. Specific thank you's to Rosiee Thor, Rebecca Schaeffer, Sam Taylor, Tracy Gold, Ernie Chiara, and Erin Luken. You read all, some, or none of INK, but each of you made a huge impact on me, whether you knew it or not.

Special thanks to my sensitivity readers, especially Vee Signorelli. This book is so much better because of your insight. If there are mistakes, I apologize and claim them entirely.

To Emilee Rudd, who gave me the cover of my dreams, and Virginia Allyn, for the wonderful map. Your art is an inspiration.

And now—deep inhale—your turn, Jessika Fleck. There aren't enough words for how much I value our friendship. You've been with me from the start: the first to read my first novel, the first to read INK, and the faithful reader of all those crappy and not-so-crappy books in-between. I feel like I've waited to thank you for years (hey wait, I have!) but I want you to know, from the bottom of my old-crone, jaded heart, that you mean the world to me. One day we're going to meet in person, and even though we're both awkward, I know it won't be awkward at all. Especially if I bring my best friend, Tanqueray, along. I love you so much I might even share with you.

To my mom for looking after the kids so I could write this book. You deserve a hundred million thank-you's, because you probably helped me a hundred million times. I truly couldn't have done it without you. And to my dad for reading Grimm's fairytales and Edgar Allan Poe to me when I was far too young and impressionable. I blame you for my macabre side entirely, and I wouldn't have it any other way.

I dedicated this book to my grandfather, because he was the first to call me a writer, long before I could claim the title for myself. He said it as if it was no big deal, as if my art was something to be proud of, even if no one else ever saw it. Some days, the echo of his words was the only thing that kept me going. Děda, you would have hated this book (so political! so strange! so violent!) but I know you would have been proud of me anyway.

To my children, Ember and Linden, my two smallest cheer-leaders in size but biggest in heart. You're both so weird and wonderful. Ember (my mini-me), I love your sense of humour, wild imagination, and fiery passion. Linden, I love your peaceful nature, sharp intellect, and infinite compassion. You inspire me every day, my loves. Who would I be, without you?

And last but not least, to my husband, Johnny. You supported this dream of mine through years of highs and lows without wavering. You believed in me when I didn't believe in myself. I'm so lucky to share this life with you.

TURN THE PAGE FOR A SNEAK PEEK
AT THE RIVETING SEQUEL!

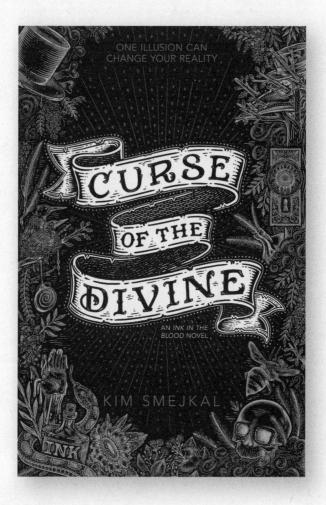

CHAPTER 1

HE'S A DEAD THING.

Celia shivered and wrapped her arms tight around her middle, clutching all her shattered pieces together so they didn't spill out like an overturned cart on the cobblestones at her feet. Watching Griffin from across the busy market square of whatever town they were in, she held her thoughts at bay with knives.

They didn't know for sure whether Diavala possessed him. In all the days since they'd left the city of Asura, Diavala hadn't made herself known; all Celia had was paranoia, suspicion, and nagging, ever-present regret. Perhaps this was what winning looked like, and Celia was just so broken she couldn't recognize it.

Still, the bees in her head insisted, *He's a dead thing.* The words kept buzzing in her mind, repeated and repeated. It might look like they'd overcome the body-stealing devil, but Celia had been fooled by Diavala before.

As a plague doctor, Griffin was certainly dressed the part. His costume was all black—hat, tight leather pants, coat of raven feathers, except for his bone-white mask with its long, stabby beak—and it seemed to give his inner death a face.

Slowly rotting on the inside but whole on the outside, decomposing by degrees. The illness inside him festering, rattling his bones, humming to him: *Diavala, Diavala, Diavala* . . .

Griffin scanned his growing audience — their baskets filled with bread and other market staples under their arms, harried looks on their faces, toes already pointed down the road they'd continue on if he didn't hold their attention — and he turned up the shine of his smile. It looked as if he was trying hard to ignore that he was competing with bread, squash, and butcher cuts of meat, and how equal the match was.

He'd been standing statue-still for a handful of moments, waiting for people to notice him before beginning his performance.

It hadn't taken long.

The town lived in another world. Market day was a bustling affair, with people moving this way and that, laughter and conversation coming from every direction, a steady hum. Tenors — the visible, ever-changing markers that signaled gender identity — shone brightly around everyone's head and shoulders, as individual as fingerprints. The sights, sounds, and smells of innocent daily life. Anything dark and beaked and ominously silent, evoking the plague and death and mystery, stood out like a bonfire.

He hadn't seen Celia yet. She stood on the steps of a bakery near the back, the scent of cinnamon and melted butter enveloping her.

When the attention of his crowd wandered too far, he'd hand

out one cheery yellow dandelion with a dramatic bow. Except for the tilt of his head when he aimed his beady-eyed goggles at someone, his deep bows were his only movement. Soon most of his small audience had one yellow tuft either tucked behind an ear, in a basket, or clutched in a hand.

Who is he? Why would he give me a flower?

And a few, *Hack, capitalizing on fame, trying to wheedle hard-earned coin. There's only one plague doctor.*

Most of Illinia knew of him now, and absurdly, his fame had grown so big, no one would have believed he was indeed *that* plague doctor. The one who had stood with the Divine when she'd revealed herself to her followers; the one who had calmly heralded her death.

With the sun miraculously shining despite the crisp autumn season, and with whatever arbitrary crowd size he was waiting for finally assembled in front of him to his liking, he began.

Celia held her breath.

A slow nod. Unclasping his hands, he swept his gaze, hidden behind those dark lenses, across every intent face. For a moment his goggled gaze seemed to land on Celia, and even though she was well hidden, she had no doubt he'd managed to see her.

He did that a lot: see her.

Always Celia and Griffin, opposite each other, circling, two polar ends of a never-ending abyss. The setting around them didn't matter at all.

He nodded at her before he began. *"'Another dawn brings shadow!'"* he boomed in his performer's voice.

One of the shoppers flinched, and the corner of Celia's mouth quirked up. His volume control was still an issue, obviously.

He shook himself off and adjusted, settling his voice into the rhythm of the poem. Dipping and lengthening and stretching. No longer words: a work of art, a painting, a story. He was used to speaking more with his body than with his words, but it was easy enough for him, animating poems already written.

Celia stopped breathing as she listened to his voice: smooth and deep, soft but strong.

> "Another dawn brings shadows
> Full of creeping things and claws.
> And our love for each other—
> Starving us and nourishing—
> Has found its perfect home."

Celia didn't recognize the poem he recited, but it seemed as if it were his own composition, just for them. Who else would understand that when love was born from the darkness, sunlight would only make it wither?

Griffin cocked his head at her. The pointy beak of his white plague doctor mask aimed at the ground like a stake, his goggles reflecting the sunlight that mocked them.

The crowd grew as he continued, his voice luring them more than his costume ever could. They tossed coins onto the purple and blue cloth at his feet; they clapped and smiled and gasped where they were supposed to. But many quickly moved on, no one staying for the whole monologue, no matter how much he inflected his voice to pierce them or lowered it to reel them in closer.

A commotion in the crowd drew Celia's attention. An elderly soul with wispy white hair like a dandelion puff shook a cane at Griffin, his peculiar tenor made of bright shades of silver with barely any nuance. Often, it took some measure of training to identify whether the proper pronoun for someone was *he, she, they,* or none at all—tenors were by nature fluid and complex, filled with an array of color and light—but this person's tenor was so uniform it would have been easy even for a Kid just learning the skill.

The plague doctor saw the shaker of the cane from the corner of his eye—Celia felt his hesitation, his reluctance to let go of their eye contact across the distance—and in that silent pause, the intruder said something. One word, over and over again, with a voice as wispy as his hair.

"Abomination."

The crowd cleared space around the old soul, giving him more room to shout his awful word. The plague doctor turned his head away from Celia slowly and smiled at him, not looking upset at the interruption, nor about the word he shouted. The old silver-tenored soul may as well have yelled *Codfish oil!* for all the rise he got from the plague doctor.

Celia had a different reaction.

She pushed out of the bakery's doorway and flew through the crowd, shoving people out of the way as she went.

When the crowd parted just so, the plague doctor looked up, perhaps catching a glimpse of her familiar black top hat, ratty around the brim from overuse, a scrap of ocean-blue fabric pinned to the underside. Because of how tiny Celia was, he might not have seen anything but the disembodied top hat weaving its way through the market crowd, approaching fast. As Celia pushed her way to the front of the group, she reared to a stop. The couple she'd just wedged herself between murmured "Excuse us!" and shuffled aside.

Celia stared at the old soul for a heartbeat, her heart in her chest hot and huge. "*What* did you say?" She stepped toward him. "*What* did you say?!"

With both hands perched at the top of his cane, he frowned at her, then lifted a gnarled finger and pointed at the plague doctor. His lips parted. But before he could utter that vile word again, Celia was in his face, looking up at him despite how stooped he was. "Don't you dare."

Something fierce had risen in her, and she had to concentrate on not unleashing a primal scream. At the old soul. At the sky.

"'For whatever's inside you,'" the old soul said, quoting a passage from the *Book of Profeta* with a defiant tilt of his chin, "'will be revealed in the end. So the Divine knows.'"

"No," Celia snapped. She'd heard enough self-righteous nonsense about the Divine's grace in her lifetime. There was no Divine, only Diavala. The trickster of a thousand faces. The one who possessed souls, used them, and then abandoned them to madness when she was done. There was nothing graceful about her, nothing good. Her religion was built entirely on lies.

Diavala was the true abomination.

But perhaps the old soul had seen something of Diavala inside the plague doctor. They'd suspected that Diavala was inside him for weeks, biding her time, licking her wounds, planning revenge against them.

It had become the perfect torture for Celia: sensing that her enemy was close, so close, but not having it confirmed.

Maybe this stranger had just confirmed it.

And oh, how Celia hated him for that. "How dare you!"

The crowd pushed closer, eyes wider and conversation quieter. The way they looked at her, nervous and skittish, it was as if they expected a brawl. Some tentatively offered murmured explanations: *He's traditional, not a fan of Commedia, thinks art is evil, slightly mad hahaha . . .*

He straightened his hunched back, then looked from her to the plague doctor again. "Abomination," he whispered one more time.

It was a dare. A taunt. He *wanted* one of them to overreact. To prove him right.

Celia's hands clenched, close to giving him what he wanted. Close enough that Griffin took a step forward and put his hand out in front of her, snapping her attention back to him.

With his hand still in front of Celia, the plague doctor tipped his hat to the intruder and smiled wide, defusing the battle with one sentence.

Abomination, the old soul had accused.

"Well, you're not wrong," Griffin said. Then he tilted his head back and laughed and laughed and laughed.

The old soul blinked and shook his head, then hobbled away, casting glares over his shoulder and muttering under his breath until the crowd closed around him, leaving the plague doctor alone again.

With another player, who'd just made a fiery entrance.

Griffin tipped his hat at Celia and stared, silently acknowledging the fiery thing in her eyes. The fear. The sadness. The hate. He tilted his head, his long hair fluttering like a waterfall at his shoulders. "Welcome to the shadows. The creeping things. The claws."

He held out a hand, asking her to join him on that bare expanse of cobblestone he'd claimed as a stage. Celia shook her head. She would have backed away if the crowd hadn't closed behind her, blocking off a retreat.

So she gave them an awkward smile. Too bad for her, she'd placed herself right in the middle of his act, and she knew the plague doctor wouldn't let her leave without a fuss.

She stepped forward into the shadows, where they lived together.

The plague doctor bowed deep. "My shadow bows to you— a tender poison, a sweet deceit—recognizing its one and only ruler."

Instead of dying, the fiery thing inside her grew bigger and hotter. It had started with the old soul and his shouts of abomination. The truth, bluntly stated by a stranger: *There is something foul inside this plague doctor performer.* But it grew and swelled beyond that initial surge of anger.

It was the thing she'd held back for weeks, rising up in revolt all at once.

This was *her* plague doctor, and Diavala couldn't have him.

He reached into his pocket and pulled out an offering: a yellow flower.

"Don't be ashamed, good ruler," he whispered. "I am your land and your possessions, your treasury and army. Claim me."

Celia met his eyes behind his mask. Despite the tint on his goggles, she could imagine the exact depth and breadth of his dark eyes. How they crinkled in the corners from his smile, how the constellation tattoo at his temple would move with the flex of his jaw.

Her plague doctor.

She found herself responding.

Improvising.

She'd been a performer too, once, and she'd been so good at it she'd cast a nation into chaos with her show. She too had been on the stage when the false Divine died.

"I can claim Death himself?" she asked. Wonder lacing her voice, she took the flower, brushing her fingertips against his as she did. Time stretched out like taffy, slowing everything down painfully. When was the last time they'd touched? So close all the time, traveling together, yet such a chasm between them.

But now everything sparked.

She pressed her hand to her chest. Slowly, like something long lost and now found, she smiled at her crowd. "If I am Death's ruler, he must obey me." She waited for people to nod, acknowledging her claim.

She turned back to the plague doctor. "Tell me everything about my kingdom," she commanded. "Tell me what it looks like, smells like, tastes like. For if I am to rule Death's land, I must understand it."

It was her own dare.

You know death. You've seen it.

Tell me. Here. Now.

More than a year earlier, he'd fallen out of a tree and died, then somehow miraculously returned. She'd asked him dozens of times — What is death like? Where are our friends? Where's . . . — but he'd deflected every question. The closer they got to Wisteria Township and every impossible hope Celia had pinned there, the more restless she'd become. He knew exactly what she wanted, but he held his secrets close.

Tell me where Anya is.

"You seek reassurance," he said sadly.

They circled each other, as if dancing.

"I seek understanding." Celia's voice cracked, and her arms wrapped around her middle again, tighter this time. Half of her was gone, and she needed to know what had happened to it.

Where is Anya?! Tiny explosions as Celia's mind bees slammed against the inside of her skull, stinging her, buzzing so loud they drowned out all other sound. *You know what I need to know, and I'm your ruler, and you must tell me!*

They must have looked ridiculous, a plague doctor circling a tiny thing like her and calling her ruler. Her face was made of a pointy chin, small nose, and big dark eyes, all framed with hair like black grass. Her tenor generally toured through hues of red and bronze, *she* and sometimes *they*, in a lazy way, slow and steady, where other people's tenors flickered and sparked. Truly, there was nothing regal or refined about Celia. Yet when she stopped moving with a hard stomp of her feet, staking a claim to the truth, the plague doctor paused, listening.

"I command it," she said. "I claimed you."

Some of the crowd became bored and moved on, but Griffin and Celia were too lost in their act to notice, weeks of tension coming out in subtext that flowed too easily, in innuendo and accusation that cut too deep.

He shook his head, the beak of his mask swinging from side to side like a slow pendulum.

Tell me where Anya is! the confused bees in her mind shouted.

The plague doctor went down on his knees in front of her. "You ask for the one thing I can't give you." It was no longer a performance. He bowed his head. All she saw was the top of his black hat, the nape of his neck where his hair parted, and the movement of his shoulders as he breathed deep. She longed to rest her hand there, on that small glimpse of skin.

She pulled her hand away before it could betray her and touch him.

Death had broken both of them, but hers was a fresh, raw wound where his was an old, jagged scar.

His head tilted, as if he were listening to the cadence of her booming heart.

The ever-present pain behind Celia's eyes got worse. "You're my tender poison, my sweet deceit," she said, her voice cracking. "I'll always meet you here, in our home full of creeping things and claws."

It was just them, and darkness. The most terrible home, but their home now nonetheless.

She barely registered when people began clapping at the finale.

When it seemed that he'd never rise, content there on his knees in front of her, hugged by her shadow, Celia pulled him to his feet. The tinkling of coins as they fell to the purple and blue cloth meant that the curtain was drawn. They accepted congratulations, smiled at their well-wishers, and gathered their things.

She didn't look at him again.